PURGATORY

Also by Jeff Mann

Poetry
Bones Washed with Wine
On the Tongue
Loving Mountains, Loving Men
Ash: Poems from Norse Mythology

Essays
Edge: Travels of an Appalachian Leather Bear
Binding the God: Ursine Essays from the Mountain South

Short Fiction
A History of Barbed Wire

Novel
Fog: A Novel of Desire and Reprisal

A Novel of the Civil War

PURGATORY

JEFF MANN

BEAR BONES
books

Published in 2012 by Bear Bones Books,
an imprint of Lethe Press, Inc.
118 Heritage Avenue • Maple Shade, NJ 08052-3018
www.lethepressbooks.com • lethepress@aol.com
www.BearBonesBooks.com • bearsoup@gmail.com
Print ISBN: 978-1-59021-375-9 / 1-59021-375-0
E-book ISBN: 978-1-59021-403-9 / 1-59021-403-X

Set in Warnock and Rosemary Roman.
Interior design: Alex Jeffers.
Cover design: Niki Smith.

—

—

LIBRARY OF CONGRESS CATALOGING-IN-PUBLICATION DATA
Mann, Jeff.
Purgatory : a novel of the Civil War / Jeff Mann.
      p. cm.
ISBN 1-59021-375-0 (pbk. : alk. paper)
1.   Gay military personnel--Fiction. 2.   Soldiers--Fiction. 3.   Erotic stories, American. 4.   United States--History--Civil War, 1861-1865--Fiction. I. Title.
PS3563.A53614P87 2012
813'.54--dc22
                                        2011048680

For John Ross, my favorite Yankee, who has shown this gray-bearded Confederate sympathizer remarkable patience. Long may we roam Civil War battlefields together.

For the people of the South: past, present, and future.

For my ancestor, Isaac G. Carden—West Virginia Pvt Lowry's Btry VA Lt Arty Confederate States Army—who fought the good fight and lived to tell of it.

—

Many thanks to Steve Berman, Ron Suresha, and Tiffany Trent for their advice and support. Thanks to Cynthia Burack, Laree Martin, Frankie Finley, Bobby Nelson, Donnie Martin, Ken Belcher, Darius Liptrap, and Kent Botkin for their friendship. Many thanks to Alex Jeffers and Niki Smith for creating such a handsome book.

—

Portions of this novel appeared as "Sarvis" in *Special Forces: Gay Military Erotica*. Ed. Phillip Mackenzie, Jr. San Francisco: Cleis, 2009.

Portions of this novel appeared in *Pine Mountain Sand and Gravel: Contemporary Appalachian Writing* #14.

"But Lucy Dare was a Virginian, and in Virginia—except in the brief, exalted Virginia of the Confederacy—the personal loyalties have always been esteemed beyond the impersonal."

—"Dare's Gift," Ellen Glasgow

CHAPTER ONE

———

Amid the whizzing of Yankee bullets, there's a sharp gasp at my elbow. "Ian, I'm hit," Sam groans. Our black-haired color bearer is bent at the waist, as if bowing to some spirit the rest of us can't see. Then he straightens, clutches his chest, stares over at me, and grimaces. Before I can do anything, Sam staggers, gets caught in the ragged folds of the flag he's carrying, spins, and falls, the Stars and Bars wrapped around him like a huge red-and-blue bandage.

"Ian. The flag," Sam moans, blood spilling from his lips. The flag's red is brighter now, as his wound wells. Inside the blue stripes, the white stars flush scarlet. "You got to save the flag." He heaves himself onto one elbow and starts tugging at the fabric swathing him.

"No! I don't want to move you," I say, easing him back against the muddy wall of our rifle pit. "You're tangled in it. Easy, Sam! Lie back."

I'm about to examine his wound when a roar fills my ears. I rise long enough to look over the breastworks. Across the field the Yanks are pouring toward us through gray sheets of falling sleet, unloading their rifles into our thin line. My God, there are so, so many of them. It's like a damned deep-blue tidal wave. Despite the brim of my cap, my spectacles are spattered with wet, making it hard to see. Still, I swallow hard, aim at the Federals, and fire. The rifle-butt slams my shoulder; the smoke fills my nose. Far in front of me, to my pleasure, a foe screams and falls.

"Damn you," I sigh, less in anger than weariness, "why can't y'all just go home?" Tearing open a cartridge with my teeth, I load up again. I'm about to aim when a Union ball chunks into the mud to my right. I duck, falling to my knees. When I look down, Sam's eyes are dull.

"He's dead, Ian. Leave him! Leave the flag." Sarge's voice is even, his hand heavy on my shoulder. "It's over. The Valley's fallen. If we don't move fast, we'll be captured."

My uncle's face is set, his gray eyes bright over the silvery flare of his moustache. He points to our left. He's right. Mounted Yanks are breaking through the trees, about to flank us. "And Early's leaving." Now

Sarge points behind us. There, atop a low hill, wild-bearded General Jubal Early and his staff are mounting up to flee.

"Rockfish Gap! Retreat!" Sarge shouts to the remains of our little company, all huddled here together in icy water behind the breastworks. "Let's go, boys! We've got to get over the bridge or we'll be cut off!"

We sprint west, through the town of Waynesboro. Around us Yankee balls are flying. Behind us are booms and shouts. Here are our horses, in a little stable owned by an old friend of Sarge's. We have few mounts, this late in the war, so we double up, as usual in times of crisis. Sarge's helping me up behind him when a young black woman appears beside us. She's shivering, a shawl over her shoulders, a dirty bonnet on her head. Her face is a shiny brown, her cheeks hollow.

"Here, sirs," she says. "Missus said you could do with these." She proffers a poke. I grab it. "Said you soldiers needed it more'n we."

"Thank y'all kindly," I gasp. "Now get inside." As if to highlight my words, a bullet sings through the air between us. The servant gives a little shriek, turns, and disappears into the stable.

"Git!" Sarge goads his horse, and we're off, through the gray town, over the bridge, through a fresh fall of sleet, and onto the road up into the Blue Ridge Mountains. It's a sad rout, our little band fleeing as fast as we can. I almost lose my cap in the rush. One arm around Sarge, one clasping my hat on my head, I look around as the wintry landscape rushes by, grim fields turn to forest, and we ascend the steeps toward the gap. Sam, damn it. Poor boy fallen in the folds of the flag he's carried so proudly for so long, the Stars and Bars become his winding sheet. But the rest of us Rogue Riders, yes, there's that shabby George, grimacing as usual, with one of the twins mounted behind him. And Jeremiah, my handsome buddy from back home, black shaggy hair flying in the wind, with scruffy Rufus clinging to his waist.

Behind us, the report of rifles continues. By the time we've reached the mountaintop, however, there are no sounds but horse hooves, men panting, and wind whistling through the gap. We're atop the narrow ridge now, winter-gray mountains rolling out around us as far as the eye can see.

"The boys without mounts are prisoners by now," Sarge says, and spits. There's General Early, on a rocky ledge, staring down into the valley with his spyglass. He curses, cocks back a flask, and curses more. Sarge dismounts, hands me the bridle, says, "Check on the boys," and strides over to Early. They begin to confer, Sarge's voice low and even, Early's occasionally rising into sharp profanity. God knows what's next for us. Months of trying to defend this valley, but there are just too few of us now. We're whipped. I'm feeling what most of us are feeling, I suspect: part of me wants to fight on defiantly to the end, and part of me wants to throw down my gun and head home to my family.

I've just dismounted and am about to check the contents of the poke the slave-girl gave me—I sure as hell hope it's food, because we soldiers are always starving—when a hand grips my shoulder. "Hey, Ian." It's Jeremiah, brushing the hair out of his eyes. His face is thin, his features sharp. He's lost his cap. "Sam?"

I shake my head. "He's gone, Jeremiah. Fell with the flag."

Jeremiah sighs. "Oh, no." He looks down the mountain toward the town. He hugs me, quick and hard, then steps back. "And are you sound? Were you wounded? Me, I almost caught a ball in—"

Rifles below. Closer. "Boys! Yanks!" Sarge shouts and points. I look down the road, and there's a little group of damned bluecoats heading up the hill.

"Shit!" Jeremiah mutters. We load fast, what's left of our little band. "Fire!" Sarge and Early shout simultaneously. Shoulder to shoulder, we pour fire down the mountain. A few answering guns, and the Yanks retreat. I guess they figure we're not much of a threat anymore, no longer worth their bother, and I guess they're right. Maybe they've had enough of a sweeping victory for one day. If Stonewall Jackson were still alive, or my hero, that magnificently bearded Turner Ashby, leading his wild horde of cavalry, we'd tear their Yankee asses up, but those days are long gone. It's March 1865. Jackson's been dead nearly two years, Ashby nearly three.

Day's about done, but we wait, arms at the ready, lined up along the wooded ridge, waiting for further attack. When, a few hours after dark, it seems clear that the Feds are probably settling into their luxurious meals by the fire—those lucky bastards and their long supply trains— we Rebs settle in, starting our own campfires and preparing what piss-ant rations we have remaining.

Sarge, striding around to check on things, counts us. Twenty-three left. Five missing, fallen, or captured back in Waynesboro. He shakes his head and chews his lower lip. "No need to pitch tents. We're moving on tomorrow," he announces before returning to General Early's campfire.

I sit on a log beside the fire and count them, my remaining mess-mates. Jeremiah, with his kind eyes and patchy black beard, has some-how, miraculously, retained his banjo in the rout and is tuning it up. He grew up just a valley over from me along the Greenbrier River back in West Virginia. We got to be pretty good friends at community events like corn-shuckings and molasses stir-offs, even working some fields and garden plots together in between trips to our favorite swimming hole. For a moment I feel some of that old desire for him I knew back home. I always feel a flicker of it in the mornings, when I see him bare to the waist and bathing, splashing water on his face, his lean chest and belly coated with black hair. Ever since my first youthful infatuation with him, I've always loved hairy men. One of the reasons I so doted on Thom, God help me. Not that I've shared that fact with any of my fellow soldiers, of course.

Here's George, a mousy little man from the Valley who's always smelling of tobacco. Behind his back, I call him Weasel-Teeth, not only because of his ugly maw but his vindictive nature. George is spitting into the fire, jaw working his customary plug. He broods, no doubt over today's rout, his lip curling every now and then to flash sharp teeth. There's a Bible in his hand, but he doesn't seem to be reading it. Instead, he stares into the flames or into the dark forest. We used to be civil. He used to look at me, I think, the way I used to look at Jeremiah, but the combination of his perpetually sour moods and his Bible rants have made his presence increasingly obnoxious. More and more, he spends time with those redheaded New Market twins. I think he en-joys bossing them around.

And here's Rufus, our ever hungry cook, auburn chin whiskers look-ing red-golden in the firelight as he simmers beans with what's likely to be the last of the bacon. As good hearted a man as I've ever known, with a wonderfully foul mouth when he's in his cups, which is as often as Sarge can procure us strong drink. I think Rufus has handled a gun only six or seven times in these four long years of war. His genius isn't slaughter; it's keeping warriors alive. Bless him, he can start up a fire and make a good meal out of next to nothing faster than anyone I've ever known, and that includes my mother and that slew of aunts back home.

Beans, cornmeal, hardtack. That's all we've eaten for weeks, ever since we left winter quarters near Staunton. We're all lean as split rails. Little left ration-wise, plus we've been on the move the last week and have been in no position to receive packages from home. God, I remember the war's first years...the boxes of cookies and fried chicken and canned milk and fruit pies my parents sent me. Damn, I just want to be home by the fire, smelling the wood charring on the hearth and one of my mother's pies baking.

"What y'got there?" Rufus nudges my elbow, sniffing at the mysterious poke I have yet to examine.

"Don't know yet," I say, fumbling it open. "Here," I say, knowing how much Rufus loves to handle food. "While don't you tell me? A slave girl back in Waynesboro gave it to me. Said it was from her mistress. The way she looked, poor haggard thing, I doubt that household could much afford it, but here it is nonetheless."

"Ah, Virginia! Her citizens take care of their brave defenders, as Sarge would say." Smacking his lips, Rufus rummages. "Let's see... Ummm... Well, lookee! Dried apples! Ain't that nice? And these funny thangs? Lil' red beads? Ain't those—"

"Yep. Rose hips," I say, peering over his shoulder. "My Aunt Alicia says they keep off the scurvy. She used to send them to me back when we got packages from home. Remember? You've made me tea with them."

"Yeah, right. Ruby-red and sour as hell, in need of about four cups of cane sugar! Helps keep off scurvy? Hell, ain't she half-Indian?"

"Cherokee, yes."

"Well, I question her judgment, if you don't mind me—"

"I do mind you saying so. Keep in mind that I've got some of that Indian blood too. What else we got there?"

Rufus can be a little backward. God knows what he'd say if he knew about my desires for men. Fortunately, he's also easily distracted by anything edible. "Oh, well, now...a loaf of bread!" he gasps. "Praise the Lord! Any sweetenin'? Yep, here's some honey. And, ummm, a slice of ham! That, hmm, well, that's it." He releases an exaggerated sigh. "I sure could have done with a..."

"Chicken pot pie? Beef roast? Half a hog?"

Rufus grins, swatting my shoulder. "Yeah, yeah. Any of that. Here, now. Y'hold onto that," he whispers, handing me the poke. "And don't let George have any. The bastard called me a hell-bound mooncalf and a heathen, just 'cause I took me a little nip last Sunday. I'm not feeling especially charitable toward him lately, Lord forgive me." Rufus spits onto the frozen ground and returns to his pot of beans.

The sleet clouds have dispersed. A few stars wink overhead. We sit in silence around the fire while Rufus cooks. Jeremiah fiddles with his banjo, plays a bar of one melody, then shifts to another, then stops. Normally, this is the time a few of us would sing, and I might even tell a bawdy story, but after today's defeat, no one's in the mood for anything but a meal and a bedroll. God knows where we'll be marching tomorrow.

"How'd Sam die?" George asks. He's put away his Bible; now he's whittling a stick with jerky movements.

"Ball in the chest," I say. "Just before Custer's men came in from our left. He faded fast, was dead by the time we retreated. Poor boy fell with the flag wrapped around him. Eighteen years old. Crazy kid," I shake my head and smile, wiping some wet out of one eye. "The boy sure could dance a jig. Don't think any of us ever beat him at cards. And that spasmodic pet squirrel of his…"

"Damned fine eating, that critter was, especially with the peanut sauce Rufus made." Jeremiah laughs. "We told Sam that miserable thing would bite him to the bone sooner or later."

"Custer," snarls George. "Sheridan and Custer. God damn them. May those names live in infamy. May they end in agony." He shakes his head and spits tobacco juice into the fire. "Too damned many of them. Our left was hanging in the air. What did General Early expect us to do?"

"He's done the best he could with what he has," I say. "We only have a thousand or so men left."

"*Had* a thousand men. Most of that number never made it out of Waynesboro." George releases another arc of brown spit. "Look around you. We're the end of it, boys, the end of it. All that's left of the grand Army of the Valley. If Sarge hadn't gotten us out of there… Damn. All those prisoners. Poor bastards'll end up in prisons up north. Elmira. Camp Chase. You think we're starving now, boys, imagine being in one of those hellholes."

"They got all the flags too," says Jeremiah, giving his banjo a mournful pluck before putting it back in its battered case. "And the wagons. And our artillery. Even got General Early's headquarters wagon. "

"Caught Dr. McGuire too, dammit. Of course they beat us. Those bluecoat bastards had thousands, as usual. Thousands. Thick as fleas. As lice." George claws his crotch meaningfully. "Legion. The Bible says it. 'Their name is Legion, for they are many.' Damn them. I hope the Lord has a special space in hell for every one of them. Especially after the Burning last fall. I know the Bible says to forgive, but, Lord, how can you forgive men who torch your home and barn and shoot your livestock?"

We've all heard this rant before, and none of us blames George for it. He lost everything when the Yanks under Sheridan burned the Valley. So did Sarge. Seems like justified hatred to me. Still, it's safe to say that we don't want to hear such words tonight. It only makes us feel more like failures. Instead of exacting grand and brutal revenge on the invaders, we're huddling atop the Blue Ridge, a broken little crew.

"Where do you think we'll march tomorrow?" I say, trying to change the subject.

"Petersburg, maybe? To join General Lee in the siege?" Jeremiah says, scratching his armpit. As hairy as he is, the lice we all suffer from must be building little villages all over him. As much as I love a furry chest, it's a handicap when the graybacks come to call. I should know, possessing some slight body hair myself. Sometimes I think I can feel the goddamn things crawling over me at night, looking for new nooks to invade. Sometimes I think about shaving off my beard to get rid of them, but as small-built as I am, my beard's one of the few things that make me look like a man.

"Petersburg, then!" George runs his hands through his hair and coughs. "Damned hair's falling out," he says, shaking strands off his fingers. "Petersburg. Lots of Yanks to kill there."

Supper spares us more of George's vitriol. "It's ready, boys," says Rufus, circling the fire, ladling beans into our tin cups. I take a bite; the beans are tender albeit few, not nearly enough to satisfy, and the bacon's tough, its taste edging toward rancid. Still, it's a better meal than I've had for days, so I eat eagerly.

After dinner, we roll out our oilcloths by the fire. I'm still hungry, and I'm exhausted and sad, thinking of Sam. Before bedding down, I slip into the darkness to piss. Here, in ceaseless wind, is a flat ledge overlooking the valley. Those flickering lights, miles down the Blue Ridge, are the lamps of Waynesboro, and, just beyond, the campfires of the enemy, a huge lake of pinprick fire. Who knew an ideal as vague as Union would bring them down here and keep them down here for so many years? Why can't they just leave us be? If we Rebs had known there were so, so many of them, would we have ever volunteered for this war?

Well, yes. I would have, though I'm bone weary of it by now. I want it over—God help me, even if it means losing. I just want to get home. I want my own little farm in the mountains where I grew up, even if I have no one to share it with. Men like me, I don't know if we're ever lucky enough to find mates. Lord knows Thom couldn't leave me fast enough.

I relieve myself over the ledge, and then I head back to the welcome warmth of the fire. There, exhausted as I am, still I do what I usually do before sleep: reread letters from home. I lie on the hard, sleet-scattered ground, wrap myself in my oilcloth, pull the packet of letters from my haversack, and study a random few by firelight.

—

CHAPTER TWO

—

November 14, 1861

My dear Ian,

I take pen in hand so as to inform you of our doings at home, as you have requested. We are sorry not to have written sooner. The harvest was difficult this year, and sparser than usual; the corn-crib is only half full. Though I am so, so proud that you and your brother Jeff are soldiers, it does make keeping up the farm far more difficult. Your father's back is no better than ever, poor soul! After the harvest, he spent a week bedridden. Since then, it has snowed every week. Please let us know if you boys need more blankets.

We miss you so. Last weekend, your Aunt Alicia had us over for fried chicken after church and we all so wished that you and Jeff were there. She made an extra batch of rolls and a dried apple pie for you two. Now that you are in winter quarters, we know where you are and have mailed a box full of such good food to you.

Susan sends her regards. She is such a lovely girl. She is making you and your brother socks. She asks after you both. I believe she is waxing fond over you, son. Perhaps when God sees fit to end this terrible conflict and you come home, you can court her. Her family is one of hard-workers and churchgoers.

Greetings to your father's dear brother Erastus, or Sarge, as you persist in calling him. He always swore he would make you a fine soldier, even if it killed him. I do hope he's managed the former without having to endure the latter! Please share this letter with Jeff, and assure him that we will write him as well. Take good care of each other.

Your Loving Mother

—

June 1862

Son,

Your mother's handwriting is much clearer than mine, and my hands are cramped up, due, I think, to too many years gripping an axe or plow, so she is writing this for me.

We are so sorry to hear of your hero's death. General Ashby was a Great Knight of the Valley, all agree. An exemplum of manhood.

We wish you were home, but you must keep to your duty. Haven't you boys whipped those invaders yet? Yanks are a spoiled, degenerate set. I've heard tell that one Southern boy can whip ten Yanks at a time. They are not an outdoors sort. Sitting in factories has made them soft.

Please find enclosed more of that odd salve your mother's sister has made. Good for wounds, Alicia says. I'm dubious. We've also sent, as you'll see, some potatoes.

The gardens are thriving, though folks farther down the hill had their stores stolen by Federal raiders. If they come up here, I will shoot them. ("I won't let him," your mother insists on adding. Her heart is a woman's heart.) We have lettuce in, and peas. The corn is growing fast. We miss your shooting skills, though, and the venison feasts you used to provide us. Our hog, however, is growing fat and will make some fine meals. We shall send you boys some salt-cured ham come November. (We have named the pig John Brown so it will be easier to slaughter. You know how attached your mother gets to animals.)

We thought of you today. We were taking a cart of wheat down to the mill to be ground and passed your swimming hole, where you and Jeff and Jeremiah spent so many hours. And then we passed the chinkypin tree, where you all used to feast on nuts.

Your cousin has sent you more books. I will forward them. (Last week, Neighbor Atkins—you might enjoy this—made a mocking comment about how much you read and how small-built you are. I reminded him of how badly you beat his son in that boxing match the spring before you left home. He suddenly seemed eager to discuss the hay harvest instead. Even your mother laughed.)

You are a fine son. Your mother tells me I should make that clear. You are as fine a son putting up hay or digging turnips as you are a scholar. I am so sorry that we have insufficient money for you to continue your education at a university. We will need you boys

*on the farm more than ever when you return. A man's fate, as you
no doubt feel deeply in your present circumstances, is rarely in his
own hands. But you have already shown, again and again, that
you put duty before desire, as a man must.*

*Stay brave. Conquer those city boys and then get home. The for-
ests you so love await you. We await you.*

Father

*PS. Jeff tells me that Susan is writing him now. She's as pretty as
a wild azalea! Why didn't you court her? As fine a writer as you
are, you could have won her over with sweet words. You had your
chance, son! (Your mother agrees.)*

*PS. Stay away from those town vixens if you get to Richmond!
They are devious and, shall we say, not of the purest fiber.*

———

October 10, 1862.

Dear Ian,

*I share your sorrow. To me, the word Antietam will always mean
the end of love and the death of hope.*

From Susan. I fold up the wrinkled paper fast. I don't want to read
this one. My eyes are tired and the firelight's dying.

I fold up my spectacles, slip the letters back into my haversack, rest
my head on it for want of a pillow, and stare up at the stars. If I start
counting the men I have to mourn, the missing faces, Sam the most
recent of that long list, I'll start to cry. I need to sleep instead. Around
a fold of oilcloth I wrap my arms.

Well, shit, here come the tears nonetheless. Stop it, Ian. You don't
want to think about death. You want to think about men, about a man
naked and willing and in your arms.

Thom, that beautiful bastard, rubbing his bare ass against me. That's
memory. Or poor blue-eyed Brandon, lying bare-chested on top of me,
nuzzling my face. That's fantasy. Both images harden my groin. I hug
on the oilcloth as if it were a lover. Sleet pats my brow and my mood
of futile ardor riles me up, but eventually I slip toward sleep, the ache
of limbs and half-empty belly grading minute by minute into blessed
insensibility.

———

CHAPTER THREE

—

General Early and his remaining men are already gone when we wake to a grim and rainy dawn. "He's off to report to Lee," Sarge says simply, after calling us out for a hurried and unkempt morning muster. "As for us, boys, the Yanks are moving our way, heading east up the mountain. We need to hide up in the woods till they pass. Once they're gone, we're heading west for Staunton. The citizens there are a mite better off than those in Waynesboro. They'll provide for us. I've told Early we'll hide in the mountains west of Staunton and bushwhack what Yanks we see in the Valley. Nelson's got a little force in southwest Virginia. With luck, we can join up with him."

No time for coffee, much to Rufus' distress. Instead, our little group has a quick breakfast of hardtack before climbing the mud-slick steeps above the road and hunching down behind evergreen walls of laurel and hemlock. "Hide the horses way up there, deep inside the laurel, boys, and feed them some of what you have in your sacks. That'll keep them quiet until the Yanks pass," Sarge orders. "If the bluecoats hear any whinnies up here, we're done for. Rufus will collect the food. Whatever you boys have that our mounts will eat. We'll replenish our stores in Staunton, I promise you."

As intimidating as Sarge can be, as loyal as we all are to him, still there are several reluctant grumbles as Rufus makes the rounds, collecting precious bits of food. When I hand Rufus the loaf of bread the Waynesboro slave girl gave me, his lower lip trembles. "I sure was looking forward to a chunk of that," he says. "But you hold onto that honey and ham, okay? Them horses wouldn't care for any of that. I'd keep the dried apples too."

Gray woodlands surround us, boughs dripping with cold rain. The wind pouring through the gap brings fog today, drifting through our bivouac. We wait inside ragged white clouds that come and go, beading our beards with tiny droplets. In between breaks in the fog, Sarge trains his spyglasses west.

"Here they come," he says just before noon. "Get down, boys, and keep quiet. If the foe discovers us, we're all finished."

Here's hoping Confederate gray blends in with March drizzle, tree trunks, and dead leaves. We drop onto our bellies onto the frozen ground, huddle inside the laurel thickets, or hide behind the thickest tree trunks, though a few of us can't resist peering over a ledge or two to watch the Yanks as they pass.

"There's Custer," George growls at my elbow. "Golden ringlets like a whore."

"Shut *up*, George," Sarge whispers.

Very carefully, I pull aside a hemlock branch and look down. They're passing, Custer's cavalry first, then Sheridan—short little bastard with a dark moustache—leading long lines of troopers. Those are the scum who burnt up the Valley last fall. With their clean uniforms of blue and gold and their robust, well-fed bodies, they look like a different species of soldier altogether, nothing like the tattered, dirty scarecrows we've become after four years of war. As close as they are and as unaware, it's a great temptation to shoot a few through the heads, but then our tiny band of Rebs would be slaughtered for sure. Twenty-three of us, thousands of them. Not exactly appealing odds.

They pass. They pass. They pass. Flashes of blue moving in and out of fog, only yards below. It looks like half the population of one of those crawling Northern cities on the march. We watch, stunned, sick, despairing. What can we do against men such as they? So many men such as they?

Finally the long line ends. The clopping of horses' hooves descends the mountain, heading for Charlottesville and who knows what sort of destruction. Sarge waits until there's nothing to hear but wind and dripping boughs before he stands, whispering, "Let's go. Keep quiet." We rise to our feet, one by one, brush wet leaves and dirt off our already filthy uniforms, and follow him down the shaly slope to the road.

"Sarge's horse ate your bread," Rufus says sadly, shouldering his haversack. "He acted like it was mighty tasty."

We mount up, two men to a horse, heading west toward the Valley Pike, which will hopefully be free of Yanks at present. We ride wearily through Waynesboro—not a citizen on the street. For a second, I remember Winchester, May 1862, the Feds routed, our triumphant entrance into that town behind Stonewall Jackson, the girls cheering us, offering us posies and fruit. Long years ago. A different world, a hopeful one. No cheering here, just empty streets and gray buildings. We pass out of town, past the rifle pits where we did our best to make a stand.

Near where Sam fell, there are fresh graves, piles of red earth in a field of brown grass. The townspeople must have buried our fallen already. I don't know which grave is Sam's, but it doesn't matter. In a war like this, all those boys were kin.

Sarge reins in his horse, pausing long enough to bow his head. Some damned Yankee, perhaps even the one whose bullet brought Sam down, has that bloodstained flag that Sam fell in. They wouldn't bury him in it; they'd keep it as a souvenir of victory. It was probably presented to Sheridan, along with all the others, in some triumphal parade. I can seem them smiling now; I'd like to beat their beaming faces in.

"Lord help this land's defenders and bless all those who've fallen," Sarge mutters, then he snaps the reins and we're off, horse hooves clopping along the muddy road toward Staunton.

—

CHAPTER FOUR

—

We limp into town as gloomy dusk gathers, as lamps flare up in windows and a chilly mist rises from the streets. The few pickets lead us to the railroad depot. It's seriously fire-damaged still, after that bastard David Hunter and his destructive passel of Yanks passed through last June, but a section of the station's whole, with dry floors upon which we're invited to sleep. Word goes out, and within the hour citizens are lining up in the brick-paved square beside the depot. By this point in the war, I doubt that they have much to give, but what they do have, they give us: cornmeal, moldy onions, coffee, molasses, dried beans, cold biscuits, warm blankets, shoes. The mayor appears, a man with impressive side-whiskers; he gives a quick, solemn speech about welcoming Virginia's defenders. Afterwards, he pulls Sarge aside—they know each other well—and presents him with several bottles of amber liquid. I'm hoping it's whiskey, and I'm hoping my uncle will share it with me, as he usually does. I've inherited a taste for strong waters from the Campbells, my father's side of the family, and as religious-righteous as Sarge can be about profanity, he's never seemed to deny himself a sip of fiery spirits when he can. It can make me silly, morose, or sleepy, but it never "embrutes" him, as he puts it. It seems only to make him a little less stern.

Of course there are no young men for me to admire among the people of Staunton. After four years of war, they're either dead, thanks to Yankee bullets and artillery, or they're starving behind the lines with Lee at Petersburg. But here come, much to my fellow Rebs' delight, a few young ladies from the female academy hereabouts, dressed for the occasion in fancily furbelowed dresses that nevertheless have seen better days. "We hid this ham from the Yankees under a sewing basket," says one with a plump-lipped smirk, presenting it to Sarge. He's in his element here, receiving the people's gratitude with low tones of thanks. He's composed in a way I'll never be, and handsome for his age—fifty—with his high cheekbones and wavy grey hair. My uncle's always seemed free of the doubts and despairs that assail me daily.

My fellow soldiers do what they always do when girls are around—they flush and flirt. Their grins grow wide and nervous, their limbs jittery. It's funny to watch, though I guess I'd act that way around a bunch of handsome soldiers. As it is, I like women, and they like me. It's good for my pride, their attentions, and I can be easy around them, since their attractions don't move me the deep way they obviously do my comrades. Several of the prettier ones circle me, making chat, touching my uniform, the handle of my sheathed Bowie knife, asking me what battles I've seen, why we lost in Waynesboro.

The poor things, they must be desperate for men, making such a fuss over smelly, muddy skeletons like ourselves. Jeremiah gets the lion's share of their attentions, not only because he's handsome, even in his present half-starved, raggedy-ass state, but because he's a charmer, a natural ladies' man. It must be exhilarating, to be open about one's desire, to be wanted by someone you want in return. Rufus, he's too awkward for such girls to find appealing, and George is too, well, homely. As much as he raves about the Bible, he probably thinks these girls are hell-sent temptresses.

After some chatter and some giggling, the cold rains renew themselves, and so the flirtacious girls depart, the rest of the citizens disperse. Sarge and the mayor head for a nearby tavern, while the rest of our crew ducks into the rail station, thankful for the shelter. There we have a cold meal of ham and bread—some elegant dowager with a gray bun in her hair brought us several fresh loaves, bless her. We roll out our blankets in the lamplight and listen to the rain—it's a comforting sound when you don't have to be out in it, as we have for most of the last four years. Jeremiah picks out "Dixie," then "Lorena." The notes of the latter make us so sad and homesick that Rufus interrupts.

"Pardon me, Mr. Jeremiah, but we don't need no more of that melancholy music! Sarge ain't here," he says, with a mischievous grin. "Ian, why don't you tell us something bawdy? I think, after looking at all them pretty girls, some of us are in the mood."

"Good idea, Rufus. Let's hear it, Ian!" Jeremiah lays down the banjo and brandishes a little ivory comb one of his female admirers must have just given him. "Meanwhile I'll just groom myself and dream of the next passel of delightful ladies." He takes it to his uneven and unruly beard, then his lank hair.

Rufus gives him a sour look. "They always did like you best. I need to find me a big-hipped little honey who falls in love with me for my biscuits... Some big girl with great big titties..."

"I ain't having none of your sinner's stories," grouses George. He moves his bedroll to the far side of the room, where he starts up a card game with the redheaded New Market twins.

"Hmm, let's see..." I contemplate my options. Well, I could tell a story about sodomites, about David riding Jonathan, or Achilles prick-spearing Patroclus, or how much I used to want to take Jeremiah's substantial cock in my mouth during those long summer days at the swimming hole, but I suspect my friends want something composed of more average lechery.

"How 'bout the one about the lass that was bitten by the trouser snake?" Rufus suggests, licking his lips. "Or that one about the saddlehorn that weren't a saddlehorn? Or the hussy who grew too fond of horizontal refreshments? Or that woman who couldn't never be satisfied? Or that one about Harrolson collecting ladies' piss to make nitre?"

"Umm, 'you have put the pretty dears / to patriotic pissing'...uh, 'when a lady lifts her skirts / she's killing off a Yankee.' Hell, I should have written that one down. I can't remember it. How about 'While one, more wanton than the rest / Seized on love's moss-bounded nest. / And cried, "Poor puss shall have a treat / For the first time of juicy meat."'"

"Hooray!" says Rufus. "'Bout time that puss was fed!" Bless him, he's as earthy a farmboy as they come. I'm about to continue when the station door opens and Sarge appears. He takes the situation in within a couple of seconds—the flushed grins, the guilty looks. "Coarse amusements, boys? Not worth of the Southland's soldiers. At it again, Ian?"

I wipe a grin from my mouth and try to look solemn. "Yes, sir." That line about juicy meat has me counting the years since I last lay with a man. My youth's flying by, I could die tomorrow, ripped to shreds by a barrage of Yankee bullets, and I have no one to touch. "The boys asked me to. I figured, as grim as things have been lately, they could do with..."

"Vulgar laughter. Yes, I see. You all get some rest!" Sarge orders. "Tomorrow we're heading west, into the mountains."

"Yes, sir" is the statement that crops up all over the room. Card decks are thrust into haversacks; lamps are snuffed. I'm about to turn to my own bedroll when Sarge says, "Come with me, nephew. I have something for you."

A scolding, I expect. Hell. Still I obey without question, as usual. Sarge leads me outside onto the station platform. We sit side by side on a bench. Rain, silvered by distant streetlamp light, drops in sheets off the eaves. Sarge pulls out two cigars, lights them, and hands me one. Typical of him: he's been alternately stern and generous with me since I was a child. We sit in silence for a time, till our cigars are glowing cheerily in the dark. He pulls out a flask now; still silent, we pass it back and forth. Before us, rails gleam in the rain. I'm surprised the damned Yanks didn't pull them all up when they occupied Staunton last summer. After all the fire damage, much of the town still exudes a strong smell of wet ash.

Sarge sighs. Always a bad sign. "I know the boys enjoy your salacious tales, nephew, but that kind of storytelling is neither gentlemanly nor Christian. It erodes moral fiber in both speaker and listeners; it's bad for you."

Bad for me, yes. It reminds me of the erotic—how hungry I am for another man's body and how hopeless that hunger is. "Yes, sir," I say, taking a long swig from the flask, then handing it back.

"I fear the Indian blood on your mother's side of the family tends you toward bodily corruption."

"Perhaps, sir," I say, puffing on the cigar. If Aunt Alicia heard him now, she'd snatch him bald-headed. They've always had a healthy hatred of one another. "Though some would regard flask and tobacco as corrupt, would they not?"

Sarge chuckles. "Spare me your slippery sophistry. These are mere manly diversions when not indulged in to excess." As if to highlight his point, he takes a long draw on his cigar. "And as lustful as your tales often are—yes, I know you tell them only when I'm absent, but George is fond of reporting them to me for some reason; you know how he's always trying to curry my favor—you yourself seem free from lust. I watched you with the young ladies today. You're handsome, nephew, despite your war-worn state, despite your perpetually disheveled hair and unshorn face. Girls like you. Yet you seem without true interest. You seem dispassionate. Why is that?"

Dispassionate? I'm half-tempted to laugh. How can I feel close to any person on this planet when I must lie to everyone? No one knows me.

"I'm shy, sir. And I'm here not to court, but to fight. Correct?"

"Yes. Good point. Well, when the war's done—God help us, I don't know how much longer our country can hold out..." He takes a long gulp from the flask, caps it, slips it into his coat, and clears his throat. "When you get home, God willing, now that that little Susan's free...after what happened at Antietam..."

The familiar knot in my throat. "Perhaps, sir," I rasp.

"Well, off to bed with you!" Sarge knows when to change the subject. He gives me one of his rare avuncular shoulder-pats. "The mayor has offered me his guest room for the night, and my age-petulant joints have encouraged me to accept his kind offer. He's promised us some horses, more provisions, and a cart. He says that little bands of Yanks have been spotted west of town, so get some sleep, for we may have a fight tomorrow. I want to get us up into the hills to recover our strength. Then we'll move south, with luck pick off some bluecoats here and there, and meet up with Nelson around Lexington or Buchanan. Sources assure me he's moving north. Once we join his force, we can turn east and add what few men we can to the struggle for Petersburg."

Sarge flicks the glowing butt of his cigar out over the rain-wet tracks, where it gives an audible hiss. "Good night, Ian." He rises. Before I can reply, he strides off into the storm.

Pick off some bluecoats. As much as I hate them—they've invaded and systematically destroyed the land I love—I've never been able to despise them the way Sarge and George do. Sarge talks about them like they're potato beetles, not men.

I sit back on the bench, pull my uniform jacket a little tighter around me, and take my time finishing my cigar. The whisky warms my head. For no good reason, I remember Brandon's maimed, hair-coated chest the night before he died. I cleaned his fresh wounds. Within the thick bush of his auburn goatee, his red lips trembled. He begged me to save him. I could do nothing. Or, rather, I did nothing.

Dispassionate, Sarge called me. What a joke. What a blessing detachment would be. At any time, but especially now, in the midst of war. Dispassionate and strong, like Sarge, that's what I wish I were: hard as an oak bole, sharp and ruthless as the blade of my Bowie knife. The rest of my comrades admire me for my sharpshooting abilities, my courage, but what would they do if they knew how I ached, what I ached for? At best, they'd probably drive me off. At worst, hell, they might string me up, if they knew what moves me most—the beards and muscles, the fuzzy solidity of other men's bodies. God help me if they knew whom I've loved. Thom, damn him. And I was beginning to love Brandon before he was killed, even though it was so clear that my feelings for him weren't reciprocated that I never admitted them. A mad, entirely inappropriate affection. A foe and a prisoner, not to mention the fact that the poor boy had a wife back home.

Maybe that's my fate, forever to find my love unreturned. To be loved by friends and kin, not lovers or a mate. Pathetic, Ian. Such self-pity. You're alive. Think of Sam wrapped in that bloody flag. Think of all the men you've seen die. You're still here yet, scarred but whole. There are far worse fates than to live without love.

"Weak bastard. Whiner," I mutter. My turn to flick what's left of my cigar into the rain. After today's long ride, my butt and thighs are sore. I stand and enter the dark station. I weave carefully in between the sleepers, through the odor of long-unwashed bodies and wet wool uniforms, through coughs and sighs, mumbles and snores. Our poor, decimated band. Such grand, heroic hopes we had. Now we're just grateful for fresh bread and a dry place to sleep. And a bedroll. I wrap myself in it and pass out.

—

CHAPTER FIVE

—

The dream disperses like fog off a frosty pasture. One second Brandon is moaning beneath me, on his hands and knees; I'm gripping his hips and shoving my cock into him just as I've always longed to do, the hard, rough way I mounted Thom. The next second, Brandon's gone, back to his shallow grave, and I'm awake, my penis hard in my pants, arms and legs wrapped around my oilcloth.

Jeremiah's gripping my elbow. "Got you one of those Female Academy girls there?" Jeremiah drawls. "I dreamed about them all night."

"Uh, yep." My lies are effortless after all these years. Concealment is second nature. I blush and adjust myself beneath the blanket.

"Sarge let us sleep late. But now he's here, and townfolks are bringing us coffee. Real coffee too, not one of those roasted grain abominations. And, Jesus, biscuits too. And some decent-looking bacon. Rufus is about to have a paroxysm!"

Breakfast's hurried, since there are rumors of Federals to the north of us, moving up the Valley Pike. At least the rain's stopped. As he'd promised, the mayor presents us with more horses, as well as a rickety cart drawn by swayback mares and loaded with the provisions we received yesterday, along with a few cabbages and two more sacks, one of beans and one of cornmeal. Sarge, no doubt tired of sharing his saddle with me, gives me command of the buckboard, so up I hop, folding my oilcloth beneath me to make the hard seat more comfortable. The young ladies of the Female Academy show up at the last minute to wish us well and see us off with a great deal of tears and tittering. One gives Jeremiah a pink handkerchief as a token.

Under gray skies, we move west along the muddy Staunton/ Parkersburg Turnpike, through the little town of West View, up through the low hills of Buffalo Gap. The road's steeper and steeper, leaving behind the fields of the Valley and climbing into the Allegheny Mountains. It's slow going with the wagon, but speed means less to us right now than the happy fact of all those provisions packed in the buckboard bed behind me. Early afternoon, we make camp in a gray hillcove high above the turnpike, a concealed place amid thick oaks and evergreens where we can watch the road below without being easily seen.

   "Tents this time, boys. We'll stay here a day or two," Sarge announces before leading a few of the boys off on horseback to reconnoiter. The rest of us set to work, the customary chores involved in setting up camp: digging a latrine ditch, gathering firewood, pitching tents. Duties done, I'm snug beneath my canvas, digging out my books, enjoying the privacy of my tent. After a few paragraphs of *The Iliad*—I'm infatuated with Achilles, swift-footed and shaggy-breasted as he is—I slip off my spectacles, cover myself with a blanket, close my eyes, and drowse. Haven't savored the luxury of an afternoon nap since we left winter quarters. For a second I think I hear distant artillery—God knows my dreams are often full of it—but then rain starts tapping the canvas above me and there's a rumble of distant thunder. Thankful to be warm and dry, I drift off.

—

CHAPTER SIX

—

The way a stone shatters a pond's smooth skin, that's how Rufus' shouts shatter my sleep. He throws open my tent flap, yells, "Sarge caught him another Yankee! He sent me to fetch you! Come on!" and disappears.

I lie there for half a minute, listening to rain pattering the tent. Despite my wool blanket, the shivering starts up again. Then I rise, pull on my brogans, check my pistol, put on my forage cap, and push out into the drizzly afternoon.

There's a commotion on the far side of camp, so I hurry in that direction. A good half of the company's standing around in the cove's cold air, staring expectantly into the leafless woods. Gray uniforms, grey tree trunks, horses' nickers, and then a telltale flash of hated blue. Pretty soon Sarge rides into the clearing, wide smile on his face, dragging the Yankee behind him.

The man's big and blond. His hands are tied in front of him and tethered to Sarge's saddle horn. He's bare-headed, cap lost in some scuffle, I guess, dressed in Union blue and muddy boots, and he's gasping and stumbling, trying to keep up with the horse's pace.

Oh God, not again. A man that young and brawny, that's the kind of prisoner Sarge tends to keep. I know what's coming next, and it makes my belly hurt. Sarge has done this before, despite the proper rules of combat. No one in the company's got the guts to object. Guess they're afraid if they do, they might end up suffering like the Yankees. Besides, most of them enjoy the spectacle and convenience of a helpless foe to focus their rage on. The war's been going on for years; despair and exhaustion make men mean.

"Ian! Get over here!" Sarge yells. I lope over just as the Yankee slips in the mud, falls onto one knee, then hits the ground face-first.

Sarge laughs and spits. He drags his prisoner a few yards on his belly just for the fun of it before reining his horse to a halt. A few of the men join him, guffawing and hawking spittle in the captive's general direction. Most of them both fear and admire Sarge; they imitate him, and sometimes, especially after last autumn's Burning, that means they're viper-vicious, especially toward the few Yankees we seize. In the past, most prisoners Sarge has sent off, as is proper, to our big Confederate prisons like Libby or Andersonville, where, with luck, they might be paroled or exchanged. Lately, though, the prisoner-exchange system has broken down, so good-looking, burly boys like this, those are the ones he occasionally keeps around to torment. Guess he finds their size and strength a challenge. He loves to see them break. He always breaks them. I try to look away, but I can't. Something inside me likes to see them suffer almost as much as he does. I guess cruelty runs in our family.

"Get him up, Ian," Sarge says, swinging down off his saddle and striding off in the rain to fetch what's needed for what comes next. I know better than to argue. Hateful as he can be, Sarge is generous to kin and has always taken good care of me. I unknot the rope-tether from the saddle horn, then stand above the Yankee, who lies prone and panting. I want to reach down and help him up, but Sarge has told me pity has no place when one's homeland is being threatened, so instead I nudge him in the side with my shoe.

"Stand up, boy," I say, mustering that hard-edged voice I've learned, tugging on the tether, "if you know what's good for you." The soldier tries to obey, pushing himself up on bound hands. He slips again, hits the mud, and curses. Then he takes a deep breath, rolls over onto his side, and looks me in the eyes.

He's the handsomest man I've ever seen. That's my first incongruous thought, despite the grimace on his mud-smeared face and the blood caking his brow. His eyes are weirdly blue, the color of burning moonshine. Many days' worth of blond beard stubble roughens his baby face. His mouth is small, with full red lips; beneath the mud and blood he's very pale; his forehead's high, with a premature widow's peak; his hair's shaggy, of medium length, a pale yellow like jonquils; his jaw is square and set. I can tell he's scared badly but trying to look brave. Hell, he looks several years younger than me, and I'm just twenty-five. Suddenly I want to help him out of this, touch his young, scared, pretty face.

Feelings are damned useless. I need to be tougher; I need to be tougher. How many times has Sarge told me that? I should hate this man, this fucking invader. "Get on up now," I say, jerking on the rope.

The Yankee licks his lips and then rolls onto his knees and stands up, looming over me. I look up at him, suppressing a gasp. He's probably twice my bulk and height. I've never been physically impressive—the puny one in my family, and more of a scholar than a soldier. My lean frame, round spectacles, shaggy hair, and scruffy black beard have never intimidated anyone, much less this blond giant, which is why I have my gun out now.

"I'm a crack shot, big man," I say, which is no lie, one of several skills I've developed to compensate for my slight size. "Don't be bolting." The Yankee looks down at me, licks his lips again, and nods. Gun in his back, I push him through the rain. Sarge is waiting. The men follow, sniggering.

—

CHAPTER SEVEN

—

"Sir, I respectfully request that you leave off. As a prisoner of war, I should be treated properly. You should—"

Sarge nods. I stuff the rag into our prisoner's mouth and try to tie it in with a bandana. The Yankee spits it out and continues his protestations, his voice a deep baritone. "Sir, *please*, I'm a private in the Union Army. You should honor the rules. I demand that you—"

Sarge backhands him, splitting his lip. "Tougher, Ian, tougher," Sarge sighs, retrieving the rag from the mud, stunning him with another slap, cramming the balled-up cloth roughly into the man's mouth, and then knotting the bandana between his teeth so tightly his stubbly cheeks crease.

This is the customary welcome given to those prisoners Sarge decides to keep. The tether's been tossed high over a tree limb and tied; the Yankee's stretched out, hands hauled above his head, swaying on tiptoes. "Strip 'im, Ian," says Sarge. Pulling out my Bowie knife, I cut the muddy coat, vest, and undershirt off our captive, first slicing the layers up the back, then circling him to tear off the remnants till he's hanging there half-naked in the cold mountain air.

His nakedness is like a poem. I don't want to feel this. The skin revealed is even paler than his face. A dense layer of honey-hued hair covers his big chest and flat belly, making a little ruff over his collarbones, feathery explosions in his armpits. Freckles scatter his wide white shoulders. The thick muscles of his torso and arms bulge in the extremity of his restraint. I want to stand here and study him. Again I want to stroke his face. The soldier looks down at me, trying to make sound against the fabric gagging him. I think he's begging. As if I'm in control here; as if I could save him. His eyebrows arch; his forehead furrows; he shakes his head; he tugs hard at the rope suspending him.

"Stand back, Ian," says Sarge and then brings the bullwhip down. Against the taut cloth the Yankee shouts. I wince. Much of me doesn't want to watch this; much of me does. No matter. Sarge always orders me to stand before the victims and watch the expressions on their faces. He says it will toughen me.

So I watch the Yankee's eyes go wild, the sweat run down his face, his white teeth gnash the gag as the whip works his bare back and the odor of blood tinges the air. For a long time, after that initial shocked shout, his pride gives him the strength to take it in stubborn silence, save for an occasional grunt as Sarge slices open more skin. His blue-flannelled legs shake, managing a tiptoe ballet, trying without luck to avoid the lash. He stares at the sky, tosses his head, stares past me into the woods. He fights the rope knotted about his wrists till they chafe and bleed, delicate red runnels creeping down his forearms. He dances more, twisting under the ceaseless whip's black tongue.

Then his blue glare falls on me and fixes. I hold him with my eyes; he holds me with his, even after he reaches his breaking point and that brave silence is replaced by deep rag-muffled shouts that soon climb higher into screams, then dip down into sobs. *Oh God, please make it stop*, he says silently, eyes growing wet and spilling over. Something about my enemy's gagged baby face, his tear-glazed stubble-scruffy cheeks, hooks me inside, in the gut. Pity for him pools, bitter in the back of my throat. *Please hold on; please be strong*, I say silently. *You're young and powerful; you can take this.* Our eyes interlock like a long handshake till his sobs dwindle into whimpers, his eyes roll back in his head, and his head drops forward. The thrashings become jerks, then a sagging tremble, and now he's silent and still.

Swish of a sword drawn. The rope's cut from the branch. The Yankee collapses into rain-wet grass, entirely insensible. Someone chortles. Sarge's striding my way, wide smile beaming beneath his bushy gray moustache.

"Clean this up, Ian." He throws the bloody bullwhip on the ground at my feet. "For now, this swine's all yours. You're excused from morning muster, prayers, drill, and the picket line for a few days so you can guard him. Keep him bound and collared but keep him alive. This one's mighty fine. I want to own him for a right good while."

Sarge turns, hesitates, kicks the unconscious man in his honey-haired belly—as if adding a postscript to a long love-letter—and heads back into camp. In his wake, the audience of soldiers disperses. For a long time I watch rain thinning the blood on the Yankee's back. Then I call Rufus over. Together we grip the tether still knotted about the big man's wrists and drag him off.

—

CHAPTER EIGHT

—

I'm damned lucky to have this roomy tent, complete with cot and camp chair, more examples of Sarge's largesse to kin. This deep into the war, not many Southern soldiers have access to such luxuries; most have to sleep out in the weather wrapped in what blankets or oilcloths they can scrounge. Once the prisoner's deposited inside and Rufus has brought me a bucket of water, I close and tie the flap. Now the Yankee and I are alone. His smell permeates the dim space: blood, mud, and unwashed armpits. I breathe him in, licking my lips, then begin my task, with some effort rolling my bulky charge onto his belly to ready him for a captivity of as-yet-undetermined duration.

First, his feet. The shackles Rufus fetched I lock around the Yankee's booted ankles—heavy iron with a foot's length of equally heavy chain between them. The key I hide in my haversack. Now there's little chance he'll try to knock me out and make a run for it—not that in his present state he's likely to.

Next, his hands. Bloodied as his wrists are, I've got to leave them bound tightly together. He's too powerful, therefore too dangerous, to be allowed much mobility or freedom. Besides, I know Sarge's ongoing orders: prisoners are always to be kept very securely and very often painfully restrained. When I check the rope about his wrists, I find it loosened from his struggle, so I tighten it, adding another yard or so of rope to secure his hands further. Wish I had handcuffs, but the pair I've used on past prisoners got lost during the company's last relocation up the Valley.

Done, I stand astraddle him—Sarge's captive, my captive. His young warrior's body is relatively helpless now. Something about his power-lessness gives me pleasure. This overcome invader's at my mercy, face down at my feet.

Now that I know he's not going anywhere, I can take my time. Gently, I remove the gag, rags bloodstained from the lip Sarge's slap split. Another urge I'd rather not host: I come close to taking advantage of his senselessness by kissing his swollen mouth but force that floodwater feeling back. Next I rinse his wounds—terrible bloody welts like claw marks across his back. No soap, this late in the war, so creek water will have to do. We're alone, and he's unconscious, and so my hands move over his flesh freely. There's delight in the density of muscle, pity in the hate-maimed skin. For long half-tranced minutes my hands tend his great body, tracing both the fresh wounds and the ridged curves of old battle scars he's received in past conflicts. It's like daubing red wine off white linen.

By now my sex is stiff in my pants, perverse demon, a throbbing I have half a mind to tend to before he wakes. Duty wins that war, how-ever—still too much to do. With Aunt Alicia's Cherokee salve smoothed over his back and bandages in place, I shove, heave, and roll his dead-to-the-world weight onto my cot—head and torso first, then hips, then legs—and cover him with blankets. Right now, I know, he needs the cot's comfort more than I do. Around his neck I lock the slave collar each of Sarge's chosen ones has worn, a smoke-black circle of iron.

My captive secured, I wipe foe-blood from Sarge's bullwhip, as or-dered, and curl it in the tent-corner to be returned later. Exhausted, I settle into a camp chair and wrap myself in a blanket against the nippy mountain night, watching my prisoner sleep and reading poetry in candlelight, prized books sent by kin back when mail still reached us. Homer first, then Shakespeare's sonnets, then a book by a Yank named Whitman.

Words give me comfort. I see myself in them. "Anger came on Peleus' son, and within / his shaggy breast the heart was divided two ways." "A man in hue, all hues in his controlling, / Which steals men's eyes and women's souls amazeth." "For thus merely touching you is enough, is best, / And thus touching you would I silently sleep and be carried eternally." Hours pass, night falls, and the long rain ceases. I listen to distant sounds—the burbling of the nearby creek, the soft laugh of my company-mates about the campfire—and wonder how many days or weeks this one will survive.

He could be dead now, still as he is. I lean over him, bending close. Yes, there's his breath, just barely. I can hear it, feel it on my face. Such thick blond eyebrows. Something about him makes me ache. I can't help myself. I touch his moist brow, trailing a finger along one round, stubble-coarse cheek. Pulling the blanket down to his waist, I rest one palm on his bare chest to check his heartbeat. I ruffle the soft hair there, finger a big satin-smooth nipple. It's been a long time since touch made me tremble so.

Sharp intake of breath. A groan. The big man's eyelids flutter open. He looks up at me, knitting his brow, then the pain floods in, contorting his face. He shifts on the cot, tries to rise, and falls back with a gasp.

Sarge told me to take care of him, and for once his orders are ones I welcome. "Lie still and keep quiet," I command, borrowing another of war's hard tones. I leave the tent, fetch my ration of spit-roasted rabbit and hoecake from the campfire, then return. The Yankee looks pretty weak yet, so I prop his head up on my haversack and feed him with my fingers. My captive's ravenous, gobbling every morsel I hold to his lips, gulping water, even sipping a bit of flask-whiskey Sarge's shared with me. Out of politeness, I try not to stare at his muscled shoulders and the deep furry valley between his pectorals. In between bites, he looks at me with a mixture of fear, hatred, and gratitude—candlelight giving his blue eyes sea-depth—muttering a sheepish "Thanks" when we're done. I guess we're both confused by this enforced intimacy. Am I his captor or his nurse? Is he my captive or my patient? Sometimes I wish the world were as simple for me as it is for Sarge.

By this time the candle's low, so I blow it out—we have to conserve everything at this point in the war—then cover him with the blanket and stretch out on the ground in my own little nest of smelly wool and oilcloth. Silence, then simultaneous sighs. Now the big blond Yankee and I begin to talk, two enemies lying side by side in the tent's darkness as if they were brothers.

—

CHAPTER NINE
—

"What's your name, Yank?" I say, studying his black silhouette against the backdrop of tent-canvas gray.

"Drew Conrad." His voice is low, tired.

"How old are you, Drew Conrad? How long you been a soldier?"

"I'm twenty. Been in the ranks a year and a half."

"And where're you from, up there in Yankee-land?"

"Hell, why should you care? I'm your enemy, that's all that matters."

"Well, yes, but we're stuck here together, so—"

"Leave me alone," Drew growls. "Don't you know you're a goddamn rebel? You've turned on your own country like some kind of nasty dog. Do you really think you scruffy backwoods boys will win this war?"

"Oh, hell," I sigh. "I don't have the energy for this. You big stupid boy, don't you bluecoats realize that the Confederacy had every right to do what it's done? You're invaders; we're defending our homes. It's the Second War of Independence, and—"

Drew snorts. "Oh no, it isn't. It's mass treason. And another thing, your sergeant's going to pay for whipping me. Don't you know that flogging a man's illegal? He's breaking the rules of war. Makes you a collaborator in a war crime."

"I'm honestly sorry about that. Sarge has a savage side, and after those sons of bitches Hunter and Sheridan did what they did to the Valley last fall, burning all those homes and farms and barns and mills—"

"You Rebs started this war, so it seems to me that Virginia is getting exactly what Virginia deserves."

"Shut up, you damned fool," I hiss between clenched teeth. Now I remember why I should be hating Yankees. "Are you insane? Talking like this to a man who has power over you? I could—"

"I know, I know. Punish me like the miserable captive I am. Fine, Reb. I'll shut up. Don't want to talk to a traitor like you anyway."

My heart's pounding. I want to punch him. Instead, I lie here, hands clenched, trying to calm down, concentrating on the play of firelight and shadow across the tent's canvas, the soothing sounds of the creek.

Across the tent, sounds of shifting on the cot. A deep groan. Another long silence. Then, "Damn, Reb, I can't sleep. Hurting too bad. We can talk if you want. Unless you want to sleep."

"I'm too riled up for slumber, thanks to you. Yes, we can talk. Except we'd damn well better change the subject."

"All right. Least I can do after you bandaged and fed me. Guess I'm not being a very appreciative, uh, guest."

More silence, like black earthworks between us. Then Drew mutters, "So what's *your* name?"

"I'm Ian Campbell."

"All right. So..." Sounds of scratching. A muffled curse. All too familiar.

I can't help but laugh. "So you have them too."

"Have what?" He sounds indignant.

"Graybacks."

"What?"

"Lice, Yank. Lice."

"You Rebs got 'em?"

"*Hell*, yes. I've had the damn things since early on in the war. Caught 'em, I think, from a blanket I foraged from a Yankee camp after First Manassas."

Drew sniggers. "A gift from Old Abe to you, huh?"

"Yeah, I guess so." I can't help but grin, scratching my own armpit. "Got used to them, I guess, though at first I was so ashamed I wanted to burn my clothes. Glad I didn't, since clothes got to be in short supply real fast. This is the only uniform I have, and I've had to mend it too many times to count."

"*I* ain't used to 'em," Drew says. "They're damned nasty. But at least I don't have to worry about infesting this blanket of yours, if you already got 'em."

"Hmmm. Well, mine have C.S.A. inscribed on their backs, so might be you'll wake up tonight with a miniature war raging over your chest and belly. And you might as well know that blanket's full of fleas too. We have damned big ones around here. Why, just the other night, here in camp, I swear to God, one of our good ole Rebel boys was fast asleep in his tent and some fleas got hold of him, intending to drown him since he'd cussed them out so bad, and had him dragged halfway to the river by the time he woke up."

I'm laughing; he's laughing. A few minutes ago, we were ready to choke one another. Now I'm lying here thinking about the hair on his chest and belly, lice or no.

"Y'all have lice races?" I ask. "When we were in winter quarters, we entertained ourselves some that way."

"Ha! Yes! Kind of funny and kind of disgusting." Across the tent, the snickering and the scratching continue.

"Sarge used to say that Yanks at Gettysburg were as thick as lice on a hen and a damn sight ornerier."

I don't know whether it's the mention of Sarge or the mention of Gettysburg, but Drew's snickering abruptly stops.

"That's enough talk of vermin. How long you been in this raggedy-ass Rebel army, Ian Campbell?"

"Since the beginning. I joined the volunteer militia that formed in our area right after that crazy old fool John Brown did what he did, trying to lead a slave insurrection and slaughter Virginians at Harper's Ferry."

The Yank begins his protest with "Now, look, Reb, John Brown was—" but I cut him off.

"Right, right, to you Northerners he's a martyr to liberty. Shut up and let me continue."

Drew coughs and nods.

"So, anyway, once war broke out in Virginia, our little crew of volunteers decided to head over to the Valley and join up with a band Sarge had gathered. Big farewell party in our holler, lots of speeches. Left wearing a fancy uniform—after a little parade and some preachers' speeches—with a passel of local boys, most of them dead now. We all were raring for a fight, eager for some action, thought we'd whip you Yankees in a month. Dead wrong about that, huh?"

"Where you from?"

"West Virginia. Southern part. Real mountainous. Mighty pretty. Along the New River and the Greenbrier River."

"Ain't West Virginia part of the Union? Why you fighting for the South?"

"It was county to county. A lot of West Virginia boys—the damned fools—are fighting for the North, us smart ones are fighting for the South. My part of the state's Rebel country through and through."

"That's going to make going back to West Virginia a little uncomfortable, isn't it? With all those triumphant Feds waiting there to laugh at you once we've beat you, Jeff Davis is hanged for treason, and you drag your whipped ass back home."

"Change the subject, Yank," I growl. "I just shared my pissant-sized rations with you, so have some manners. You Feds might be lucky enough to have decent provisions, but everything here is in damned short supply."

Drew clears his throat and scratches some more. "All right. Uh. West Virginia...do you have slaves?"

"Lord, no. We can't afford luxuries like that. Any work that's done around our farm, we do ourselves. Same for all the hill-farms round about there. Hell, I hadn't even seen black folks till we visited Sarge—he's my uncle—and Aunt Ariminta in the Valley when I was ten. Their cook was a Negro. Her name was Sapphire. She was fine looking for a woman her age. Always wore purple or red. Sarge can be pretty mean—as I fear you've discovered—but he treated her well. Don't know whether it was because she was a good cook and housekeeper or whether he felt like he ought not to misuse valuable property. Either way, I liked her right much. She was mighty sweet to me. And she made the best damned corn pone you'd ever sink teeth into. Especially with butter and Damson preserves on top."

"Do you like 'em?"

"What? Who? Corn pone?"

"Negroes. Some of 'em want to fight with us bluecoats, but we white boys won't stand for that."

"You abolitionists seem mighty confused to me," I snort. "You want the slaves all freed—after you Yanks sold 'em to the South for decades, I might add—but you don't want to fight with 'em or live near 'em. Hell, I heard Old Abe wants to send 'em back to Africa."

"I'm no abolitionist! I don't care about Negroes. They scare me, to be honest. Those black, shiny faces... I saw them in Harrisburg every now and then. I ain't fighting this war for them! I'm fighting it to keep this country together!"

"And I'm not fighting it for them either. Like I said, my people don't have slaves. I'm fighting it to keep you damned invaders out and to keep our liberties! I—"

"All right," the Yank groans. "On to other topics of discourse."

"Yes. Gladly."

"Tell me, uh, what family do you have?"

"Father and mother. We have a little hill farm near the Greenbrier River. My older brother Jeff..." I don't really want to think about Jeff. "You? Where you hale from?"

"Pennsylvania. Central mountains. West of Harrisburg. It's...beautiful there."

Another bout of silence. I know what the big torn-up Yank is doing right now. I know it as well as if he were saying it. He's thinking about home, aching a little before he starts up again.

"So, Ian, you're a farm boy? Then you should see our farm. I'll bet you'd be mighty impressed. Lord, it was looking good when I left; that was September of '63. Big fields of potatoes and corn. My family puts on some big meals. Do you have scrapple in those Rebel-lousy mountains of yours? Or pickled beets? Damnation, I could do with a big breakfast of fried eggs and scrapple!"

"I could too. This company's been subsisting on next to nothing for a long, long time. We've been back in the hills so long mail doesn't catch up to us, so the packages of food my family used to send—oh, pies and jam and potatoes, that was all so good!—they don't get to us any longer. The beef ration we get's downright mean; might as well be mule like those poor folks were reduced to eating down at Vicksburg, thanks to that son of a bitch Grant."

Drew warns, "Now, Reb, you said we shouldn't talk about—"

I choke back my anger. My country's lost so much, it's hard for me not to wish every Yankee straight to hell. "Right. Yes. Well, at any rate, I don't know how long that impressive-big frame of yours, spoiled as it is on Federal food, is going to hold up on the few rations we'll be able to spare you. But, back to your question, yes, we eat all those things, pickled beets and scrapple. Sounds like you Pennsylvania farmers may have been stupid enough to vote for Lincoln but smart enough to run a fine farm. Are you Yanks smart enough to bake biscuits? That's what I miss most about home."

"Not so much biscuits as homemade bread...with butter and honey, since we have a few hives..."

"Oh, *that* sounds good. We raise bees too. And tap sugar maple trees. And make preserves from berries. Always loved me some sweet. I'm always hankering after sweet." I rub my belly, wondering why boys with so much in common are enemies.

Drew sighs. I sigh. His belly rumbles.

"So what about your family?" I ask. "Talking about the war just makes us angry, and talking about food just makes us hungry, so let's discuss something safer."

"Well, my mother and father are still alive, and I have three older brothers. They're all in the U.S. army, still fighting, last I heard. Two sisters at home...sweet, pretty little things, both younger'n me. I—"

A bout of campfire laughter interrupts Drew. When he begins speaking again, his deep voice shakes. "I miss my mother. She cried a lot when I left. She's not too well, either. I wonder if she'll pass on before the war ends or if I'll survive to get home. One of your Confederate bushwhackers almost got me in the head last week. Now I'm here in shackles. My family's going to be so ashamed, especially Father."

What's youth worth when it's wasted on war? The sorrow in his voice makes me want to reach across the gap between us and comfort him, but that impulse is one I resist. Kindness is a trap, Sarge always says.

For a few minutes, we leave off speech. I mull memory and regret, and I have no doubt my Yankee captive's doing the same. It's part of what comes of being a soldier so far from home. I think about my mother's gray hair and lined face, my father turning over earth and following the plow-horse along furrows. I wonder how their health is, how the farm's coming along without me, what my father's planted yet. I think about the old orchard, the way wasps swirl about rotting windfall apples in autumn. I remember the wildflowers down by the banks of the Greenbrier in spring—dog's tooth violets, bluebells, the elfin umbrellas of mayapples, the snow-white blossoms of bloodroot and the gold-green fronds of ferns. I hear the sparkling gush of swallow song, smell the rich dark of the smoke house with its curing hams. I see the ramshackle barn, feel the nest of loft-hay I made every summer just under the tin roof, where I could lie listening to storms and drowsing to the patter of rain, where I lay with Thom at last.

I'm just about to drowse off when the Yank shifts, emits a hoarse groan, and says, "You still awake, Reb?"

"Yep."

"Thinking about home?"

"Good guess, Yank. Yep."

"Me too."

"So how'd you end up a prisoner anyway? None of the boys told me how Sarge caught you."

"I was part of a patrol west of Staunton. We knew your General Early had evacuated the town a few weeks back, so some of us Federals were sent to clean up any lingering Confederates, maybe watch the railroad."

"How long has your detachment been in the Valley?"

"Since...since right after those burnings you mentioned. I'd taken mighty ill about then, last fall it was—the flux, camp itch, couldn't sleep, couldn't aim my pistol worth a damn I had the shakes so bad, plus I'd lost my mount—so some higher-placed kin took pity on me and had me transferred. Wintered near Winchester. Anyway, we'd seen some Rebel skirmishers on a hill near Staunton, so we headed after them. Last thing I remember, my borrowed horse was shot out from under me and I hit the ground hard. Must have knocked me out. When I came to, I was surrounded by gray uniforms, my hands were tied, and your Sarge was pouring cold water on my face. Why is your crew of Rebels in this area anyway? I thought we'd cleaned up...I mean, I thought, after the battles last fall, that you Rebs had about abandoned the Valley to Federal control."

"Well, after we lost that battle at Cedar Creek—"

"You fought at Cedar Creek?" Drew sounds excited.

"Yes. Terrible rout. Everybody in our company barely escaped capture."

"I was at Cedar Creek too."

"Hell. Really?"

"Yes, I was part of that great counterattack behind Sheridan. We really sent you butternuts flying."

His obvious pride makes me grit my teeth. "You know why you whipped us so bad?"

"Yes, I do," Drew says softly. "I'm sorry. Didn't mean to rile you. I heard about you poor bastards and the food."

"Did you now? You with your well fed muscles and good looks? What did you hear?"

"Look, Reb, I apologize. Would you give me a drink of water, please?"

"What did you hear? Tell me, and I'll fetch you that water."

Drew shifts on the cot, groans, then says, "All right, we outnumbered you bad, but you might have tore us Feds up despite the odds, but...I heard you were hungry and so you didn't..."

"We didn't pursue you fleeing fools because we were starving."

"Yes," Drew murmurs. "That's what I heard afterwards from some of the Confederate prisoners we took that day."

"If we hadn't stopped to plunder your all's camps..."

"You crazy Rebs might have won. I admit it. You're a bunch of savage bastards, that's for sure. That cry you Southern boys give—like a wolf's howl, or an owl's—always puts a shiver down my spine. I was running full out that day, with all my buddies in blue, before Sheridan turned us around."

I rise, fetch my canteen, and hold it to Drew's mouth. He gulps and gulps. He lies back. "Thank you."

I return to my smelly nest of blankets and curl up against the cold, remembering that October day. "I hadn't eaten anything but parched corn for a week before that battle. And, as much as I hate to admit it, a rat my messmates and I shared."

"A rat? Good Lord. Were you Rebs that bad off?"

I snort. "Yes, thanks to Mr. Lincoln and Generals Hunter and Grant and—

"All right. Don't start up. What'd rat taste like?"

"Like young squirrel. We caught it in a barn and roasted it over the campfire. Better than bullfrog."

"Ack," says Drew.

"But, damnation, what we found in those Yankee camps of yours...my hands were trembling that day from sheer starvation, hard for me to load my damned rifle, and then there you Yanks went, retreating in total confusion, and we thought we'd beat y'all, and officers begged us to pursue y'all, but we just couldn't stand to pass up those victuals. It was early, you remember? Just after dawn, and the Yankee campfires smelled of breakfasts just prepared, standing ready to eat. Bacon and flapjacks, dear Jesus..."

"Enough about food! So where has your company been ever since? You call it a company, by the way, but I ain't seen but twenty or so men. Our companies are around one hundred."

"Well, we *were* a lot larger. We're an odd collection, we Rogue Riders. Semi-independent, like partisan rangers, since Sarge has some kind of sway with folks in Richmond. For much of the war, we've been aiding the Stonewall Brigade, though occasionally Sarge would take us off on little raiding jaunts near the Yankee lines, back when we had a goodly number of horses. Most of the boys were from the Valley, a few of us, as I've said, from southern West Virginia. We were all volunteers; no trashy conscripts here. Never any artillery. Mainly infantry these days, though at the start we had some fierce horsemen. General Ashby—Lord, he was a handsome man, and a great hero, he was Jackson's cavalry chief, died early in the war at Harrisonburg, shot through the heart, I cried and cried when I heard—well, anyway, he was mighty impressed with us. I wish I could be more like him."

I lie back, close my eyes, and remember that black beard, those dark eyes, that terrible day near Harrisonburg. I was half in love with Ashby, I think. "Well, so, we have very few horses left these days—hell, we can hardly feed men, much less horses. I'm surprised the cart mares we have survived this long. What with short rations and sickness—the flux has killed a lot of us, and pneumonia, and camp fever—for, as you're unlucky enough to discover this very night, it's hard to keep warm, there are never enough blankets and tents. Last winter quarters, the flux came through, ran all over the camp. "The Virginia Quickstep," we called it, trying to make a joke of it, but there was little laughter soon enough, just cussing and moaning. I was laid up for three weeks, barely survived. Seven men died. Thanks to Abe Lincoln's cursed blockade, we have no medicines left, save for what we can make ourselves from roots and such. Also, a lot of us died at Antietam and Gettysburg and... all the other battles. We're twenty-three men, about a quarter of what we were."

"And you keep fighting? Got to admit you Rebs have stamina. So where did you go after Cedar Creek?"

"There wasn't much left of General Early's army, so Sarge led us boys up into the western hills. We went into winter quarters near Staunton in November, left there when we heard we were needed at Waynesboro to back Early again. Lost there too, as I'm sure it gives you pleasure to know. That was the end of Early's Army of the Valley. Another narrow escape; I almost ended up in your shoes, a prisoner of war, but Sarge got us boys out of there. So we're hiding up in these western hills again, sending what little cavalry we have down into the Valley to harass you Yanks when we can, till Sarge figures out what move to make next."

Drew shifts again, his shackles clinking. "Hey, Johnny Reb? I want to hear more—listening to you helps me focus on something other than how I'm hurting from these welts—but, well, may I please have more whiskey? If you can spare it? I heard you Southerners could be a mite hospitable to well-behaved guests."

I chuckle. "Such flattery. Such sweet talk. Certainly, Billy Yank. It'll probably help the pain." Pulling the flask from my haversack, I take a swig and hand it over. The conversation continues, interrupted occasionally as we pass the flask back and forth, Drew's bound hands brushing mine.

"So, Johnny, where you been wounded? I have me a few battle scars, and I've only been fighting for half the war."

That's pride I hear, like a little boy too shy to boast outright. "I know you've had wounds. I cleaned you up, remember? I saw your scars. Tell me about 'em, then I'll tell you about mine."

"Well," begins Drew. "That half-moon on my ribs? A saber at Yellow Tavern. This on my arm? A bullet at Trevilian Station. This one on my shoulder, another bullet right before we took Staunton."

I recognize those battles. Suddenly my heart gives a sick jolt; the back of my neck crawls. "So you were cavalry? For Sheridan?"

"Yes, sir! Till one of your slimy bushwhackers got my horse late last fall, till I fell ill and got transferred. That was a fine mount, a—"

"Were you one of those Yanks who helped Sheridan burn the Valley?" I growl. "Because, if you were... God help you. Sarge lost his wife then, Aunt Ariminta. She was killed by a Yankee skirmisher. It must have been an accident—for what coward would shoot a woman?—but ever since her death Sarge has abhorred you Yanks even more than before and has slaughtered and tortured as many of you as he can get his hands on. He lost his farm too, to Federal firebrands, and all his livestock, as did several other men in this company. We all saw the aftermath on the way to Cedar Creek. It was a goddamned smoking holocaust."

Drew hesitates for a second, then gasps out, "No, Ian. I—I was never part of that, though I saw it happen. It—it was terrible. I'm very sorry about your aunt."

I hear him gulp more whiskey. The hand that returns the flask to me is shaking.

"All right. I'll choose to believe you, just because having to take care of someone who had been a part of that is too abominable for me to stomach. I think that's enough talk anyway. Do you think you can sleep?"

"Yep, Reb, yep," Drew mutters. "I think my exhaustion, with the help of your good whiskey, is overpowering my pain."

Drew's words trail off. Soon I can hear his breathing shift into sleep. I roll over, curling deep into the sound of his snore and the purl of the creek, and close my eyes against the dark.

—

CHAPTER TEN

My slumber's fragmented. The prisoner mumbles and thrashes on and off all night. His shackles clatter as he tosses and turns. Bad dreams, I assume; they afflict many a soldier. I would comfort him if he weren't an enemy.

Finally come dawn and reveille's bugle. I snuggle deeper in my blankets, happy to be excused from morning muster. In the pale light, only feet away he's sleeping soundly on his side, facing me, my prisoner, my charge. I listen to him breathe. Beneath my uniform, I'm hard with morning, as usual. This uncomfortable situation isn't helped when I fetch my spectacles, the better to study Drew's face. I want to feel and taste that swollen lip, that beard stubble like scythed wheat. Against my better judgment I try to imagine him naked, as I tend to do with handsome men. If it weren't for my Cherokee aunt, Alicia, as well as certain poetry I've read, I'd believe what Presbyterians like Sarge say about such desire: hell-sent, demonic, banned by Leviticus, et cetera, ad nauseum. As it is, I simply keep my feelings to myself and hope someone with similar longings might come along.

Someone big and beautiful like Drew. But not a Yankee, not a prisoner. Still, I can't resist imagining it: doing with Drew what I did with Thom in the barn one rainy night, that autumn before the war began, Thom bent over the hay bale gasping as I took him from behind. I stroke myself for a while, remembering Thom, then visualizing Drew's bare chest and the honey fur spreading there, how his muscles bulged as he fought the rope he hung from, the way his teeth bit down on the gag, how our eyes locked and held during his whipping, the way his round cheeks glistened with tears. And then suddenly I go limp, remembering how I locked that metal collar around his neck as if it were his predecessors' fate, knowing that big farm boy's hairy body is one I will soon enough be digging a grave for, not making love to. No way for him to escape the same doom of those boys before. I might as well be lusting after a cadaver.

As if my morbid thoughts serve as a warning cornet, Drew's eyes flicker open. He stares at me staring at him, gives me a bleak smile, and mutters, "Morning, Rebel. You going to let me loose today?"

My smile is no doubt equally dismal. "Not today, no." Rising, I leave the tent to fetch stale biscuit and a cup of bitter campfire coffee. Beneath a dripping tree, Sarge is leading morning prayers, an event I'm usually expected to attend and am glad to be missing. Returning, I find my prisoner sitting on the cot's edge and tugging at the collar around his neck.

"What's this for? I ain't your damn slave. This is no way to treat a prisoner of war."

"Sarge's orders," I say, standing over him.

"You not going to untie me?" Drew says, twisting his thick wrists around in the rope.

"No," I say.

"How'm I going to eat then?" His frown's sour as unripe crabapple.

"Open up," I say, holding a crumbly bite of biscuit to his mouth.

"I ain't a child," he snorts. "Don't you feel like a damn fool feeding a full-grown man as if he were—"

"I've done this before. It's necessary. Be quiet and do what I tell you, boy, or you don't eat," I say sternly. Sarge would be proud, plus I have to admit I enjoy ordering around a man of considerably greater size and strength. I also enjoy feeding such a man: it underlines for both of us how defenseless he is, how dependent on me.

"Goddamn you," Drew mutters, then parts his lips to take the biscuit.

I sit by him. We eat in silence, chewing biscuit and sipping from the shared cup, without the interruption of further protest. I get out the dried apples the slave girl in Waynesboro gave me and we have a few of those too. When we're done, I order Drew onto his belly on the cot. He obeys, leg irons clinking. I remove the bandages from his back to soothe his wounds with more of Aunt Alicia's herbal salve. He winces, curses, grinds his teeth, then thanks me as the medication, seeping in, gives his pain some relief. I rebandage him and am about to cover him with the blanket, when he sits up, pale face flushed. Hanging his head, he mutters, "I need your help, Reb. I've got to, uh, relieve myself."

—

CHAPTER ELEVEN

—

He's tethered again, with a rope attached to his collar, just in case he's fool enough to try to run despite the chain hobbling his ankles. I grip both the tether and his arm, leading him through the gray morning, my pistol loose in its holster just in case. Beside me, Drew, bare-chested, shivers in the cold and shuffles in his shackles as we move slowly past a group of my jeering compatriots, buddies of mine who would gladly beat Drew to death if they weren't so fond of me and so afraid of Sarge. Drew keeps his head high till we leave the camp, but then my big proud prisoner's head is drooping again and his quiet pleas have turned to downright begging.

"Please, Reb, just untie my hands and let me get behind a bush. I promise I won't try anything. You have the gun; you have me shackled. What can I do?"

"My name's Ian, remember?" I say. "Ian Campbell." From here I can smell the creek.

"Yes, Ian, right. Please don't make me do this, Ian. Don't shame me this way. A man shouldn't have to be seen while—"

"If you shut up, Yankee, I'll lead you a bit upstream where none of my company-mates will see you. If you don't shut up, we can go back and have you give the camp a show."

I might as well have stuffed another rag in his mouth, as quiet as he abruptly gets. No sounds but the chinking of the leg irons, a cardinal's cry, the creek's purl.

A good ways from camp now, a grove of winter-bare willows, limbs sagging over the stream. "Behave, all right?" I say, touching my holster. Drew nods. Eyes blank, he gazes over my shoulder as, standing before him, I unbutton his uniform pants and drawers and tug them down to his knees, exposing thick thighs—more pale skin coated with fine golden fur—and his sex, small with humiliation and the March chill, hiding in its sleeve of loose foreskin. I want to take it in my hand, but my prisoner's frightened enough, so I say "Go ahead" and step aside to allow him that small independence. Holding his member in one bound hand, he pisses into the creek, steam rising off his relief.

When he's done, blushing furiously he mutters, "Now I need—" Nodding, I push his clothing on down to his ankles and help steady him on the wet stones as he squats into bodily necessity. His calves tremble; he swallows hard; he leans on me. For a second I think he's going to burst into tears, but then he's done. "Stand up and bend over," I say. He does. There, in March's silvery light, are his bare buttocks, even paler than the rest of him, and, like the rest of him, coated with fine blond hair growing thicker and darker in the cleft. Another sight I want time to study, but to spare his feelings I move fast, wiping him clean with a cloth I've brought for the purpose, then dropping it into the flow of the creek.

I've buttoned him up and we're turning back to camp when he says, "Thanks for not letting your camp-mates watch. I'm sorry you had to, to clean me. It's got to be nasty to—"

I cut him off, feeling shame roll off him like campfire smoke and so trying to be casual. It's out before I realize what I'm saying. "Forget it. I've done it before with others Sarge has kept."

Drew stops in his tracks and looks down at me. "Others?" he asks. "Does your sergeant regularly treat prisoners this way? Whipped, bound, and collared like slaves? What others? Where are they?"

The man has a right to know. If I can wipe his ass, I can tell him the truth. "Follow me," I say. Tugging on the tether, I lead Drew to a mossy rock by the stream. He's shivering again, his big nipples erect with the cold, so I push him down into a patch of sun before I sit beside him and start to explain.

—

CHAPTER TWELVE

"Four. There have been four of them. In the last six months." I can feel Drew's gaze, but I don't meet his eyes. I look instead at pewter-gray light riding the creek.

"Sarge—he's really a captain, but everybody calls him Sarge—he's always had a mean streak, but ever since his wife was killed, ever since the Feds burned the Valley last September and torched his farm, he's been downright vicious. If he gets hold of a Yankee soldier, once in a rare while he keeps him. Especially if he's, uh, as f-finely built and handsome as you." I clear my throat, feeling suddenly foolish. Picking up a stone, I rub it between my fingers and then lob it into the water.

Drew laughs softly. "Thanks for the kind words, Private Campbell. Go on."

"Sarge has his fun for two or three weeks, till the prisoner dies on him after such steady abuse, or till Sarge gets bored and murders him. I'm in charge of them while they last. I keep them tied, I feed them, I mend them as best I can for Sarge to beat on and break down again. And eventually I bury them."

"What were their names?" Drew's voice is steady.

"Brandon was first. Irish boy from Boston. Blue eyes, auburn goatee. Big and hairy like you. Like I said, the ones Sarge chooses are all good-looking and strong."

"How did he go?"

I stand up, take a willow branch between my fingers, and stroke the buds. Just a trace of the coming green. "Sarge strangled him with his bare hands. Made me watch. Poor Brandon was pretty weak by then. He didn't put up much of a fight."

"The others?"

"Gregory from New York. Michael from New Hampshire. Christopher from Maine."

"How did they go?"

"Haven't you heard enough?" Finally I look at Drew. He's sitting with his elbows on his knees and his face in his hands. A shaft of sunlight falls across his bandaged back. He's so beautiful. How I wish we both were free and happy, naked together in my bed back home.

"Tell me. Please." He gazes at the ground now, as if he's addressing his request to the earth.

"Sarge pistol-whipped Greg. He lingered for a day, then died. Mike wasn't around long. Sarge gave him to the men; he'd been real smart-mouthed, so they beat him to death. And Chris just wasted away from daily floggings, exposure, and starvation."

Drew glares up at me. "And you watched all this? Didn't try to stop it?"

"Sarge is my uncle!" I shout. "My aunt was murdered! You all are enemies and invaders. And if I objected, well, I *have* objected, and..."

"And?"

"What do you think? I grew real fond of Brandon, the first one. He was sweet-tempered and so, so scared. We got to be friends. I begged Sarge not to whip and starve him. I tried to sneak him food. Sarge told me I'd be strung up with Brandon and flogged if I didn't shut up and do what I was told. So with the others I was too afraid to—"

"Couldn't you help them escape?"

"I'd have to have run off with them. I was in charge of them. If they got away, I'd have been blamed. I know Sarge is my kin, but if I disobeyed him like that, he'd—"

Drew's face falls into his bound hands again. "So you can't help me? So I'm going to end up like them because you don't have the courage to help me? I've never done anything to you, Rebel Ian. After talking last night, we already know how much we have in common. I'm just a farm boy like you who wants to make it home."

My eyes are wet. I wipe them dry with the back of my hand. There is no rejoinder to what he says. He's right.

Drew spits into a pile of dead leaves at his feet. "When will your uncle be entertaining me again?"

"Today, most probably. I'll try to get more food into you before then. I have some cheese back in the tent. To endure all he no doubt has in mind, you're going to have to keep your strength up."

"Let's go then." Drew stands up, looming over me. "I'm damned fond of cheese." His breath clouds the air. The patch of sun's long gone. "Please take me back to the tent; I'm really cold." Rubbing his bare chest with one roped hand, he shudders. His big nipples are still chill-stiff, and goose pimples scatter his arms. I want to take his hand, try to comfort

him, and promise to save him, but instead I take up the tether and lead
his chained-up shuffle back to camp.

—

CHAPTER THIRTEEN

—

Cheese, stale biscuit, blankets. In camp life, simple pleasures mean a lot. Drew doesn't make a fuss this time when I hand-feed him; now that he's heard about his likely fate, I think he's just thankful for kindness in any form it might come. Leaving my half-naked prisoner to warm up in my cot, I scrounge us coffee by the fire, plus a couple pieces of hardtack from the little hoard our cavalry stole from a Yankee camp a few weeks back. It's getting colder. The sky's a churning gray. A few flurry flakes skim the rising wind. Rufus tells me there's word the company might be moving soon, heading higher up the mountain.

Drew and I have barely finished the lukewarm cup and I'm feeding him the last of the hardtack when Sarge parts the tent flap and shoulders inside. I stand at attention, half-chewed cracker in my hand. Drew sits up stiffly on the cot, eyes wide with fear. Sarge smiles at him—I know that smile all too well—then turns to me.

"Don't you all look cozy? You two could be schoolmates...or morphodites."

"S-s-sir," I start, hating that habitual stutter that takes over when I'm scared, "I'm just f-f—. You told me to keep him alive, sir."

"Yes, yes." Sarge waves a dismissive, shut-up-now hand. "Coddling him, looks like, giving over your cot. How's he healing, Ian? Using your Injun salve?"

Drew breaks in. "Sir, please. Please observe the proper—"

Sarge looks at him as if he were an earthworm that had just uttered a blasphemy. His eyes go hard, but then he smiles and turns to me again. From his pocket he pulls a rag and a long length of rope.

"Ian, please be sure to keep this pig mannerly. I want him gagged whenever he's in my presence. I never want to hear him speak again."

I take the rag and rope from him. I turn to Drew. Apology in my eyes; humiliation and pleading in his.

"Go ahead, Ian. You know what to do."

I need to give Sarge a show of firmness. If he realizes how much I pity Drew, he'll remember how fond I grew of Brandon and how weak that made me. So I pull my pistol and press the barrel against Drew's ear.

"Open your mouth, boy, or I'll open your skull."

Drew closes his eyes and obeys. Sarge chuckles. Holstering my gun, I stuff the rag in. I tie it in place, centering the rope's length between Drew's lips, wrapping it around his head till his mouth's stretched wide and cord-covered, then pulling the rope ends tight and knotting them behind. When I'm done, Drew swallows hard and hangs his head, entirely stifled.

"Just right," says Sarge. "Very pretty. That'll keep him quiet. Keep him that way for a while. We're going to be on the move tomorrow. Today, though...the men need a little fun. I think this Yankee can give it to them."

—

CHAPTER FOURTEEN

—

Brandon, Greg, Mike, Chris, now Drew. I've had lots of practice tying a man so well he can barely move, no matter how big a frame he sports. Drew groans, straining against his restraints, but, under Sarge's watchful eye, I've given the hapless farm boy little leeway.

The flurries have stopped for now; there's a weak sun by late afternoon. We've been packing up the camp for most of the day; we're due to head up the mountain in the morning. Now it's suppertime. I'm picking mold from a cold hoecake and smearing it with a little lard borrowed from Sarge's store. In between bites, I'm savoring swigs of the whiskey that Sarge has kindly shared. I want to feed Drew, but Sarge has ordered me not to. Rations are too low to waste on pigs, he said.

While I eat, I watch Drew struggle and fall limp, struggle and fall limp. The rag-and-rope gag's still in place; probably a good thing, since he'll need something to bite down on when whatever pain Sarge has planned begins. His hands are still bound together; his feet are still shackled. But now he's bent belly-down over the camp sawhorse, face nearly in the dirt, round blue-flannelled ass in the air. I've run through a lot of rope getting him tied down to the heavy wooden frame in a manner tight and thorough enough for Sarge's satisfaction: cords interlace his arms, encircle his chest, waist, and bandaged back. He can do no more than wiggle a few inches in any direction, thanks to me. So he stares at the ground and waits for whatever's to come. Sarge's whip, no doubt.

During the six hours Drew's endured this, my buddies have taunted him with regularity and marked him with many a slimy gob of spittle. During that time, when he's not been staring at the earth, probably wondering how soon he'll be beneath it, my Yankee's been craning his neck to look for me. Since I've been as kind as I can, despite my military duty to the South and my familial allegiance to Sarge, I guess I'm Drew's anchor now, the one sympathetic face in camp. I've tried to stay away, to focus on packing, because it hurts me to see him publicly shamed, but here I am again, sitting where he can see me, a camp chair a few yards in front of him, where, if he lifts his head, our eyes can meet.

What was I thinking, ever regarding him as an enemy? He's just a boy who's suffering, whose agony I'm abetting. I felt this same unwelcome warmth for Brandon, feelings I think Sarge sensed, which is why he took such pleasure in throttling Brandon and forcing me to watch. It's so much easier to think the way Sarge thinks, especially with Sarge in charge. Yankees are pigs; Yankees are scum. Ever since I saw big sweet Brandon die, I've tried hard to believe that. But now, when I look at Drew's bandaged back, the futile ripple of his biceps against his bonds, the rope I've tied across his pretty mouth, the blue pleading in his eyes...hell, his helplessness haunts me, and his body's a lodestone drawing my eyes. He's this camp's Christ. Sarge is always talking about Christ, insisting on group prayer every morning, preaching compassion and cussing fleshly desire. Can't he see he's doing it all over again, crucifying an innocent?

Fuck this. My big bound blond Yankee needs a friend. No one's looking now; it's meal time, so most of the camp's chewing the literal fat around the fire. I stroll over to the sawhorse casually. Drew looks up at me and groans. Pain furrows his face. The rope's cutting the corners of his mouth, tinging the stubble on his chin red-gold.

"Don't look at me," I whisper. "Just look at the ground. I don't want anyone to know I'm speaking to you. All right?" Bending over, I pretend to check the tightness of his bonds.

Drew gives a slight nod.

"Don't nod. Someone might see. Just clench your hands for Yes, let them go limp for No. You holding up?"

Drew's hands clench.

"Good boy. You hurting pretty bad?"

Drew's hands clench.

"I'm truly sorry. You hate my Rebel guts?"

Drew's hands clench and fall limp several times.

I chuckle. "Yes, no, yes, no? Yep, I understand. You're one conflicted Yankee giant. Now listen. I'm not going to help you escape. If I do, I won't make it home. Sarge would whip and probably hang me for a traitor, nephew or no. But I'm going to make your time here as easy as I can. If I treat you rough in front of others, it's because I'm afraid Sarge will think I'm weak and assign you a much more brutal keeper.

But when the two of us are alone, however often that might be, I'll take care of you. I promise. Understand?"

Clench.

"In other words, when I'm cruel to you, I'm not only trying to save my own skin. I'm also trying to spare you worse cruelty at another's hands."

Clench.

"You know I don't hate you. If we'd met in another time, we could have been..."

Clench.

My messmate Rufus is strolling curiously over with a steaming cup. "All right, good and tight," I say loudly, tugging at the rope around Drew's waist.

"Want some soup?" says Rufus, proffering me the cup.

"Yep," say I, giving the sawhorse a sound kick before heading over to the campfire to spend time with my buddies, my camp mates, whose intense love for their land and their families has made equally intense their hate for this battered stranger bound to a sawhorse in the falling dark.

—

CHAPTER FIFTEEN

—

"Not me this time. This time, you're going to do it," Sarge says again, gripping my shoulder. "Show me you're strong. You need to be strong to scourge evil."

Several men have dragged the sawhorse and its trussed-up burden from the black edge of the woods into the campfire's circle of light. Packing's done for the day; now it's time for the fun Sarge spoke of. These men want something different tonight. They're tired of fiddle music.

"First time for everything, Ian. Let's see how much you hate these Northern bastards. Remember what they did last fall. How they burnt the Valley." Sarge smiles at me, offering me another swig of whiskey.

I take that swig, then another, and then another. With a frame my size, it doesn't take much liquor to hit me hard.

Now I unbutton Drew's pants and drawers and pull them down to his ankles, just as I did by the creek bank this morning. I mutter, "I don't have a choice. Understand?" In answer, Drew clenches his fists. I take in the sight of his round ass, firelight glistening on the golden fur there, and his trembling thighs. The campfire smoke stings my eyes. Then I pull my belt from its loops. Around me, the men's jollity falls quiet. Sarge pats my arm and steps back.

I double over the belt and lift it. I'm about to bring it down when I remember the Yank's tear-wet eyes, how wild and frantic they grew as Sarge whipped him. As if in answer, Drew lifts his head and releases a sharp sob.

I lower the belt. "I'm sorry, sir. I believe I'm too drunk."

"Ian. Remember all his kind has done. To our nation. To our family."

"Truly sorry, sir." I sway there, trying to meet Sarge's glare and failing. "Just can't."

"Oh, for God's sake." Before I can slip the belt back into my trouser loops, Sarge snatches it from me. "Give me that, nephew. I'll do it then. Stand back." Doubling over the leather, he snaps it, then brings it down hard across the helpless Yank's beautifully bare ass.

—

CHAPTER SIXTEEN

A fter another hour of drinking, I can hardly stand. Sarge pushes me down into a sling chair. The belt's wiped off, snug again around my waist. I stroke the leather and focus on the fire. About me men stretch out, drinking and talking in the welcome warmth. Logs crumble; sparks spit and shoot up into the sky. A few stars glint like cold eyes between running racks of cloud.

"One more?" says Sarge, holding up the flask.

"N-no, sir, think I've had enough." The men, trees, and tents appear in duplicate. Drew I can't see. They've dragged the sawhorse back out into the night, somewhere behind me. A single Drew is enough to split my heart. A double Drew I couldn't bear.

He didn't scream this time, only grunted and gasped, no matter how hard Sarge beat him. Part of me loved the way he jerked under the blows and his muscles bulged in their bonds. There was something beautiful about how his buttocks' whiteness reddened and bled. I wanted to kiss every wound my uncle inflicted. Did that Roman soldier feel the same confusion, flogging Christ?

"Sarge sure tore that poor Yankee up," Rufus says. He's whittling in the firelight, a wooden bird with folded wings.

"Shit, yes," George says. "He sure frailed that fucker good. Made him bleed, just like he deserves. I can see his big white ass from here."

When George is sober, he's all pious, even helping Sarge to lead morning prayers and occasional prayer meetings, and he's a fine horseman, but his mouth gets real nasty when he drinks. Like most of our men from the Valley who lost their homes and barns in Yankee raids, he's exceptionally savage to Federal prisoners.

"Except his ass ain't so white now." George sniggers, pointing over my shoulder. "Looks like pokeberry-stained paper, all those bruises coming up."

The smoke keeps drifting this way, pinching my eyes wet. From a woozy distance I hear Sarge's orders.

"Leave the prisoner out there till morning, Ian. You've coddled him too much. And tomorrow, I don't care how he's hurting, he walks on a tether beside or behind your cart, he doesn't ride in it, understand? No food tomorrow either. Time we started breaking him down."

"Yes, sir," I mumble, sagging back in the sling chair and closing my eyes.

"Yeah, big ole ass gleaming out there in the woods," says George. In between slurps on his flask, he fingers a loose tooth. "Boy's hairy as a goddamn bear. Needs hurt some more. Sarge, lemme beat him next. Fuck, think I'll poke him. That'd make him cry. You couldn't make him cry, Sarge. Bet I could. Just ram him like a woman. That'd—"

The resounding sound of a slap opens my eyes. Dizzy, I sit up. Sarge is standing over George; George is cradling his cheek in his hand.

"You will not be 'poking him,' George. What kind of Christian are you? Disgusting! God hates sodomites; you should know that. What you're suggesting is an abomination. I will be beating him next, not you. Get out of my sight."

Murmuring apologies, Weasel-Teeth rolls onto his hands and knees, thinks twice about further verticality, and crawls off.

"What good is my insistence on morning prayers with a man like that?" Sarge sighs. "Good night, Ian. Remember what I said. No more coddling foes." Fetching a blanket off the ground, Sarge covers me with it.

"Yes sir. Thank you, sir," I slur, staring up at the stars. When I close my eyes again, the sling chair rocks like a rowboat. I'd vomit if I had the energy.

—

CHAPTER SEVENTEEN
—

I wake to my own shivering. The fire's low; my company-mates have dispersed to their tents or lie snoring by the embers. It's night's core, the cove completely silent. I stand unsteadily, still a good bit drunk, wrap the blanket around my shoulders, and stumble off.

"Need to check on the prisoner," I say to the shadow of a passing sentry.

"Sure, Ian." It's messmate Jeremiah. Nodding, he moves on.

Dark as it is, I can make out my Yankee only dimly. He's as he was, bound to the sawhorse, pants still around his ankles. He's facing the forest, back to the camp and my approach. The footsteps he hears across dead leaves could be anybody's, Sarge with a whip, George with a stick.

"It's Ian. Don't be afraid." Drunk as I am, my caution and my self-control are reduced, so my cold hand does what it pleases, stroking his cold hip. Even in the dark, I can make out the bruises. "Are you awake?"

Drew lifts his head and nods. I can tell by the odor that he's pissed himself after so many immobile hours across the sawhorse. Beneath my hand he quakes violently. Fear or cold? Probably both.

Poke him, that's what George said. Yes, God. Poke him. But only if he wanted it. Like I rode Thom back home in the barn. Maybe I could make him want it. Abomination, no. Fuck the preachers. It's the sweetest thing I've known.

I sway a little closer, then cup his right buttock in my hand. Drew jerks and mumbles. Skittish mount. "Easy, easy, buddy boy." Shit, I'm still slurring. "I'm not going to hurt you. Just checking your wounds." I run my palm over one buttock, then the other. Gentle, gentle. Hard welts, proud flesh, dried blood. The hair, so soft across each swollen cheek. And here, in his cleft, thick tangle I finger. Sweat-moist, even in this cold. Terror-sweat. I want to cherish him, rape him, save him, break him.

Drew jerks again, hard enough to rock the sawhorse. He shakes his head and mumbles another muffled plea. Can't make out the words but sure comprehend the abject tone.

"No need to be scared. I ain't gonna—. Here, *here*, buddy boy, see what I brought you." Unshouldering my blanket, I spread it over his nakedness.

"I'm sorry. I'm so sorry Sarge beat you again." Hunkering down, I touch his face. The stubble's becoming a beard.

Drew doesn't resist. In fact, he leans his cheek against my hand. Tenderness of any kind must feel like God's grace when you're tied bare-assed to a sawhorse, beaten with a belt, and left to suffer in the cold mountain night. "I just want to take care of you," I say, stroking his lips and the rope layered between his teeth. "I won't do anything you don't want. I just want to t-touch you for a while. C-can I touch you for a while?"

Drew nods, slumped over the wood, no protests left. I sit cross-legged on the earth and fondle his beard. I caress the hairy nests in his arm-pits and the muscles of his arms. I take his bound hands in mine and squeeze. When he squeezes back, I start to cry. He joins me. For a long time we snuffle softly together, two weeping farm boys far from home, holding hands in the dark. Then footsteps sound nearby, a sentry's. I strip the blanket off Drew, pat his shoulder, and return to my tent.

—

CHAPTER EIGHTEEN

—

Hard going, these half-frozen switchback mountain roads. From this ridge-top, we can see for miles. A big Federal troop is heading in our direction, so say the scouts. The Yanks have had control of the Shenandoah Valley since last fall, so we're avoiding the Valley Pike as much as possible as we move south, crossing a few low western ridges to get out of their way, men who would want to rescue Drew and shoot a Southern boy like me through the head. It's even colder up here in the foothills: rotten snow banks beneath the hemlocks, rocky streams iced along the edges, a few flurries lashing our faces.

As ordered, Drew's trudging beside the buckboard, still shirtless, his bloodstained wrists tethered to the frame. I look over every now and then to check on him as he stumbles stiffly along, face set in a bearded frown. I've convinced Sarge to remove the foot-shackles that might slow our prisoner and thus the entire company's pace, so Drew manages to keep up, despite the pain of his wounds. There was no time this morning to salve and bandage his ass, just enough time to unrope him from the sawhorse, remove the gag, and tether him to the cart. We have a long way to go, a long steep way, and as I guide the mares over ruts and around curves, I find myself praying hard, praying that Drew makes it, even if survival simply means more suffering.

Sarge has stood firm—no food for the Yankee today—but when we take a break, I'm allowed to give Drew water. I lead my tethered captive off the road, to a cliff-jut of rock overlooking the blue-gray valley, so he won't have to see men around him eating. He wants to stand or kneel, considering the savaged state of his buttocks, but I lay down a doubled-over oilcloth, since Sarge and his objections are nowhere in sight, and Drew eases his behind, with many a flinch, onto the makeshift pillow. The wind's strong at this height, so I sit to the windward side of him to shelter him what little I can. We sip water from the canteen till we've had enough. I'll eat my own lunch ration later, when we're on the move, so he won't see me. Maybe some hardtack will ease this whiskey-after-math pounding in my head. Maybe I can sneak him food tonight.

"You were pretty drunk last night," Drew says, staring down the valley at a distant plume of smoke. His face is drawn and tired, but he smiles anyway, a crooked smile, wry, sheepish.

"I needed the whiskey to..."

"To get up the guts to beat me?" The smile's sad now.

"Yep. I've never beaten anyone. Sarge has always done it. I figured he always would, as much as he enjoys it. Don't know why he wanted me to do it. Guess he sees a softness inside me he wants to drive out. Guess he sees I don't hate you like he does." My hands' will and mine are beginning to diverge again—the coppery fur on Drew's forearms is gleaming in a sudden sunbeam and I want to stroke it—so, as substitute, I snatch up a dead stick at my feet and methodically peel off its husky bark. "I'd ask you to forgive me, but I don't deserve it."

Drew's laugh is low. "Forgive you for tying me down so I'd be easy to beat or for stroking my ass like you love me?"

I break the stick in half and toss it over the cliff-edge. I stand up. "Sometimes, when I'm drunk, I get confused. So I apologize for both. Come on, Yankee, let's go back." I lift the tether and tug.

Drew tugs back, tipping me off balance. "Sit down, Rebel boy, Rebel Ian. I've got something to say." For once I'm the one who obeys, settling back on the stone.

Now it's Drew's turn to fiddle. He retrieves a dry leaf from the ground and picks at it with thumb and forefinger. "It wasn't so awful being beaten. I could feel you there, sharing my suffering somehow. I knew you...don't hate me. It hurt bad, surely. But even as that very belt you wear split my skin and bloodied me, even as I could feel how much your uncle despised me, I could also sense your concern and caring, Reb. I could feel your kindness almost as much as his cruelty. If I had any doubt of that kindness, that doubt was banished later on, when you covered me with the blanket—that felt damned good after all those hours of being exposed to the cold. And when you touched me, that felt good too. At first I thought, the way you were fingering my behind, that you were planning to...and I was surely scared. But I was wrong. And, if you want to know," Drew says, crumbling the leaf into tiny particles and letting them drift off on the wind, "here's the skull-bald truth. Your touch was of some comfort to me in the cold and the dark."

Stunned, I'm spared the attempt at an answer, for there's Rufus bounding over to announce our departure. "Git up, Yankee," I growl for Rufus' benefit, rising and tether-tugging Drew to his feet. Wordlessly he follows me to the wagon. I knot his tether to the frame, and we're off again, following the windy ridge, the two of us one story among many in the company's slow gray column.

—

CHAPTER NINETEEN

—

"This stick'll do," says Sarge, taking his Bowie knife to a straight section of low-hanging white oak branch. "Bark needs to be left on. I want it rough. Get a little blood going."

"Yes, sir," I say, hiding my heartsick queasiness. After Brandon, Greg, Mike, and Chris, I know what's next on the agenda for Drew.

The company's settled in a hill cove much like the last, a day's march south of Staunton, a day's march north of Lexington. The weather's taken a turn for the worse, though: the intermittent flurries have turned to light, gusty snow. Now that the camp's set up, the men are busy getting fires going, digging out rations, making bean soup and coffee. After a long day of travel, with little but water and hardtack, those simple smells are downright delectable.

Torture, though, for Drew, to smell meals denied him. He's kneeling in the slowly whitening grass, hands still tied in front of him, ankles once again shackled. After hours of walking up and down slopes with no refreshment but cold water, he's looking pretty whipped and weak. With his big arms, he hugs his bare chest in the thickening snowfall. I've seen this before: after a few days of bondage, torture, exposure, and starvation, the prisoner's anger and defiance crumble like stream banks in flood. Hanging his head, Drew waits for what pain Sarge might have in mind and what small mercies I might be able to arrange.

No mercy tonight, that I've been told. Sarge hands me the short stick; the rope I already have in hand, and the long wooden rod that we've used before on other prisoners. "If he gives you any trouble, let me know, and I'll send a few men over to hold him," Sarge says, then heads toward the campfire for his meal.

I stand before Drew for half a minute before he looks up, exhaustion in his eyes. "Doesn't look like bean soup to me," he says, smiling weakly in the dusk.

"No," I say. "You need to come with me."

"They still won't let you feed me? Right now I'd kill for a wool shirt and a piece of pie."

"No food for you. And you need to spend another night outside. This is going to really hurt. But you can take it."

Drew shakes his head, then lifts his face into the slow fall of snow.

"I'm going to put you right outside my tent. If I get a chance, tonight I'm going to sneak you some food and cover you with a blanket when no one's around. That's the best I can do."

Drew reaches over and fingers the rod in my hands. "I know what you're going to do. We use this punishment too. A few times I even helped. The men were all sobbing like children by the time we released them."

Grabbing the frame of the cart, Drew pulls himself to his feet.

"You know better than to fight me, right?" I say, looking up at my blond giant.

Drew sighs and rolls his eyes. "I know better. Your Sarge is wearing me down good, and hell, it's only been a couple of days. As much as I want to get away, well..." He lifts one foot off the ground and rattles the short chain connecting his feet. "And, good as you've been to me, I don't want to get you in trouble." He's briskly rubbing his breast, blue-white now with long hours in the cold. Those chill-stiff nipples again. I want to warm them with my mouth.

"Come on," I say abruptly. Taking his wrist-tether, I lead him first to the latrine-trench to relieve himself before his long immobilization begins, then to my tent, which I've pitched at camp's edge in hopes of relative privacy. Risking Sarge's disapproval, I lay down an oilcloth on the hard ground before we begin.

"You need to sit down now," I say. "The cloth should help ease your butt."

Drew lays one hand on my shoulder. "Wait, please," he says, desperate. "Is this some kind of test? Is God punishing me?"

"I don't know. I'm sure Sarge would say so. My Aunt Alicia's Cherokee, and I like her God a lot better than Sarge's. Thanks to her, I see God in places other folks don't."

"I want you to tell me about that sometime," says Drew, gripping my shoulder hard as I help him sit stiffly down. "Damnation, my ass hurts," he mutters, shifting uncomfortably. "Any chance for salve tomorrow?"

"Yes, I hope so. I have a good bit left."

"That'd be wonderful. It surely helped my back." Looking up at me, Drew musters another grin, mere minutes from the pain he knows is near. "So you wouldn't mind rubbing it on my butt, huh?"

Amazing. The beautiful bastard is downright flirting with me. "No, Yankee boy." I chuckle and blush. "Whatever helps soothe your hurt. I'm selfless that way."

Our grins match for a moment before Drew drops his head and lifts his hands, muttering, "Go ahead. Do your duty." Using the length of tether, I tie his wrists together more firmly. With more rope I bind his already shackled ankles very closely together.

"Draw your knees up and wrap your arms around your legs. You know how it's done."

He does what he's told. I'm about to insert the rod over his elbows and under his knees when he says, "Wait, please. One more minute. I just want to... You'll be near, promise? I don't want to be alone all night." His voice is lower, huskier than I've ever heard it.

"Promise. I'll be here in my tent. I'll only be a few feet away."

"Will you talk to me some, while I'm out here? Please?"

"Yes, Drew." His arms are so thick with muscle that it takes me a while to work the rod through. Finally it's in place; we're both silent as I circle and knot rope around his elbows, forearms, and knees to hold the rod in place. He's going to be hurting badly real soon. The lean and limber boys I've seen endure this punishment have taken it a lot better than muscle-bound ones like Drew.

Drew's down to a hushed whisper now. "Oh, God, I—I'm really afraid. I'm afraid I'll break and cry and shame myself. I don't think I can take this all night."

"I know. Cry if you need to. Hell, we wept together last night, right? There's no shame. Just cry quietly so the others don't hear you and come over here. They're sure to mock you or worse."

I hold the rough oak stick up. Before I can lodge it in his mouth, in a rush Drew chokes out, "You're my only hope, Reb. I don't mean the hope of escaping, I mean, just...while I'm here, hope for kindhearted-ness. You asked before if I—if I'd forgive you for touching me. Look, now I—I'm begging you to touch me whenever you can, as tenderly as you can and as often. It's all I have left."

We stare at one another for a moment before I nod, brushing his hair with a palm. "I'm going to tie this pretty loose, so it doesn't cut your mouth too bad." Drew whimpers as I insert the stick between his teeth as gently as I can. The last lengths of cord I loop over the ends of the stick, tying it in place, knotting the ends together behind his head.

Done. He rocks a little in his bonds, testing them. He sags and sighs, biting down on the stick-gag bit. Snowflakes gather on his bunched shoulders and melt. "I'm going to fetch myself some food," I say, brushing flakes from his forehead, "and pilfer a little for you too." Leaving my prisoner bucked and gagged in the snow, I head through violet twilight for the nearest campfire. What you've come to own, I'm beginning to learn, you must care for.

—

CHAPTER TWENTY

—

More cheese, more biscuit, dried apples, a little cold soup in a coffee cup, all of which I'm hoarding to feed Drew later. But not now. Sarge is sure to be over at some point to make sure his orders have been properly carried out. So I wait. I lie belly down on my cot, tent-flap half open to keep an eye on Drew and, beyond the sideways silhouette of his trussed-up form, the rest of the camp. Quietly, by candle-stub light, I read parts of *The Iliad* to my captive and sip from my flask. The story's new to him; I'm hoping the excitement of the epic will distract him from his pain. I'll stay up all night if I have to in order to help him through this hell.

Listening, Drew's very still, though occasionally he stretches his limbs as best he can in such a constricted position and whimpers softly. Sometimes he shifts his weight onto one buttock to give the other some relief or he works his no-doubt numb hands around in their rough bracelets of rope. For the most part, his head droops, chin on chest. Every now and then he lifts his head to look at me, though I can't see his face in the dark.

I leave off at the spot where the story seems uncomfortably relevant: the great Greek warrior Achilles has just heard of his beloved comrade Patroclus' death and, in grief, covers himself with ashes. It's full dark now; the snow's tapering off, the gusts dying down. Moonlight comes and goes through flitting clouds. When my pocket watch marks midnight, it should be safe to turn traitor long enough to feed my captive.

Blowing out what's left of the candle, I leave us in the dark. Beyond Drew, I can make out the distant forms of a few men still drinking around the fire. Someone's playing a banjo, probably Jeremiah, enjoying himself a little before he starts his sentry rounds.

"Uhh," Drew groans around his bit.

"You're really suffering?"

"Uh." Drew nods and sways.

"Cold as hell, too, I know."

"Uhhh."

"You still want me to talk to you? Will that help?"

"Uh huh!"

"All right." I roll onto my back and tug the blanket over me. The warm weight of it feels like guilt, since I know Drew's so cold. Staring at the black canvas above me, I begin. I'm not much of a talker, but here's a damned good excuse to try.

Small things first. In between whiskey nips, I give him some background on *The Iliad*, since tonight I started reading mid-story. I tell him about *The Odyssey*, how the hero makes it home. I tell him about how pretty these hills look in the spring and promise him he'll live to see the green, the bloom of sarvisberry and dogwood. I tell him about my first boxing match, and the country ham and sweet potatoes my family enjoyed during my last Christmas at home. I tell him about Thom and what close friends we were for a while, though I leave out the sweet sodomy we shared in the barn and the fact that Thom wouldn't speak to me afterwards and moved west soon after that. I tell him about how bad these camp biscuits are and how fine my grandmother's are back home.

I pause, roll back over on my belly, and check my watch. Two hours till midnight. "More talk?" I ask. Drew grunts and nods. He's started a rhythmic rocking in an attempt to warm himself. Behind him, only a couple of men are left around the campfire's low glow. The snow's entirely stopped, the sky clear. Moonlight paints purple shadows across the fallen white. I'm sleepy, a little drunk, but I need to keep talking. Drew's holding onto my voice like a drowning man does driftwood, or, more to the point, like a freezing man does tinder and a flint. So I ramble on, sipping my flask, moving closer and closer to risky, whiskey-frank topics. Despite his youth and strength, I don't know how much longer he'll survive, and, as much as he depends on me, I know he's not likely to divulge my feelings to the others, so what I mumble now approaches deep things I'm afraid to admit.

"Keep that rocking up, buddy. Move your fingers and toes around too, to keep off frostbite. Be patient; I'll bring out the blanket in just a little bit. I have some cheese and biscuit in here for you, and some cold soup. I'll feed you real soon. Just hold on."

Drew's rumble of affirmation. Shivery call of a screech owl. Whiskey burning my throat.

"So you like *The Iliad*? I saw a drawing once, of Achilles and Patroclus, in a book. One was bandaging the other's war-wounds. Some things

I've read say that... men could be together in different ways then, that warriors who fought side by side would take comfort in one another."

Long silence, then another grunt and nod. Remotely, Jeremiah's banjo sounds, the first mournful notes of "Shenandoah."

"Big as you are, buddy, you look like Achilles or Hercules, like a Greek hero in chains. I wish I were as tough and strong as you. Tomorrow I'll salve your butt and back and bandage you up, I promise."

Bit-bent mumble of gratitude. More rocking in the dark.

"You wanted to know more about where I see God? Well, right now, in this snow, and the bare tree trunks, and the moonlight, for sure. The campfire too. And my body, and your body. And, and y-your beard, and the way your muscles knot up when you struggle, and the marks on your back, and the hair on your chest."

"Uhhhh?" Drew grunts, lifting his head. Surprise or query? If only I could see his face, know for sure what he was feeling. The rocking ceases, then starts up again.

Drunk and bold now, these mutters of mine. "I wish you were in here with me, buddy, all hairy and warm. I know you're so cold. I wish I could hold you, rub your muscles into ease. I'm glad you find my touch a solace."

The moon's shifted. Now its light illuminates Drew; in its gleam his bare skin looks blue. He rocks in silence, my broad-shouldered soldier, my brave slave. "I wish I had you naked," I whisper, closing my eyes. "I wish I had you home."

—

CHAPTER TWENTY-ONE

When I wake, it's deeper dark, the moon passed over. *Goddamned fool*, I think. *Drew's out there starving and freezing, and you fell asleep beneath your cozy covers.* I'm about to fetch his food from the tent-corner in which I hid it when I hear again what must have woken me: a ripping sound, followed by a deep groan.

Cautiously I peer past the tent flap. There's a man standing over Drew. Too dark to make out a face, but I can tell it's Sarge. Drew looks up at Sarge and shakes his head; against his gag he's begging brokenly, last vestiges of pride shattered. Sarge bends down, grips Drew's jaw in one hand and with the other tears a strip of bandage off Drew's back. Another rip, another groan.

"S-sir?" I say, crawling out of the tent. "What are you doing?" I want to break my uncle's jaw but, of course, think better of it.

"Ah, Ian. Just helping you change his bandages." Another rip, more pale cloth hanging from Sarge's hand. "Tomorrow, perhaps, we'll open these wounds up. Unless you object to another beating. You seemed squeamish the other night, when I invited you to take your belt to him. Surely a soldier as brave as you've proven yourself to be over the last few years of war should savor an enemy's suffering."

Suddenly it's there in such a challenge, in another of Sarge's endless invitations to cruelty: how to keep Drew alive longer. I bend down, take hold of a bandage, and rip. Drew gulps back a sob. In the starlight I see his white teeth gnash the stick-bit. Sarge laughs, pulling off another strip. I do the same. We take our turns till Drew's back is bare, wounds dark against his back's pallor even in such dim light, like illegible words cut into the surrounding snow.

"Sir, I apologize for my weakness. I was very drunk. And, to be honest, since it was you who lost so much during the Burning last fall, and since you do clearly savor his suffering, I think you should reserve the privilege of beating the prisoner for yourself," I say. Now I'm feeling like Odysseus: not the strongest of warriors but sometimes the most devious. "This Yankee's been a powerful trial to me; I'm ready to see him punished whenever you say it's fitting."

"Excellent, Ian! Finally you're being a proper nephew. You might not have been born with strength, but you can certainly achieve it," says Sarge. "Till tomorrow, you can start by tightening this pig's bit. He's chewed it half loose."

I obey, unknotting the gag. Drew winces as I secure it tighter; warm drool spills over the bit, dripping onto my hand.

"Just one more thing tonight. This poor Yankee looks mighty cold, so I'm going to warm him up."

The previous prisoners endured this too. There's nothing I can do without risking the hope I suddenly see. I stand silent as Sarge unbuttons his trousers, pulls out his penis, and circles our prisoner. The piss splashes across Drew's face, over his shoulders, and down his back. My Yank sputters and gasps, heaves and shakes. The bitter odor fills the air. Sarge chuckles, "How's that, boy? How's that? Warmer now, I'll bet." Finished, Sarge wipes his dick across Drew's cheek, then buttons up, pats my back, wishes me a good night, and disappears into the dark.

Drew waits till Sarge is safely off before he breaks down, cursing and crying against his gag. I hunch down and grab his hand. He shakes me off. "Listen to me," I say, gripping his jaw just as Sarge had. I can feel streaks of saliva half-frozen on his bristly chin. "I did *not* betray you. Listen to me. I think I know how to make things a little easier on you and how to keep you alive a little longer."

His sobs cease as abruptly as one of Jeremiah's banjo strings sometimes snaps. Wiping the tears and urine off his face, I explain. "If Sarge thinks I enjoy seeing him torture you, maybe he'll let me keep you alive longer. It'll mean regular whipping and restraint, the sort of things you've already endured, but it might mean fewer nights out in the cold and it might mean more food." It's a gunpowder mix, this amalgam of tenderness, pity, and desire I feel, stroking his wet beard.

"Sarge's been after me since I was a little boy to lay down my books and get mean, to toughen up and turn ruthless. This way he might think he's succeeding; he might want to keep his big blond whipping post around longer. What do you think?" I ask, pressing my face to his. "It's better than dying in just a few more days from starvation and exposure."

Drew's head bobs with more energy than I thought he had left. I squat there for another few minutes, warming his hands in mine, till

I'm convinced everyone's asleep and the sentry isn't likely to pass by soon. Then I loosen the knots behind his head, ease out the stick-bit, and fetch food and blankets from the tent. Shawled in wool, my Yankee Achilles gives a throaty growl and falls to, hurriedly gobbling the cheese, bread, and spoonfuls of soup I lift to his lips. I stand guard by him for a long time, while, despite his bonds' discomfort, he drowses exhausted in the blanket's long-awaited warmth. When a sentry's tread alerts me, I reluctantly remove the blanket, rope the bit back into Drew's mouth, tightly, in case Sarge checks again, and slip back into my tent.

"That's all I can do for you tonight, Yank," I murmur, tying the tent flap half open again so I can see him and he can see me. "Tomorrow I'm going to talk to Sarge."

Drew nods. "Thank you. Thanks. Thank you. Thanks." His words are distorted by the stick I've tied in his mouth, but I can make them out nevertheless.

Lifting my flask, I take a last swig. I slip off my spectacles, pull my blanket up to my chin, and fall asleep knowing how fortunate I am.

—

CHAPTER TWENTY-TWO

Rain. That's the patter of rain on the tent. And something else, below the rain's rhythm, some other sound, nearby but barely audible. I roll over, slip on my spectacles, and listen. Through the tent's entrance I can make out Drew's shape in the dim gray that heralds dawn. His head's down and his shoulders are shaking. Behind him, in the camp, no one's in sight.

I crawl from the tent and kneel beside him, in the lingering smell of urine, the must of dead leaves growing sodden in the rainstorm. Drew's sobbing, very quietly. This long agony has finally broken him just as it did the others. Why is it that, broken, he's even more beautiful? The sound of his suffering makes burning embers crumble and flare inside my chest. I stroke his temples; he lifts his pain-twisted face to me; around us the rain drums down. He's bound, he can't fight me; he needs me too badly to betray me. And so I do what his naked woe demands that I do. I kiss his forehead, his streaming shoulders, his bearded chin. I kiss the stick-gag between his lips, then, as best I can, the lips themselves. Drew pushes his mouth against mine and sobs harder. Rain's speckling my lenses; my fingers roam his chest hair, his torso's hard curves.

Footsteps. I look up, and there's rangy Jeremiah on another of his rounds, leaning against a sapling, watching us in pre-dawn light the dove-gray hue of his uniform. My friend from back by the Greenbrier, who hoed beside me the same hilly acres, who surely shares the same sense of sin as all our people. But what I see in his face is not a scowl of disgust but a sad smile.

I'm up and stuttering now, trying to explain—"I-I-I w-was just..."—but Jeremiah strides over, grips my shoulder, and shakes his head. "Ian, take comfort where you can find it. To hell with those preachers back home. And help this poor bastard as best you can. I won't tell." With that, he's gone, just a crunch of leaves receding in the rain.

As if Jeremiah's understanding gives me some long-awaited permission, I crouch down, unknot and remove Drew's gag. Laying it on the leaves, gently I wipe blood from the chafed corners of his mouth. Then I grip him by his metal collar, pull his face to mine, and kiss him again, full on, hard and fast. He parts his lips, whimpers, and our tongues nestle together for a few sweet seconds. He tastes like iron and salt-rising bread. I pull away, looking into his eyes, running a fingertip over his swollen lower lip.

"Please," Drew gasps. "Oh please, Ian, please! It hurts so bad. Please get me out of this."

"I will. I'm going to untie you and fetch us some food. We're going to have a proper meal together. But first I have to speak to Sarge."

—

CHAPTER TWENTY-THREE

I don't know what power keeps the stutter from my words this morning, but I'm thankful. I sit in a sling chair in Sarge's tent and explain, as calmly as I can, my requests. He gives me only the edge of his attention as he shuffles papers on his camp desk.

I begin with what he wants to hear. "Sir, will you be beating the prisoner today?" My voice is tight with counterfeit eagerness. "That boy deserves to suffer."

"Tomorrow, Ian. As much as I want to string the Yankee up and flog him bloody, I'm heading down the hill with some of the boys to rustle up provender. We'll need some provisions to get the boys to Lexington."

Another day for Drew to gather his strength, thank God.

"Certainly, sir. I'll wait. But may I ask permission to—"

"What, what?" Sarge asks, impatient. He's poring over a map.

"Sir, I want to get the prisoner out of the elements and feed him. I—"

Suspicious cock of the head. His gaze abandons the map to fix on my face.

"Now, Ian, if you're going soft, as you did with that other bluecoat—Brandon?—I'll have to give over the prisoner's care to someone else. George has volunteered to take the Yank off your hands. He's older and firmer, despite his unseemly behavior when in his cups."

Now I've really got to be convincing. George will beat Drew and most probably, cross-eyed drunk one night, rape him. "Sir, I'm not going soft. I want the Yankee out of the cold because, to be honest, if he suffers frostbite and loses toes, he'll be more of a trial to lead around. And, since he's forbidden to ride a cart when we break camp—"

Sarge nods. "That makes sense. Go on, go on."

"I want to feed him so, well, I want to keep him alive for a while to—to torment. When I watch you beat him"—I stroke my belt—"his suffering...nourishes me, I guess the same way that you took righteous pleasure in the pain of those other prisoners."

Here's the truth embedded in my manipulative lies. It's a mystery, not only why I've come to care for Drew, but why it gives me such pleasure to see him bound and sunk in deep hurt. Maybe there is a demon in me.

"Since I'm your kin, I'm finally... Well, you know, sir, what they say: blood tells."

Chin cupped in hand, Sarge studies me for a long stretch in silence. "And you will prove to me your loyalty and kinship by making him suffer as I would make him suffer?"

"Yes, sir, I will prove it. At my hands he will bleed and weep." Blood and tears, yes, Sarge and I both cherish them, though I suspect for different reasons.

Sarge, smiling, drops his eyes back to the maps at hand. "You have my permission to warm and feed him, though I expect you to keep him well bound. Tomorrow, when I return, I will break him again with the lash."

"Thank you, sir." A quick salute, and I'm out in the rain, striding back to my tent as fast as I can.

—

CHAPTER TWENTY-FOUR

I can hear the muffled cussing from a good distance away. When I round the tent, I see the cause of it. That damned ferret, George, is standing beside my captive and snickering as he roughly slaps the sides of Drew's head. Though I left Drew ungagged, George has apparently seen fit to force the stick-bit back in, against which Drew growls protest. Just as I shout, "Get away from him!" George slams a boot into my helpless giant's side.

"You miserable fuck," I say. Human weasel he might be, but George still has ten pounds on me. No matter. There's not a man in this company who can outbox me. Been a while since I got a chance to demonstrate my skills. I'm on him in an instant. My right fist rocks his jaw, knocking out a scurvy-loose tooth; my left follows, catching him in the belly. He doubles over, gasping, loses his footing on rain-wet fallen leaves, and hits the ground hard.

The bastard scrabbles about in the mud, whining and snarling, trying to gain a foothold. I give him a kick in the side to match the one he inflicted on Drew. He grabs a sapling, pulls himself to his feet, and snarls, "Damn you, Ian! You're a goddamn Yankee lover. I'm going to tell Sarge. I'll make you pay!"

My fists are up again. There's battle-lust hazing the edges of my vision now, like a red tunnel with George set in its lucid center, in the focus of my hate's sights. I get this way when someone threatens someone I love. "Tell him, swine. And I'll remind him how much you want to 'poke' this here Yankee. You remember what he thought of that?" I laugh and spit into the leaves at his feet, then lunge forward, feinting another punch. George yelps, turns tail, and he's off, limping toward the camp. When he's disappeared among the tents, I shake the remnant rage from my head and sink to Drew's side.

"You all right?"

"Uh huh," he grunts, red-faced and teary-eyed.

Drew smells like tobacco. How the hell did that happen? Then I notice the brown juice streaking Drew's cheek, the brown liquid dripping off Drew's chin, and remember Weasel-Teeth's fondness for the plugs of chewing tobacco the army rations out.

"I've won you some relief, big man," I say, wiping the smelly spittle off his face. "And I won't let that swine hurt you again."

First I remove the gag, next the ropes binding the rod between the crooks of Drew's elbows and the backs of his knees; now I remove the rod itself, releasing my captive from his hours of agony. Drew's face contorts as he slumps onto the ground on his side, stretching long-constricted limbs. "Jesus," he sobs between gritted teeth. "Oh, Jesus, it hurts."

"Easy, easy," I say, unknotting the ropes about his ankles. "It worked. Sarge says to keep you bound, so I've got to leave your hands tied and your feet shackled, but he's given me permission to feed you and warm you up. Let's get you into the tent."

That proves to be a difficult proposition. Having been bucked that long and that tightly, now my prisoner can hardly move. He tries to crawl on hands and knees—stiff as an old man, emitting whimpers that break my heart—but can't even manage that. Welcome albeit cumbersome burden: I grip him beneath the armpits and laboriously drag him into the tent. Inside, I try to get him up and onto the cot, but he's hurting too much. He collapses on the tent floor, curls up, covers his face with his hands, and cries, louder and harder now that we're alone and there's no chance of mocking witnesses. I soothe him as best I can, in tones usually reserved for children; I rub his joints' throbbing till his tears subside. Sighs of thanks, then he passes out. I cover him with a blanket and stroke his moist face. For a while I guard his sleep, then head out into the unceasing rain to fetch us what food might be found. I will comfort my captive while I can before Sarge returns and the pain begins again.

—

CHAPTER TWENTY-FIVE

Drew sleeps all day. His slumber is restless with what must be night-mares. Occasionally he mutters and tosses. Occasionally he jolts awake, wide-eyed and panting. I reassure him; he settles down, groans, curls into a big ball, and sleeps again. While he snores and mumbles, I nibble on biscuit, sip on sour rose-hip tea Rufus has simmered for me. I read, nap in my cot, and listen to rain shift to hard sleet at the approach of dusk. I've scrounged more bread and cheese for our supper, to share whenever Drew wakes. I've also borrowed a little more whiskey from my uncle's stash. I figure, if Sarge expects me to keep our big captive uncomfortably bound, the least he can do is help me keep my conscience and Drew's pain-tattered senses somewhat liquor-dulled. Word in the camp is that Sarge and several of the men are gone on their reconnoitering mission and that George, surly and bruise-faced, has accompanied them. Good news, because, vindictive as George is, he's sure to be plotting what revenge he can. Only vigilance, my fists' skill, and my kinship with Sarge will protect Drew and me from Weasel-Teeth.

It's near dark again when Drew shifts, groans, and opens his eyes. He looks up at me, snuggles into the blanket, and sighs, "God *damn*, this is cozy. Helluva improvement over last night."

I smile. "How do you feel?"

Drew stretches and winces. "Pretty bad. Stiff as ice and twice as brittle."

"You need the latrine?"

Drew shakes his head. "Naw. Haven't had enough food and drink lately..."

"You hungry?"

"*Hell*, yes." Biggest grin I've ever seen him muster. He sits up stiffly, arranging the blanket about his bare shoulders.

I hold out biscuit, cheese, and dried apples. Instead of taking them, he looks up at me. "You can feed me if you want. With my hands tied and all, I, well, I'm used to you..."

My throat's suddenly too tight to speak, so I say nothing. Instead, I sit cross-legged beside him and hand-feed him his cold supper. Occasionally, his moist lips brush my fingertips.

"Thanks for driving off that bastard," Drew mutters, gulping down cheese and a mouthful of the now-cold tea. "If I hadn't been tied," he says, working his thick wrists around in their encircling rope, "I'd have..."

"I know, I know, you're the Yankee Achilles. Big as you are, you'd have broken him across your knee. Wish I had your muscles."

Drew laughs softly. "You did all right for a little guy, Rebel... Patrok...?"

"Patroclus," I correct.

"Yeah, Patroclus. So we're army buddies, huh? Greek warriors together. Too bad we're on different sides," Drew sighs. "Though, good as you've been to me, it doesn't feel like we're foes. But anyway, you have quite a pair of fists."

The admiration in his voice makes my cheeks glow. "T-thanks," I say. "You-you're my responsibility, and George is a cur. I've been charged to keep you prisoner, b-but"—how I hate to stutter, but this close the rich smell of him is unnerving, a mix of sweat, mud, and piss-wet wool—"as my prisoner, you deserve my protection too."

The food's gone now, though our bellies both rumble yet. We settle back into our damp blankets, me on my cot, Drew on the ground, trying to get warm, watching what's left of the light fade beyond the canvas pitched above us.

"I'm still hungry," Drew says.

"Me too. There's no other food to be f-found." I stretch out, trying to stabilize my tongue. "Sarge will be back tomorrow, and my guess is that he and the boys will have tracked down victuals of some sort from local farmers. They're masters at foraging and confiscating."

"Listen, little Patroclus," Drew chuckles. "If you let me loose...well, all right, I know you can't, but...well, if I survive this somehow and get home...and if the war ever ends, then...you hie your ass to Pennsylvania, and my family and I will treat you like a prince. We will feed you well; these damned days of stale hardtack will be a distant memory."

"That sounds mighty fine to me," I say, proffering my freshly replenished flask.

Drew's fingers fumble over mine as he takes the flask from me. He enjoys a long slurp before passing it back. "Let me tell you how it'll be. I hope you like bacon, pork roast, and ham, because we have quite a few pigs. Oh, and sausage too, and ribs simmered with sauerkraut. And potatoes! My mother sure knows how to cook up potatoes! Fried potatoes and potato cakes and potato dumplings...and dried corn and green beans, and baked chicken and chowchow and scrapple...have you ever had molasses pie? Or dried apple pie?"

"If you don't shut up, I'll have to gag you again," I chuckle, rubbing my belly. "Is this how you take your revenge on me? Those menus are reminding my innards of all I'm missing. I feel like a hollow sycamore trunk.

"Well, I can play this game too, Achilles. If I could drag you back to West Virginia on your tether, get us both home safe, we'd be able to tuck into pinto beans cooked with ham hocks, with cornbread and kale on the side. We'd have fried potatoes there too, and fried cabbage and corn pudding, and half-runner beans with bacon grease. And for dessert, maybe apple stack cake or cherry pie with cream."

"Oh damn," Drew groans. "Lead the way! I'll gladly tolerate the tether for a heaven like that!"

I suck down another flask-sip and sigh. "But as it is, we're stuck with hardtack and homesickness and eternally damp blankets. Just say your prayers of thanks that we have this tent. A lot of my buddies have to sleep in the open wrapped in oilcloths they've stolen off dead Yankees."

Drew gives a matching sigh. "I guess we're both bound, huh? You to me, me to you, both of us to this war. How long since you've been home?"

"Two years. Not many furloughs in the Rebel army. And lately, no pay either. Not that Confederate money's worth anything anyway. You?"

"Six months since I was home. Few furloughs for us either, though we were still getting pay. I used to cry in my tent at night, I missed my family so much. But I hardened up some, got at least a little used to it. Back home we were taught that hardship was God's will, his way of testing our strength."

"We were taught that too. I guess the war's both your test and mine. You've taken more than I ever could. I've never been whipped or bucked. No way I could take it."

"I didn't take it. I cried when your uncle whipped me, and I cried when I was bucked. I break easy, Ian." Drew's voice is low, shaky. "I may look strong, but I've got this scared little boy inside me. His tears shame me again and again."

"But you survived. You're here still yet. You're still strong and brave and..."

"I ain't brave. I'm terrified. I'm terrified that soon I'll be strung up again for your buddies to mock and abuse. I'm terrified of that lash your uncle used. I'm afraid that nasty little man who slapped me around will get hold of me in your absence, and you won't be there to help me, and—" Drew's voice cracks; the rush of words ceases, like a stream vanishing over a precipice.

I shift from my back to my side, speaking now not to the tent's pitch but to his silhouette on the ground. "Makes sense that you're scared. But I'll be there, buddy. You're my charge. I'll keep an eye out, I promise. I'll do what I can to protect you." I reach down and pat his bare shoulder, hard whiteness off which the blanket has slipped. For a second I think about crawling off the cot and lying on top of him, but I don't think either of us is quite ready for that.

Instead we lie there, side by side in thickening nightfall. Another screech owl is lamenting somewhere, that weird shiver of descending notes, what a ghost must sound like. Seemingly inexhaustible sleet taps the tent.

"Drunk yet?"

"Yes, thank God," Drew chuckles. "Thank God and thank you. When I'm drunk, I'm not so scared. How about you?"

"Yes indeed. Small as I am, it doesn't take much."

"So when does the torture start up again?" Drew's voice is flat, calm. The question's like a tack shoved in my temple.

Shakily, I pass the flask back. Not much left; I can tell by the weight. "Tomorrow. Sarge will be back from his reconnoitering."

"Him or you?"

I know too well what he's asking, despite the verbal shorthand. "Him. It'll be him from now on, I think. I don't think that, well, I *hope* that he won't pressure me again to beat you. I told him that, after all he's lost in the war, he deserves the pleasure of wielding the lash. I t-told him I wanted you fed and out of the elements so you'd keep alive and strong, so he c-could beat you." Goddamn tongue. Weak fool. "I t-told him that I was b-beginning to enjoy—"

"Seeing me beaten?"

"Yes."

"And do you?"

"Yes." God, I'm so glad I'm drunk.

"Why? I know you don't hate me. Why do you enjoy seeing me suffer?" He tugs at the iron collar about his neck and rolls onto his side. We stare at one another in the dim light.

"I-I don't know. S-something about how s-strong you are, how hand-some." I want to look away but I can't.

"You like this too?" Drew lifts his hands, looking pointedly at the rope that's bound them for days now.

"Y-yes," I sigh. Now I drop my gaze to the tent floor.

"Why?"

"B-because I...b-because you..."

"Stop stuttering and look at me."

I do. I can just barely see Drew's face in the last of this day's light—this bitterly cold day in March 1865, one of a long, long series of days, I'm suddenly aware, that have faded and passed into the dark. To my surprise, he's smiling.

"Finish up the liquor first," he says, passing me the flask.

One last gulp and it's gone.

"Who am I going to tell?" Drew whispers. "I owe you my life. I just told you I used to cry like a child in my tent. You've seen me sob several times now. You wiped my ass. I'm ashamed; you're ashamed. All right. We'll live with shame together. Please tell me." To my amazement, Drew reaches up, brushing my cheek with one hand—briefly, gently—before settling back down and tugging the blanket up over his bare shoulders. Gazing at me, he waits.

"I don't know why," I admit, forcing myself to return his gaze, despite my throbbing urge to turn away and look at anything—ground, tent-side, the insides of my own eyelids—rather than face him. "You're so strong and handsome that—you're the kind of man I've always wanted to be, and—when I see a man as brawny as you made weak, a man with a body so powerful, your helplessness makes me feel strong, and, oh hell, I don't know!" The stutter's gone from my tongue, but in its place is a quivering along my limbs, the way a horse's hide shudders beneath a farrier's touch. "You're like Achilles, but you're like Christ too, half-naked, bound, and wounded, and, yes, damn you! I admit it! I want to keep you tied, so I can feel strong and in control. I want to take care of you, protect you, but, yes, I want to hurt you too. There's been this crazy spirit in me since I was a child; it mixes up kindness with cruelty. Ever since I saw that man in our barn one night when I was ten... That's where it started, I think, where I first felt..."

"What? You felt what? What did you see?"

"That's another story. Maybe I'll tell you later. My body hankers for things my head can't comprehend. I want to bring you to tears and then comfort you, hold you, wipe those tears away."

Pressing my face into my blanket, I squeeze my eyes shut. "I think you're beautiful. I think you're beautiful bound. Your face...your body, your blood, and your tears. So's the collar around your neck and the rope around your wrists. If I had my druthers, I'd own you. I'd take you home to West Virginia, keep you safe, and keep you prisoner. I'd treat you like a comrade and a slave. My heart's a monster's heart. Is that enough? Have you heard enough?"

For a good while, there's no sound but that of sleet on the tent. He's collecting his voice to curse me, surely, or collecting his strength to lunge at me, despite his restraints, and bludgeon me senseless. He won't get far in those shackles. The sentry will bring him down with a bullet before he reaches the woods.

"That's enough, yep. Thank you," Drew says. "Would you *please* look at me?"

"You're one bossy captive." I lift my face from the cot, suddenly all obedience, to study the pale features of his face and his eyes, their blue hue nothing now but deeper shadows in the dwindling dusk. "Did you...this morning, D-Drew, d-did you mind me kissing you? It didn't d-disgust you?" Questions of great consequence always give my tongue the craven shakes.

"I kissed you back, didn't I?" Drew says firmly. "Ian, don't you remember? I told you your touch was a comfort. I told you I could sense your caring beyond the blows of that belt. I can't explain any of this, except that...I feel things I can't make sense of either."

Drew sits up now, cross-legged by my cot. The blanket drops to his waist; his scent washes over me. Wrapping his big arms around his torso, hugging himself in the cold, he continues. "I think it has to do with that little boy inside me. I get so tired of being what all my muscles make people expect of me. I get tired of trying to be brave, of always being strong. I *like* how you...how you take care of me, take charge of me. I asked you to keep hand-feeding me even when I could have fed myself, remember? Sure, I want to get away, I don't want your uncle and his cronies to humiliate me, I don't want to die—but I've come to depend on you, and that feels good. If it takes regular beatings to keep me alive, I'll suffer that."

Drew reaches over; again his hand brushes my face. Now his fingers caress my beard. I sigh and close my eyes again, trying to memorize the moment. I'm as starved for touch as he is. Making love to Thom back home in the barn was a long, lonely time ago.

"You're no monster, Ian. You're my defense. You're God's grace. You're keeping the monsters at bay. Maybe, if we get through all this, after the war we can be real friends. Free to live as we please."

Speechless, I nod. His fingertips are warm and callus-rough. They graze my lips and stroke my brow.

"If I don't make it, will you be the one to bury me? Like you did the others?"

A nod's all I can muster. I swallow hard. What feels like woodchips are caught in my throat.

"Good," Drew says. "That'd be fitting. Will you write a letter for me and, if I don't survive, take it to my family when the war ends? And some keepsakes? This ring my father gave me?"

His hand rests on my cheek. I grope for it and find the band around his left middle finger. I lift his hand to my mouth and kiss it, first the ring, then the palm, then the back of his hand, hair soft against my lips. "Yes," I croak, like some kind of stunned bullfrog.

"Would you do me one other favor? Before the sun comes up, your uncle gets back, and you have to watch him whip me?"

"Yes," manages the bullfrog in Confederate gray.

"Get down here. Please."

I can't move. It's too unbelievable. The world never gives me what I want most. Never. I lie in my cot clutching his hand and staring into the now-complete darkness.

"Please? Ian? I'm cold as hell, and I need some solace in the face of tomorrow. You said that Achilles and Patroclus gave one another comfort. You said—"

I drop his hand, roll off the cot, and fall to my knees beside him.

"I just want—would you just hold on me a while?" Drew mumbles. "I'm so cold, and I'm scared, and I feel so defenseless, and tomorrow those men will be laughing at me while I bleed and break and cry, and—"

Something flexes and swells inside me, something strong, like birch roots slow-splitting stone. "Roll over," I say, nudging his flank.

Drew obeys, curling up on his side, back to me. I slide against him, tugging my blanket off the cot to supplement his; I pull the doubled wool over us, tucking it around his bare shoulders. Then I do what

I've ached to do for days: I slide one arm beneath his neck, wrap the other around his bare torso as best I can, considering my significantly smaller frame, and hold him close, his broad back pressed against my uniform jacket. Surely he can feel the physical evidence of my excitement against him, hard inside my wool pants, but, if so, he makes no objections, and besides, it's my heart and not my groin that rules tonight. As much as I want to make love to him, it's comforting, not fucking, he's asked for, and that's what he'll receive. I may be an accomplice to torture but I still have some honor left.

We lie together at last. No words, just the pattering of sleet and the rhythms of breath. We would seem ridiculous to most, a small man wrapped protectively, possessively, around an enemy soldier twice his size, but there's no one here to see. I fondle Drew's beard, the hair upon his bare breast, the welts ridging his back. He snuggles even closer against me, gives a little sob, and commences snoring. I stay awake for a good while, thinking hard, wondering how I might save Drew, thanking God for the deep balm of body warmth, before sinking into sleep myself.

—

CHAPTER TWENTY-SIX

I feel before I see or hear. Pressure against my chest, softness against my face.

I open my eyes to blackness. It's night's heart. There's the sound of sleet, continuing its impatient tap on the canvas. And here, pressed against me beneath the covers, is Drew, a darkness denser than the night's. We're lying side by side now, and face to face. His hands are pressed against my torso. That softness brushing my face is his lips. Drew's kissing me and rubbing his unshaven cheek against mine.

I cup his fuzzy chin in one hand and grip his roped wrists in the other. Lightly, I kiss him back. He sighs and snuggles closer. He kisses me again, shyly, tentatively.

"You don't have to do this if you don't want," I whisper. His breath is warm on my face, aromatic with whiskey. "Most men would think that this is sin."

Drew chuckles. "You think I'm kissing you 'cause I'm angling to get loose? You think I'm going to brain you in the midst of an embrace and shuffle off into the sleet? You think I'm giving up my sweet favors, as the ballads say, to insure your continued good will?"

"Well, all that has crossed my mind. I've made it pretty clear that I, well, that I love...looking at you, t-touching you..." I kiss him again, harder this time. "...tasting you. You don't need to kiss me to secure my protection, buddy. That's yours freely. Don't do this if you don't—"

"Give over the guilt, Reb. I ain't angling for anything, and I ain't no whore swapping kisses for favors. I'm kissing you 'cause I want to, 'cause you're good to me. Besides," says Drew, running a fingertip along the ridge of my nose, "you're not the first man I've kissed, Private Campbell."

He reads my silence correctly. "Shocked, huh?" he snickers. "Guess your Yankee Achilles has a few surprises left. I'll tell you a story if you help me piss. That whiskey moved right through me."

I toss the blankets back, help Drew crawl outside, lift him to his feet, and lead his stiff, shackled shuffle to the wood's edge. The sleet patters us, sharp little pins. He unbuttons his trousers and turns away from me. I study the tapered muscles of his back, a pale blur in the night, then turn away as well. The dual sounds of our piss drum the ground.

Back in the tent, we crawl, teeth chattering, under the blankets. Side by side again, we're stroking one another's faces in the dark, wiping off the melted sleet, shivering till the warmth our bodies create together builds back up.

"This feels damned good, little Reb. Fine distraction for me, considering what I've got coming to me tomorrow."

"It does feel fine," I sigh. "More soldiers ought to have the sense to try this. Two men's body heat's a damn sight better than one, especially when the blankets are so everlastingly moist. As for tomorrow, we'll get through that together. Right now, don't you owe me a story?"

"Will you do me one favor first?" Drew's manly voice slips into that soft tone of pleading I've already come to cherish after only a few days together.

"Surely, if it's possible."

"Oh, it's possible. Would you strip to the waist and then hold on me some more? Then I'll tell you about my wrestling buddy."

"I, uh, I, well..." is my less-than-articulate response. Drew's one sweet surprise after another, that's for sure.

"You read Homer and that's the best you can do? Come on, Reb. I've been shirtless and shivering for days, ever since you cut my clothes off me. Least you can do is join me for a time, skin to skin. Come on, be brave. I'll keep you warm."

First my uniform jacket, then my undershirt, both tossed on the cot. "Damn, it's cold," I grunt. Half-naked now, I burrow against him.

"Now you know what I've been going through, or at least part of it," Drew says, slipping his bound hands around my neck and pulling me close, till his beard-soft cheek is pressed against mine. "How's this? Comfortable, little captor?"

"Stop calling me 'little.' Yes, this is sweet," I say, fondling the fur on his face. "Sweetest thing I've known in a good long while. You're a regular honey-hive, big man."

"And you're a beer-cask of compliments. At the very least, you make me smile in hell. And, by the way, if you can call me 'big,' I can call you 'little.' So you want this story?"

We're joshing with one another like longtime drinking buddies. Guess this is how we hold off the thought of where we are and all that's inescapable and inevitable. Fine with me. "Yep, get on with it," I say, nuzzling his neck. I want to touch his chest, his loins, make love to him like I did Thom so long ago—who knows how many more days together God has allotted us?—but fear and shame hold me back even now in the face of his obvious affection.

"So, the wrestler. Back home in Pennsylvania, I was always winning the wrestling contests. We'd have 'em at fairs, after church socials, you name it. I'd made quite a name for myself in the county by the time Rob and his family moved into town. We were pretty evenly matched, but every now and then he threw me. He was about my size, about ten years older, with a bushy black beard already going gray around the edges. I liked the way he looked, I liked his big build, the hair on his body—he looked like a black bear when he stripped down, all muscled-up, fierce, and downright splendid. I used to spend time with him, help him around his farm. He was a fair companion."

"So, you and he kissed?"

"I'm about there. Hold on. One October night, Rob and I were drinking too much cider. His wife and child were abed; it was late. We were in the stable, checking on the horses...we got to wrestling around." Drew breathes deep before recommencing. "We tore off one another's shirts, laughing like the drunk bastards we were. He pinned me on my belly with my arms twisted behind me. I got, uh, hard. I always got hard when he pinned me. I could feel the hair on his body as he shoved me into the straw. His hair tickled my bare back; the straw tickled and scratched my face. Somehow I got out from under him. But Rob just laughed some more, slammed me up against the wall...and then he got to kissing me. I kissed him back. I think he wanted more, 'cause his hands were rubbing me down there, but...I wasn't ready for more, and wasn't entirely sure what more would entail. I did savor the kissing, though. I savored it a good bit more than kissing on the silly farm girls my parents were always after me to court."

"Did it ever happen again?"

"Naw, we were both sort of bashful and bumbling around one another after that. We only wrestled a few more times afterwards. By then I was letting him win, after putting up a credible struggle, just 'cause I liked the feel of him straining and sweating atop me, holding me down. Like I said, losing to him always got me hard. The next summer he busted out his back baling hay and had to give up wrestling. Got himself a farmhand, so we didn't have much cause to keep company after that.

"So, you ain't the first man I've brushed lips with. You ain't the first man I've slept with, either: back home, we brothers all had to share beds. You are, however, the first man I've snuggled with like this. Also the first man to rub salve on my back, to feed me with his fingers, and to help me shit in a stream. Not that I'm complaining. The devil might have sent me your uncle, but the Lord surely sent you. You're indeed a boon and a treasure. I won't forget it. If I survive your Sarge and this war, I'll reward you yet."

We leave off words for a time, beard nuzzling beard. Encouraged by his blessed amorousness, I finger his thick chest hair, the hair coating his flat belly.

"That feels mighty fine," Drew sighs. "I do appreciate how you touch me."

"For a guy as shoulder-broad and chest-deep as you are, you're certainly thin," I say, patting his lean middle. "Every boy in the company is half-starved by now. At least Sarge has agreed for the nonce to let me feed you what little we can spare."

"Belt's been pulled in two notches since I joined the army," Drew says. "I used to have me a little bit of a gut when I joined up. All that pork and pie I told you about. Long gone now, goddammit, though we Feds sure eat better than you skinny Confederates.

"So, Reb...your turn," Drew says, dropping feast-nostalgia for inquiry. "Did you ever kiss a man before?"

"There was...yes, I have. His name was Thom."

"That guy you mentioned to me before? Your friend from home. Was he as handsome as me?"

Even in a night this dark, I can see the pale crescent of Drew's grin.

"Just about. You're damned full of yourself, buddy," I reply, grinning back.

"Would you be treating me so good if I weren't so handsome?"

The pale crescent expands. It's a gift to laugh together on the eve of tears.

"Hell, no," I say. "Or so strong." I use the latter confession as an excuse to squeeze the dense flesh of his right arm.

"You Southerners surely have honied tongues. I suppose I'd be dead by now if I were homely or puny," Drew says. "Now get on with your story."

"Not that much to tell. He and I got stuck in the barn one evening during a hard rain, ended up spending the night sacked out in the hayloft. First man I kissed. Last man I kissed. Before you."

"Was kissing all you did?"

"No," I say.

"So you do know what 'more' is, then? The 'more' that Rob wanted and I wasn't prepared to give?" Drew's fingers play over the back of my neck.

"Yes," I admit. "I found out a good bit that night. Don't play so innocent, Yank. Every man's got a cock, a mouth-hole, and an asshole. Think hard, and you'll figure it out."

Drew snickers again. "Yeah, I think the asshole was what Rob was after. Wasn't going to give that up."

"Thom did."

"Really?! How did you...?"

"After we both used our mouths—"

"You mean you and he...? You sucked...?"

"Yep. Sure did. The doing of it wasn't half-bad, and the receiving of it was damned grand. After a long while of that, I bent him over a bale. I used spit. I went real slow. He hurt for a while, and then he started to...well, it gave him pleasure."

"Really? And it gave you pleasure too?"

"Hell, *yes*. What do you think? He was hot and tight there. It was like my own hand, but twice as fine."

"I ain't ready for anything like *that*," Drew says. The fingers grazing the back of my neck stop their roaming. "I don't need no more pain right now."

"You aren't ready just yet? Or never?" I say, patting his flannelled butt.

"Are you saying I owe you that, after all the things you've done to help me? I told you I ain't no whore."

"No, I'm not. I'm saying taking Thom like that was wonderful, and that...yes, I'd like to take you that way too, but I'm not going to force you just because you're my prisoner. I'm not going to do such a thing just because I can. Sodomizing the unwilling is not the kind of suffering I savor. If you're ever ready, if we get a chance to be somewhere safe...if you were to give yourself to me that way, it would be a gift and a rapture. Right now, this is enough," I say, licking his chin and lower lip.

Drew's wet lips mash against mine. Our tongues roll together. Another long silence, as our mouths lose themselves in wordless pleasures. Finally, breathless, we pull away.

"You smell good," I say, nuzzling his armpit. "I love how you smell. It gets me a little giddy."

"Hell, I stink like unwashed soldier-sweat and your devil-kin's piss!"

"I'll fetch us a bath soon. Meanwhile..." Breathing deep, I nuzzle more. The feathery hair tickles my nostrils. "Your pits smell like barnyard straw and salt-rising bread."

Drew giggles like a little boy. "*Stop* talking about bread. You're a torment. Salt-rising with apple butter..."

"Hot biscuits with honey," I murmur.

"Shut up!" Drew soft-slaps my back.

"All right, all right. No more food talk."

Drew, sighing, presses his bearded cheek against mine and strokes my shaggy hair.

"God, it's good to be in here together. Outside it's all sleet and mud, cruelty, cavalry... I'm so sick of all of it. This is so good, Ian. It's as close as I've been to home since I left home."

"Me too. I haven't touched a man like this since Thom left."

"He left?"

"That's another thing I didn't tell you before. After that night, he wouldn't speak to me again. He moved west right after that."

"Was it 'cause you took him that way? From behind?"

"I assume so...but I didn't force him. He showed me how. He begged me to."

"He was ashamed to face you, then?" Drew's fingers recommence their slow exploration of the back of my neck and the long-unshorn locks of my hair.

"Yep, that's it. He couldn't face what he wanted. I was pretty sad for a long time after he left. I was mighty fond of him." Absentmindedly I caress the curly silk across Drew's torso, then settle one hand upon his breast. There, now, his heartbeat, slow and steady.

"I can tell you cared for him, Ian. I'm sorry. Think I know how you feel," Drew says. "I felt pretty sad when Rob and I stopped wrestling and working together. Sometimes I caught myself wishing...he didn't have a wife and child so he and I...could just homestead together."

Stroking Drew's chest-pelt, I count his heartbeats for a while. I leave off at one hundred. That long line of numbers is finite, I know, but it's in my power to extend it, if I can only find the cunning and the courage. "We need to get some rest, buddy. Tomorrow will be torture for both of us." Reluctantly I slip from his embrace.

"All right." Drew fumbles for my face, pats it, then his fingers drop to my bare chest. "You got some hair there, little man," he mumbles, tugging gently at it. "Nice near-naked. Nice." His touch has me even harder.

Now his fingers stop their ranging. They find a focus, stroking a zigzag across my breast.

"I figured you'd start finding them sooner or later, if I ever took my shirt off in front of you and if I was ever lucky enough for you to want to touch me," I say.

"That's right. That first night, you found my battle scars, I told you about 'em, but I never got a chance to hear about yours. Tell me, Ian. Please?"

"That there you're feeling on, that was a bayonet at Antietam. Jeremiah—he's a bit of a poet—says it looks like 'a white lightning bolt in the black storm clouds of my chest hair,' since hair doesn't grow on scars. I was in the camp hospital for a while with that. Saw the piles of limbs after the surgeon left; thanked God I still had my hands and feet. A fever almost took me, but I recovered. And this," I say, taking his hand and leading his forefinger to my belly, "this was grapeshot at Fredericksburg."

"Hmmm, feels like a bunch of little mole hills," Drew murmurs, tapping the scars with his fingertip, then ruffling my belly hair. "Little mole hills and pasture grass."

"Nice. Nigh as poetic as Jeremiah," I say, laughing. "And this," I say, rolling on my side, "on my back, deep graze of a bullet at Chancellorsville. Very close call."

"Damn. How many do you have?"

"Three more. I'm pretty shy out of combat, but I'm a wildcat in battle or boxing, as Sarge likes to say. This here, along my right forearm"—Drew's fingers fumble about, then find the healed-over long slash—"was a Yankee dagger, hand to hand combat, at Gettysburg. Here"—Drew's finger circles the little pit on my right shoulder—"was a bullet, also at Gettysburg. Being carted out of there along those rutty roads was far worse agony than being shot. And there's more grapeshot scars here, " I say, patting my trousered right thigh. "That's from Fisher's Hill."

Drew sighs. "Damn, I'm glad you survived these." To my surprise, he kisses my scarred chest. "I'm so sorry, Ian. That men I might have known, men from my state, might have... Buddy, I'm so, so glad you survived."

I lie still, heart welling with thanks, patting his head. Gently he moves me about, his lips meeting my old wounds one by one. When my eyes well up, hurriedly I wipe them dry.

"My turn," I say when he's done, voice shakier than I'd like. "Maybe, if you're lucky, you can get to the one on my thigh some other night." Nudging him onto his back, I straddle his legs and begin my own exploration. "Here," I pat his ribs, the slat-bones prominent beneath my touch, "this big slash...Yellow Tavern?" My lips brush the half-moon, left by a saber that, more accurately wielded, might have finished him.

"Yep. Good memory." Drew grips my shoulder and squeezes.

"Black day. Jeb Stuart was mortally wounded there, dammit. Well." I caress a pit on his arm, very much matching the one on my shoulder. "Trevilian Station?" Bending down, I kiss it.

"Right. Your test is almost over."

"And this on the shoulder—oh, I know all these very well, having salved and bandaged you—was outside Staunton." A final kiss, before I stretch out on my back and he curls against me, head heavy on my shoulder.

"Speaking of Staunton," Drew murmurs, fondling my chest hair, tracing again the scar there, "I guess we've left out another kind of sharing soldiers do. May I ask...if you're not too tired..."

"What?" I say, but I think I know what's coming. "Go ahead."

"Well, outside Staunton was where...where I...first killed a man. I mean, before that, I'd seen battle, and I'd shot at many and many a Reb, but, what with all the powder-flash and smoke and noise, hell, you know how it is, you load up, you charge, you aim, you fire, but rare is the time, in such confusion, that you see a man fall and know beyond a shadow of a doubt that it was you who brought him down."

Drew's finger wanders down to my belly button, circles and probes it, then his big arm falls across my chest and he snuggles closer. "I was cavalry at Yellow Tavern—pistol and saber—and I know I wounded a goodly number—and then again at Trevilian Station—but near Staunton, the man whose ball caught my shoulder, I think he even might have been a civilian, 'cause he was dressed that way, well, the blow knocked me off my mount but I scrambled up, I looked him in the eye—he had a musket, was trying to reload—and I...I shot him in the head with my pistol."

"And since then? Any others?"

"Yes. Confederate skirmishers and bushwhackers around Staunton. Men like you, hiding up in the hills and harassing us every now and them. I've shot them. Without hesitation. Them or me, right? Shot them or...one man, my saber, well...that's enough. Except...a lot of my buddies, we were all real tender at first, but they seemed to harden up, get used to the...necessity of killing. It *is* war, after all. But I never seemed to grow that tough bark. It's like they turned into men and I'm still a little boy. Every time I touch this shoulder scar, I think about that man gushing blood in a field outside Staunton and how I stood over him, staunching my wound, till he stopped kicking and twitching."

I run my fingers through Drew's beard and sigh. "My turn, I suppose. Well, I have hardened up. Not as hard as Sarge wants me to be, especially when it comes to prisoners. I mean, you all are pretty helpless, you shouldn't be tortured, but...men who've come at me with gun or sword drawn, well..."

"'Wildcat in war,' were those the words?"

"Yes. This red rage comes over me, like I'm moving through a mist of blood. In mythology I've read, they talk about Vikings who went berserk, so I guess it's like that. I've always been this way, sort of quiet and peaceable, fond of books and forest walks, but when I'm crossed, when someone threatens those I care for...and I care for the South, and this company, so...I've killed and killed and killed. Small as I am, you might not believe me, but—"

"I believe you," Drew whispers, his words tickling my neck. "I know how you dealt with George when you defended me. I'm just damned glad that you and I didn't face one another on the battlefield. Big as I am, I don't know if I would have walked away from that."

"The first was a man about my age but twice my size who almost gutted me with his bayonet. I shot him through the heart with the pistol Sarge gave me when I joined up. They were all blue-coated young men like you, for the most part, though a few were older, men in their prime, probably with wives and children at home. And I, hothead mountain boy, a crack shot thanks to years of hunting deer back home...I..."

"That's enough, Ian. I'm sorry I asked. I truly am. Let's get some sleep now. Just hold me, all right?"

I nod, staring into the dark, counting the men and the battles, my throat dry.

"Glad you found me," Drew says sleepily. Scooting down, he curls up, rests his big head on my scarred chest, and sighs. "Can hear your heart." Then he's gone into sleep. I'm left with the sounds of sleet and his breathing. His breath is like the distant soughing of pines.

—

CHAPTER TWENTY-SEVEN

—

Dawn, and the sound of campfire clatter and chat. No reveille in Sarge's absence. The sleet's tapping has stopped. I'm lying on my back. Drew's bound hands are tucked up against my side. His head still rests on my chest; my left arm's numb beneath his shoulders. Carefully I extricate myself, making sure he's tucked in warmly before pulling on my undershirt and jacket. Leaving him to sleep, I head off to fetch coffee.

Outside, it's still gray and damp. Melting ice drips from bare twig tips. There's a welcome warmth to the breeze, though. About time. If I were home, I'd be helping my father sort his garden seeds.

"No biscuit left," says Rufus. He's sitting dejectedly near the fire, rubbing his hands, waiting for the coffee to brew. "Lord, I hope Sarge gets back soon. He's bound to bring supplies."

I nod, biting back words. Rufus would certainly not understand why I hope Sarge takes his sweet time returning to camp.

Coffee's done. I pour two cups, handing one to Rufus. It's especially bitter, Rufus explains as he heads off to curry the horses, because our coffee stores are so low that we're having to extend them with ground roasted acorns. I'm grimacing and about to search for some kind of sweetening when Jeremiah taps my shoulder.

The fear must show on my face, because Jeremiah is quick to push me into a camp chair near the fire and whisper, "Be easy, Ian! I ain't telling anyone." He looks around to make sure there are no eavesdroppers before pulling up a chair and continuing in a low voice.

"D'you remember when my older brother John left home?"

"Yes, I do. Just before the war began? He must have been about the age we are now, right? One week he was helping us with the corn shucking, and the next week he was gone. You never did tell me why."

Jeremiah takes a deep breath, rubs the scruff on his chin, and stares into the fire. "I saw my brother John do the same once, the same as you, you know, with that Yankee? John was kissing his friend Bobby in the springhouse. John had to leave home because I told. Our father called him a blight and a sodomite, cast him out, told him to leave and never come back. He hasn't. We don't know where he is."

I rise, pour a cup of acorn-coffee for Jeremiah, and sit back down. He takes a sip and grunts. "Tastes like the war.

"At any rate, Bobby disappeared soon thereafter. I hope he followed John and found him. I hope they're together somewhere, in Richmond or making a new life out west."

"Is that why your banjo songs are slow and sad so often?" I say.

Jeremiah grins. "Yup, I guess. The boys are always begging me to play jollier, huh?" He takes another sip, makes a face, and says, "That's why I ain't going to tell on you, Ian. You're my friend. I recognize kindness when I see it...even if your version of kindness means treating that giant Yank like a threatened damsel, which is nigh onto accurate, since we know what happened to the last several Feds that Sarge fixed on. You better watch out after ole Weasel-Teeth, though. He and the others won't be so understanding...and Sarge, well, if he gets wind of this, he'll throttle your big friend with his bare hands like he did that poor Boston boy. Sooner rather than later, too."

My turn to take a sip, black liquid bitter as what surges up in my gullet now, frothy gorge of fear and hate. "George? That goddamned ferret? What did he say?"

"He told ever' body about you punching him, knocking out a tooth, in defense of the prisoner. You may be Sarge's kin, Ian, but watch out. The boys all like you, 'cause you've always been nice to all of 'em, and you haven't taken advantage of your kinship with Sarge—save for that sweet little tent we all envy—but if George keeps on talking, well..."

I rise, uncurling the sudden fists I find my hands stiffened into. "Thanks, friend. I won't forget this." I grip his shoulder, fill my cup, then head back to the tent. Maybe Drew will like this acorn-swill better than I do.

—

CHAPTER TWENTY-EIGHT

—

Drew's still asleep when I enter the tent. I sit in the camp chair, cup warming my hands, and watch him, still disbelieving last night. That he asked me to hold him all night and that I did, that we cuddled and kissed and touched one another, those are blessings reserved for others, not me, not an unkempt mountain boy from down by the Greenbrier. I can't say why I find beauty where I do, but I guess I'd better be thankful that there's any beauty left, after these many months of slogging camp-life and savage wartime. All this must make me a sodomite indeed, this longing to pull off Drew's blanket, lie atop him, and wake him with the weight of my body and my kisses.

Drew stretches now, rubs his eyes like a little boy, and looks up at me. For a second, he looks confused, as if he can't recall how he got here or who I am, but then I can see memory sparkling in his blue gaze. He grins, a wide white grin, happy, mischievous, then sits up to take the cup.

"Beware," I say. "It's nasty. Got acorns in it. We're about out of real coffee, and there's no breakfast."

Drew sips, makes a face much like Jeremiah's, sips some more, shakes his head, and stubbornly sips some more. In the silence his stomach rumbles. "Drew," I begin, "last night was, well, thanks for—"

Drew chuckles. "My very sentiments, sir. Now how about that wondrous salve on my tore-up butt?" Grin widening, he rolls over on his belly, rump in the air. "Just salve, though. As I said last night, I ain't prepared to give up my cherry right just yet."

I'd do anything for a man with a face and body like that. "Surely," I say, reaching for the haversack where the jar of salve's kept. "Those wounds do need tending." As much as I'd relish riding him, just massaging his bare ass will be distilled bliss.

That's when we hear the commotion of horses. A few cheers go up. A stern, all-too-familiar voice shouts orders. Sarge has returned to camp.

Drew's eyes widen. "Oh, no." He swigs the last of the coffee and hands me the cup. "I'm ready," he says.

"Listen to me," I say, bending forward to grip his arm. The thick muscles flex and tremble beneath my fingers. "Make as much noise as you can when he beats you. Just let go. Struggle and scream. That's what Sarge wants: a real spectacle. Don't try to be stoic. Let loose. I've promised Sarge both your blood and your tears."

Drew squares his jaw, seizes my hand, and nods.

"Take it as long as you can, bawl like a baby, give Sarge what he wants. He wants to see you broken, so break." What is on my lips unsaid is that I want to see Drew broken too. Beauty broken down moves me like none other. But I think Drew knows that by now.

"Then pretend to pass out. When you do, he'll stop. Salve and a bath are waiting for you on the other side of this."

"And more nights like last night?" Drew sounds like he's asking for another piece of cake. He's squeezing my hand so hard it hurts.

I can't help but smile, despite our situation. "Yes, big man, I promise. As long as Sarge lets me keep you out of the cold and as long as you welcome my touch, that's the way your nights will be spent."

I drop his hand, adjust my uniform, slip on my cap, and am halfway out of the tent—greeting Sarge seems like the politic thing to do, especially if George has been bad-mouthing me during their foraging mission—when Drew says, "Wait, Ian. One thing."

"Yes?" I say, turning. He's sitting cross-legged amid oilcloths, hugging himself again, the golden pelt on his breast curling in a shaft of sunlight the parted clouds and tent flaps permit.

"If the time comes, if your uncle wants proof of your loyalty, will he ask more of you?"

"What are you saying?"

"I'm saying, will you be the one to…when he tires of me, will he order you to execute me?"

I drop the tent flap. The shaft of sunlight vanishes. A big, broad-chested boy looks up at me in the sudden shadow just this side of spring, speaking with utter calm about the likelihood of his violent end.

"And if so ordered, will you obey?"

"No, I—"

"If I have to die, Ian, I'd just as soon a man who cared for me was to be the one. If you have to do it, just make it fast, please? I'm begging you. I don't want to shame myself any further."

"No one's dying," says a firm voice I've never known before. "Especially after last night. No one's dying this time." I part the tent flaps and step out into the sun.

—

CHAPTER TWENTY-NINE

Sarge has done it again, whether by charm or coercion. We haul off the cart several bags of beans, coffee, bacon, field peas, and corn meal. Rufus, in between armloads, does a little dance of jubilation. George is nowhere to be seen.

I'm helping Rufus mix up some corn pone when Sarge taps me on the shoulder. "Come with me," he says. I follow him to his tent, head prickling and belly pinching. How did the man who used to take me hunting and teach me how to box become this thing I so fear?

Inside, Sarge settles in behind his desk; I take the proffered sling chair. As is usual for our conversations, his attention is for the most part reserved for the papers he's shuffling through.

"Welcome back, sir. Looks like you were successful in fetching supplies. You've always been a wonder at foraging. God knows all us men were depending on you. The food hoard was next to empty."

Sarge is like most men: he lives for praise. He gifts me with a sidelong smile.

"Yes, indeed. In fact, I've got some presents for you, nephew." Sarge gestures to a bucket by my chair. In it, I make out a flask, a waxy rectangle, a poke, a couple of jars, and something with a metallic gleam. "Whiskey and your own coffee store. Soap and a little sorghum and honey."

"Many thanks, sir! I'll very much savor—"

"At present the Valley's fairly free of Yankees. Day after tomorrow, we move south, keeping to the back roads. We'll pitch camp near Lexington. On the next day, or the next, if there are no Feds in evidence, we'll head along the Pike towards Buchanan, at the base of Purgatory Mountain. Word is that Nelson's forces can meet us there in a few days. After we join up, we can traverse the Blue Ridge, get to Lynchburg, then head on to Petersburg. The city's still in a state of siege; the least we can do is try to help. See here?"

Sarge shakes out a map, tracing with one finger a line I can't see. A map of allegory, perhaps? Moving from Hell to Purgatory sounds like a shift in the right direction.

"Yes, sir. I'll be sure the men are ready to—"

"What condition's your prisoner in?"

"Pretty weak, sir. He's had little food. He's still in pain from the night he spent bucked."

"If he isn't mobile, he'll have to be left," Sarge says. "Like we left the others. Enemies don't deserve the luxury of a cart-ride."

In my lap, I clutch one hand with the other to hide the trembling.

"No, sir, certainly not. But he's mobile. I'll tether him to my cart as we did before. As I've said, I want to keep him around so that you can—"

"George spoke to me last night," says Sarge, dropping the map and shaking out another. "He said you punched him in defense of the prisoner. Even dislodged one of his teeth."

"Sir, you know that George is—"

"Why did you do that, Ian? Seems nigh-treasonous to me."

Always a bad sign when his glance falls on me and fixes. It's always taken a good bit of my meager courage to meet his eyes. But this is a question I expected.

"Sir, George was drunk. He was abusing the Yankee, which is, of course, certainly allowable. I know you've let the boys work out their frustrations on prisoners before, and it's a fine outlet. But I think that George was planning to...well, you recall what he said by the campfire that night. George wanted to 'poke' the prisoner, you recall?"

Now I reach for that word, the one Sarge has used, Jeremiah's father has used, with such crawling contempt, the word that describes the secret desire that Weasel-Teeth and I seem to share. "Isn't that called sodomy, sir?"

"Yes. Yes, it is." The awful rifle sights of Sarge's attention return to his maps. "All right, Ian. All right. But you should know that George has been complaining around the camp and in our overnight bivouac. Now some of the boys are wondering why the prisoner is allowed to luxuriate in the shelter of a tent while they sleep out in the elements. The weather's improving; spring seems near; there's little likelihood that the prisoner will suffer the frostbite you fear. I'll allow you to shelter him until we get to Purgatory Mountain. After that, he stays outside. While we have sufficient supplies, you may feed him. But when those supplies dwindle, starve him. I won't have him coddled."

Tight grip of lichen on gravestone, my clenched hands in my lap. "Yes, sir."

"Ian, do you know why I've always given over the care of prisoners to you? The ones I keep?"

"No, sir," I say. But I'm lying. I think I do.

"Because you're too kind, Ian. Just like your parents. There's a weakness there, a legacy of weakness. Each prisoner is a test. Will pity make you weaker, or will duty make you stronger? You were weak with that Boston boy, Brandon. I strangled him for your sake. You were stronger with the others. This one...what is his name? No matter. George says you're weak, though your words and actions so far indicate the firmness I've always prayed you'd develop. Watch yourself, nephew. Compassion is a deadfall. Especially in wartime."

Sarge looks up. "I anticipate being on the move a great deal in the next few weeks. I also plan for the prisoner to be whipped and bucked often, which means he'll weaken fast. Strong as he appears, he's liable to last another week, two at the most, before he becomes too much of a burden. As soon as the prisoner can't keep up, he dies. Do you understand? When that time comes, I expect you to dispatch him. You're old enough for that duty now."

Execution. Drew was right. Here's one future announcing itself: my pistol, the one Sarge gave me when I joined up; tiny movement of my crooked forefinger; a fiery flash, an aureole of smoke; that golden head I've stroked and kissed sundered in a second, temple oozing red.

In my throat's a dam I force words past. "Yes, sir," I say, bowing my head.

"And this afternoon, I will give the camp a fine show with the bullwhip. You have it, do you not?"

"Yes, sir. It's cleaned, as you ordered. It's in my tent."

"After lunch, then. That's all. Enjoy your coffee and whiskey."

"Thank you, sir." Picking up the bucket of gifts, I stand.

"Oh, and Ian? There are handcuffs in the bucket too. They'd been lost. George found them. Please apply them to the prisoner. No use taking a chance that he'll work his wrist-ropes loose. When you need to leave him alone, be sure his hands are cuffed behind his back. That should insure his continued presence in our little camp. Might as well keep him gagged too, unless he's being fed. There's no reason to permit him speech. No one cares what he has to say. I interrogated him when I first captured him. He knows nothing we need."

Nodding, I depart. Outside, frayed clouds disperse. Spring's almost here. Soon, the sarvis will be blooming, and the redbud trees. Sarge's words have made the sun's warmth a curse. Soon, we will reach Purgatory, and Drew and I once again will sleep apart. Soon, unless I act, Drew will be dead.

—

CHAPTER THIRTY

———

Drew and I say little, sharing fresh corn pone and coffee in the tent. I sit in the camp chair; he sits cross-legged at my feet. I offer no information; he asks for none. He has the bullwhip to endure today, so what Sarge said this morning I'll relay some other time. I dribble honey on the pone and hold it to his lips. He thanks me, chews, and gulps coffee. Outside, my compatriots are laughing, a little giddy with the sudden sun, the apparent departure of winter.

The paltry portion of pone's done. Now I hold out the handcuffs. "Sarge found these," I say.

Drew lifts his head, looks at the cuffs, hangs his head, and holds out his roped hands. "Go ahead," he says, so I do, locking the metal about his wrists, then unknotting and removing the bloodstained ropes that have bound Drew's hands since he first was captured.

"When?" Drew mumbles.

"After lunch," I say. We both gaze at the bullwhip in the corner, curled up like a black snake.

"Do you want me to salve and bandage you now?"

Drew shakes his head. "Might as well save it till…after. Suspect I'll be needing it from head to toe by then. Do you have enough?"

"Yes," I say. "I got a jar of it from Aunt Alicia last autumn, and I made a good bit of it too, while the herbs were available. I have enough for…a goodly number of uses yet."

"A goodly number of beatings, you mean." Drew stares at the ground; I stare out the tent flap.

"Yep," I say. I hold the cup of coffee to Drew's lips and he slurps. A little dribbles from the corner of his mouth. I wipe it off his soft-bristled chin with the back of my hand.

"Sorry," I say, "that there was so little pone. I had to fight the boys for what measly bit I got. They get surly if I fetch two helpings, 'cause food's so sparse that they resent every bite I reserve for you. 'Good food wasted on the Yankee pig,' to use their words. So we'll just have to make do, sharing one portion."

"It was good, Ian. You're mighty kind to share your food with me," Drew says. "I love honey on cornbread. We had hives back home."

"The key to your ankle shackles is in my haversack," I say, "which is where I'll be keeping this cuff key too. If you were to knock me out, tie me up, and make a run for it... If you're careful, you could make it past the sentries."

Drew stares at me hard. "What's changed? A couple of days ago you said you weren't willing to help me escape."

I'm not ready to tell him about Sarge's new orders quite yet. Tonight, during the salving, maybe.

"A couple of days have made me care more. For God's sake, man, last night we—"

"Wouldn't you be shamed and punished if I got away? Wouldn't your uncle be suspicious?"

"Perhaps."

"Ian...?"

"All right, yes," I say, gulping the last of the coffee. "A prisoner escaped once, on Jeremiah's watch. This was soon after Jeremiah and I joined up. Sarge tracked the Yankee down in the woods and shot him. Jeremiah spent the next ten hours bucked and gagged as punishment. He broke just like you did."

"Is that what would happen to you? You're the bastard's kin. Wouldn't that fact spare you?"

"Probably. Not necessarily. Sarge is big on fairness. He hates being accused of favoritism. And he knows the boys envy me my tent and the little extras—like this coffee, or the whiskey he shares with me. But spending a few hours bucked and gagged would be worth it if you could get away."

"No, Ian. No." Drew grabs my hand.

"Would you rather I bury you?"

"If I run, why can't you run with me?"

"I can't leave my company-mates. I won't run like a coward. This is my home, these mountains. And I intend to help in the defense of them. As much as I care for you—" I stroke his hand, then release it.

"You're no slave-owner. You're a hillside farmer's son like me," Drew says, shaking his head. "Why are you even *in* this war? Use those keys tonight. We'll make our way north; I'll take you home. My family will treat you like a hero."

"I'd be the soldier of an enemy nation if we made it to Pennsylvania, big man. You'd be obliged to turn me in."

Drew's head keeps shaking, more emphatically now. "No, no. I could hide you till the war ends."

"Too dangerous for you and for your kin. And I'm in this war because these are my people, because my homeland has been invaded—"

"By boys like me!" Drew snorts. "To keep this country united, and to—"

"To drive boys like me into submission. Who the hell are you Yanks to force us into a union we no longer want or believe in?"

"You Rebs are so frigging stubborn and stupid. So high and mighty, so frigging proud. You make me want to spit. How can you continue to—"

"Shut up, Drew," I say. I hate how my voice shakes when I'm angry. I sound like a little kid.

"Why? Don't you want to be in a rage when your uncle whips me? Won't that make it even easier to watch? Won't that make it easier to shoot me through the head sometime soon?"

"I've had enough of you," I mutter, rising. "Sarge says to keep you gagged and to lock your wrists behind your back when I leave you alone. Keep still and don't fight me."

Drew shrugs and frowns. I offer him a hand; he takes it; I help him up off his haunches and onto his knees. Squatting by him, I unlock the cuffs. Obediently he clasps his hands behind him. I lock the metal in place, then stand over him. He tugs on the cuffs; the muscles of his shoulders and biceps swell and relax. He looks up at me with a bitter grin. "Now I'm even more defenseless. Just how you want me, right? Uncomfortable, on my knees, half-naked, and at your mercy?"

I'm hard inside my pants. The bastard's always right. It takes all my willpower not to push him to the ground, straddle him, and kiss his lips bloody. Instead I fetch rag and rope from my haversack. I bunch the rag up and hold it in front of his face; Drew gives me a glare but opens his mouth. As before, I work the rag in, then secure it with several feet of rope pulled tight between his teeth and knotted behind his head.

Done. My captive stares up at me, angry and scared, blinking his eyes of burning blue. He's so beautiful, so pitiable like this. I'd like to keep him this way forever.

I borrow Sarge's hard tone for the first time in days. "That'll shut you up. I'll be back when it's time."

With that, I turn my back on him and push through the tent flap. The sun's bright; it hurts my eyes. After so many gray months, my senses are accustomed to winter's dimness. The cardinal flying through the corner of my vision looks like a bloody bullet.

—

CHAPTER THIRTY-ONE
—

No bloodroot yet. No bluebells, no dog's tooth violet, no coltsfoot. No sarvis blooms, or redbud, or the wild crabapple. Only the willow's yellow-green buds convince me that spring is near.

Walking in the woods has done no good. Drinking whiskey has. It's smooth, a nice accompaniment to the half-cooked field peas I'm having for lunch. I make small talk with Rufus by the campfire. George passes silently, giving me a venomous look. Then Sarge's hand is on my shoulder, his orders are lodged in my ear, and it's time to prepare the prisoner.

In the tent, Drew's curled up on his side. He looks at me once, then avoids my gaze. I take in the sight of his gagged, half-naked helplessness. At precisely the same time, tenderness floods my chest and lust flexes between my legs.

"It's nigh about time. We have half an hour. You want some food?"

Drew shakes his head.

"You need the latrine?"

Drew nods.

"Up," I say, cupping a hand beneath his elbow. He rises unsteadily to his knees, then his feet, staggering a bit before finding his balance. Parting the tent flaps, I lead my captive outside. Drew blinks against the sunlight, lifting his face into a warm breeze moving up the mountain. I grasp his arm, leading him to the camp's edge, past the latrine trench, into the woods and over the side of the hill for some privacy.

"Here all right?" It's a little clearing among mountain laurels, their evergreen leaves offering shelter among the otherwise still-bare trees.

Drew looks around, finds us alone—no other witnesses to his humiliation—and grunts, "Uh huh."

"You need to...? Both?"

Drew nods. His blue stare's begging.

"No, I'm not going to uncuff you. We're doing this together."

I could certainly release his hands long enough to allow him the brief luxury of bodily independence, but I don't want to do that. Part of it's

my remnant anger, I guess. Part of it's seeing him so vulnerable; part of
it's the power I feel in reminding him of how a captive as strong as he
depends on a captor half his size for the most basic necessities. Part of
it's the chance to touch him in his most private places.

That shamed droop of his handsome head, so pathetic, so moving. A
giant in shackles. Now I'm remembering another book of myths, on the
shelf in my bedroom back home. Prometheus, the fire-giver, chained to
a mountainside where an eagle chews his flesh in slow, sweet gobbets.

Standing before Drew, I unbutton his trousers. Here it is, small bulge
inside his underclothes. I pull it out, limp thing nestled within its bush
of hair, sparse inches' worth. I should step back now, aim it for him, allow him release, but instead I cup it in my hands. And in my hands it
begins to swell. Spring bud, freshet after rain, little sapling the passage
of years plumps up to hard-girthed trunk.

We both stare at its growth for a few seconds, then I look up to find
Drew gazing down at me. His mouth may be packed with rag and rope,
but he can still muster a smile. I look around, checking the woods. Still
no one in sight. Smiling back, I gently rub the flesh expanding in my
hands. He closes his eyes, pushes himself against me, and sighs. I take
the head between right thumb and forefinger, grip it tightly, and stroke.
The thing's gifted with as heroic a proportion as the rest of him. I lick
my lips. Drew shoves his flesh into my fist and groans.

"Ian!?" Rufus's voice. The sound of distant footsteps in leaves. "Sarge
is looking for you. He says to git on back here. It's time."

I turn, and there's Rufus trudging over the hilltop, about fifty yards
away.

"I'll be right there," I shout. "The Yankee had to take a piss."

Rufus is sweet but he's simple-headed. Why Drew and I are using the
middle of a laurel thicket instead of the latrine-trench doesn't seem to
occur to him. He waves again and disappears back over the hill.

My heart's pounding; Drew's cock has shrunk into its formerly puny
state. A few more minutes, and who knows what Rufus might have
seen? Another few strokes, and I would have been ready to drop to my
knees and take Drew into my mouth.

"Shit," I mutter. "Not much time, Yank. Better get to this." Sarge's stern
tones again. I'm always acting tough when I'm really scared, acting angry when I'm really hurting.

I aim his sex, the urine arcs into the sun, the forest floor steams. I
pull his pants around his calves and help him lean against a tree. Drew

squats, eyes firmly shut, forehead bunching up. Pressing my shoulder against his to steady him, I whisper, "This is nothing. We've done this before."

I clean him; I button him up. Back toward the camp I lead him. Quick duck into my tent to fetch the whip. Holding it out of his sight. Passing lines of tents and the pursed lips of soldiers. Approaching the appointed place and time.

"I'm sorry we argued. I've always been too prideful for my own good. And I'm sorry for what's about to happen." I talk low, so only Drew can hear.

We keep walking, eyes fixed ahead, on the whipping tree, a distant oak on the far side of camp. Drew's arm is trembling in my grasp. Boys I've spent years of my life with, drinking and eating with, fighting beside, are spitting on the ground as we pass, saying things we both refuse to hear. If Sarge decides to remove Drew from my charge, he won't last more than a day or two before the boys beat him to death.

"I feel such a tenderness for you, Drew. I want to take care of you. Tonight, afterwards…I'll care for you tonight. I promise I'll ease you, I'll soothe your wounds."

Drew stumbles over a stone. I steady him. Someone laughs. Drew straightens with a stifled cussing, then we continue. The oak grows, the trunk thickening, the limbs spreading wider, gray clawing clouds and fracturing sun.

"Remember what I told you. Give Sarge a show. It might help lengthen your life. I'm trying to give us time, so somehow I can save you. You believe me? I'm coming to care more about you than about this war."

We both stop walking. Drew stares over at me. Trust, doubt, and terror mingle, moistening his blue glance. His teeth grip the rope.

"I mean it. I intend to save you. Somehow. If I can. Do you understand?"

He grunts, nods, then stares straight ahead again. We continue walking. The row of tents ends, and here's the oak above us, and, about us, parentheses of men come to see Drew bleed beneath the lash.

—

CHAPTER THIRTY-TWO

Sarge's pistol is beautiful. Rich walnut grip, brassy trigger, and long barrel the color of blizzard-bearing clouds. It's polished to a high sheen, as Sarge's weapons always are, like the gleam of sunburst breaking through that same snow-heavy storm. The mouth of it's pressed against Drew's cheek. Drew and Sarge glare at one another, then Drew looks away. Hard to hold the devil's eyes, Aunt Alicia used to say.

To me, Sarge says, "Cuff his hands before him." To Drew, Sarge says, "You, pig, keep still."

Behind Drew's back, I turn the key, easing the metal off his wrists. In obvious pain, Drew stiffly edges his arms to his side, takes a long breath, then holds his hands together and lifts them toward me. The chafed skin's scabbed red and oozing. Across those wounds I close the iron with twin snaps, twin key-twists.

"George, string him up," says Sarge.

Here's George now, face flushed and smiling. He circles Drew's cuffed wrists with rope, tightening it roughly till Drew flinches. He tosses the rope over a branch, tugs Drew onto his toes, and secures the rope to the trunk. My Yankee hangs there before me, wide back naked and quivering.

All's ready now. Sarge takes the braided leather lash from me. "Much of the skill's in the wrist. One works the shoulders first, then the upper back. If you can curl the whip around to catch the chest or belly, so much the better. Watch now," he says, patting my shoulder. "Perhaps one day you'll find sufficient strength to take a turn."

I nod. He snaps the whip back, then forward. The black lash disappears, reappears for a mere second across Drew's left shoulder with a cracking sound that makes me jump, then vanishes again. In its place is a red welt scrolled across white skin, joining the marks Sarge made the day Drew came to camp.

Drew's made no sound. He sways on his toes, utterly silent. He stays silent as the whip leaps forward again—arc of a rattlesnake I once saw strike a dog—and paints a matching welt on his right shoulder. If only I were facing him as before, so I could hold him steady with my eyes.

"One can make a kind of art this way, Ian. With skill and practice, one can mark an enemy up with a kind of symmetry," Sarge says, grinning. "And if you step just a bit closer"—he does, then lifts the lash again—"and angle the blow just so, you can catch him with the whip's tip on the front or side." Again the whip parts the air too fast to follow. Again that awful cracking, like a lightning strike. This time, Drew gasps. His head jerks back, then forward, then droops.

George ambles over to the prisoner. "Good one, Sarge," he says, running his hand over Drew's nakedness. "You caught him across the left breast and side." He steps back and stands there now, staring up at Drew's face, close, just out of the whip's reach. "Sir, see if you can mark him that way on the other side. I'll wager you can do it, sir."

"Ah, a challenge!" Sarge's arm angles back, then forward. Another whipcrack. Another gagged gasp.

"Yes, sir! You did it! Perfect! He's bleeding!" George shouts. Even from this distance, I can make out the jubilant gleam in his eyes. What Drew sees now is that red, evilly rapturous ferret's face.

I lose track of the number of blows Sarge delivers. I try to concentrate on the skill being demonstrated just so I can impress the entire company with my supposed enthusiasm for this. I try to keep in mind my purpose: if I can convince Sarge of my cruelty and loyalty, maybe Drew will live a little while longer, albeit welted, bruised, and bleeding. But Drew's gasps and George's flushed face defeat any rational focus I might muster, as a gridiron of welts appears, line by line, across Drew's back.

"Would you like a turn, nephew?" says Sarge, offering me the whip.

I take it. It's heavier than I remember. I carried it to this whipping place only minutes ago, but somehow it's twice as heavy, as if the flesh and blood it's eating this afternoon were like the overabundant feasts that can make a man fat.

I hand it back, trying to suppress the quivering that runs along my fingers. "No, sir. As I've said, after all you've lost, this is a righteous pleasure you shouldn't have to share."

"Yes. All I've lost." Lips set, Sarge grips the lash and gives it a shake. Every time he tortures or kills a foe, he must be remembering Aunt Ariminta: all the years they shared, her sudden death last fall. He never, never mentions her, but surely she haunts him just as powerfully as

Drew has come to haunt me. Perhaps, if Drew were taken from me so brutally, I'd be as full of hate as my uncle is.

"Lay it on, sir!" George shouts with glee.

"With pleasure," Sarge says, recommencing his efforts.

Part of me is here, listening, obeying, watching Sarge's arm swing back, then forward, hearing the crack, seeing the body before me jerking and swaying, the snowy skin staining like parchment smudged with scarlet ink. Part of me is in Drew, taking that sharp tongue across his back again and again, biting down on rope, staring down at George, fighting back screams, feeling youth's skin part and trickling blood tickle.

Sarge stops, panting softly. I stare at his handiwork as at a tapestry hung up for my inspection. The muscles of the snow are all red now, pretty parallel bars, red raspberry juice. And still Drew isn't crying. Why the hell isn't he doing what I told him to do? He's simply swaying and jerking, infrequently releasing a soft gasp or groan. This is not the show Sarge wants.

As if Sarge were reading my mind, he says, "You promised me the Yank would give us blood *and* tears, nephew. Let's carry on. Let's see if I can catch the belly or chest once more."

My uncle swings. I feel Drew's right nipple open up. His breast is dripping not mother's milk but warrior's gore.

My uncle swings. I feel Drew's golden-hairy belly open now, red furrow of plow in clay.

"You should see his face!" George laughs. "Lord, does this boy hate us!"

No time now, no seconds or minutes, just Sarge's rhythm. Right, then left. Right, then left. Right, then left. Stepping forward and back, forward and back. Breast, belly, shoulders, back. Breast, belly, shoulders, back. Breast, belly, shoulders, back. Our captive's gasps become whimpers, and now he's silent, and now his spastic jerks beneath the whipcrack have become a heavy slumping.

"Sarge?" George has left his long study of the prisoner's face and strolled over. "He's passed out. You look tired. May I try? Why don't we drop his pants and mark him up below?"

"That's enough," I say.

Both men look down at me, frowning.

"The prisoner's unconscious. He's had enough. I won't have him die on me."

"Sarge! I told you that Ian's gone soft on this pig. I told you—"

"Shut up, Private." Sarge tosses the dripping whip onto the ground. The grass beneath the whip is faintly green. "Ah, that was glorious. That was enough. Yes, Ian, cut him down. You can nurse him and treat him easy today and tonight. Tomorrow, though, buck and gag the man again."

George sputters, then falls silent beneath my uncle's cold stare. Sarge strides off. Jeremiah steps forward. He props the unconscious prisoner up while I untie the rope from which he hangs. Released, Drew slumps on Jeremiah's shoulder. "Shit, he's massive," Jeremiah grunts, lowering him into the grass. Jeremiah takes one arm, and I take the other. He's almost too heavy to move this way, but Rufus joins us, and laboriously we half-drag, half-carry him to my tent, depositing him on the ground inside.

I thank Rufus. He nods and heads off. "Good luck with him," says Jeremiah, patting my shoulder as he leaves. My Yank lies on his belly, hands thrown above his head. I ungag him and, as an afterthought, work an oilcloth beneath his dead weight. I trace the wounds across the arch of his back. I lift my stained fingers to my mouth. His blood tastes like all men's blood, the blood that flooded my mouth in boxing matches when I was younger and often lost. It's salt and iron. I rub it across my forehead, across my lips, across my tongue.

—

CHAPTER THIRTY-THREE

"Damned fool," I mutter. "Why did you have to be so frigging brave?"

Unconscious still, Drew's in no position to respond. He's a mountain of bare skin I'm daubing blood from. Water I've heated over the camp-fire steams in a pail, growing foamy with the precious soap Sarge gave me earlier today. The white cloths and the water slowly redden. The wounds Sarge inscribed streak Drew front, sides, and back, as if my big Yank had been waylaid by a bear.

I'm wiping blood from the deep slashes crosshatching the small of Drew's back, where, astride his spine, a little patch of yellow hair spreads, when he groans and shifts. "Ian?" he mumbles, lifting his head. Then "Oh, God," he gasps, pressing his face against the oilcloth beneath him, agony stiffening the body beneath my hands. "Oh God, oh God."

"Easy, buddy, easy. These wounds really need to be cleaned, salved, and bandaged. Can you take that?" I run a finger between his shoulder blades, where purple and red paint what once was freckled white, where swollen stripes groove what was smooth. "I'll take it slow; I'll be as gentle as I can. It really needs doing."

"Yep," Drew says. "Get on with it."

"Want some whiskey? I got a flaskful."

"Courtesy of your devil-kin, right? Hell, yes."

I slip the flask into his hand. Cocking his head to the side, he takes a long drink. Then he corks the flask, hands it back, and buries his face in the oilcloth once more.

I recommence the washing and the ringing out. Drew hisses. His fingers claw the grass in slow motion. He shakes his head slowly. "Goddamn. Goddamn." I wipe him dry, as lightly as I can, and spread the salve across his welted shoulders, his upper back, down his spine, over his lower back. Drew shivers and groans. Beneath my fingertips, the muscles knot up and slacken again and again.

"Done," I say. "Roll over. Your chest and sides are pretty ripped up too."

With agonized slowness, Drew begins to move. "Easy, easy," I say, helping him. "Arms over your head."

On his back now, Drew's blinking up at me, grimacing, then looking down, half-dazed, at the gashes crisscrossing his chest and belly. Blood's stained the hair a ruddy gold, the color I imagine Bronze Age armor might have been, the breastplate worn by Achilles. "Good boy," I say, gently cleaning the thick mounds of his torso, the hunger-lean belly, concave beneath his rib cage, and the ribs themselves, prominent after months of war ration and days of Sarge's enforced starvation.

Beneath my ministrations, Drew lies back, closes his eyes, and sighs. Occasionally he gives a jerk or flinch as the washcloth meets some particularly deep wound, but for the most part he's still as my hands guide the wet, pink-tinged rag over his great body. This, it occurs to me as I daub clotted blood from the slash that Sarge's effort cut across his right nipple, is how a hero should be shaped. When I try to gauge what exactly has me so enamored, what combination of line, shape, and color has driven me into devotion, all I can come up with is the way that Drew combines a hero's frame with a boy's vulnerability. That's what has seized me up so utterly. One side of me is praising God; one side of me is damning myself for a fool.

"Clean my armpits too, Ian, please," Drew whispers. "I'm tired of my own stink."

"The soldier's life does encourage an aromatic high state," I laugh. "If I ever get you back to West Virginia, there's a swimming hole I'll have to take you to. Damned sweet spot after an afternoon's haying." I scrub the furry nests beneath his arms, then, as an afterthought, unbutton my jacket, shrug off my undershirt, sit by Drew's feet, and scrub my own armpits, chest, and face. Sunlight's slanting against the side of the tent, and the air inside this closed space is warm, a welcome change after months of sleet-moody skies.

Eyes open now, Drew watches me down his body's long length. "You're using that water to wash? It's blood-dirty now, ain't it?"

"Yep, guess so. Easier than heating up another bucket, though. Water's still warm. I don't mind. Besides, your blood's my fault."

Drew smiles. "You ain't Cain. You're Ian. But your uncle sure did beat the hell out of me."

"Yes, he did," I sigh, scrubbing my forehead. "And why the *fuck* didn't you cry? You are one stupid boy. I told you to—"

"Hand me that flask, will you?"

I do so, then start in on the scolding again. "One of the reasons he felt obliged to whip you so damn long was 'cause you wouldn't cry. And I *told* you to pretend to pass out. Did you? Seemed to me you were really unconscious."

"Right about that, Reb. I managed a dead faint, for sure." Drew's eyes range over my exposed chest. "You sure have a fine little form for a scrawny kid." He flourishes the flask in my direction. "Here's to my Confederate captor, jailor, nurse." He takes a big swig. "Between your salve and this liquor, I'm sure to heal up fast."

I look down at myself, at the hard muscles, the wet smudges of black hair upon my breast and belly. Nothing heroic here, nothing special, nothing that a man as splendid as Drew would find worth loving. He's got me smiling, though, and almost off the subject. Stubborn, I veer back.

"I'm no kid. I'm five years your senior. Anyway, back to the topic at hand. He wouldn't have hurt you so bad if you'd only have—"

Drew rests a forearm over his eyes. "I could sense you there," he says quietly. "It was like before, when he took the belt to me. It hurt bad, but I could feel you there, inside the pain, and that kept me warm, gave the punishment some meaning...and, hell, some of the things I've done, some of the orders I've obeyed, well, maybe I deserve to bleed. Look, Ian, I know I should have let myself break; it would have been easier on us both, but don't you understand? I hate these men. They hate me. I don't want to give them the pleasure of my tears. I'm harder than I was when I was first whipped. Hell, it's only been a few days, but..."

"Keep talking," I say, dipping up a waxy clump of salve and smearing it along a gash in his side. "Just keep your voice down. Sarge told me to keep you gagged, remember, and I don't want him to catch us talking. You'll be in George's keeping fast if I'm caught disobeying orders. And George won't be interested in your scruples regarding the sanctity of your 'cherry,' as you call it."

Contempt twists Drew's face. "That bastard makes me want to puke. Well, anyway, that's about all I wanted to say, except...at the same time that this abuse is making me harder inside, it's breaking down my body. I don't think I can take many more beatings like the one today."

"I should tell you now, Drew. Sarge has said when you get too weak to keep up—we're going to be moving a lot in the next few days—that we'll have to..."

"I understand. I'll be left in a shallow grave like one of those poor bitches in the ballads, right?"

A welt across his belly now, bisecting his navel. My greasy fingers part the fur, following the swollen trail the braided leather left. "Yes. And he means to keep you bucked and gagged a good bit till we leave. So that..."

Drew nods. "Pretty soon I won't be able to walk. As soon as I slow your company's progress down, I'll be on my knees in the mud on the side of the road and your pistol will be pressed to my head."

"That's not going to happen. I'm not sure how, but we're going to get you out of here before that time comes. One more thing, buddy." The damaged flesh is hot beneath my fingers. Bruises are darkening like mud puddles beneath his skin. "Sarge says, since the weather's warming up, after we get to Purgatory Mountain, you'll be kept outside as before. Which means..."

"We won't be able to hold one another at night." Drew's voice catches. "Oh, damn, Ian, your touch was the only thing getting me through all this. I won't last long without you."

I put away the salve, take a drink from the flask, and cork it. "We have a few nights yet, I think. Depends on how fast the company moves. A night near Lexington, probably, then another on the way to Purgatory. We need to make that time count. Meanwhile, if you'll sit up, I'll bandage you."

"You got any more salve?"

"Yep. Why?"

"Hell, Reb, you ain't forgotten, have you? When I got my butt beat bloody a few days back, you promised to salve me down there, and you *still* ain't gotten around to it. From what you've said, time's awastin.'" The smile on Drew's face is strained, but it's a smile nonetheless.

"For a man who's never done more than kiss, you're sure eager to get my hands on your ass," I mutter. "You'll get your salving down below. Tonight, I promise. Right now, you should nap, get your strength up. I need to leave you alone for a few hours. Promised Jeremiah I'd help him gather and chop wood. You hungry? I'll fetch you some food."

"Once you're done with the wood," says Drew. "Until then, yeah, I'll get some sleep."

"I'm not going to cuff your hands behind you like Sarge ordered. If he checks on you, I'm going to tell him you're just too torn up. Right now, though, you need bandaged."

When Drew sits up, I begin, unrolling long strips of cloth and wrapping them over his wounds. He's been so thoroughly worked over that the bandaging takes a long time, and by the time I'm done his torso is almost entirely swathed in cotton.

Drew looks down over the strips of white, shaking his head. "I'm already a corpse wrapped in grave clothes."

"You aren't a corpse just yet. Here, get up on my cot."

Some effort and a lot of wincing, and Drew's settled in for the afternoon. Before I leave, I tug a bandana from my back pocket. "You're supposed to be gagged, so..." I knot it loosely about Drew's neck. "Put it in your mouth if you hear someone nearby."

Drew, damn him, pulls the bandana up and grips it between his teeth.

"You know how handsome you are like that?" My hand seems to have a will of its own, stroking his golden-bearded cheek.

We stare into one another's eyes. I lean over and kiss his gagged mouth, then pull the bandana down over his chin, leaving it to hang about his neck.

"You like me with a rag in my mouth, don't you, Reb? Another thing that makes you feel powerful and protective?"

"You're mocking me."

"No, sir, I'm not. I'm just asking what pleases you. After all you've done for me, least I can do is please you."

Such a simple word, "sir." Nevertheless, it makes my face flush and a shiver climb my spine.

"You're flirting with me like a—"

"Whore? Like a whore? No, Private Campbell. Like a buddy. A buddy who's hoping you'll lie atop him tonight while we still can. A buddy who's helpless, who knows you savor his helplessness, but who's nevertheless hoping you'll save his life."

I pull the rag back up over his chin, centering it between his teeth. "I'm getting you home, Yank. If not your home, then mine. Here are my promises: I'm going to salve your ass and somehow I'm going to save it too. Now lie down and shut up."

"Yes, sir." That's what he's mumbling. With that, my captive does what he's been told, falling silent and curling into the blankets. I love his obedience. It moves something inside me, as if a log dam were dislodging, allowing a river to rush into its ancient, customary channels. Leaving him in the tent, I head off to help Jeremiah with the wood.

—

CHAPTER THIRTY-FOUR

Jeremiah's good with an ax, far better than me. The maple he's downed splits neatly beneath his swing. For a time, we work side by side without speech, making a goodly pile to feed the cook-fires. When we take a break, sipping water, the talk begins.

"How's the Yank?" Jeremiah hones his ax with a stone.

"Pretty weak, in a lot of pain. He's still unconscious in my tent."

Jeremiah nods. I take his lead, scraping a whetstone across my own blade. It smells like pine out here, and moldy leaves, a welcome change from the camp's smells of damp wool, unwashed bodies, the latrine-trench, moldy tent canvas, and wood ash. Through the trees, I can make out the blue-gray horizon of distant hills.

"In a few days we head for Purgatory Mountain," says Jeremiah, eyes on his blade. "Wild place, I hear tell. Bear and painter-cats still live up there. Prowl down the slopes and kill cattle."

"Sounds like home," I say. "My Granny was always talking about hearing painter cats on the ridge above her place. She said they sounded like women screaming. We're used to wild, aren't we? Remember when your Daddy drove that bear cub from the orchard with a hoe?"

"Yep, he hates to kill things." Jeremiah musters a faint smile. "I always got to butcher the hogs come November. But Ian, you know there might be more'n big cats screaming back home." He spits, wipes his mouth. "Isn't that why we're in this war? To keep marauding Yankees out? If the Yanks have invaded...back home, there's women screaming. Our kin. Folks we love."

We fall silent. I try not to imagine. "I don't think so. I hope not. The last letter I got, when we were in winter quarters outside Staunton, said the Yanks had left them alone so far."

"I pray you're right, friend. All right, let's get this wood done. And we should do some packing up after this."

"Surely. Though I'll need to feed the prisoner first."

"Think he'll make it to Purgatory?"

"I don't know. He's young and strong, but..."

A whetstone scraping metal seems like a small scream. It sets my teeth on edge.

"Word is he'll be spending all day tomorrow bucked and gagged. I know what that feels like. Will he be able to keep up when we decamp?"

I shrug, trying to be nonchalant. But Jeremiah's the one who caught me kissing Drew. Why am I trying to hide how I feel from an old friend from home?

"Are you planning to help him escape?"

I look up. Jeremiah's eying me calmly.

I put down my whetstone and ax. I stand up, looking out over the valley.

"George has been talking so much about how you're a Yankee-lover that some of the men are getting wary of you. And I've been asked to keep especial eye on your tent at night when I'm on sentry duty. So have some other men."

"By Sarge?"

"Yep. Ian, I'll have to shoot him if he runs. I won't want to, but—he don't mean as much to me as he does to you."

"What do you mean by that?"

Now Jeremiah lays down his whetstone and ax as well. He strides over and rests his hands on my shoulders. "Friend, I ain't no fool. I've known you since we were brats weeding corn in the garden and picking blackberries in the dell. I remember how you looked at Thom back home, before he up and left. It's the same way my brother used to look at his...friend when he thought no one was watching. The way you look at that Yankee, it's the same. Only harder. There's something deep there, Ian. Don't you know what it is?"

I shake my head, wiping some wet from my eye. Somewhere in the woods nearby, a mourning dove sobs. Rain crow, we call it back home. The sound means rain's on its way. Or grief.

"You're falling in love with him, man. Face it. You've got to root that out of your heart. He'll be good and dead mighty soon."

"Love?" I turn from Jeremiah with a snort. "I've only known him for a few days."

"Yes. But war...everything's faster, grander in war. It's like God's whetstone, sharpening our edges. It—it's like a still. The sour mash gets run through, comes out fire."

I can't help but laugh at Jeremiah's metaphors. That doesn't stop him.

"Since he was caught, you two have spent constant time together. You've had to feed him, help him piss and shit. You've had to watch his suffering and dress his wounds. You've had to sleep in the same tent. Friend, we're all half-starved and homesick, all crazy as hell and craving some comfort. So it's no wonder you're feeling strong things. But, Ian, it's treason if you help him get away. Any man in the company would be obliged to shoot down both of you."

I pick up my whetstone and rub its rough length along my palm. "Jeremiah, I fear you're right about all of this. I'm not asking you to help me, nor asking you to allow him to escape. Just don't tell anyone what you know. About how I feel."

"I won't, Ian. But are you? Going to let him loose?"

"I don't know. I thought I might, but with the suspicions you describe..."

"He won't get far. You won't get far. My advice is to enjoy him while you can but prepare yourself for parting. And pray. Who knows? I suspect during wartime the air's thicker than usual with prayers, but despite that clotted babble the Lord might hear you yet."

—

CHAPTER THIRTY-FIVE

Drew's ravenous again. I feed him slivers of squirrel that Rufus shot and bean-broth poured over crumbled cornbread. Leaving him curled on the cot, as comfortable as a gagged and cuffed man covered with lash marks can be, I range around the camp helping my company-mates begin packing for the move to come. At dusk we leave off our efforts, gathering about the fire for supper. I do my best to be sociable, the self I was before the prisoner came. I have doubts to allay.

If my companions suspect me for a Yankee-lover, I can't see it in their eyes. Field peas and stewed squirrel finished up, we pass flasks; I tell a few vulgar tales the boys have heard before but ask for again. Lots of laughter; a couple of palms pounding my back with uproarious appreciation. For a few hours, it feels like old times. Jeremiah, bless him, abandons his usual mournful tunes to lighten the men's moods with some banjo jigs. Only George is clearly suspicious, watching me from across the fire as he chews a mouthful of tobacco. We glare at one another through the sparks and smoke before his glance skitters sideways. He spits into the fire and moves off into the darkness.

I try to head to bed several times, but the boys, pressing drink on me, demand more stories. "Tell us the one about the country girl and the city girl in the diddling contest! How about that ant and elephant tale? Or the one about the preacher and the street-whore?" When I'm done with those rank entertainments, Jeremiah launches into his version of "Bile Them Cabbages Down." Rufus does a little dance; someone joins in on harmonica; the boys clap in time. Then Jeremiah and I sing along to his version of everybody's favorite, "Home, Sweet Home"; after a verse, all the boys join in. I can almost believe that I'm truly part of all this, can almost forget that I've got a much-bandaged Yank in my tent fearing for his life.

My feet have a little stagger on by the time I leave the fire, carrying a pail of more warmed water. Beyond the circle of firelight, it's the thick dark of country midnight; I stumble a few times, sloshing water on me, then lean against a tree to regain my balance. It's a sarvisberry, I think.

I finger a twig and can feel the buds swelling with the new year. Taking a deep breath of cold air, I look up the trunk, into the branches and past them into the sky. Above us, there's the Dipper and the Bear, those constellations my Daddy taught me when I was a child. They look like mosaics of ice set against burnt-black wood. I wish I could heave Drew over my shoulder, climb this tree, and just keep going, up into those stars where no one could hurt us, where our bodies would interlock and burst into flame and, embracing, hang in the heavens forever.

"You asleep?" I whisper, putting down the pail inside the entrance and closing the tent flaps behind me. I bump into a tent pole, curse, fall to my knees, and crawl over to the cot. Here's Drew, warm wooly hill beneath my fingers. "You sleeping, big man?"

"Huh uh," Drew mumbles. Fumbling in the dark, I find his face, pull the bandana out of his mouth and down over his chin. I kiss him, sloppy and hard, then tug the blanket down to his waist and rest my head on his bare chest.

Drew chuckles. "You're drunk as a lord. And smelly as a still."

"How you been? How you feeling, boy?" My lips range through his chest fur, find the satin-smooth circle of a nipple, and kiss it.

"I slept good and hard. And I feel better already. That Indian salve of yours really helps." His fingers stroke my hair.

"That cot can't hold us both. Get down here." Tugging the blanket off him, I roll onto the ground on the nest of oilcloth. "And drop your pants while you're at it. Get bare-assed. I owe you more salving."

"About damned time," Drew rumbles. Silence, then the sound of trousers slipped down over thighs.

"I left that jar of medicine under the cot. Fetch it, Yank."

Rattle of the shackle chain binding his feet. "You sure are domineering when you're drunk, Private Campbell. Or is it 'cause you figure, since you got me collared like a slave, you can order me around?"

"That's it, yes. I already told you I'd like to take you back to West Virginia and own you, now didn't I? Get on down here, boy. Stretch out on your belly."

"Yes, *sir*!" Drew says. That word again. Drew's intonation is ironic, but I'm exhilarated nonetheless. More shackle-clink, then he's bumping my arm with the jar of ointment and lying heavily down beside me.

"Got to clean you up first." I shake my head, trying to disperse the whiskey-fog. "Uhhhfff, drank too much." With awkward effort, I light the candle-stub. Dipping a cloth in the warm water, I gently rinse his buttocks and the cleft between them. Drew spreads his thighs as far as the short length of shackle chain allows, rests his head on his arms, and says nothing save for little moans of gratitude as I wash him thoroughly, rinse him, and pat him dry.

"Jeremiah told me something today. Said that, thanks to George's evil talk, some of the men are suspicious. Said sentries have been ordered to watch this tent," I say, sliding a palm lightly over his buttocks. They're hard and curved, covered with soft fuzz; scabs my belt left make rigid paths across them, like the trails the habitual hooves of cattle cut along the slope of a hill on the way to a pond or salt lick. The nearness of him sobers me up, or, rather, replaces one intoxication with another. "Even if you were willing to 'overpower' me, make a run for it, and leave me to face the consequences, I'm pretty sure you'd be shot down."

"All right, Ian," Drew says. He stretches his cuffed hands above his head and presses his cheek against the ground. "I wasn't willing to go that route anyway. Don't want you suffering for me."

The end of words for a while. I uncap the salve and spread it smoothly over his right ass cheek. My fingertips trace the scabs with unguent and massage the swollen bruises. Drew sighs with pleasure.

"We leave for Lexington day after tomorrow, Purgatory Mountain a day or so after that. If you can make it to the mountain—you'll be tethered to the cart again, and it'll be hard going, even harder since you'll be bucked all day tomorrow—maybe there I can figure out how to get you out of this."

When I move my attentions to the left buttock—there's an especially bad swelling here, spreading across the curved muscle and over his hip—Drew winces, lifts his head, and looks back at me, here where I kneel between his spread legs. "I sure wish I could say I ain't afraid to die. But I am afraid. Could we just be here now and not speak of such things? I want to savor what time together we have left. If we keep talking of what's to come, I might piss myself."

"Sure, buddy," I say. "I'll shut up."

Drew nods, then presses his cheek against Virginia earth again, closing his eyes. I dip up more salve, anoint more bruised and scabbed flesh, gently kneading him. "That's some splendid touching, Reb," he murmurs. "You surely know how to soothe a man."

Finished with the salving, I cap the jar. But now my fingers veer back to his body, stroking the lush bush in the valley parting his buttocks. The hard warmth, soft skin, and thick fur of him are irresistible. "I can't touch you enough," I say, eyes lowered and ranging over the gift of his nakedness. "I so badly want to lie with you."

"You ain't about to rape me, are you, Reb?" Drew says. I can't see his smile, but I can hear it in the tone of his voice.

I lift my hand, about to protest. Drew says, "Hell, I'm joshing you. Keep that up. It feels wonderful."

Permission granted, I snuff the candle and continue my rapt exploration. I stroke the fine tufts of hair in his crack, tug on them tenderly, rest my cheek against one buttock and stroke his crack-fuzz some more.

"Ian? I ain't ready for that over-the-hay-bale fucking you and Thom did, but...other than that, since we got so little time, you're welcome to...take your pleasure of me. Do what you want, whatever pleases you. I trust you. I know you know what you're doing. You got me all trussed up. This Achilles ain't going anywhere. So use me. Show me how it's done. Just break me in slow, okay?"

My lips are on his ass-cheek now. I kiss it softly, brushing my chin-beard over it. Drew lifts his loins off the earth, pressing himself against my face.

"My guess is I'm due to meet my Maker real soon, so...this side of the grave, I'm yours."

Gripping his lean hips, I part his ass-cheeks with my thumbs. I rub my chin along the crack.

"You hear me, Ian?" Drew groans. "I'm yours. Fill me up with kindness before I got to die."

What I do next I never did with Thom. It's something I've never thought of before, never heard of. But it seems right. His flesh smells like soap and blood, the salve's herb-infused lard, and the grassy musk that clings to men's crevices and secret parts even after a bath. I spread his ass-cheeks further and lick the fuzz growing there.

Drew gasps. "Ian, what are you—?"

"I'm taking my pleasure, boy. You gave me that permission. You're a feast. I'm feasting on you."

My tongue trails the crack, then drops deeper. Drew bucks back against my mouth; I grip his hips harder. Then my tongue-tip finds his tiny opening and laps it. There's a musky bitterness like black walnuts we used to crack and hoard at home, a musky sweetness like sorghum we used to boil down from green sugar-cane juice. My tongue circles his tight spot. I fumble for his balls, find them, grip the base of them in one hand, wrap my other arm around his waist, and push my tongue into him.

Drew's making too much noise, I realize dimly. The tent brims with his loud rapture. I lift my head long enough to whisper, "Stuff your mouth with that rag and keep quiet, fool. We don't need an audience." Then I'm on him again, brushing his crack with my beard, prying the edges of his opening back with my thumbs and wedging my tongue into him more deeply.

Drew obeys. He's quiet now, only making an infrequent cloth-crammed grunt as he pushes back against my face and I explore him further, mouth and nose buried between his buttocks. We rock together for long minutes. I've shifted my grip from his balls to his very hard penis and have started stroking him when, outside, there's the shuffle of footfalls in dead leaves.

I push him to the ground, unholster my pistol, and listen. There's the shuffling again, nearer now, then stopping, then recommencing only to recede. I part the tent flap and step out. There's nothing to see but tree trunks, their thin columns black against black. Nothing's unusual but a telling odor. I find it by its strong scent, three yards from the tent: a moist plug of chewing tobacco, recently spat out.

—

CHAPTER THIRTY-SIX

"Do they call this spooning where you're from?" Drew asks.

"Yep," I reply. "Can't imagine a better way to spend a chilly mountain night."

We're lying side by side in the tent's pitch dark, speaking in whispers. My chest is pressed against Drew's bandaged back; my lap cups his butt; my arms embrace him. He's nigh onto naked, trousers still around his ankles; I've stripped to the waist just so we can lie skin to skin. We curl together beneath the covers, afraid to do more than cuddle until we're sure whoever might have been listening—most probably George—has not returned.

"I cherish the pressure of your body against my back," Drew says, snuggling closer. "Makes me feel safe."

"Ha! How a little guy like me could make a golden colossus like you feel safe is beyond me."

"I saw you take out George. You were on him like a catamount. And didn't you tell me—well, warn me, rather—that you were a crack shot when we first met? Not to mention a battle-berserker?"

"Yep. Guys my size got to compensate."

Words taper off. I stroke the thin hair on his temples, the denser hair upon his cheeks and chin, while we listen to night sounds. Somewhere nearby, birds ruckus in a treetop roost, then settle down. There's a slow soughing that comes and goes—mountain wind through hemlock or white pine. So far, no repetition of leaf-rustle, no further indication of a spy.

"Tell me about the man in the barn," Drew says. "The one you mentioned before, when you were trying to explain why...you like to see me tied."

"All right. As much as I want to do more than talk...I want to pleasure you all damn night, Drew, while we're still here together...I can't get enough of how you feel and smell and taste, but..."

"I know. You're afraid someone's listening. You think George is out there, waiting, hoping to hear something damaging, something he can tell your devil-kin."

"Yep. He might have already heard you moaning. Hell, if he even heard us talking, we'll be in trouble, since I've been ordered to keep you gagged. George is angling to be...assigned you, I think. If that happens..."

"I won't last but a few days. I know that too. I can see the evil in his eyes. So, here, now"—Drew grips my hand and kisses it—"look, we're together, this is enough. Just hold me, buddy, and let's talk. We still got a few nights, God willing."

"And tomorrow night, let me get this clear, you'll be ready for more than kissing, right?"

Drew laughs low. "Yes, sir. Count on it. It's true that, before tonight, I'd never done anything with a man—or a woman, for that matter—but kiss, but I was certainly relishing your Southern hospitality earlier this evening. I think you could tell from the racket I made. Your tongue's a treasure, Reb."

Slipping one arm over his hip, I tug at the hair around his navel. When did touching get to be so easy?

"All right, big man. So, you want the story about what I saw in the barn when I was ten. The man was an outlaw. My father had caught him trying to steal a horse from our stable. They'd scuffled; Daddy punched him out. He tied him up in the barn, set my older brother Jeff to watch him, and rode off to fetch the sheriff. I was curious, of course, so in the middle of the night I sneaked out of the house.

"It was summer, I remember, hot, a night full of lightning bugs and the sound of whippoorwills. Jeff wasn't all that pleased to see me—he didn't want me near the prisoner—but I offered to fetch water and food from the house when Jeff wanted it, so he let me stay. He thought it was funny when I said I wanted to help him guard the man, since I was so young and puny, and I guess it was funny, though even then, I suppose, I had a protective streak when it came to those I cared for."

"Thank God for that," Drew murmurs into the dark.

"Well, but, when I saw the man, my feelings got confused...like they are with you. Divided loyalties, or, rather, in that case, family loyalty mixed with some kind of fascination I'd never felt before."

"I'm assuming, since you're telling me this to explain how you like to see me with metal locked around my wrists and ankles, that you liked looking at him?"

"Damn, yes. He was about your size and about your age, with black eyes, eyebrows like a crow's wings, and thick black hair that kept falling over his face when he woke from his stupor and started to struggle. His beard was just as black, and bushy, as if it hadn't been trimmed for a year. He was hairy like you, and muscled too. I could tell 'cause Daddy had torn his shirt open in the struggle. What I saw across his chest was not skin's white but wooly black, as if he were half-animal. Daddy had hogtied him—hands bound together behind his back, then cinched to his roped feet. He made a lot of noise when he came to, once he realized his state and figured out the law was on its way and he was liable to be hanged. When he got to cussing Jeff—nobody messed with Jeff, he was a hothead—Jeff kicked the man in the side, pulled a bandana from his back pocket, and, with some effort, 'cause the man fought like crazy, gagged him."

I fondle the cloth still knotted loosely around Drew's neck. He nods. "I'll chew on that all night if it pleases you. Once the story's done. So what happened then?"

"The outlaw kept struggling and screaming, rolling around over the straw, trying to get loose, till Jeff kicked him a few more times and then pulled a knife and held it to his throat. He settled down then. I fetched Jeff some water and some cookies from the house, and a blanket for myself. I curled up on the blanket; Jeff sat on a bale, ate and drank, then whittled a bit. I studied that prisoner half the night, till sleep finally came to me. I watched his chest hair glisten with sweat; I watched his muscles strain against the rope; I watched his teeth grind the rag; I watched his eyes glow with anger and fear."

"All those things you've studied in me, right?" Drew kisses my hand again.

"Yes. And I was hard for the first time, down below. At least the first time I can remember."

"But not for the last time?" Drew nudges his butt against me, where he can no doubt feel the stiffness between my thighs.

"No," I chuckle. "Definitely not the last time. Sorry. The story kind of riled me up. So, at any rate, that was when all those things got melted up together in my mind: beards and chest hair; ropes and gags; sweat and struggle; powerlessness and fear. Seeing that outlaw marked me, you know? The way they say trauma can mark a baby?"

"What happened to the man?"

"Oh, Daddy showed up that next morning with the law. The horse-thief put up more of a fight; word was he was from a wild family even farther up the mountain than us. The sheriff pistol-whipped him, knocking him out. Last I saw of him he was tied over a packhorse's saddle, blood stringing from his mouth. I heard they hanged him later. A year or so after that, when I first learned how to...use my hand to relieve myself, it was that trussed-up outlaw I thought of."

"What about Jeff? Is he in the Rebel army? Sounds like he would have made a fearsome soldier, as tough and mean as he sounds to be."

"Jeff's dead," I rasp. "The Yankees got him at Antietam. It's real hard for me to think of him or speak of him. Real hard. That's why I haven't mentioned him much."

"Oh, damn. Ian. I'm so sorry."

"He and I volunteered together. We fought side by side in this company for over a year. I hated Yankees for a long time after he died. Wasn't till I met some captured Feds, got to know them a little, saw them suffer under Sarge's hand—especially big handsome Brandon...I was feeling some of this tenderness for him by the time he died—that I started to winnow out whoever shot my brother from...men like you."

Pulling Drew closer, I press my face against his bandaged back. My body soaks in his warmth the way my washcloths absorbed his blood. "Let's get some sleep, boy," I say. "Tomorrow will be hard for you."

"Surely, Reb," says Drew. "Will you gag me first?"

"What?" Surprised, I rub his soft chin. "Are you sure?"

"Yes, sir. I know you enjoy it. I don't care why. It doesn't hurt me. It makes me feel...cared for somehow. The more helpless I am when I'm with you, the more control you have over my limbs and even my speech, well, the more I know I have you to protect me, the more I know you feel obliged to protect me, the more... I don't know. Hell. Just put the rag in my mouth and hug me close till morning, all right?"

I oblige. I loosen the bandana's knot, push the center between his teeth, and pull it taut.

"All right?"

Drew nods.

I knot it behind. "Not too tight?"

Drew shakes his head.

I fondle his face for a while, his bearded cheeks, his moist lips, the cloth growing damp between his teeth. Then I close my eyes and pray. I pray for courage. I pray for Jeff, for Drew, for all the young men out under the cold skies, huddled under oilcloths and by campfires, or rotting in graves, their pine boxes collapsing, their uniforms molding, their splendid bodies melting down to bone, their graves sinking in woodland or field, innumerable little depressions like a finger might make in clay. I might have loved so many of them, living or dead, if we'd been given a chance to meet.

"I'm falling in love with you," I say. "I'd do anything to save you, Drew. I've fallen in love with you." The words wing out of me sudden, the way a hawk, out of nowhere, swerves surprise through the sky.

Drew's silence is a solid thing, a sharp bayonet that could open me up and tear out the frailest parts of me. But then his silence becomes a sigh, something liquid like dew or the sweetness a country boy can sip from a honeysuckle flower.

In his hard grip, the bones of my fingers ache. The cloth blocking his mouth and obscuring his words makes no difference. His response is clear. "I love you too," he says. I wrap my body around his like a husk about a walnut, a shell around a seed. I rock him in my arms till he's fallen asleep.

—

CHAPTER THIRTY-SEVEN

I'm up with reveille, leaving my captive to slumber. Overcast skies, but warm. A flurry of chickadees skirts me. Over the newly fed fire, Rufus is frying hoecake. I'm pouring coffee when Sarge appears beside me. Unasked, I pour him a cup. We sit side by side in sling chairs, sipping while the hoecake cooks. I wait for his words, dreading them. An ill wind blows no good, that's what Aunt Alicia used to say about him.

"Today, Ian, I'd like you to join the other men for drill. Then help them complete packing. We'll be leaving for Lexington tomorrow after breakfast."

"Yes, sir. What should I do with the prisoner? Won't he need to be guarded?"

"No need for you to guard him. He'll be in full view of all the men. I want him bucked and gagged in the middle of camp, not by your tent. I'm sure you're tired of watching him every day. You've had to miss drill ever since we captured him. Bad for a soldier to miss so much drill. Makes you dull and clumsy and likely to fumble or fall in battle."

Drew suffering in full view, at the mercy of any passing man's taunts or abuse? My belly's a pang clenched around coffee. It takes all my skills in dissembling to muster the sound of gratitude. "Thank you, sir. It'll be a relief to be free of him for a while."

"At night you may tend him in your tent. But remember, once we reach Purgatory, he's to be denied further shelter. As I said, spring's almost here, and soon frostbite will no longer be a threat. Let the prisoner spend what time he has left under God's wide sky...as so many of our boys must. And if he can't keep up tomorrow, on our journey, I expect your pistol to send him to his reward. If we're on the move, no need to bury him. Just drag him into the woods. Let the crows eat him. Fit fate for pigs like him."

"Here you go," Rufus says. A square of hoecake steams under my nose.

"Eat up, private," says Sarge. "Lots yet to pack. You'll need your strength."

I might as well be chewing dirt. Suddenly there's no taste to anything. Only swigs of coffee save me from choking on the cornbread crumbs. Sarge finishes his coffee and hoecake; Rufus fetches him more of both. I rise, poke at the fire, and turn toward my tent. "I should get ready, sir," I say.

"One thing, Ian. George spoke to me this morning and told me something odd."

Sarge's tone of voice is sufficient to cause Rufus to retreat. Now my uncle and I are alone by the fire.

"George said he couldn't sleep last night and decided to trade sentry watches with Travis. He said he heard talking in your tent long after dark, along with a strange moaning. Why was that, Ian? My order was to keep the prisoner gagged."

I make a grand show of pouring myself another half-cup of coffee. The words Drew and I exchanged last night make me feel like an oak, with a taproot nothing can dislodge. Can it be that the scared little boy is me is gone? No, I doubt he'll ever depart, but somehow there's less of him now.

"Sir, the Yank needed water. When I ungagged him so he could drink, he started to cry. He knows he's likely to die soon, so he broke down. I let him cry for a while; that must have been the moaning George heard. Then the prisoner asked me to pray with him. For a while I did, before he calmed down and I gagged him again, as you'd ordered. I hope, sir, as a Christian man, you won't object to me permitting a prisoner to pray."

"No, Ian. He has reason to pray, surely, for his no-doubt myriad sins and for the rapidly approaching release of his soul. All right. Buck and gag him over there"—Sarge points down a line of tents to a clearing near his own quarters—"and then prepare for drill. Don't interfere if the boys have some fun with him. That's one of the reasons we're keeping him, are we not? He's been kept sequestered and sheltered long enough."

"Yes, sir," I say. I drink the last mouthful of coffee too fast. It burns my tongue.

"And Ian? Give him no lunch. For his dinner, all we can spare is some hardtack that's gone to the weevil. Don't untie him till he's sobbing. You hear me? The men will savor his tears. I'll tell you when you may release him." Sarge pulls out his pocket watch. "About nightfall, I think. A good twelve to fourteen hours should break that boy like a dry twig."

—

CHAPTER THIRTY-EIGHT

—

The drill goes on and on, as tedious as usual. A couple of hours in the morning, a break for lunch, then another two hours in the afternoon. The maneuvers blur in my mind; my rifle grows heavier and heavier. I keep thinking about Drew, how he fell to his knees in front of me, clasped my legs with his cuffed hands, and buried his face in my uniform jacket before I led him from the tent to be bucked. I keep thinking about the scared little whimpers he made, so quietly only I could hear, as I bound him in the clearing and tied the stick in his mouth. I keep thinking about how I had to leave him there, as vulnerable as an infant, the morning after the night I told him I loved him. I keep thinking about how I looked back once, to find him still staring after me, blue eyes wide and wet.

Drills over, packing begins. Now's the perilous time, when men whose presence up to now had been required at drill disperse to their different tasks, some of them drifting in Drew's direction. I concentrate as best I can, helping Rufus load up camp chairs, leftover firewood, cots, and canvas. From here, where we're loading the cart beneath the tree where Sarge whipped Drew, I can see smoke rising over the few tents but can't see the clearing where he waits. There's an occasional laugh from that direction, but not the moans of pain or the muffled protests I dreaded. He's either been left unmolested— highly unlikely, against all odds—or he's biting down on his bit and trying to be brave while my company-mates abuse him.

It's the latter, I know in my gut. Even from here, I can feel his pain and his yearning, invisible but tangible, like this soft breeze on my face, in the same way that I could almost feel his agony as Sarge bullwhipped him, as the lash slashed his back and breast. It's as if a rope still joined my fist with the collar locked around his neck, as if our bodies were somehow still tethered together. He's aching not only to be freed from a position of long humiliation and agony but to see my face.

I stop lifting boxes of hardtack into the cart. Panting, I wipe my brow. I stand still, staring in Drew's direction, feeling for him in the distance.

A breeze catches dead leaves, spinning them into frantic little circles before they slow, eddy, and descend. Cloud shadows and sunlight drift their dispute over the camp. I look up into the sky, and there's a hawk drifting over, riding a current of air down into the valley. I rub my chin, lift my hand to my nose, and breathe deep. My lover's scent is faint but warm, his body's musk lingering in my beard and on my fingers.

It's all so clear now, as if the winter sun were burning doubt from my vision like frost melting off windowpanes. Drew's here, inside me, blood oozing from his wrists, his face bruised from the blows of fists, the stick-bit cutting his mouth as he mumbles my name. Christ, how blind I've been. Why has it taken me this long to recognize a miracle, sent by a God far kinder than He who brought on this war? Two foes, both so far and so long from home, have found some semblance of home in one another's arms and in my musty little tent. Christ, what a coward I've been. Why has it taken me this long to realize that saving Drew is worth any risk or consequence?

By the time Rufus and I have the cart packed with as much as it will hold, the sun's slanting over the camp, pale orange of late afternoon. I try to take my time, approaching Drew's clearing, eager to see him but fearful of what I'll find. Veering around a tent, I almost run into George. A smile creases his face, showing off the sharp brown teeth. "Your friend's a fine entertainment," he says, snickering. "He's been snuffling and mewling like a brat for a good hour now."

"Motherfucker," I snarl, giving him a hard jab in the ribs with my elbow as I pass. As much as I'd like to slam his face into a stone until the skullbone's exposed, getting to Drew is more important now.

Drew's alone, hunched and bent by the rod and rope that bind him into the tight package that bucking makes of a man. But there's plentiful evidence of recent company. The strong smell of piss pervades the clearing. Fresh piss streaks his back, darkens his trousers, bedews his boots, and puddles about him. There's telltale tobacco juice in his hair and across his shoulders. His bandages have been torn off, making little piles of stained cloth—red-brown of blood, yellow of piss, dark brown of tobacco-spit—all around him. When he lifts his head, he's staring at me with one eye only; the other's blackened and swollen shut.

"Oh, buddy...oh, goddamn." When I touch his shoulder, his face crumples. He breaks down, sobbing and shaking. Then he's jerking his head at me, pointing one index finger back the way I came.

"You want me to go? You want me to leave you like this?"

"Uh huh. Uh huh." Drew nods emphatically. He points again, then bows his head between his arms to hide his damaged face.

Something shatters inside me. Old promises, old faiths. "I'll be back at nightfall to release you. Tonight I'll—"

Greenbrier's coiled in my gut and knotted around my tongue. Turning on a heel, I stride off. Two of my company-mates pass me, smiling: those redheaded twins from New Market. Hardly any beard yet; they can't be more than eighteen. Yankees burned their home last fall, so, like George, their hatred is especially deep. Behind me, sounds of them taking their fun: something hard striking flesh, Drew's groan, a boy's laughter.

In my tent, I press my face into a blanket so no one can hear me weep. Then, spent, I sit on the edge of the cot, clean my pistol, sharpen my Bowie knife, and wait for nightfall. I see a way home now. The next chance I get, I need to study Sarge's maps.

—

CHAPTER THIRTY-NINE

When Drew's sobs subside, I unlock his shackles. It takes a long time
to tug his smelly boots off, his piss-soaked trousers and drawers.
Their bitter odor fills the tent. Again, after so many hours bucked, he
can barely move. How he'll recover fast enough to keep up tomorrow
only God knows. But now my battered Yankee lies entirely naked, save
for collar and cuffs, in the light of the candle stub. He is, of course, as
beautiful as ever, despite the blood and bruises, but I keep my lust to
myself for now. The lover can come later. Right now, what's needed
yet again is the healer. I roll and heave him this way and that, soaping,
scrubbing, kneading, salving, bandaging, doing what I can to reverse
the damage of the afternoon. His breath catches, as if hung on something, then sluices out of him in great sighs. He's stunned, unrespon-
sive, a great stone I move up and down, back and forth.

What I can't salve, of course, is his pride. Hours of painful bondage
and abject humiliation at the hands of my company-mates, those facts
mere soap and water can't erase. It was full dark when Sarge gave the
order to release Drew. By then, both his eyes had been blackened by my
compatriots' fists, his mouth chafed bloody by the stick-bit, his wrists
chafed bloody by the ropes. By then, my Yankee Achilles had been used
as a piss-pot and a spittoon by half the camp. And, after fourteen hours
bucked, he was sobbing without check, uncontrollably, in so much pain
he'd lost all caring or awareness of what his many jeering witnesses
might see or hear. He cried harder when I unbucked him and helped
him stretch his limbs. He kept crying as Rufus and Jeremiah helped me
drag him to my tent.

Now he's quiet, lying on his back atop the oilcloth, beneath the quilt
I brought from home, blond head propped on my haversack. His eyes
are closed, both swollen shut. The weevily hardtack Sarge ordered me
to feed him I've soaked in cold coffee till the bugs floated to the surface.
He tried to eat it, got down a couple of bites, then gagged and threw
it up. I've managed to get only a few sips of whiskey down him. This
does not bode well for tomorrow's relocation. He'll be not only stiff and

sore from today's long restraint, but he'll be weak from lack of food. If he collapses, if Sarge commands me to kill him, well, someone will die indeed. I won't know until that moment, if it comes, whether it will be Drew or Sarge.

I sit on the cot, chin in my hands, elbows on my knees, and study him. His face is a little boy's bruised up after a brawl. I try to imagine him as a child, a farm boy in Pennsylvania, smiling as he climbs a tree or greedily gobbles a piece of pie. I try to imagine us meeting some-where else, in some other time, some decade less full of cruelty and death. I try to see him limping into the new campsite, safely arrived at Purgatory. I try to see him home with me in West Virginia, cuddling against me in my old bed.

My hands, I realize, are wringing one another the way my mother's used to when she was anxious, the same gesture she used to twist rags dry. I wash them in the rapidly cooling water with which I bathed Drew—smells of sweat, piss, blood, pain, and chaw-spit. He's snoring softly by the time I'm done, exhaustion swallowing him like a hill-gap at day's end does the sun. He'll be safe enough here, while I visit Sarge to express interest in our coming remove and to study his multitude of maps.

Leaving Drew's urine-moist boots outside the tent's entrance, I wash his fetid pants and drawers in the stream, then hang them over a near-by sapling's limb. I empty the pail of water in the latrine-trench, then head for the fire. My uncle's there, relaxing with the majority of his men. Rufus is annoying everyone with his attempts on the harmonica. George, playing cards with his New Market buddies, gives me a jagged grin. I spare him a glare, then settle into a chair beside Sarge, accept his proffered flask, lean back, and close my eyes. Now that I've decided what I have, it's more important than ever that I act as I did before the Yankee came.

"Sir, I'd like to have a better sense of where we're going tomorrow. May I examine your maps?"

Sarge rubs his chin—freshly shaved, looks like—then his bushy gray moustache. It was black when I was a child. I used to tug on it when I sat on his knee. I've known him all my life. Some of my strength I've learned from him. What I plan to do he will never forgive.

"Certainly, Ian. The relevant one is on my desk. You're welcome to examine it tonight. We'll be heading off at dawn. How's the prisoner?"

"Unconscious, sir. Pretty beaten up. The boys used him hard."

Sarge laughs softly. "Then he's served some purpose on this earth. Will he make the march tomorrow?"

"I think so, sir. We'll see. May I find some new trousers and a shirt for him? His own pants reek. I don't want to have to smell his stink. You know several of the boys, while he was bucked..."

Another laugh. "Only fitting. Using a foe as a chamber pot is a high pleasure in this life. I won't allow him upper garments; let the scum stay shirtless and suffer from the elements. But for decency's sake, yes, I think we have some leftover trousers somewhere, ones big enough for him. Those ones that Jebediah left when he got caught in the crossfire near McCormick's Depot. They're liable to be packed, though. Look for them when we make camp outside Lexington. You'll have to tolerate his smell till then, or simply tie him up outside."

"Yes, sir. I'll keep him in the tent tonight, just because he's in such bad shape. He can wear his own clothes till Lexington."

Someone cheers. Jeremiah is tuning up his banjo, and poor tone-deaf Rufus has given up his musical attempts. I stay by the fire for several songs, sprawling in the chair as if I were drunk or entirely relaxed, before bidding Sarge good night. Jeremiah gives me a nod as I leave. George, it seems, has retired. The New Market boys, inveterate gamblers, are quarreling over their card hands.

The big map I need's already unfolded across Sarge's camp desk, where he said it would be. The candle lantern flickers and starts; shadows hunch up and recede in the corners of the tent. I find the present here, tonight, this mountainside south of Staunton. I find the approaching future here, near Lexington, then up the pike to Purgatory. Then, in maps charting ranges to the west, I find a farther future—fate, luck, and smarts allowing—here, up the James, up Craig Creek, over this mountain, then down the New River. The days to come, I'm beginning to see, are not a ravine we're dumbly driven down. They're limbs to climb, if we have sufficient strength and reach.

—

CHAPTER FORTY

"Ian?" Drew's voice is small, scared. It's pitch dark in here, but at least the smell of piss is diminishing. "Is that you?"

"Yep," I say, sealing the tent flaps behind me before peeling off my jacket and undershirt. Unsheathing my Bowie knife, I put it atop the cot, within easy reach.

Feeling around for him, I brush his shoulder's hard bulge and hot skin. He's here on his side, curled into another of his frightened balls like a sowbug does when it's alarmed. "Just keep quiet. George is ranging around somewhere, so I got to keep you quiet." I kiss him hard before pushing one balled-up bandana into his mouth, then tying another between his teeth and around his head. I settle in behind him, spooning him beneath the quilt.

"Pretty soon you'll be spending the night outside, boy," I say, smoothing the bandages I've bound across his back. "So tonight, considering how badly you've suffered today, I'm going to make you feel as fine as I can. I know you're real sore. All you got to do is lie there and stay silent. All right? Let me know if I hurt you, if you don't like what I'm doing, if you want me to stop. All right?"

"Uh huh," Drew mumbles, snuggling closer.

"We've waited long enough," I say, mouth pressed to his ear. My arms circle his thick torso; my fingers play with the hair on his breast. When I find his nipples, he gasps, pressing his ass against my groin and thrusting his chest against my hands.

"Shhh, shhhh," I say. "You like that, huh?"

Drew nods hard, then sighs, then gasps again as I rub and flick the nubs of smooth flesh, hard little islands in a sea of soft fur.

My trouser-pent cock's bumping his buttocks now, rubbing his crack. As much as I want inside him, I've promised him not to go that far, so I focus on his nipples instead. My long-reined-in excitement makes me rougher and rougher; the rubbing and stroking become a hard tugging, pinching, twisting. If I'm hurting him, he seems to like it, tossing his head, emitting tiny moans. I clamp one hand over his mouth, pull his

head back against mine, and knead the big mounds of his chest like biscuit dough before narrowing my attentions to his nipple-nubs again.

Now my hand ranges over his famine-flat belly, the indentation of his
navel. I wish I were there, the day he was born. I wish I were there to
hold him in my arms, to cradle and comfort him as if I were his father.
Well, I can do some of that now. I'm sifting his pubic hair, running a
finger up and down his erection till he's shuddering and half-repressed
groans well up beneath my hand. "Shush," I say, kissing the back of his
head and squeezing his stiff penis in my fist. "Keep real quiet, or I'll
stop."

No groans now, just hard breathing through his nose, as I stroke the
thick column of his sex and tug at his scrotum, an oriole's nest sagging
with the weight of two precious eggs. Silently he rides my hand, cock
sliding in and out of my grip like a dagger being impatiently sheathed
and unsheathed.

"It's time to taste you," I murmur. "Roll onto your back; stretch out.
Keep your hands above your head or I'll tie you down. I don't need
touched right now. Touching you is sufficient pleasure tonight."

I climb on top of him, my fuzzy warrior, my naked man-mountain.
Cupping my hands beneath his head, I lift his face to my lips. I kiss his
cheeks, his cloth-stuffed mouth, the swelling around his eyes. Then
I'm sliding down his body's long length. He's like a river in high summer, all white water welling, riverweed waving, hard mossy stones. My
mouth roams over him, tugging on his body hair with my teeth, tongue
searching amid the soft foliage of his breast till one nipple's found, then
another. I suck, lap, chew. His arms are around me. I force his hands
back over his head. I suck, lap, chew. He's groaning once more; once
more my hand falls over his mouth. My other palm's a celebration,
grasping his cock, peeling back his foreskin. Silenced, he bucks, fucking my fist, nodding beneath my hand. His breast-hair tickles my nose,
then his belly-fur, then his crotch-bush, as I slip lower, wrapping my
arms around his waist, resting my head on his prominent hipbone.

"Cover your mouth with your hands, boy. I'm going to finish you, and
no one must hear. Promise me you'll be quiet."

"Uhh," Drew grunts, cupping his palms over his lips as ordered.

With that, I take the head of his penis between my lips. It's salty, a
mite soapy from his earlier bathing, already aromatic with the animal flavors of sex-musk and private sweat. Drew bucks into me; his
cockhead fills my mouth. I take him in, inch by inch, tongue flickering

over the head, up and down the shaft. He thrusts; I choke, take a deep breath as if I were about to swim underwater, and gulp in his entirety. I bob on him, choke, surface, seize air, go under again. One hand clutching his sac, I pull, massaging the orbs inside the loose folds of flesh, then pull a little harder. Here's the rhythm, here's the taste of him I've longed for, better than any feast of meat, stew, sweet, or biscuit, honey on cornbread, maple syrup on buckwheat cake, moonshine or wine. I stop sucking him just long enough to lap my own forefinger wet, then resume. Saliva spills from my mouth, tickling my chin.

"On your side." We shift yet again, my cheek on his thigh, his flesh humping my mouth, my lips sliding tightly up and down him, my hands kneading his ass. My moistened finger finds his crevice now, and, within that overgrown grove, the tight spot there my tongue has known before. My fingertip circles and tickles that sweet gate, then nudges, then rubs. For a second he forgets himself, a low growl seeping beneath cloth and his own obedient grip. Then he's silent, hammering my throat harder as the tip of my forefinger slips inside him. His thighs stiffen, his hands grip the back of my head, he heaves against my face, and my mouth floods with the milk of him, surge after surge I gulp down. He tastes like sarvis berries, marigold petals, prayer. If prayers were solids, not sounds, this is what God would taste, what God would learn to crave.

My boy's patting my face, rubbing my shoulders. I ungag him, rearrange the blankets about us, lie back on the oilcloth, and pull him to me.

"My God, Ian, my *God*. I've never felt anything so sweet in all my years." He curls beside me, head on my shoulder, his pants subsiding.

I chuckle. "That's just what I was wanting to hear. We've both been waiting for that for a long time."

"I never knew that men could...love like that. Never knew it could be so damn good."

"My guess is that men have been loving men that way from the beginning of time. At least that's what I gather from some books I've read." I stroke the fur about his navel. "Now you know what you've been missing, buddy. I'll be giving you more of that as long as I can."

Drew shakes his head and whistles low. "*Hell*, yes! It does help. It is a healing balm indeed. Even better than your salve. Those nasty preachers back home, I think they rage against sodomy just 'cause they want it and are too ugly to have it."

I'm in the midst of another chuckle when a tentative hand cups the lump in my pants.

"Ian? May I? I'm sure beholden. I think I'm ready to try…ready to taste you. I'd very much like—"

"No need for that tonight. Tonight I've had bliss enough. Next time, perhaps. We need our rest now."

"Ian, next time? Aren't our nights together running out?"

"No words, Achilles. Except these: you make it to Purgatory, and, I swear, we'll share the same and more. Your days of suffering are approaching an end. When we get to Purgatory, somehow, I don't know how yet, I'm leaving Sarge and this company behind. And you can be damn sure I'm taking you with me."

—

CHAPTER FORTY-ONE

They're gone when I leave the tent for reveille: Drew's boots, the pants and drawers I'd left outside. I cuss, range around the tent, and find nothing. I have no doubt who took them, but there's no time to track George down or demand them back. After morning muster, the men begin packing up the last few tents and cook pots. Rufus is passing out cold hoecake, pouring the last of the coffee, and dousing the little fire left with water. When he pours my cup, he says, "We're heading off in half an hour. And here." Rummaging in a basket, he looks furtively around, then hands me a little package wrapped in handkerchief and string.

"Two pieces of hoecake. One for you; one for your poor Yankee. And listen here! Inside's a nice little slice of bacon I been saving for you all too. Sarge told me to give you that nasty hardtack to feed him, but, hell, Ian, it's wormy. The boy was tormented real bad yesterday, by George and the New Market twins in particular. I feel sorry for him. I hope he makes it."

I pocket the food fast. "I'm beholden, Rufus. Don't suppose I should hug you now?"

Rufus grins. "Naw. Save that for some big-tittied pretty back home. Anything to peeve George. Sarge, he's a great man, and he's brung us a long way, but George has been rattlesnake-mean to me since I joined up. He ain't fit to tote guts to a bear. If helping that big Yank drag his poor tore-up ass to Purgatory sours George, well, then, I'm happy to contribute."

Drew's sitting on the cot, the quilt shawling his shoulders, when I dip back beneath the tent flap. "Here, here," I say. "Rufus gave us some treats. Eat up. We're about to leave."

My Yank licks his lips. He fumbles with the kerchief, opens it, and stuffs his mouth with crumbly hoecake. "Dear God, bacon!" He chews off half of it faster than I've ever seen him eat anything.

"One of these days, my Northern friend, you and I are going to sit down to a groaning board together. Maybe sooner than you think." I love watching him eat. That's it again, what charms me so: the little boy inside the thick-muscled man.

"But, uh, Ian?" He holds up what's left of the bacon and the second hoecake.

"Aw, no, I had mine by the fire." At this point, I'll lie to anyone, even him, to keep him alive.

"Yeah? Well, hell, you've fetched me a feast then!" Grinning, he falls to. The few crumbs that fall from his hands he fishes from the grass with a tongue-moistened fingertip.

"How you moving today? Think you can make the trip?"

Drew rubs his elbows, then his knees. He licks a greasy remnant of bacon off his palm. "I'm mighty sore. Joints like an old man. But even an old man will keep moving if it means he'll stay alive."

"Good boy. But here's a complication. I got something not so nice as bacon to report," I say, handing him my cup of coffee to finish. "Your boots and clothes are gone. Stolen last night. My fault. I left 'em outside after I washed 'em. Never thought that anybody'd take 'em."

Drew's face falls. "Oh, Jesus. Oh, damn. What? I got to walk to Purgatory barefoot and naked?"

"Well, the naked part would please me, just 'cause you're so damned pretty," I say, mustering a half-smile. "But the barefoot part, that would give George and my uncle and the many rat-faced and small-souled boys in this company too much delight. Sarge gave me leave to find you another pair of trousers, but not till we get to Lexington. Meanwhile, let me see here..." Flipping open my haversack, I start rummaging for scissors and spare bits of cloth.

—

CHAPTER FORTY-TWO

If Drew's torment reminded me of Christ's before, it does even more so today. During his week of captivity, his beard has filled out and his hair has grown shaggier. He's like a German-blond version of Jesus. This morning he's white, bruise-violet, and gold, a cuffed, rag-gagged, black-eyed savior wrist-tethered to my cart, trudging beside me along the road to Purgatory. He's naked, save for slave-collar, layered bandages—those with which I've plastered his lash-maimed back, those which I've knotted into a makeshift loincloth about his hips—and a spare undershirt I've torn into pieces and bound about his feet. All that are missing are the crown of thorns and the Cross. Or rather, those take another form, the racked and bruised body he carries stiffly down the road.

The day's travel is all downhill or on relatively level terrain, the only blessing I can discern. Leaving the western hills, we descend into the Valley, following switchbacks through gray groves of trees, then head south along back roads skirting the hills, wary of Yankee troops or ranging Federal scouts. Here and there, like dark scars on the rolling valley floor, are the reminders of last fall's raids: burnt farmhouses and barns, scorched fields and pastures, ruined orchards charred blacker than Drew's bruises. Occasionally, as we pass a new ruin, George or the New Market twins gallop up long enough to curse Drew and slash him with their crops. Drew grits his teeth around the rag, hangs his head, and makes no protest. Fresh blood streaks his shoulders and back. I shout them off, but, as much as I despise their cruelty, it's hard to blame them. I've heard their stories around the campfire: their farmhouses torched, their stores stolen, their livestock shot, their kin left homeless.

The sky grays over; a cold breeze picks up; in late morning a small rain falls and doesn't cease. My uniform jacket grows heavy, cold, and sodden. My Yankee stumbles often, on rocks or sticks, as our company makes its way down the uneven road. Occasionally he falls. When we cross a thigh-deep stream, he slips on slick stones and goes under. The men behind us jeer and applaud. I rein in the cart-mares, vault off the buckboard, and haul him up. He sputters, gasps for breath, and rights himself with difficulty. The creek's gray rills off his bandaged back and drips from his beard, droplets winking in dim rain-light.

Up the Valley of Virginia we make our way, south toward Lexington, as rapid a march as we can manage. The company pauses at noon, in a leeward dell thick with pines and sheltered from today's chilly gusts. Drew slumps to the ground by a cartwheel, leans against it, hugs himself, and closes his eyes. I let him nap in the slow rain, waking him just before we leave to pull the rag from his mouth and press a few fragments of hardtack into his hands. "Don't look, just eat," I whisper. Hardtack, Sarge has always been fond of saying, is best consumed in the dark, where infesting insects can't be seen. Drew nods, stares over my shoulder, and chews. I adjust his makeshift footwear, already half-tattered and pink with blood, daub new wounds the crops inflicted, replace the rag between his teeth, and we're back on the road.

The rain falls fast and steady into late afternoon. We're only a few hours from Lexington, say the scouts, when, in a vale between two low hills, where a rill's made thick mud of the road, the cart jolts, tilts, and comes to an abrupt stop. Its right rear wheel is stuck. I urge the mares, but they're as weak with short rations as we are. The cart rocks a bit, then stubbornly returns to its hindering ditch. Rufus appears, puts his shoulder to it, and has no success. Jeremiah joins him. The duo shouts and grunts; I lash the mares. The cart lurches forward a few inches, then sinks deeper into mud. My messmates try and try; two more men lend their efforts; two more men grab the mares' bridles and pull. The mares strain and steam in the rain. The cart sinks deeper.

"Uhh." It's Drew, gripping my elbow. He tugs at the rope tethering his wrists to the buckboard. He arches his eyebrows; he cocks and flexes his great arms.

I stare at him for a few seconds, growing hard beneath my wet trousers—I can't help it, for, in all this cold gray of landscape and sky, he's a hairy golden colossus, a veritable sun god. Then, nodding, I unknot his tether from the cart frame. "Rufus, get up here and lead," I say. Rufus obeys. Hopping down, with the tether I guide Drew to the back of the cart. Jeremiah and the other men step back; Sarge and George ride up, frowning, no doubt curious as to the cause for delay.

A little crowd is gathering around us, curious to see what my Yankee can do. Drew stands there for a full minute, rain rolling down his back, gauging the situation. He gives the buckboard a few exploratory nudges. Then he turns, looks up at Sarge, and lifts his cuffed and tethered hands.

Sarge tugs on his moustache, then nods. "Yes," says Sarge. "Free one hand, Ian. George, watch him."

I fetch the key from my haversack; George unsheathes his pistol and points it at Drew's head. I remove the rope-tether and unlock one wrist. Drew rubs it briefly, then digs in his heels, gripping the buckboard with both hands. When he's got sufficient purchase, Drew nods.

"Go," Sarge shouts. "Gitty-up!" Rufus yells. Snap of the reins. We all watch as Drew's broad, bandaged back strains, muscles popping up beneath the hate-torn skin as he bends into the task. His white teeth gnash the gag; he gives a long groan; his face contorts. He gives another shove, then another. The wheels creak; the frame shakes; the cart inches forward. Drew props his crop-bloodied shoulder against the frame, growls, pushes, pants, gives a great heave...and the supply-heavy cart bumps forward and rolls out of the rut, so abruptly that Drew falls on his face into the mud.

A few men cheer; a few clap. The crowd disperses in the thickening downpour.

"Well, I'll be damned," George mutters, lowering his pistol.

"Good for something then," says Sarge.

I help Drew to his knees, then his feet. He's smeared with brown-gray from brow to bloody-bandaged feet. He wipes mud from his nose and beard, wrings out his rain-sodden hair, then looks up, first at Sarge, then at George. He smiles around his gag, an expression full of pride and menace. George lifts the pistol again, as if Drew had just voiced a threat. Drew snorts. He turns toward me, stretches his frame, muddy muscles bulging, then smiles at me. This smile is just as proud, but full too of fondness mixed with triumphant glee.

"Impressive strength, yes," says Sarge, begrudging admiration in his voice. "And more proof he needs to be kept bound. Cuff him."

I've just secured Drew's free hand in the rusty bracelets when there's a commotion in the front of the line. "Sir!" a man yells. We all turn to see her, the first woman we've encountered in days, since we marched exhaustedly through the streets of Staunton. She's about forty, I'd guess, short and bedraggled, dirty dress clinging to her thin frame, gray fabric spotted with faded blue flowers. Her gray-streaked hair's pulled behind her head in a messy bun. She's running toward us, clutching a small

cloth bag. She slips in the mud, almost falls, rights herself, then drops
to her knees in front of Sarge's horse.

"Sir," she says. "I heard your shouting from over the hill. Have you any
food to spare?"

Sarge's brow furrows. "Madam, very little. We're on our way to
Lexington, and—"

"I'm Mrs. Trent. Sir, look!" Opening the bag, she dumps the contents
into the mud. "My children and I have been living in the woodshed
since the Yankees burnt our house and gardens last autumn. We're
nigh unto starvation, but we're proud nevertheless. I'm not asking for
charity; I'm willing to trade. My children and I have been scouring the
country for these. Can't you use them? Aren't they worth at least a bit
of bacon or a cabbage or two? I'm the widow of a Confederate soldier,
sir. He died at Gettysburg. I—"

The woman emits a choked sob and falls silent. Rising to her feet, she
places a hand on Sarge's boot, staring up at him.

"Ian," says Sarge, clearing his throat. "Please count them."

I kneel. I pick through the Minié balls, returning them to the poke
one by one. "Fifty, sir."

Sarge sighs. "Mrs. Trent, we owe you greatly for this ammunition.
With any luck, each one will find its billet in the heart of a Yankee,
among them hopefully the men who burnt your farm. Rufus, fetch Mrs.
Trent some cornmeal, some side meat, some field peas, and what beef
we have left. Mrs. Trent, better luck to you. I wish we could spare you
more. Our country owes women like you a debt too great ever to pay
in full."

"Bless you, sir!" Mrs. Trent pushes strands of hair out of her face.
Sarge and George ride off; Rufus begins rummaging through boxes on
the back of the buckboard. Mrs. Trent studies Rufus' every movement,
eyes gleaming, chest rising and falling rapidly. It isn't until Rufus has
the bag filled that Mrs. Trent notices the near-naked giant standing
cuffed and gagged by the cart.

"A prisoner? He's a Yankee?" Mrs. Trent stiffens, staring up at him.
Before I can respond, Drew nods.

The little woman is just tall enough to slap Drew across the face if
she reaches high and rears up on tiptoe. And so she does, fast and hard,
before I can stop her. Then she grabs the poke, murmurs, "Bless you"
to Rufus, swivels, and heads off down the road. Drew bows his head,
refusing to look at me. The order to move passes down the line. I rope

Drew's wrists to the cart frame again, stuff the little poke of bullets in my haversack, and we're on our way to Lexington.

—

CHAPTER FORTY-THREE

—

It's still raining, just coming on dark when the tents are finally pitched in a sheltering grove of pines edging a field near Lexington. The rain's washed off some of the road-mud that matted Drew, but he's racked with shivers, leaning feebly against the cart as Rufus and I unload the last of the supplies. After untethering my Yank, I foot-shackle him, help him relieve himself in the woods, then help him crawl into the tent, where he slumps facedown on an oilcloth and passes out. I tuck a blanket about him, wipe mud from his hair, and for a few minutes watch him sleep. Leaving him there to recover from the march, I'm about to help Rufus gather firewood when Sarge rides up, clad in greatcoat, cap cocked against the continuous drizzle.

"Ian, I'm heading into town to visit some old friends and to see the damage that Hunter and his men inflicted last fall on the Virginia Military Institute. I also want to pay my respects at Jackson's grave and fetch more provisions. I'll be back tomorrow morning. Where's the prisoner? I assume he's appropriately restrained. His display of strength today just convinces me that he'd be a great cause of damage to us given a chance."

"In my tent, sir. He's collapsed. I have him shackled, cuffed, and gagged as is usual. You did say I could shelter him till we got—"

"To Purgatory, yes, yes. But what happened to his clothes? Hasn't he been near naked since we broke camp? It was unseemly for Mrs. Trent to see him in such a state of undress."

"His boots and clothes have been stolen, sir. I'd rinsed them and left them outside to air out last night, but this morning...no sign of them."

Sarge laughs, a full-throated sound. "Ah, some of the boys are having their fun. Can you blame them when blackened evidence of Yankee depredations are all around us? Well, we should be safe here for a day or so. The scouts tell me that few Federals are in the area. Most of them, I suspect, are helping that devil Grant lay siege to Petersburg. Since it's Saturday, I've given all of the boys save those on picket duty leave to head into Lexington and spend the night if they'd like, perhaps to join me in church tomorrow morning. God knows we all could benefit from a little break from camp life. If you want to join us, just cuff the prisoner's arms behind a tree and leave him. Rufus has offered to watch the camp."

It takes some effort to conceal my relief and delight at Sarge's imminent absence. "Thanks, sir, but I'm really tired. I think I'll stay here and write some letters to post before we leave for Purgatory. I might read a little too."

"The Bible, I hope. Other books are of no consequence." With that, Sarge nods, wheels his horse, and heads off into nightfall, toward the distant lights of town.

Rufus and I have a little pile of wood collected by the time the rest of the boys, including George and the vindictive New Market twins, ride or stride out of camp. Jeremiah lingers long enough to help Rufus and me start up a fire before he announces his disinterest in campfire cuisine and his intention to spend the night in town. He cocks his foraging cap over his brow, studies his face in the tiny mirror we pass around when or if we shave, smoothes his beard, and winks at himself. "Either of you boys got any wages left?" he asks.

"No," says Rufus, dejected. "I lost it all to the New Market twins and their cursed cards."

"I do, Jeremiah. A little left. Why?"

"I'll tell you later. Right now, I got me a lady to see. If you're lucky, you'll get to meet her tomorrow." Then he's off, across the field and over the crest of the hill.

Rufus can't read, his harmonica playing is far from tuneful, and he's not much of a talker—can't tell a story worth a damn—but the man sure can cook. With the paltry supplies we've got, he's soon got an aromatic pot of beans going and some cornbread too. We sit together in camp chairs by the fire, the occasional breeze shaking raindrops from the dense pine boughs above us. I pull out my flask to share. It's very quiet, save for the sizzle and spark-spit of the fire.

"Just the three of us in camp tonight, Ian," Rufus says, rubbing his rusty chin-whiskers and sipping. "I'll take the pickets some food here in a little bit. Thanks for staying with me. You can bring your poor Yank out if you'd like. Sarge won't be back till morning, nor the others neither, I reckon. I won't tell if you want to make him comfortable."

"I think he needs his rest, Rufus. What with all the beatings and little food, well, I'll rouse him later."

Rufus nods, then his face lights up. "Forgot!" He rises, bounds over to his tent, rummages, then returns. He's holding a little tin in one hand and what looks like pale green goose quills in the other. "This," he says, lifting the tin, "is bacon grease I been hoarding, and this," he says, waving the quills, "is wild onions I spied near the road right after that poor woman waylaid us. Both'll make this mess of beans tastier than usual. Good to keep off the scurvy too, I hear tell."

He stirs both ingredients in, then hunkers down to turn hoecakes frying in the skillet. I take a flask-swig, welcome warmth on this cool, wet evening, then realize I have my own hoarded luxuries to offer. "You like sorghum?" I ask.

Rufus grins. He straightens up and wiggles in an awkward approximation of a jig. "Oh, Lord. You got some? I ain't had much in the way of sweetening since winter quarters."

"Would you rather have honey?"

Rufus' eyes widen. "Can I have a little bit of both?"

"As long as you don't tell the others. Sarge can be mighty strict, as you well know, but he is generous to kin. And I don't want to share my little cache of secret sweets with men who are so unkind to the prisoner."

Rufus nods. "Oh, no, I won't say a word! And they have been mighty unkind. It ain't Christian."

I leave him near to salivating by the fire, crawl into my tent, and feel around for my haversack. That's when Drew, a big black bundle, rolls over and mumbles my name.

I feel for him, find a knee, then an elbow, then the softness of his beard. "You awake, huh, big man?"

Drew gives a rag-muted grunt. His cuffed hands find mine in the dark and squeeze.

"You hungry? We got a little feast on the fire."

"Ummmmmm," growls Drew, squeezing my hands harder.

"Come on out, boy. It's safe for a change. Sarge and George and most of the others have gone into town. There's pickets, so I can't get you out of here right yet, but I can feed you pretty well."

Drew's stiff from his past torments and the long day's march, so I have to help him as he crawls from the tent, painfully rights himself, and staggers the short way to the fire. Twice he trips; twice I catch him before he falls. I've never seen him weaker. Rufus rises, staring up at him with mingled awe and pity, then offers him his chair. Drew proffers one cuffed hand; Rufus hesitates, then shakes it. I help Drew ease himself into the chair. His legs shake like an invalid's. He leans back, takes a deep breath around his bandana gag, and closes his blow-blackened eyes.

"Beans'll be ready directly," says Rufus, fetching another chair, then bending to stir the pot.

I look around. No one but us, true. Nothing visible but trunks of pines, pine needle beds, dripping branches, empty tents, and, far off, across the field and down the hill, the lights of Lexington. For the moment, any source of cruelty has moved off. And so I pat Drew's shoulder, loosen the bandana's knot, and pull the gag from his mouth. "Thanks," he grunts, looking up at me with a weak smile, the first time he's really met my eyes since Mrs. Trent struck him. I offer him the flask. He takes a sip, then slumps deeper in the chair, sighing with gratitude in the face of this sudden and unexpected reprieve from discomfort.

I warm my hands over the flames, then sit beside Drew. He stares blankly at the gray smoke drifting off the campfire and trailing down the moist breeze. Today's triumphant display of strength seems to have sorely overtaxed him. I think only the thought of imminent nourishment is giving him the strength to keep his eyes open. "I'm Drew Conrad. You're Rufus, right?" Drew mumbles.

My messmate flinches. He seems startled to be directly addressed. "Uh, yes, sir! Rufus Ballard." It occurs to me only now that no one in the camp save I has heard much of Drew's voice—other than his cloth-muffled moans and screams beneath the whip or his bucked-and-gagged sobs—since the day he was first brought to camp. "I—I'm glad to make your, your acquaintance," Rufus stammers.

Drew smiles, wry and crooked, at Rufus' phrasing. It's as if they were meeting in an elegant parlor or a church social. "Well, I owe you, Rufus. I know you have cause to hate my guts, and I admit my fellow soldiers and I have given your people nothing but hurt, but I do thank you for providing me with a special breakfast this morning. That bacon was a real delight, and it helped me endure the march. And this fire you've made feels mighty nice after trudging in mud and rain all day."

"I try not to hate anyone, sir. It's my Christian duty to love anyone, even a damn Yankee. Uh, begging your pardon!" Flushed, Rufus fumbles about, fetching tin cups, ladling beans, flipping hoecakes. Soon he has a wooden plank heaped with the little corn cakes, each of which he's smeared with a light layer of bacon grease.

"Now where's that sweetening you promised me?" Rufus gives a little hop of anticipation.

"Ah, right. Forgot," I say. A quick return to my tent to fetch the haversack, and I'm pouring black dribbles of sorghum and amber dribbles of honey on the cakes. "You want uncuffed while you eat?" I say, offering Drew a cup of beans. I raise an eyebrow at Rufus. He's wide-eyed, clearly startled at the thought of an enemy so huge suddenly unbound.

"Naw." Drew exhales, then chuckles. "No point. Don't want to scare off Mr. Rufus here. And you'd get in trouble if the pickets showed up, or anybody returned from town. Plus, it's not like I have the strength at this point, were I uncuffed, to overpower you men and get back north in these." He lifts one bandaged foot off the ground and jingles his shackle-chain. "I'd just as soon you feed me, Reb, as I've grown accustomed to it. And I fear that I might make a mess in my present state of feebleness." He lifts his hands in their rusty bracelets. The shaking is visible even in the irregular flicker of firelight.

"All right." I pull my chair closer to Drew's and commence feeding him. Rufus looks on for a few fascinated seconds, amazed at what must be to him an incongruous and absurd sight, then his own hunger bests his curiosity and he falls to, grunting appreciatively over the quality of the sweetening. Drew and I stare into one another's eyes in silence as I lift spoonfuls of beans to his mouth, then bits of hoecake. All is as good as Rufus had predicted: the bean broth is rich with flavors of bacon and onion; the hoecake is golden-brown; the sorghum and honey are sweet reminders of better days back home. But, though my Yank smacks his lips and smiles, taking the food with murmurs of eagerness and thanks, there's despondency in his eyes I've never seen before.

In the absence of competition from our messmates, we each devour second helpings, though our famine-shrunk stomachs won't allow us more. For a while, we pass the flask around till it's empty. Rufus sighs and drowses, scratches vigorously, settles down, and begins to snore. I add more wood to the fire. Drew falls asleep, seized by fatigue obviously bone-deep, and soon his snores mingle with Rufus'. I fetch some poetry from my haversack, a book my cousin in Washington sent me just before the war began, one I've read and reread, *Leaves of Grass* by Walt Whitman. The poems may be by a Yank, but they make me feel less alone.

My favorite section's named after a plant we have back home, growing on my grandparents' farm. It's a pond-dweller, a kind of reed, sprout-

ing a funny little penis like a Jack-in-the-pulpit. We call it sweet flag;
Whitman uses the Latin, *Calamus*. The word makes me think of Drew,
his hairy groin, the taste of his big cock in my mouth last night, the
taste of his thick juice. Tonight, if I can rouse him from his stupor and
his sadness, perhaps I'll taste him again.

"We two boys together clinging, / One the other never leaving." I'm
entirely enrapt by the words—how perfectly they reflect passions I once
feared no one but I ever felt—when a hand taps my shoulder. "Night."
It's Rufus, standing by my chair. "I'm taking food out to the boys on
picket duty and then hitting the hay."

I nod. Rufus dips up beans, wraps hoecakes in handkerchiefs, and
departs. I read further. When thickening raindrops begin to pimple the
pages, I close the book. For a few minutes, I lie back in the chair, watch
the fire as it hisses and steams under the onslaught of heavier rain, and
study my Yank as he sleeps.

"Up, Drew," I say, shaking his shoulder. "Let's get you in the tent. The
rain's getting harder."

Drew jolts. I've helped him half out of the chair, cupping his elbows,
when his legs buckle and he falls to his knees in the pine needles.

"Sorry," he says.

"Let me help," I say.

"In just a minute," he says, leaning against me, face buried in my uniform jacket. For long seconds he gathers his strength. At last he tries
to rise; again he fails.

I lay my hands on his shoulders, pity clogging my throat.

"I can't, Ian. It's all catching up to me. Freeing that cart was the last of
my old strength."

I look around the circle of firelight, the night blessedly free of hostile
faces. I kiss the top of his head. "I know, buddy. Can you crawl?"

Drew nods. He squeezes my thigh with one hand, then falls onto
hands and knees. I follow him as he creeps beneath dripping pine
boughs, first to the latrine-trench, then to our little tent.

—

CHAPTER FORTY-FOUR

—

"For the one I love most lay sleeping by me under the same cover in the cool night, / In the stillness in the autumn moonbeams his face was inclined toward me, / And his arm lay lightly around my breast— and that night I was happy."

"That's amazing," whispers Drew, his head in my lap. I sit cross-legged, leaning against the cot, reading him poem after poem from *Leaves of Grass*. I've washed and salved Drew's hurts—thank God none of them are festering yet—though his bandages are too soiled to reapply and I'm finally out of the torn rags I've been using to wrap his wounds. At his request, for the first time since we've shared this tent, I've stripped off not only my muddy brogans and uniform jacket, but also my trousers and underclothing. We're both completely naked, draped in smelly blankets, in the light of the candle. Since no one's in camp tonight save Rufus, it's a chance I'm willing to take. Leering George and snooping Sarge are in town doing who knows what? George is probably deep in his cups and gambling. Sarge is probably growing even bitterer as he tours the torched remains of his old school, the Virginia Military Institute. I have very vague memories of those grand buildings from a visit in my early childhood. They looked like crenellated castles. Word is the Yankees have left little but ashes.

"Do you think this poet is like us? That he's felt for other men the way we've come to feel about one another?" Drew asks. Taking my hand, he lifts it to his lips.

"It certainly seems so. Before I read his poems, I wondered if Thom and I were the only men in the world who felt such things. I thought that warriors in *The Iliad* might have shared such passions, but modern men did no longer. Sometimes, when I recalled what Thom and I had done together, and how he fled in shame, I thought perhaps the preachers' words were true, that I was harboring an unnatural vice, that I was indecent and immoral. But when I got that book in the mail— from a kinsman in Washington who was always trying to encourage my education with the same zeal that Sarge has always encouraged my soldierliness—then I knew that there were others like me. A 'brother-hood of lovers,' Whitman says."

"Speaking of love, sir," Drew says, smiling up at me. "I'd sure like to pleasure you tonight the way last night you pleasured me, but I don't think I have the strength yet." His hands brush my chest hair, grazing a nipple. "I feel like a wood-whittler's twig, Ian. Every day peels off a bit of me, and soon I won't have nothing left. Will we march tomorrow? I don't think I can make it."

"I don't think so. Sarge made no reference to leaving tomorrow, and, what with a hard-drinking Saturday night in town, many of the men will be too worn out with their entertainments to march anyway. With any luck, tomorrow will be a day of rest for you. Unless Sarge orders you bucked."

"Lord, no. I don't think I can take that again. You saw how shaky my limbs are. Though tonight's meal surely helped."

"You need more sleep, boy," I say, smoothing his shaggy, mud-mat-ted hair. "Enough poetry." I blow out the candle, then pull the blankets over us and pull him to me in our now customary spoon, his back to my chest.

"Damnation." Drew scratches his side, then his crotch.

"Lice or fleas?"

"Fleas, I think. Giving me some of that Southern hospitality."

I scratch my armpit, then my breast. "You've gotten me started."

Drew laughs. He snuggles back against me. We lie there listening to the patter of rain for a bit. Then Drew says, in a small voice, "Ian?"

"Yes, big man?"

"Could you ever hate me?"

"What sort of question is that? I've already told you that I love you."

"Well, in this war I've done things I ain't proud of. Things I ain't told you."

"I could say the same. I've spared you many a detail of how my deer-hunting skills have brought down a slew of your cohorts."

"But this...some of this is different." Drew takes my hand, pressing it to his chest. Beneath my palm I can feel his chest hair, the muscle beneath that, the heartbeat beneath that.

"Drew, don't fret. Get some sleep. We can talk tomorrow."

"All right," Drew whispers. "I'm sorry I ain't up for loving. I just feel so feeble..."

I hold Drew close while he falls asleep, lines of Whitman's washing through my mind. "You give me the pleasure of your eyes, face, flesh, as we pass, you take of my beard, breast, hands, in return…I am to see to it that I do not lose you." I fondle Drew's thickening whiskers, his navel, his soft cock. Then my own weariness seizes me; my thoughts grow mazy; I drift off to the sounds of Drew's soft snores and the patter of rain on canvas.

—

CHAPTER FORTY-FIVE

What I do I do half-asleep, half-aware, operating on sheer instinct. Drew's groans wake me to myself. My right hand's clamped firmly over his mouth; my left hand's working his cock; my own cock's impatiently bumping his bare ass. Drew's thrusting into my hand, then rubbing back against me. His tongue wets my palm.

"Oh, hell," I whisper, ceasing all these randy operations as soon as I'm fully awake. "I'm so sorry. I want you so badly that even in my sleep…"

Drew gives a low laugh. "I ain't complaining, Reb. I feel a little better now anyway. It was a sweet way to be nudged from my slumbers, and I reckon we should use what time together we have, especially with the camp nigh-empty."

"So you're saying…"

"To keep on, please. Touch me some more, Private Campbell."

I obey, kissing the scars on his back, cupping the fuzzy flesh of his chest in my hand, fingering a nipple. I'm stroking the hairy cleft of his ass with a fingertip when Drew sighs, "You want inside me bad, don't you, Reb?"

I sigh in reply. "Mightily."

"One day, maybe. Perhaps that'll be your reward for helping me escape. In fact, it's a deal. You get me my freedom, and…you can…take me any way you please."

"Uhhffff! Boy, I'm hard to bursting. Really?"

"Yep!" Another low laugh. "Is that sufficient motivation?"

"Yes, indeed! But I thought, only days ago, you'd proudly boasted that you were no whore."

"I ain't whorin'! Why, this is a gentleman's agreement."

"A deal then," I say. "Hell, yes! For tonight, though, I know you're weak, so why don't you just roll over on your back and lie still while I taste you as I did last night?"

"A deal indeed." Drew obeys. I start my trail of kisses on his brow, spend a good bit of time kissing his mouth, then his nipples, then his belly hair and hip bones. Now, as slowly as possible, I sheathe his cock in my mouth. He sighs and thrusts; his cuffed hands tug at my beard and hair, then rest upon my head. Within minutes, he's finished on my tongue, I've finished in my hand, and we're spooning again, both sound asleep.

—

CHAPTER FORTY-SIX

Sunday morning. I wake before him. I sit beside him and watch him slumber, my boy, my lover, my captive. I touch his scars ever so lightly. I pore over him as if he were a beloved book, my private Bible: his tangled hair, his mussed beard, the long golden lashes of his swollen eyes. He's as fine as any sonnet I've put to memory. "For thy sweet love remembered such wealth brings, / That then I scorn to change my state with kings," I whisper to myself before dressing and leaving the tent.

Rufus's hunkered over a skillet frying bacon. Dependable as ever, he already has coffee brewed. I join him by the fire and pour a cup. It's good, thanks to Sarge's recent success at foraging—not that acorn swill we've had lately.

"The last of the bacon," Rufus announces sadly, flipping the meat. "Got one piece per man. Plus I'm soaking some hardtack to fry in this grease. Should make it tastier. And softer. I'm always 'fraid I'll break a tooth on the stuff. Don't know how the Yanks stand it. Let's pray that Sarge finds us more victuals in town."

It's a gray morning, but at least the rain has stopped. Bacon done, Rufus is frying the hardtack and, at my request, simmering rose-hip tea when we hear hoof beats. It's George, riding over the crest of the hill and across the field. His old gelding, a sickly dun, is about as pleasing to the eye as he is. He comes to a halt at the forest's edge. Waving a bag, he shouts, "Y'all git over here. Sarge sent you this." I glare at him, then, turning my back, pour another cup of coffee. Rufus obediently scurries over. They talk for a bit; I add a stick of wood to the fire. Then George gallops off. Rufus lopes over, toting the bag, face fallen.

"Sarge sends word that he's staying in town for a while yet, to attend church, says the boys should all be back in camp by late afternoon. This here's some cornmeal. He says he'll bring some cabbage and some beef this evening."

"Well, that's good news, right? We've been starving for good beef for weeks. Why're you moping?"

"George brought this too. He told me what it says." Rufus pulls a folded paper from his pocket.

I open it, recognizing Sarge's blocky letters.

> *Dear Nephew, I will return by nightfall. My friends have been, despite their reduced circumstances, most hospitable, so I should return with provisions sufficient to get us to Purgatory. Do not, however, waste food on the prisoner, unless it be that hardtack gone to the weevil. I would prefer that he be bucked and gagged once more, especially now that I have seen the ruins of my old school and have heard firsthand the suffering inflicted on the good citizens of Lexington. But since it is Sunday, you may show him mercy if your conscience so dictates, and knowing your over-soft heart, I rather think that it will. Rather than bucking him again, you may let him spend God's day bound to a tree. I would also suggest that you read him the Bible and perhaps encourage him to pray for forgiveness. He, like all his kind, has much to repent for. And his days on earth are strictly numbered.*
>
> *Your Uncle*
>
> *P.S. Find enclosed a few bills, in case sutlers come to camp and you would like to treat yourself to some small pleasure.*
>
> *P.S. You may use my Bible, if you please. It's in my tent, on my camp desk.*
>
> *P.S. Tomorrow we leave for Purgatory.*

I stuff the money in my pocket, crumple the letter, and toss it into the fire. Hardtack's sizzling in the skillet. "I'm sorry, Ian," Rufus mutters. "I like your poor Yank right well. Don't seem a mite different from us. Let's us give him a good breakfast anyway. I ain't tellin' nobody. And I'll find him those trousers you were asking about. No reason for the man to spend what time he has left looking like a savage."

I nod. If I spoke, I fear my voice might crack. I stand by the fire while Rufus browns the hardtack. I'm praying, as Sarge suggested, though these prayers are silent. I'm thanking God for kindness.

"Smells like bacon," Drew says, blinking up at me sleepily as I enter the tent bearing our breakfast.

—

CHAPTER FORTY-SEVEN

Sitting on a stump beside Drew, I read it from beginning to end. The Book of Job is some comfort, though it disturbs both of us that Job's first family stays dead; his faith only wins him replacements. "Mighty hard to replace you," Drew says, grinning as I lift a cup of water to his lips.

I've made my handsome prisoner as comfortable as Sarge's orders allow me. His hands are still cuffed before him, his ankles still shackled. He's got on his new trousers, a very loose fit I've cinched with a rope, though he's still shirtless, a fact I both savor for the sight of his manly chest and regret due to the chill air he's exposed to. I've seated him at the base of a little pine, on a cushion of moss, and tied him to it by wrapping several lengths of rope around his chest and arms and knotting the bonds not too tightly behind the trunk. I intend to spare him the gag till Sarge returns. I *was* ordered to pray with him, after all.

"Do you believe in heaven?" Drew says. "Other than that provided by Rufus earlier. That bacon was so good, and even the hardtack and that sour tea were welcome. I mean the afterlife the Bible promises?"

"I guess I do...though lately I think it has less to do with angels than with the taste of honey and hoecake and gold-haired Yankee nether regions."

Drew winks at me. "Well, yes. But seriously, Ian. If I end up shot through the head, and if you end up blown to bits by artillery or taking a Minié ball outside of Petersburg, do you think we'll ever meet again?"

"Maybe. Maybe we'll end up making love for all eternity. Or eating pies for all eternity. After the suffering we've seen, God owes us as much. My Aunt Alicia's Cherokee, and she thinks after we die, we blend with mountains and forests and rain. That sounds pretty fine too." I wink at Drew. "Maybe you'll end up an oak, and I'll be the summer thunderstorm that moistens your roots."

Drew chuckles. "You Southern boys are a hot-blooded bunch. My root surely was moistened last night, and with praiseworthy skill. I—"

A sound interrupts Drew, a sound I haven't heard since we left Staunton. Somewhere nearby a woman's laughing. It's a high, shimmery sound, like chimes.

I turn. There, cresting the hill now, now flowing through the field toward us, is a woman, from the looks of her in her mid-twenties, with Jeremiah by her side. Her hair is black, heaped atop her head and framing her face in sausage curls. She's holding his hand and laughing.

Rufus is out of his tent in a flash. He stands nervously by the fire awaiting our visitor's approach. "Wait here," I say to Drew, rising. "I believe I will," Drew says, flexing his arms against the ropes, then dropping his cuffed hands heavily into his lap. "Ain't going nowhere, Reb. Company's too fine."

"Too clever for your own good, you Yanks," I mutter. By the time I reach the fire, Rufus has offered the mysterious lady a camp chair, which she's apparently declined due to the width of her skirts, and poured her a cup of coffee. Jeremiah looks like his brief absence from camp has refreshed him considerably. I've never seen the boy with a wider smile. I do believe that he and our guest might have celebrated Saturday night in a manner at least somewhat similar to how Drew and I marked it.

"This here," announces Jeremiah, "is Miss Pearl. She's been showing me around her fair town. She's a true admirer of soldiers, a solid patriot. In fact, she's here to help us keep our strength up."

Miss Pearl gives another bell-like laugh. Her lips and eyes are lightly painted. Her buxom upper half is fitted into a tight velvet jacket of deep purple. Below, her hoop skirt fans out in shades of purple and black. Her tiny hands are gloved in white.

"I-I'm Ian Campbell, ma'am. Welcome to our camp. We haven't had the b-blessing of a lady's company in weeks. To what do we owe this pleasure?"

"Well now," Miss Pearl says, after taking a tiny sip of coffee, "Jeremiah—he's an old friend—said you boys might be standing in need of certain comestibles, and, well, the local sutlers are bound to be out here, and they're *terrible* people, charging poor soldiers like you simply outrageous prices, and... Oh! Who's that!?"

She's pointing at Drew, who's watching her with the same fascination she's evoked in us. As much as I love men, especially beautiful men like Drew, I'm as starved for female company as much as any of us after years of camp life and war.

"That's our prisoner. He's a Yank we caught up near Staunton," says Jeremiah. "He ain't a bad man, just deluded by Lincoln like all the rest of them. We ain't had a chance to send him to Richmond and prison, since we been up in the mountains for weeks. Ian here has charge of him."

"Mercy! I ain't—I haven't spoken to a Yank since they came through last fall, damn them...oh, forgive my language! It's just that, I watched the Institute burn, and Governor Letcher's home too. That vile toad Hunter had his men take the torch to building after building...it's just hard not to hate." As Pearl talks, she edges toward Drew. Curiosity seems to be greater than resentment. "Though I know our Lord said to love our enemies... Mercy, he's big!"

"Would you like to meet him?" Jeremiah asks. "He's well-tied. He can't hurt you."

"Well, for heaven's sake, he's half-naked. But...well, yes. Please introduce us." Miss Pearl, eyes wide, finishes her coffee, hands Rufus the cup, and, with a swish of skirts over pine needles, accompanies Jeremiah and me to Drew's side.

For a few seconds, they just stare at one another, the little woman in fine clothes and the bare-chested Yankee tied to a pine. Then Drew clears his throat and says, "Hello, ma'am. I'm Drew Conrad. I apologize for my present appearance. Can't be helped, as you might imagine." He shifts in his bonds, tossing back the muddy hair hanging over his eyes; a few drops of lingering rain fall from the boughs above. "But I'm glad to meet you nonetheless. Ain't seen much of women since I left Pennsylvania. You are very pretty, ma'am."

"Mercy! I was led to believe that all you Yankees were rude-mouthed brutes, especially after Hunter's beastly raid through here. But you're a gentleman, and a handsome one too!"

Drew smiles very briefly, then the smile vanishes. He hangs his head, clears his throat again, and looks up at her, something desperate in his blue eyes. "Ma'am, I would like to apologize to you for any distress my fellow Federals caused. I'm truly sorry. I've gotten to know Ian here pretty well, and he's been mighty kind to me—in fact, all these boys you see here have been kind to me, as the rest of their company has unfortunately not, but I ain't complaining, that's the facts and the nature of war—but ma'am, I know what we Federals have done has sorried you all, and I truly, truly regret any part I've played to bring you or any of these here Rebel boys grief. I do pray that this damn war—sorry, ma'am,

I was never known to swear until recently; army life does coarsen a man—I do pray that this war is over soon, and that, like Job, you are able to recover all you've lost."

Drew's voice is shaking. Just when I think he's about to burst into tears, he drops his gaze to the ground. "Please do forgive me," he whispers, then falls quiet.

All of us stand around Drew, stunned into silence. Then Jeremiah laughs, a nervous sound. "Damn, Yank! You just made up for all those days with a gag in your mouth! That was a pretty speech."

"Pretty, and much appreciated." Pearl pulls out a handkerchief and wipes her eyes. "Honey, honey," she says, "they have you collared like a slave. And your poor eyes are black! And where'd all these scars and welts come from? Your chest and shoulders look like you've been wrestling with a big-clawed bear."

"Our captain is mighty hard on prisoners," Rufus says. "He's 'specially bitter, since he lost his wife and his farm during the Burning."

"And we're out of bandages, ma'am," I say. "I'm sorry you had to see his wounds. At this point in the war, every little thing's a luxury."

"Well, Lord! That's why I'm here!" She pats Drew's shoulder, then arches an eyebrow at Jeremiah. "Shall I?"

"Yes, indeed, Pearlene." Jeremiah smiles and steps back.

"Now you boys just look away for a minute," says Miss Pearl. "You too, Mr. Yankee."

We obey. There's a great rustling of fabric, some thudding, then more rustling. What could she be doing?

"Behold!" says Miss Pearl. We open our eyes. We stand amazed.

There, deposited in the carpet of pine needles before us, is a veritable commissary. Rufus falls to his knees and pats item after item, mumbling with reverence. "Oh, Lord God, a ham. Coffee... And, oh, ma'am, are these fried pies?"

Miss Pearl beams. "They are! Apple! Made just yesterday. And that flask there is full of homemade spirits to warm you boys up on gray days like this. And here's cloth for bandages, and blackberry extract for the flux, and even some isinglass plaster to doctor wounds."

"Oh, Lord, canned meats?!" Rufus gasps. "And beef jerky?"

"Pearlene here has specially made skirts, you see," Jeremiah says. "She's smuggled many a toothsome tidbit across Yankee lines."

Miss Pearl giggles and curtsies, rustling her great ruffled bell of crinolines. "I just want to take care of our beloved Confederacy."

"Ah, yes," I say, suddenly remembering Jeremiah's query about wages yesterday. "But—I risk giving offence by bringing up the subject of money in the presence of a lady—what amount would you require?"

Miss Pearl blushes. Jeremiah says, "How much you got?"

I fetch my haversack, fish my last wages from it, and add to them the bills Sarge sent me. As worthless as our Confederate currency is these days, I fear it won't buy us much.

Jeremiah receives the money, counts it, and hands it to Miss Pearl. She strokes it with her gloved hands, counts it, and sighs.

"Well..." The dubious expression on her face has Rufus on the edge of despair and has me remembering the myth of Tantalus. "I don't think I can—"

"Oh, ma'am! I got no wages left at all, but there's this!" Rufus, still on his knees, fumbles a pocketknife from his trousers.

Pearl takes it from him with a sad smile.

"Here's my contribution," Jeremiah says. "No money either, after last night on the town"—Miss Pearl purses her lips and nods—"but I have this." He digs into his pocket and lifts something gleaming into the light. It's a blue cameo brooch. "Would you accept this, Miss Pearlene? It was my grandmother's. I've been carrying it around the whole war waiting for some lady fair enough to deserve it." Taking her hand, he lays the jewelry gently in her palm.

"Oh, well...is that jet around the edges?"

"Yes, ma'am, I believe so."

Miss Pearl studies it with great care; she strokes it with a finger. Then something in her seems to give way. She and Jeremiah exchange smiling glances. "Oh, honey, this'll do. As long as you spend the day with me. And as long as this boy here fixes me lunch." She pats Rufus's arm. "And as long as you all share some of this with your poor prisoner. He's so well mannered I can't hardly believe it. I'm giving y'all an extra discount just because his apology moved me so."

"Miss, how about I heat us up some ham and fried pies? Would that lunch suit you?" Rufus is staring up at her as if she were the goddess of abundance, which, at this point, I suppose she is. "With more coffee?"

"As long as you slip just the tiniest dram of spirits into that coffee. For all of us. It'll be our Sunday celebration. We'll have us a little toast. I would toast to the victory of our new nation, but I wouldn't want to offend you, Mr. Yank. How about 'To the end of the war'?"

"Yes, ma'am," Drew sighs. "I suspect we can all agree to drink to that."

—

CHAPTER FORTY-EIGHT

—

"I ain't sharing this stash with the others, especially that son of a bitch George." Lunch done, Rufus, mildly drunk and so more profane than usual, is hiding our new Pearl-bought provisions. "Ain't no one gonna know about our Sunday festivity but us."

In twos or threes, the boys trickle into camp all afternoon, sluggish after their Lexington immoderation. Most take to their tents; the more vigorous head into the forest to hunt squirrels. Rufus, secure in the knowledge that our prizes are well hidden, snoozes by the fire. Jeremiah and Miss Pearl take a rustic promenade about the field and forest, billing and cooing like doves, before Jeremiah escorts his lady back into town. Drew and I talk and nap; I read to him, alternating Shakespeare sonnets with the Song of Songs, letting poets of the past declare my love for me. When no one's looking, I stroke the matted hair out of his eyes and hold his cuffed hands. The metal has kept his wrists chafed raw, so I salve them.

"Sure wish Miss Pearl had her some brogans beneath her skirts to go with all that food." I'm applying the newly purchased cloth to Drew's feet. "I'll bandage up the rest of you tonight once I've freed you from this tree. Getting that isinglass plaster is mighty timely, since I'm running low on my salve."

"Ham and pie, damn. Finest meal I've had since you captured me," Drew sighs. "That Miss Pearl was an angel. She smelled like jasmine. She was a real lady."

"I think she fancied you, boy," I say. "She has good taste." I look him over: his blackened eyes, his straggly hair and beard, his bruises, welts, and scars, his prominent ribs and blond torso-pelt, the still-bulky muscles of his chest, shoulders, and arms. "Raggedy-ass prisoner that you are, you're still the handsomest man I've ever seen. You look as sweet as those pies tasted. Hell, I'd rather taste you than pie any day or night."

"Flattery, flattery. I told you you ain't getting up my ass till you get me out of here." Drew grins, wiggling his butt against the moss.

"Agreed, Achilles. You're a damn tease. But let me ask you...why did you say all you did to her? All that about forgiveness? You've never been in Lexington, have you? God, certainly you weren't with Hunter?"

"No, Ian, but there's things I still haven't said. Could we wait till tonight? When you hold me again?"

"Sure, boy. Let's just enjoy our time without Sarge and George and the others."

I've just started another section of the Song of Songs—"His arm a golden scepter with gems of topaz, / his loins the ivory of thrones / inlaid with sapphire, / his thighs like marble pillars / on pedestals of gold"—and am splitting a piece of beef jerky with Drew when the day goes all to hell. George rides up, dismounts, spits a gob of tobacco into the fire, then, red-faced, strides over.

"I seen what's left of the Institute," he snarls. "It's nothing but goddamn ash. Sarge is all tore up about it. Your kind did it, Yank. I'm gonna take the whip to you when Sarge gets back."

Drew glowers up at him. I rise, taking my customary position between Drew and any danger. "The Yank apologized just this morning to a Lexington lady who was here."

"Lady!" George snorts. "Soiled dove, you mean. A venal Cyprian. I seen her and Jeremiah in town. I seen her face paint and her preening. She ain't no lady, she's a whore."

"You shut your mouth, you black-hearted bastard," Drew says low. "If I weren't tied, I'd break your back over one knee. She *was* a lady. Don't you dare dirty her name."

"*You* shut *your* mouth, Yank. I'm gonna make you bleed soon enough. Ian, why ain't this man gagged? Why is he even allowed to speak? Sarge told me that he ordered you—"

"Sarge also told me to observe Sunday with prayer and Bible reading, which," I say, pointing to the book in Drew's lap, "is what we were doing. Seems to me you've always been more cruel than Christian."

"I'll have you know I'm a lay minister back home. And what do you know about Christ? Consorting with damn Yankees and strumpets."

"Don't you call her that!" Our shouting has roused Rufus, who strides over, dander up, face as ruddy as his chin-whiskers.

"Oh, get away, little man." George gives a dismissive wave. "Go sort some beans or stir some gruel."

"You can suck my ass," Rufus says and swings. His fist catches George in the shoulder. George staggers back against a pine trunk, then turns to run. Rufus tackles him. They roll around on the ground, Rufus punching, George screening his face with his forearms and screaming.

"Goddamn you! Get off me! I'll have Sarge hang you by the thumbs!"

The New Market twins show up now, George's mealy-mouthed minions. One grabs Rufus by the shoulders, trying to haul him off George. I catch the first twin in the chin, sending him flying. The second lunges at me; I get him in the gut. Both sprawl whimpering in the pine needles.

I turn just in time to see George, with a few desperate kicks, break free of Rufus' hold. Staggering over to Drew, he drops beside him. Seizing Drew by his shaggy yellow hair, he jerks his head back, pulls a penknife, and holds it to his throat. "I'll cut him," George gasps. "Y'all leave me be, damn you. I'll cut him. I'll slit his Yankee throat. Y'all are whore-mongers and Yankee lovers."

I step forward, lifting clenched fists. "George, if you hurt him…"

"Sarge will thank me. He's incited a camp riot, that's what I'm going to say. He's liable to die in the next few days anyway."

George's hand shakes. He nicks Drew. Fresh blood dribbles. Drew hisses, "You're a goddamn coward. You're a dead man if I ever get loose."

That's when Jeremiah's voice sounds quietly at my elbow. "That Yank may be a prisoner, but he's a decent man. Now you get away from him, George, or I got a ball with your name on it."

Jeremiah's musket is shouldered, the hammer cocked. "I got to camp just soon enough to hear what you said about my lady Pearlene. Brave enough to insult a woman, huh? Impressive. Now if you want to keep your rat teeth intact—not to mention your eyes, ears, brain, and filthy tongue—you'd best pocket that piss-ant blade, get up slow, and take to your tent. For you're a foul thing through and through, and I'd take some pleasure in cleaning the camp of you."

George does as he's told. Muttering "Whore-mongers, every one," he rises, puts away the blade, and limps off into the trees.

Rufus cackles. "Thanks for the help, boys. The ole polecat should keep his distance for a while now. Next time he has a mind to insult a lady, he's likely to think twice. And, hell, he ain't gonna tattle to Sarge. Too afraid of being punished for fighting, I 'spect." He gets up, brushes off his trousers, and says, "Y'all get extra helpings tonight. After supper, meet me behind Ian's tent, all right? I'll give you seconds. As for George, if he's fool enough to take food at my fire, he might find his beans seasoned with grubs." Snickering, he heads into the forest, apparently with insect hunting in mind.

"Thanks, Jeremiah," Drew says, as I daub at his throat. Luckily it's a very shallow wound.

Jeremiah nods. "Glad to do it. Thanks to both of you for being so good to Pearl. She's had a hard time of it, and, well, if she weren't so pretty, she might have starved by now. If I get through this war, I hope to get back this way. Want to see a lot more of her."

He uncocks his musket, takes a few steps away, stops, and turns. "You know, I hope to have with Pearl what you boys have together. I'm glad y'all got one another. I'll pray for you both." Then he's gone into the shadow of the pines.

—

CHAPTER FORTY-NINE

—

"Sorry about this," I say, pulling the bandana from my pocket. "Sarge just got back. I'll sneak you supper later. It should be good."

Drew nods. Without protest, he takes the roll of cloth between his teeth, hanging his head so I can more easily knot the gag behind. Now he leans back against the tree, gazing serenely at me, the expression in his blackened eyes as limpid as a child's.

For a good while I'm busy, helping Rufus unload the cart a very thin civilian has driven into camp in Sarge's wake. Here, as promised, are beef and cabbages, even a few turnips and some onions, some dried corn, a few bags of cornmeal and beans, and a few jugs of whiskey. Grim-faced, Sarge supervises us. At nightfall, after ordering a meal brought to him and asking not to be disturbed, he disappears into his tent with a newly arrived scout. I jog over to check on Drew, afraid that George might sneak out into the dark and finish what he tried to start this afternoon, but my Yank's fine, sagging in his bonds and napping.

By the fires, the men gather, eager for fresh food, a welcome change of menu. The talk is all about the Institute's charred ruins, Sarge's cleverness in fetching provisions, the bad news from Petersburg, the ongoing seige. Rufus roasts chunks of beef on twig-spits over the fire, fries cabbage, stirs leftover beans, and bakes skillet cornbread. The whiskey jugs make the rounds, a rough-edged stuff, not half as smooth as Miss Pearl's. To our mutual disappointment, George decides to eat at another campfire rather than risk Rufus' culinary revenge. "Damn," whispers Rufus. "Now what am I gonna do with these grubs? They're all tickly inside my pocket. Guess I'll keep 'em for later."

"Your Yank needs fed. Want a distraction?" It's Jeremiah at my elbow, licking beef grease from his fingers. The meal's done, and, other than our secretive Sunday lunch compliments of Miss Pearl, it's the best we've had in recent memory.

"'Twould be much appreciated," I say. "I surely would like to smuggle him some of this beef."

"Watch this." Tossing down his empty plate, Jeremiah begins scratching vigorously, first at his crotch, then at his armpits. Unbuttoning his jacket, he pulls up his undershirt and claws his bare midriff. Cursing, he picks at the black mat of his belly hair. "Got one!" he shouts. "Beastly grayback! Let's have a race! Which of you men has lice as swift and agile as mine? None of you, I'll bet!"

It's a free-for-all. Rebs love a wager. Everyone's plucking and waving vermin, eager to join in. Soon white cloths are laid down on the ground; lice are lined up and let loose to competitively crawl. Sarge sends word to keep the noise down. I take in the spectacle for a few minutes, then wink at Rufus. He meets me behind my tent, slips me an aromatic kerchief still slightly warm, then returns to the fun.

"Boy? Wake up, boy. I got you a fine meal." It's very dark under the pines, but I can make out the silhouette of Drew's broad shoulders against the trunk he's tied to.

"Ummmm," Drew says. With one hand, I fumble with the gag's knot and tug it out of his mouth. "I'm awake, Reb. Had me a little sleep, but the aromas woke me right up. The smell of that beef has my stomach growling awful. You did bring me some, right?"

"Oh yes! Thanks to Jeremiah, who's challenged everyone to a lice race, and Rufus, who's saved you this." I open the kerchief to find seven nice-sized chunks of beef.

"That's what all that noise is about?" Drew says, biting into a morsel I hold to his mouth. "Ummmm." He chews and chews, groans and swallows, then, like a baby bird, opens his mouth for more. A few cheers sound behind us.

"You want me to fetch you some cabbage and some beans now? And one of those hidden fried pies?"

"Yes, please," says Drew, gulping the last of the beef. "I'd be most grateful."

Back at the fire, the lice races continue. Jeremiah appears to be winning. He looks up at me, face flushed with laughter. The vermin make their agonizingly slow way across the course. "Nigh epic, I'd say," I mutter before winking at Rufus again, then meeting him around the back of my tent for more food.

"I'm full. I'm really full," Drew says, downing the last of the fried pie. "I can't believe it. With all I've eaten today, I might make it to Purgatory yet."

"Sarge is holed up with a scout, so I'm going to untie you now and get you to the tent. Let me join the boys by the fire for a while so as to waylay suspicions, then I'll be in."

"Can we have that talk tonight?" Drew says, voice tight.

"You bet, boy," I say, unknotting one by one the ropes circling his torso and arms. When my hands brush his erect nipples, he shivers.

Drew seems stronger, just as he said. He walks to the latrine-trench and then to my tent without a stagger or a stumble. I have him nestled in blankets and, thanks to Miss Pearl's largesse, his wounds covered with precious isinglass plaster and fresh bandages, when banjo music begins. By the time I get back to the fire, a stag dance has started. The boys look awkward, dancing with one another, shuffling in time to "Gal on a Log." A few titter and curtsy like girls, inspiring more laughter. One bewails the absence of a bonnet. I'm just imagining how sweet it would be to dance with Drew, and the second song, "Leather Breeches," has just begun, when Sarge's voice, hoarse with annoyance, rings out. "Quiet, boys! I have a guest here!" Within minutes, the party breaks up, groups of three or four switching to less roisterous entertainments.

"Many thanks," I say, passing Jeremiah on the way to my tent. He's hunkered down with a few boys over hands of cards.

"No trouble at all. I won me enough money to treat Pearl to another bauble next time I'm in town. That grayback was a regular Mercury."

—

CHAPTER FIFTY

"I got to tell you this," Drew sighs. "And if you can't forgive me, I'll un-derstand. You've been wonderful to me. And if, after tonight, you leave me to my fate, well, I guess I got it coming."

"God, boy, what could it be?" My nape-hair prickles. Drew and I are spooning in the dark, both shirtless. He's curled up into a tighter ball than usual, as if he were preparing for blows. There are no sounds in camp but fire-crackle, pine-sough, and an occasional muttered conver-sation over cards. When Sarge tells us to shut up, we shut up.

"You asked me once... Well, I lied to you once, I...about something real important, but then that pitiable lady slapped me, and then I met Miss Pearl and heard about Lexington burning, and I know you've risked a lot for me and plan perhaps to take even greater risks for my sake in the future, considering all you've promised about Purgatory Mountain..."

I prop myself up on one elbow. It's too dark to see his face. "What is it, for God's sake? You're scaring me."

"I was just afraid that...if you knew, if the camp knew, it'd be the end of me for sure. If I'd told you then, Ian, we never would have become friends, we never would have had this." He fumbles for my hand, seizes it, and presses my palm over his breast. Beneath its hairy curve, his heart is racing.

"I'm just so afraid you'll hate me, and now that thought is worse than being beaten to death by your company-mates. But I got to tell you now."

"Say it," I croak. Suddenly my voice is a raven's voice, tight and dry. "Tell me."

"I...was part of it. The Burning. I lied to you. I was part of it. Part of Sheridan's cavalry. I helped burn the Valley."

I push away from Drew. I stand, bumping my head against the tent canvas. I sit down heavily, cross my legs, and put my head in my hands. "Oh no."

Drew sniffles. "You can tell 'em. Let 'em end me. I deserve whatever I get. I been choking on this since last fall, when it all happened, when we were ordered to do it. To burn the houses, the barns, the mills. It's been like a chunk of burned wood wedged down in my throat, down deep in me. And when I met you, and you were good to me, and now we're...together like this...well, that chunk's just swelled and swelled, and some nights I'd wake in your arms and I couldn't barely breathe, and sometimes the smell of the campfire would take me back there, and then I saw that poor woman selling bullets for food, and Miss Pearl, the look in her eyes when she described how Hunter had come through, and I just have to spit it out now, Ian, I got to."

Drew commences to cry, small whiffling sobs half-suppressed, the sounds of a big man ashamed of his own tears but too broken up to suppress them entirely. Part of me wants to do as I have done lately, to rest a hand on his shoulder, to ease him. Part of me, something new, will not permit me to do so.

I rise. I pull on my undershirt, my jacket, my cap, and my brogans. I push through the tent flaps. Jeremiah and a few boys are still sitting by the fire, poring over their cards, passing a flask. I pull up a camp chair and sit by them. Jeremiah looks up at me, cocking an eyebrow of inquiry and concern. I shake my head. "Bad dream. Pass me that flask, boys."

I'm warmly drunk after a while. Jeremiah loses two hands, then wins three. Every now and then he looks up at me, forehead furrowed. I watch the logs crumble, the orange embers smothered by ash. "Consumed with that which it was nourished by," that's the Shakespeare line. One of my favorite sonnets.

"Night, gentlemen," I say, rising to weave off into the woods. Here's the pine I bound Drew to. I sit down on the moss bed where he sat. I lean back against the trunk. The boughs and the clouds are too thick to see stars. I cock my cap over my eyes, hug myself as I've seen Drew so often do, and take a little nap.

—

CHAPTER FIFTY-ONE

Drew's no longer weeping when I reenter our tent in the very first seep of light before dawn. He's lying silently on his back, cuffed hands making a little prayer-tent on his blanket-covered chest. I fall to my knees beside him. For a while, we simply gaze at one another.

"Go on," I say.

"What?"

"Tell me about it. I want to know. I want to know what it was like. To do that."

"Oh, no. Please."

"You said you wanted to choke up that charred wood, Yank. Here's your chance. Tell me. You'll be gagged again soon enough."

Outside, birds are peeping in the trees, heralding dawn. War and winter have both seemed endless; I can't remember the last time I heard a bird sing. Somewhere nearby, there's a scraping sound, then the sound of water being poured into a pail. It's Rufus, no doubt, starting up the fire, getting coffee ready, and breakfast, to get us through the day's march to come.

"I did what I was told. We all did. And what we were told to do, word was, General Grant had told General Sheridan…to make the Valley so bare a crow flying over would have to carry its own provisions. There were some girls at Edinburg, they begged us to spare the mill, said it was the town's only livelihood, so that one, we extinguished the flames, but the others…"

"Go on. We don't have much time till reveille."

"Oh, Ian. God. There were bonfires everywhere, for we left not a barn intact. The smoke shut out the sun. There were women and girls screaming, tearing their hair, watching their houses flare up and then die down to ash. One woman I saw was laughing, crazy with grief, and couldn't stop. We stole wagons heaped with food; we shot horses, cattle, sheep; we burnt acres and acres of wheat and corn. I shot dead four different bushwhackers. Is that enough? Have you heard enough?" Drew's stifled sobs start up again.

"Don't cry. Someone might hear. Finish it."

Drew coughs, gulps, and wipes his eyes. He lies there, cuffed hands clasped on his chest like an effigy on a tomb. He clears his throat and continues.

"We were told we were exacting God's righteous revenge on a fallen people, the way the Israelites did in the Bible, but I knew better. Every time I smell smoke, part of me wants to vomit. I deserve every beating your Sarge has given me. In fact, I'm thankful for it. When I bleed, I can focus on that, and forget those faces, those women, those staring children. It was after that that I got the shakes and got transferred to the area around Staunton. It wasn't until we met, and...you held me at night, that I could sleep more than a few hours at a time without my nightmares waking me up."

Reveille sounds. "Stay here and keep quiet," I say.

I join morning muster. I feed Drew a quick breakfast of hoecake and jerky in the tent, each man avoiding the other's eyes. Tents are struck; last items are loaded on the cart. The Yank's mouth is gagged, his ankles unshackled, his wrists tethered to the cart. Jeremiah tips his cap to the distant church spires of Lexington, and we're off up the pike. A fairly fast march, for Sarge wants to make Purgatory by nightfall.

—

CHAPTER FIFTY-TWO

A dead man's sprawled facedown on the edge of the pike. There's a gaping hole in his side—probably left by a Minié ball—and the ground about him is rust-brown with old blood. His fingers, curved like claws, are sunk deep in mud. He's dressed in Rebel butternut. I roll him over. He's stiff, eyes wide with surprise, face contorted in a scowl. Black-haired, scruffy-faced, about nineteen years old, he looks like a younger version of myself.

Sarge, frowning, rides up to study him. "The scout warned me about this. He said there might be a few bands of Yanks roaming around. We shouldn't have come up the Valley Pike. We need to get off onto a back road as soon as possible."

I eye the corpse's shoes greedily—even with what I know now about Drew's past, looking out for him has become a habit—but they're far too small for the big Yank, and George confiscates them quickly enough, along with the dead soldier's belt and forage cap. Someone's taken the boy's gun already, but the bayonet's lying in the grass; George greedily seizes that as well. Jeremiah and some of the other boys bury him quickly—a shallow grave in an adjoining field, two sticks tied together to make a marker—then our little band hurries up the pike between rolling hills, past weed-filled, untended gardens, past the ruins of burnt barns and homes, past the skeleton of a cow. At a crossroads, Sarge consults a map, then leads us off the pike and toward the shelter of the western hills again.

Drew keeps up today. Yesterday's ease and unusually filling meals have rescued him from his feeble state. He trudges on beside my cart, eyes straight ahead, ignoring me, gritting the rag between his teeth and grunting with pain every so often as the terrain punishes his bandage-wrapped feet with stones or thorns. I try not to look at him, but I catch myself studying his half-naked body again and again, as we follow a little stream-skirted road west and then south. One minute, I look at him and see him in the blue uniform he wore the day we met; I see those women of the Valley screaming in the sparks, cinders, and

smoke. Another minute, I look at him and see the beautiful blond giant
I've cradled in my arms after a bloody beating, the frightened boy I've
made love to, the broken soldier whose guilt-wracked sobs filled our
tent last night.

Lunch stop, in a neglected orchard by a ramshackle farmhouse. I expect another poor woman to dash out, desperate for provender, but no
one appears. A few crows settle in the limbs above us as Rufus doles
out stiff squares of hardtack. "Sarge said to make it quick, boys, so this
is all you get," Rufus says apologetically. "Damn stuff's so hard you
could knock a bull down with it. Tonight, though, I'll make us cush and
parched corn, I promise."

It's late afternoon when Sarge leads us along yet another small road,
this one skirting a high, swift stream. The sky's overcast, the air's moist
and chilly, and light gleams on the rock-ruffled water like gray gunmet-
al. The road narrows as we pass through a little glen squeezed in by low
ridges with steep slopes. Over us, the limbs of pawpaw trees, still bare,
stretch and mingle, twigs brushing together in the breeze like black
finger bones. I'm looking at Drew as he hangs his head and picks his
barefoot way over potentially painful obstacles, trying to make sense of
what he said last night, thinking of how good tonight's cush will be, and
realizing, despite the shock evoked by his confession, how much I want
to brush the muddy hair from his brow, when I hear it, the pop I've
heard from triumphant First Manassas in July of '61 till that last hopeless battle near Waynesboro only days ago. Someone's firing on us.

"Yanks! Up on the ridge!" That's Jeremiah shouting ahead in the line.
There's another pop, above us, there where a puff of smoke marks a
musket's ignition. Jeremiah curses, drops his gun, grabs his left arm,
and falls to his knees.

I'm off the cart seat in a second. There are few places to take shelter in
this narrow dell—a few rocks behind which most of the company have
already fled—so I seize Drew by the arm, slice his tether with my Bowie
knife, and shove him beneath the cart. "Stay here," I growl, then, my
head down, lope over to fetch Jeremiah. Another pop; a familiar whizzing past my eye. A few more inches, I think with utter calm, and that
ball might have taken off the right side of my face. Jeremiah's bleeding,
teeth clenched, face knotted up with pain. I haul him to his feet and
tug him toward the cart. More balls sing past us, audibly pocking the
mud about our feet. There's the thudding of hooves—what cavalry we
have probably trying to outflank our attackers—more popping gunfire,

and then a scream, shrill and short. We duck beneath the cart, joining Drew, who's lying on his belly in the mud. Clearly relieved to see me unharmed, Drew seizes my hand and squeezes hard. There's the dull sound of balls embedding themselves in the buckboard bed above us. A few more bullets kick up small explosions of mud around the cart, a few feet from our faces.

I look at Drew and Jeremiah, both wide-eyed, one bleeding. I can't stay here. The men shooting at us from the ridge may be Drew's Federal compatriots, but if someone doesn't stop them, they might well kill us all, Drew included.

First, though, I help Jeremiah remove his jacket, then his undershirt. He's very lean, his chest and belly covered with rich black fur; dimly I remember that other world, back home, our youth, how I loved to look at him when we swam naked in the river. Long, long ago. Now there's a hole clean through the flesh of his upper left arm, bleeding copiously. I tear off my own jacket, then my undershirt. As old and tattered as all our clothes are—who can afford a new uniform this deep into the war?—it takes very little effort to rip one sleeve off my undershirt.

"Bind his wound with this as best you can," I order Drew. "I'll be back."

Drew shakes his head, trying to grab me by the belt, but I elude him, rolling out from under the cart before he or Jeremiah can stop me. I check my pistol in its holster, cock my cap, then race up the hillside.

The red mist is here again. I rush through its tunnel, the gray slope and woodland smearing into swirls of crimson. Someone needs to die. I'm young and strong, despite months of low rations. I dodge from one thick tree trunk to another, panting and cursing. More singing balls, the thump of them against wood columns sheltering me. Behind me, another scream. Drew? Jeremiah? No, they're smart enough to stay where they are. From the far side of the ridge, hoof beats and shouts. Sarge is taking their rear.

Teeth gritted, I zigzag bare-chested up the slope. A volley of balls. This rock ledge, a nice haven. Pause. Deep breath, deep breath, deep breath. Up again. Bowie knife I hip-pat, at the ready. Up, up. And there's the blue—blue uniform, blue eyes—a mere boy, could be Drew with that golden hair—aiming. The mouth of the musket, a black trumpet flower. Flare of fire. The merest edge of something catches my right side. A pang, the sudden, expected wet. And, aflame with luck, I'm atop the ridge, slamming into the Yank. We roll together. He's bigger by far, like most men, damn my size, but I box his temple, he grunts and falls. Before he can rise, my knife's in his chest. I would stab and stab, but there are others and I turn to them. One's got his pistol aimed at me. Sarge's saber flashes; the Yank's hand and firearm roll off together. From behind, arm about my neck now. I twist and punch. Growling, I push off the weight. I pull my pistol and fire. The man at my feet now, gasping, is gray-haired as my father. I kick him nevertheless. I kick him and kick him, and then he stops gasping and I stop kicking and the shouting atop this ridge has ceased and it's very quiet now and now I wipe the drool from my beard and the blood from my bare side.

—

CHAPTER FIFTY-THREE

"Foes don't deserve the dignity of a grave," Sarge says. "You boys, toss the dead Yanks in the creek. You all, load our wounded in the cart. The rest of you, bury our dead at the base of that boulder."

I'm grateful for orders. I'm too numb to do more than what I'm told.

"All of you, work fast. One of those Yankee swine escaped, and we're in serious trouble if he makes it to any of his compatriots nearby. We need to leave this place as soon as possible and find a safer spot to pitch camp. It's too late now to make Purgatory by nightfall."

One of the New Market twins, badly wounded in the belly and bleeding freely, is moaning in the cart. Jeremiah's bandaged up, as I'd ordered, his arm in a sling. It's a flesh wound, painful but not mortal, thank God, the bleeding nearly staunched. He slumps on the buckboard seat, waiting for our departure. Two of our company, both from Winchester, are dead: a skeletal man named Bob, shot through the chest, and an older man named Edward, shot through the head. They never said much; they had their own mess and kept to themselves. Now they're fitted into the earth side by side.

George indulges in his customary corpse robbing, confiscating the dead Yankees' guns and cartridge boxes, then their uniforms and shoes. Stripped, their corpses lie splayed on the earth in nothing but underclothes. Sarge has ordered my prisoner uncuffed long enough to help me dispose of them. Drew and I haul the five dead Federals down the hillside one by one and give them to the stream. When we get to the last man, the first one I killed, I retrieve my Bowie knife from his chest, wipe it off on my sleeve, and slip it into its sheath. Drew bends over him, takes a sharp breath, then hunkers down beside him and touches his gray child's face. My big Yank gazes up at me, blue eyes wide with surprise, white teeth sunk in his rag-gag.

From the dead grass, I fetch my forage cap lost in the struggle. Near it lies the Yankee hand Sarge cut off. The body it belonged to has already been washed downstream. I leave it where it lies.

"You knew this boy?" My voice is wispy, hollow.

Drew nods. He grabs the soldier's shoulders; I grab the feet. The body swings between us like a hammock as we slip and slide down the hillside's carpet of dead leaves, across the mud-rut road, and to the stream. It gurgles grayly over smooth rocks.

"He shot me," I say, staring at the water, then at Drew. "I'm sorry," I say. Drew nods. We swing the body, gain a little momentum, then release it. There's a soft splash, then the blue uniform and gray face are cupped by the current and carried off.

My wound is only a nick, but it's bleeding profusely, a little scarlet waterfall down my side, staining my trousers, moistening my underclothes. Drew turns from the stream's busy coursing to me. He touches my ribs. He cups up water from the stream. He washes away the smeared blood, wiping his fingers on his borrowed trousers. He tugs off one of the cloth strips crisscrossing his chest and back, one of the new ones Miss Pearl sold us. Tightly, tenderly, he bandages me. The white strip blooms with slow red, as if a poppy were spreading its petals against my skin.

From the head of the newly formed line, Sarge shouts the order to march. I slip on my one-armed undershirt, then my wool jacket with its damp scent. I cuff Drew, tether him to the cart, climb into the buckboard seat, and we're off at a rapid clip, bouncing over the rough road. Jeremiah winces as we hit ruts; he leans against me. Occasionally I wrap an arm around him to steady him. Behind us, the wounded New Market twin groans with each jolt. "God! Oh, for God's sake, take me out! Take me out and leave me to die on the roadside! Please!" Eventually, he passes out, and there are no sounds but the tramp of men, the creak of the cart, the purling of the stream, and the caw of crows in treetops.

—

CHAPTER FIFTY-FOUR

I do what I can. Save for what little we bought from Miss Pearl, we have no medicine, thanks to that damned Federal blockade, and I'm almost out of salve, having used so much of it after Drew's beatings. I doubt that salve or isinglass would make any difference anyway. The wound in his belly is too deep. I can't stop the bleeding. I'm no surgeon. The nearest town is Buchanan, at the base of Purgatory Mountain. Sarge has ridden there to try to find a doctor. I fear his efforts are for naught. The wounded New Market twin is fading fast.

He lies on a cot by the fire, covered in blankets. His name is Ben. He is, I think—I've always gotten the two confused—the one I punched in the chin outside Lexington when he tried to pull Rufus off George. His brother is William. They're both pale, freckled, red-haired, and sharp-featured. But it's easy to distinguish them now. One is significantly paler than the other.

William hovers around Ben, face tear-streaked. He falls to his knees by the cot and holds his brother's hand. Ben smiles up at him, then closes his eyes, drifting in and out of a doze. I dip rags into hot water Rufus has boiled up, wring them out, and press them against Ben's belly, trying to stop the bleeding. Ben groans. The cloths rapidly turn red. I wring them out again, soak them in hot water again, apply them again. Ben gulps down water that George proffers, swallowing eagerly but with visible effort one tin cup full, then two, then three, then four. I cup his brow in my palm. He's very cold. He grits his teeth in pain, shudders, then musters another weak smile. "Thanks, Ian. Thanks, George," he mutters. "Yeah, thanks," William says, nodding. George, tight-lipped, stalks off to fetch more water.

Briefly I leave Ben there, in his brother's care, to fetch my flask of whiskey from the cart. A few sips are bound to ease him. Our new camp is pitched atop a low hill, in a grove of pines like the one near Lexington where we met Miss Pearl. It's sheltered to the east by a razorback ridge Sarge hopes will keep Yankee troops on the Valley Pike from noticing us. To the west are mountains we're poised to retreat to, if necessary, high horizons edged now with sunset's pale gold and apple green. When I get to the buckboard, I find Jeremiah curled up in the cart-bed beneath an oilcloth, fast asleep. Drew's asleep as well, exhausted with another day's foot-march. Obeying Sarge's hasty orders, I've cuffed my Yank to the cartwheel. He lies on his side, head lolling in the grass, dead to the world. Fetching a blanket from the cart, I cover his snoring frame, remove his gag, and slip my haversack under his head to serve as a pillow. Sarge has more important things to worry about tonight than insuring the prisoner's discomfort.

By the fire, Ben takes sips of my whiskey with grateful murmurs. As promised, Rufus prepares cush—frying chunks of leftover cooked beef in bacon grease and adding crumbled cornbread—then parches corn. Ben takes a few bites of cush, refuses the corn, asks for more water, gulps and gulps, coughs violently, and passes out. The remaining members of the company talk low around campfires. Night falls; stars glimmer among the pine boughs. Someone tries to pluck Jeremiah's banjo with a singular lack of success. Rufus breaks out his precious stash of Miss-Pearl coffee and makes us a pot. Conversations flare up and die down in the firelight. We eye one another, eye the wounded man on the cot. George chews tobacco and spits into the fire, hissing wads that put off acrid smoke. Ben's breathing grows loud, irregular, shallow. William sits cross-legged by his brother's cot and mumbles prayers.

Leaving William to apply compresses, I take Drew and Jeremiah dinner. Both are famished. I check Jeremiah's wound, wash it, rebandage it, and tuck him back into the buckboard bed. I lead my Yankee into the woods, where we both relieve ourselves, then to my tent. He crawls in, curls up on the oilcloth, and sighs. "Can we talk, Ian? I need to—"

"Later. I think Ben's dying. I need to watch him. You just stay in here and keep warm, keep quiet. I'll be back eventually."

I'm halfway back to the fire when I hear the commotion. By the time I reenter the circle of firelight, William's sobbing, his face buried in his hands. Ben's eyes are fixed on the starry sky. George is scowling, spitting another tobacco wad into the fire. Sarge returns with the Buchanan doctor about the time that William thumbs his brother's eyes closed and covers his face with a blanket.

—

CHAPTER FIFTY-FIVE

—

"Ben's gone," I say, shouldering aside the tent flaps.

Drew's deep voice is a mere whisper. "I'm sorry, Ian. I really am. Despite the way he treated me."

I feel for Drew in the dark, find the coarse wool of a trouser leg, then sit beside him, wrapping my arms around my knees. "He was easily influenced. They both were. If George hadn't been around... Well, he's gone. It's too late. He was your age. We'll bury him tomorrow morning. William won't stop crying."

As if eager to prove my words, a racked sob reaches us, then the murmur of fireside voices attempting to comfort, then a few more sobs tapering into silence.

"Ian, I want to talk about what I told you last night. I can't stand this coldness between us. Are you going to tell the others? You should. I'd rather be beaten to death than live thinking you hate me. You've got to believe me, I bear that guilt every day and night, what I did to all those poor people. Can't you forgive me? I can't forgive myself, but if you could, well, it would make a big and blessed difference."

Outside, the fireside sobs start up again. I rock in the tent's dark. "When it comes to tears, everyone has to take a turn."

"What?"

I sigh. "Next it could be me crying over you, or even you crying over me."

"Yes, I know. But—"

"That man I stabbed to death today, who was he? How did you know him?"

"He was... I don't know how he ended up in this area. Last time I saw him he was at...during the Burning, at Edinburg. His name was Jimmy Wise. We used to drink and play cards together in the camps. Like you and I, he was at Cedar Creek. I didn't know him well."

"And what was he like?"

"He...well, he could tell a joke. He could throw a snowball better'n anyone. He was from New York. He was always cussing the bad beef and the hardtack."

"And"—I take a deep breath—"did he have a family, young as he was?"

"Yes, Ian. He got a furlough last fall and went home to get married. Came back all flushed and happy, shared with me little cakes his new wife had baked."

"Well," I say. "Well." I tug off my upper garments, then slip down beside Drew. He gives a great sigh, grabs my hand, and nestles back against me.

"Seems to me we're both guilty as hell," I say. "Tarred and feathered inside, that's what it feels like. I guess that's what duty does for you, at least in times like these. Difference is...you were obeying orders when you torched the Valley, and my guess is you'd have been shot if you disobeyed. Me, today, I...I was protecting you, and Jeremiah, and my company, yes, but it was that berserk rage again, that 'wildcat in war.' I get hot to kill. I swing and stab and shoot. Once that killer in me gets awake, I can't stop. I get that way when I defend...friends and kin."

"And lovers," says Drew, placing my hand on his fuzzy breast.

"Yes," I say. Burrowing my face into his unkempt hair still scented with mud, I press my lips to the back of his neck, tasting both his skin's salt and the metal of the slave collar. "You forgive me, I'll forgive you."

"Yes," Drew murmurs.

"And speaking of deals, I still want up your ass once I get you somewhere free and safe."

"Yes." Drew laughs softly, rubbing his butt against me. "Long as you go slow."

"Ummmm, I'll try." Growling softly, I bite his shoulder and stroke the wool covering his firm behind. "I'm sorry I was cold to you. I'm so glad we're together."

Outside, William's weeping starts up again. Drew and I snuggle closer, listening. Finally the jagged sounds of sorrow cease, and we fall asleep.

—

CHAPTER FIFTY-SIX

Drew's kisses wake me before reveille. We lie there on our sides, brushing lips, nuzzling beards, fondling one another's hard nipples, rubbing trouser-pent hard cocks together. I'm just about to unbutton Drew's pants when there are footfalls right outside the tent. I push away from him fast and am reaching for my Bowie knife when I hear Rufus' voice calling my name.

I crawl out, still shirtless. Rising to my feet, I rub my eyes and scratch my armpits. Here's hoping the bulge in my pants isn't as obvious as it feels. Rufus hands me a cup of coffee with an apologetic air. "Sarge says you should help with the funeral and leave the prisoner cuffed in the tent. Says, since you read better'n any of us, you should recite a psalm. Don't worry, I'll give the Yank—uh, Drew—I'll sneak him some breakfast. Got a little cush left over."

I dip inside the tent long enough to fetch my shirt, jacket, and cap. "You heard all that? Rufus will take care of you."

Drew nods, smiling. He gropes his own crotch, whispering, "I'll be fine. I'll save this for you."

The morning bugle sounds. I join the others for muster. When we disperse, Sarge beckons. I follow him to his tent. Inside, he leafs through his Bible. Outside, there's the sound of shovels displacing dirt. "This one," he says, pointing to a page. "Yes, sir," I say. "Dismissed," Sarge says, with more than usual clipped curtness.

I settle by the fire, reading over the psalm, sipping a second cup of Miss Pearl's coffee—what a luxury to have the real thing instead of those nasty brews made from acorns, roasted rye, or sweet potatoes. Across the fire, George is sharpening a bayonet, probably the one he took from that roadside corpse. His face is flushed. He ignores me; I do the same to him. Rufus has returned—hopefully from feeding Drew—and is spooning me out a plate of cold cush when George rises. He points the bayonet at me. "I ain't forgot what I saw in Lexington, those black ruins, and all those ashes up and down the Valley. Now Ben's dead, thanks to Yankees. Mark me, Ian. I'll see your big boy bleed a good bit yet." He hawks a great glob of brown juice into the fire, where it hisses like a viper. Before I can respond, George stalks off.

—

CHAPTER FIFTY-SEVEN

First sun in days, albeit still March-chilly. William sits in a camp chair by the head of the grave, head bowed, hands clenched together in his lap. Sarge stands beside him, occasionally patting his shoulders' slump. The rest of us collect about the grave's foot, what's left of the Rogue Riders. Only twenty of us now, down from ninety, picked off battle by battle, or from lingering disease, left to rot in holes in the ground much like this one. Half of me listens while Sarge prays over Ben's grave. Half of me pictures absent faces, remembering my brother Jeff, remembering boys who began with us in the swelling patriotic hopes of '61, boys we've buried in hurried ceremonies like this after Manassas, Winchester, Malvern Hill, Antietam, Fredericksburg, Gettysburg, Cedar Creek. I remember too those Yankee prisoners before Drew, boys as innocent and as guilty as Ben, as Drew, as me, all buried in shallow graves I helped dig. I pray inside my head, for a future with my big golden Yank, one safe and free and far from here.

Sarge falls silent. I'm next to speak. I open the Bible, look down at the freckled face in the earth—we have neither the time nor the materials to fashion a coffin—then begin.

I will lift up mine eyes unto the hills, from whence cometh my help.
My help cometh from the Lord, which made heaven and earth.
He will not suffer thy foot to be moved; he that keepeth thee will
*   not slumber.*
Behold, he that keepeth Israel shall neither slumber nor sleep.
The Lord is thy keeper; the Lord is thy shade upon thy right hand.
The sun shall not smite thee by day, nor the moon by night.
The Lord shall preserve thee from all evil; he shall preserve thy
*   soul.*
The Lord shall preserve thy going out and thy coming in from this
*   time forth, and even for evermore.*

"Amen," Rufus says. I hand Sarge his Bible and return to the half-circle of men at the foot of the grave. A few lift shovels, the rest of us preparing to disperse, when George says, "Wait." He's shown up late, halfway through Sarge's prayer, a tardiness I find odd, considering what cronies he and the twins were. He's also moving unsteadily, as if he's been drinking despite the early hour. Beneath a big, floppy-brimmed hat I've never seen before, his right eye's inexplicably blackened, but there's still a strange satisfaction in his expression, a tight smugness, entirely inappropriate for the occasion.

"May I, Sarge?" he says. When Sarge nods, George moves to the head of the grave. The lay preacher in him just can't resist the opportunity, I guess. From a tree, he's broken a little branch with buds just opening, and this he drops onto the chest of the corpse. He clears his throat again, takes off the hat with a grand gesture, sweeps his eyes over our little assembly, scowls at me, and begins.

"Gentlemen," he says, "I'll be brief. Ben, our brother in the great fight 'gainst Northern tyranny, has been laid low, as have so many of our company-mates since this conflict began. Those same invaders who've done burnt our homes and farms have murdered him. This should harden our resolve. This should make us ruthless. This should make us thirstier than ever for Yankee blood. We have much to avenge."

A few boys behind me grunt assent. Sarge nods. Rufus rolls his eyes and makes a disgusted face.

"Do y'all need further proof that all Yanks are monsters? Seems to me that *anyone* who befriends a Yank, who shows a Yank *any* kindness..." George continues, glaring at me, but William's murmur interrupts what promises to be a tirade with me in mind.

"'T'won't help. 'T'won't help." Rising, William clutches a handful of earth and sprinkles it over his brother. He kicks at a clod of earth. Dislodged, it rolls into the hole. "He's gone now, ain't he? Deader'n a doornail, ain't he? Yankee blood ain't going to help, fool." Tears streaming down his face, he turns to George. "Now, just you be quiet, fool. You led my brother and me into unkindness and hatefulness, and now he's dead."

George snorts, grabbing William's arm. William shakes him off. Sarge sighs.

"Sir," William says, turning now to Sarge, "I would much 'preciate leave to take this sad news home to my kin. I would so much 'preciate..." Choked up, he falls quiet and sits down in the camp chair, hiding his face in his hands.

Sarge hesitates for only a second. "Yes, son," Sarge says, "you can go home. We can't spare you a horse, but we can spare you provisions. Rest up till tomorrow, then be on your way, and God bless you."

William nods. "Bless *you*, sir," he says. Taking a shovel from one of the men, he begins filling up the grave.

I'm heading back to my tent when George sidles up. "I had a whole sermon all prepared just for you," he hisses. "A regret you didn't git to hear it, Yankee-lover. Sorrow's made William all weak. And speaking of Yanks, just where *is* yours right now? Not where you left him. *Told* you I'd make him bleed a right bit more before he ends up in a hole like poor Ben."

"Oh, God, you damned son of a bitch. If you've hurt him—" I grab for George, but he's ready for my response, leaping out of my reach and dodging off between the trees. Frantic, I race to my tent. It's empty. Drew is gone.

—

CHAPTER FIFTY-EIGHT

"I don't know where he is, Ian. I fed him breakfast, left him in the tent, and went to the funeral," Rufus says. "I'll help you look. Let's spread out."

I've made half a circuit of the campsite when Jeremiah runs up to me, face grim. "You looking for your Yank?"

"Yes! Lord, man, have you seen him?"

"Yep. Check in the woods behind Sarge's tent." I'm about to race off when Jeremiah grips my forearm.

"Prepare yourself, Ian. Someone's treated him awful bad."

I tear off. My throat aches as if invisible fingers were encircling it.

He's here where Jeremiah said, in the shadow of the pines. He looks up at me, face twisted. I squat down beside him. His eyes fill up with tears and overflow. Someone—can there be any doubt who?—has torn off his bandages and bucked him with rope and wooden rod. Instead of the usual stick-gag, a bayonet has been wedged between his teeth and tied tightly in place. The sharp edges sink into the corners of his mouth. He's drooling blood. His pained panting blows bubbles, flecking his lips with red foam. His blond beard's stained and dripping.

"Oh, buddy..." I say, touching his shoulder, then patting his bent back. He winces, whimpering. "What...?" I say. My hand is wet. I stand, step around him, and see, across his bare back, a big X cut into him from shoulders to waist, bleeding profusely.

I'm fumbling with the knots behind his head, trying to loosen the bayonet, when Sarge appears around the corner of the tent. "What are you doing, nephew?"

"S-sir, George has moved the prisoner without warning me. And surely this treatment is too vile even for a foe. I'm taking this blade out of his mouth. And look at his back. A pig or dog deserves better."

Sarge steps forward, grabbing my hand. "Yes, a pig or dog does. A Yankee doesn't. You didn't see the remains of the Institute at Lexington. George and I did. I attended school there, Ian, and now it's a pile of blackened wood and ash, as is—have you forgotten?—my home. And now another of our company has fallen, thanks to this fellow's friends in blue. I gave George permission to do this. It's a way of commemorating Ben, a strong way, not the soft way William has chosen. You will leave the prisoner to suffer. You may fetch him after supper. Not till then."

I shake off his grip. I step back, pointing to Drew's maimed back. "But, sir, this is outrageous. This man is a human being. Surely you—"

"*Enough*, Ian. After your fine fighting yesterday on the ridge, I was so proud of you. But now...I don't like your tone. The same old weakness— I see it again and again—and now, I think, for the first time there's defiance too. Unseemly. You owe me obedience, do you not? I'm your captain, your elder, your kin. And my saber saved your life mere hours ago, did it not? Did it not?"

What can I say? He saved my life indeed, and right now I wish he'd never been born. Mute, I nod. I look not at his face but to his right, concentrating on the play of sun and shadow in the pines behind him. I don't dare let him see the naked hate in my eyes.

"How many times have I saved your life now, since this long war began? Two? Three?" Sarge waves at me dismissively. His voice is low, cold, and even. "I've tried to be a second father to you, to make a man of you. I'm weary of it. Take yourself off now. Don't come back till nightfall. I mean it. George has lost one of his best friends. He's angry. It's a righteous anger. It deserves an outlet. It cries out for blood. Blood it shall have today; blood it shall have in future."

I take a step toward the camp, fisted clenched, but Sarge can gauge my intentions. Bushy brows knit, he waves a warning finger, as if I were a child being scolded for some thoughtless prank. "And Ian, leave George alone. This punishment was as much my idea as his, though I gave him the pleasure of implementing it. If you start a fight with George, I'll not only cut this Yankee's throat myself—ah, I can tell from your face that his fate is of great concern to you—but, I swear, though you may be my kin, I'll have you hung by your thumbs or bucked and gagged like him. As it is, this little fit of insubordination has earned you picket duty today from lunch till supper. Now get along with you."

It's all I can do not to curse him. I'm turning away when he adds, "We leave for Purgatory tomorrow. If the prisoner can't keep up, you'll be required to shoot him."

Sarge shoves aside his tent's flaps and disappears inside. Within the tent, something fragile crashes into something hard and shatters. I sink to my knees by my boy. I pull a kerchief from my pocket and wipe the oozing blood from his mouth, wipe the tears from his cheeks, wipe the streaming blood from his sliced-open back. I look around, make sure no one's watching, then kiss the top of his head. "I'm going to hold you tight tonight, in our tent," I whisper. "And, when we get to Purgatory—you got to be strong and take this, hold up just another day or so, till we get there—I'm going to set you free or die trying."

Against the cruel gag, Drew groans. He nods once, then bows his head. I leave him there. I return to my tent. I have a brief, silent cry, determined not to give anyone the satisfaction of hearing my grief. Then I borrow an ax from Jeremiah and head out to gather firewood. Every log is George's face. The blade cleaves his nose and sinks into the black muck of his brains. I have a goodly heap split by the time Rufus announces lunch.

—

CHAPTER FIFTY-NINE

The hours crawl. First, lunch, some fried hardtack Rufus brings me, which I hurriedly chew before starting my watch. Then the miserable hours of picket duty, the slow creep of sun descending with afternoon, as I pace the perimeter of the camp, then along the crest of the hill, then back, keeping an eye out for Yankees who—since the sound defeat of General Early's forces, at Fisher's Hill and Cedar Creek, and then at Waynesboro, that last pathetic attempt of ours—have just about ruled the Valley, damn them. I smile at myself, feeling that old stab of resentment against the boys in blue even though now my entire existence seems wrapped up in the welfare of one of those very foes, a lover whose efforts with the torch have helped starve the new nation I'm defending.

By evening, my eyes are tired and my feet are aching. It's suppertime at last, the campfires starting up, flickering among the rough columns of pines. There's the sound of footsteps in fallen leaves, and Jeremiah appears, one arm in a sling, grasping a pistol with his free hand, his face drawn in the dying light.

"You're excused, Ian. I volunteered to relieve you. Go get something to eat."

"You're wounded, friend. You ought to be resting, not marching picket," I say, but he waves me off.

"I'll be fine. Your big Yank bandaged me up right nice. He was real careful with me. The boy ought to study doctoring." Jeremiah taps his bandaged arm with the pistol butt. "Just a scratch. Hardly hurts. I'm just a little weary is all. But Ian? Sarge said to leave the Yankee tied just yet. He said he'll send for you tonight when he's ready for you to fetch the prisoner. And Ian?" Jeremiah's voice drops. "Look here."

He holsters the pistol long enough to pull a bundle out of his back pocket and offer it to me. "I've been saving this," he says. Eyebrow arched, I take it, unfolding the cloth to find a blackened little chunk of beef, a tiny square of cornbread, and a piece of greasy hardtack.

"What—? But Jeremiah, like I said, you're wounded. You need to keep up your strength. Why would—?"

Jeremiah looks around, then says, even more softly, "Rufus and I been talking. We know your Yank is in the worst shape ever, after what George did today. The boy's lost some blood; some of the men are angry over Ben and, as you might imagine, have been roughing up the prisoner while you been out here on picket. And we know we all have another long march tomorrow, and, well, I know how sore your limbs get after being bucked for hours 'cause I suffered it once, and... Rufus and I are afraid your Yank won't be in any shape to make the march. And...Ian, I followed you to Sarge's tent, and I heard him tell you to shoot the Yank tomorrow if he can't keep up."

My legs are wobbly. I sit on a stump, placing my rifle across my knees. I take a deep breath, hang my head, and nod.

"We, uh...well, we care about you, Ian, and we know—well, I especially know—that the big ole Yank is, uh, important to you, so Rufus and I thought, well, your Yank needs this food even more than I do, so..."

"Oh, Jeremiah..." I begin, but he'll have none of it.

"Now, just get on. Get on to dinner. I'll be fine here."

I give Jeremiah a quick hug. He winces.

"Sorry, sorry," I stammer. "I forgot!"

"That's all right. Now get on now. I'm gonna spend the evening thinking about Pearlene. That oughta keep me warm." He scratches his crotch vigorously, then his beard. "Just hope I didn't leave her with these frigging graybacks. She'll twist my dick in a knot if I did. On the other hand, heavy as her skirts are, the damn things would probably smother 'neath them." Snickering, Jeremiah marches off.

By the fire, Rufus serves me up soup beans and parched corn. "I heard about Drew," Rufus mutters beneath his breath. "I got you a little surprise to take him later. And I fetched me some fresh bark-grubs just in case George—"

As if on cue, George saunters over and plops himself into a camp chair. He's wearing his new hat.

"Lord, lord!' Rufus says, his face gleaming with amusement. "Get out from under that! I know you're in there! I can see your legs!"

"Shut up and cook," George growls, tugging irritably at his moustache.

"Take them mice outta your mouth! Take 'em out! No use to say they ain't there! I can see their tails ahangin' out!"

"Shut *up!*"

"What Yankee corpse you steal that fine headgear from?"

George flushes. "Shut up!"

Grinning, Rufus turns his back, tending to the food.

"Nice. A lay preacher, a base coward, and a grave robber. The combination makes sense to me," I say, leaning back in my chair. "If it weren't for Sarge, I'd have you facedown in that fire right now," I say, voice as even as possible.

George purses his mouth, staring at the flames. "I did hear that you and Sarge would be having y'all a little talk," he says, glaring up at me, lips twisting into a thin smile.

I pat my open palm with a clenched fist and smile back. "I don't know where you got that black eye, but it becomes you. Very pretty. At some point, Sarge or not, you might receive another to match the first."

George's face falls. "Here, here," he sputters at Rufus, "fetch me some vittles, damn you, and make it quick. I'm famished."

"Yes, *sir,*" Rufus drawls. With exaggerated slowness, he shakes some parched corn onto a makeshift plate made of half a canteen. "*Certainly,* sir. Why don't you start with this? I'm sure cutting on a helpless man has worked you up quite the hero's appetite. You're a true knight of the Southland."

George snorts. "I didn't ask for conversation, you greasy whoremonger. Gimme that food." Snatching the plate, he crams a handful of corn into his mouth.

Rufus turns from him, cocks an eyebrow my way, and smiles. Before he ladles out beans, I see his hand burrow in his trouser pocket.

"Here we go, hero," Rufus says, handing George the steaming cup. "I do hope it's fittin' to eat."

Rufus and I sit back, chewing our portions. We watch George. He makes a face at us, swallows a few mouthfuls of beans, and makes a face even more vividly unpleasant than before. "Look at those sharp lil' teeth," Rufus whispers. "I'll bet he could chaw through pianer wire. Puts me in mind of a skunk skull my uncle has on the mantel back home."

George snarls, "What y'all lookin' at?" A few last hurried bites, a few finger-scrapes of the cup, before he drops plate and cup by his chair and rises. "Damned nasty," he growls. "You're a sad excuse for a cook, Rufus Ballard. I ain't eatin' at your mess no more. Them beans were bitter as gall."

"Oh, sir, I'm *ever* so sorry," Rufus says, with a giggle and a flutter of his hand. "Son of a bitch," he says to me as George disappears behind a wall of wood smoke. "Cutting on that poor big boy. He's damn lucky I didn't piss in 'em. He don't *know* bitter."

—

CHAPTER SIXTY

"Yes, take him away. He stinks like a sty." Sarge passes me on his way to supper.

"Drew," I say, squatting beside him in the dusk. "I'm here to help you."

My Yank doesn't respond. He does stink, of blood and urine. From the thoroughly sodden state of his pants, I'm guessing the urine is both his and that of various hostile visitors who came by while I was on picket duty. His head sags upon his breast, shaggy hair veiling his features. I cup his bearded chin in my hand, lift his head, and brush the hair away from his face. His eyes are closed. A black bruise stains his swollen right cheek. Another mars his right temple. His honey-blond beard is stained red with gory slobber, as is the hair matting his chest and belly.

"Drew, wake up, please," I say. His eyes stay closed.

"Oh, God," I say, fumbling loose the bloody bayonet bound in his mouth and then the ropes and rod imprisoning his limbs. I lower him onto his side in the pine needles. He lies there in his cuffs and foot-shackles, limp, entirely unmoving. None of the usual agonized sobs. I press my hand to his chest. Nothing? I press my fingers to his throat. There, yes, a faint throbbing.

He's very hard to move, but I don't want to leave him alone long enough to fetch Rufus, and Jeremiah's still on guard duty. Cupping a hand under each armpit, careful to keep his fresh wounds off the rough ground, slowly I drag him through the pines to my tent and into it. His back is crusted with dried blood, but at least the bleeding's stopped. I light a candle and study his bare chest's shallow rise and fall. I leave long enough to fetch water and some cold supper should he wake. I clean his bloodstained beard. I wash, medicate, and rebandage his mutilated back—how many times have I performed these actions since he was first brought to camp?—then blow out the candle, hold him beneath the blanket, and indulge in another very quiet cry.

When I hear Rufus whispering my name, I hurriedly wipe my eyes before opening the tent flap. "Here, here!" Rufus says, looking worriedly over his shoulder before giving me a little bundle much like the one Jeremiah gave me. "There's a hoecake I been hoarding for Drew, and a tiny bit of bacon, and"—Rufus sighs—"a fried pie."

"Oh, thank you, Rufus!" I whisper, gripping his hand. "You're a real friend."

"That's all right," Rufus says. "I feel mighty sorry for that boy, even if he is a bluebelly. You tell him ole Rufus hopes he makes it, and to enjoy that pie. It's the last one," he says regretfully, eying the bundle as if he were having second thoughts about his culinary self-sacrifice. "Figure he'll need all the strength he can get to make it to Purgatory now." With that, he turns and disappears into the dark.

Hours pass. Sounds of a harmonica, some boys singing, then all that dies down. It's very late. I curl up against Drew, listening to the continuing blessing of his breath. I'm on the edge of a doze when he shifts, groans, and whispers my name.

"Here. I'm here."

"Water," croaks Drew. He rises on one elbow, sways, then lies down again. "Ian? Water? Ian?"

"Here, here!" I say, reaching for the canteen. "Let me help you." I slip an arm beneath Drew's head, angling him upright. He sips. Then he gulps. Then he coughs. Then he gulps some more.

"Put me down," he sighs. "Dizzy. Need to lie down."

I lower his head onto the oilcloth. "Here, Drew. You need food. You've been roughed up pretty bad, and you need to get your strength up. We have a long march tomorrow." I fumble for the food-bundles in the dark. "See, Rufus and Jeremiah gave you this from their own rations." I break off a bite of hardtack and hold it to Drew's lips. "You need to eat, buddy."

Drew sniffs, then takes a tiny bite. He gags. He rolls away from me and vomits onto the ground.

"No food."

His arms are shaking in my grip as I help him stretch out again. I sit cross-legged beside him and ease his head into my lap.

"Why'm I so s-sore? Where are we? Why's my head hurt? An' my arms and legs? An' my back? An' my mouth?" His pale eyes stare up at me in the dimness of the smelly tent. His words are slurred. Did the bayonet damage his tongue?

"We're in my tent, Drew. Don't you remember today?" I whisper, smoothing his shaggy hair.

"No, I don't. Las' I 'member was..."

Drew clutches my hand. "I can't 'member. I'm afraid." A little sob breaks out of him. He rolls over, burying his face in my lap.

"You're sore because you were bucked again. And George, he...cut you. Don't you remember? He cut you on your back. You lost a fair bit of blood. And he tied a bayonet in your mouth."

Drew shakes his head. "I don't. I don't. I don't 'member. How could I forget? Wha's wrong with me?" His hand squeezes mine till it hurts. "Oh, my head!"

"Here, I think, is what's wrong." I touch his bruised temple. "I think someone struck you here. Men lose their memories sometimes in battle when they're hurt in the head. Do you remember your name?"

"Yes." Releasing my hand, Drew rolls over again, looking up at me. "Drew Conrad."

"And you're from..."

"Penns'vania."

"And you do know me, right? You used my name."

"Yes, Ian. I know you. Ian Campbell. How could I ever forget you? You're...you're my lover."

Even in these circumstances, to hear him say the word makes my heart leap. "Do you remember what we did last night?"

"You...we listened to that boy crying 'cause his brother died, and you hel' me, and I felt sorry for tha' boy, and his brother who died, but being close to you made me feel safe."

"And, a little while back, you promised me what if I helped you escape? It was something very important."

Drew's grin is a white crescent in the darkness. His hand squeezes mine again, more gently. "My, my ass."

We both laugh. "I guess your mind's pretty much all right," I say. "Except we have to march to Purgatory tomorrow."

"I don't think I can, Ian. I don't." Suddenly Drew tries to rise. "Help me. I needa piss. Lemme see if I have the strength to..."

I help Drew up onto his hands and knees. He sways, groans, crawls forward a couple feet, then drops to his elbows. "Oh, no," he says. He vomits again, this time on the oilcloth.

"I'm so sorry," he sobs. "I'm so, so sorry. It's nasty."

"It's all right, boy. It's mostly water. Here." I wipe off his bristly chin, then the soiled oilcloth.

"Piss. Gotta piss," he gasps. "Please help." Trembling, he crawls with my aid out of the tent. "Something loose in my head. A drum in there, and a bell ringing. I'm so dizzy and weak. Please help me up."

It takes us a long time to get him upright. Slowly he rises, with many a wince and a groan. The lower limbs of a nearby pine lend support. I can't help but laugh at the difference in our sizes. "Sometimes I really wish I were the big one and you were the small one," I pant, leaning against him to steady him as his cuffed hands fumble with his trouser buttons.

"Tha's how it feels, halfa time," Drew says, pissing in the needles. "You're big, I'm small." His words are still slurred, as if he'd had too much to drink. "When you hol' me, I'm small and safe." He staggers, throwing his weight against me to keep from falling.

"You surely don't feel small right now," I say. "You feel like an avalanche. Uhhhhfff! Why did I choose a Yankee giant to fall in love with?"

"Don't think there's much choice in it, Reb." Finished, Drew sinks to his knees, cock still hanging from his opened pants. "Okay, okay, done." Stiffly, he crawls back into the tent. I follow him into our fetid little cave.

"Drew, you really need to eat. Tomorrow you've got to walk a long way. Sarge said—"

"Sleepy," he mutters, collapsing onto his side. "No food, or I'll puke. No, no food. Gotta sleep. Tired a' hurting. Thanks for helping me. So tired all a sudden."

By the time I've tied the tent flaps, he's snoring. I sit there in the combined odors of vomit and urine and watch him slumber. I want to wake him and tell him he's got to walk to Purgatory tomorrow or he'll get a bullet in the head. I want to shake him awake and force him to eat. Instead I lie on my side and take his limp cock in my mouth. I suck it gently, nibbling tenderly on the foreskin. I take one ball, then the other, then, with some difficulty, both into my mouth. Then I return to his cock. It smells and tastes like piss, sweat, and stale body musk. It smells and tastes wonderful.

"So sweet," Drew whispers. His hands find the back of my head. His penis grows half-hard. He thrusts into my mouth. "Love you, Ian," he mumbles. "Lil' Reb. So sweet." Then his hands fall away, his cock goes soft, and his snores start up again. I lie there, his limp flesh filling my mouth, and think. Unless I come up with something fast, this will be our last night. If we break camp tomorrow, Drew is doomed. He'll nev-

er make a long march in this shape. If he could be given just one more
day to recover, then...

Somewhere nearby a horse nickers. And then I know what to do.

"You'll be all right here," I say, as if he could hear me, gently slipping
his cock and balls back into his pants and buttoning him up. I head
out to the fire. Rufus is curled beneath a blanket near the dying embers. Here and there, other men sleep soundly beneath ratty oilcloths.
I bend, giving Rufus a shake.

"What?" he mutters. "It ain't time yet for breakfast, damn you." He
rubs his eyes, then smiles sleepily. "Oh, it's you, Ian. What's going on?"

"Shhhh, Rufus! Will you help me with something?" I whisper. "It's really important. But it'll be risky."

"Well...sure. What is it? If it's important, well, sure."

"Wait here. I'll be right back. I need to ask Jeremiah something first."

"Okay. I'll be right here. Don't rush." Rufus nods, lies back, and closes
his eyes. "This fire surely does feel fine."

Overhead, the stars are glittering. I use their light to pick my way
as quietly as possible through camp and out into the woods to find
Jeremiah.

I hear his voice before I see him. "Who's that?" he says. "What's the
password?"

Cut against the night is a lean silhouette. No doubt his pistol is aimed
right at me.

"It's Ian," I say. "Jeremiah, please help me. I really need your help."

—

CHAPTER SIXTY-ONE

—

Yankee guns pop above me, on the crest of the hill. I lean against the stone wall, biting a cartridge open before stuffing it into my musket and tamping it in. An enemy bullet embeds itself in the earth by my bent knee, throwing up a little explosion of shredded leaf mold. Another bullet chunks into a tree trunk behind me. Smoke drifts across my eyes and climbs up my nose. Coughing, I aim and fire. The musket kicks back into my shoulder. Another wave of smoke envelops me. Above, a shell screams and explodes in the forest behind me. On the hill high above, little fires flash and fade, like a field of love-drunk lightning bugs, another rain of balls pocking my stony shelter of a wall. There's an aching in the back of my skull, a black space, a sticky mud puddle, a patch of tar. The blue's rolling down the hill like floodwaters, like an angry sea's advance no one can stop. I look around for help, but none of my company's near. I'm surrounded by the gray of smoke and tree trunks, not my Rebel buddies. I fumble in my cartridge box, but it's empty. Then the smoke thickens, opens its maw, and takes me in. I hack and retch, eyes asquint, stinging and watering. My hands are too weak; the gun drops from my grasp. I fall onto my side; the ground's soft with brittle leaves, hard with broken rock that bites into my ribs. I roll over, groaning. With one hand I reach back to rub the tar from my scalp. Someone grips my shoulder, shouting. Smoke stuffs my mouth, a filthy rag.

"Ian!"

I open my eyes. I'm looking at dead oak leaves and amber pine needles, a rock green-gray with splotches of lichen, and young grass blades glimmering in sunlight. My skull's pounding. I lift my hand into my vision; the fingers are smeared a vague pink. I groan again, curling myself into the frightened ball Drew's made of himself so, so often. Then hands touch me again, rolling me onto my back, wedging something soft beneath my head.

"Wait here now. I'll fetch you water."

I know that voice. Someone I used to play with back home, search the dells for May apples and bluebells and dog's tooth violets down by the river in the spring. Sweet to see naked in the water. Wet pale gleam of his lean hips, wet dark gleam of his dripping belly hair. Friend for years. And, last night, his big gift. The risk he took for my sake, and Drew's.

It's morning. We're still here. We're not yet on the road to Purgatory. I smile, rubbing more blood from my scalp, feeling the hard swelling beneath my rumpled hair. I roll onto my belly, I locate myself here, by the campfire—breathing in its smoke must have awakened me—then look over toward the paddock where our few, slowly starving horses were kept. Yes, they're gone. And by the empty paddock, the cart, listing and useless. One big wheel missing.

"Here now." It's Jeremiah, my savior. He helps me sit upright and lifts a cup to my mouth. Cold water. Good. It feels good in my dry mouth and throat.

"Did we do it?" I whisper, looking around to find no one within earshot. "Is Drew all right?"

"We did it. Everyone believes that last night the camp was almost bushwhacked by some roaming Feds before you and I heroically chased them off. And Drew's fine. He's still sleeping in your tent. Sarge and the others are too busy trying to find the horses to bother him. In fact, you and I are the only ones in camp other than your Yank. Everyone's scouring the woods, even Rufus, who'll hopefully lead 'em away from the spot where we hid the wheel. Sarge is furious, and you should have heard George cussing." Jeremiah gives a low laugh and lifts the cup to my mouth again. "Want some breakfast? Rufus made coffee and fried hardtack before he left."

"Surely," I say, gingerly massaging the lump on my head. "You certainly made this look convincing. It certainly *feels* convincing."

"You told me to hit you hard. So I did. It wasn't easy, bringing a musket butt down on a buddy's head, even at his request...but I think we saved your bluebelly. He's already had breakfast."

"Really? He has an appetite? Last night he threw up everything, including water."

"I think our little delaying tactic has saved his Northern ass, Ian, just like you'd hoped. With any luck, by the time they find the horses and someone heads off to fetch another wheel, Drew will be in good enough shape to make the march. Just be ready to lie to Sarge as good as Rufus and I did."

The hardtack tastes good, softened somewhat by its hot bacon grease bath, though the coffee is another sad substitute made from roasted grains. Jeremiah and I share a cup, making occasional faces of displeasure, before I rise unsteadily, head pounding, and make my way to the tent where Drew waits.

"Boy?" I say, crawling inside. Drew's on the cot, asleep. I bend over him, touching his bruised cheek. His blue eyes open. He smiles. Reaching up, he tugs on my chin-beard, then softly explores the back of my head. I wince and grimace.

"Big damn bump. Jeremiah told me what you three did last night while I was unconscious. He also told me why: that your devil-kin was going to have me shot if I couldn't march. Guess I owe all of you now. Hurts, huh?"

I nod. "Some. Not too bad. Small price to pay. Jeremiah had to make it look like Yanks had knocked me out. Otherwise I'd be first on the list of Sarge's suspects."

With a clanking of shackle-chain, Drew rolls stiffly off the cot and onto his knees. With his cuffed hands and big arms, he makes a circle I slip inside. I wrap my arms around his waist and lean my head against his naked chest. We hold one another for a long time before he swallows hard and whispers, "I'll make it now. Thanks to you."

"Are you sure? How do you feel?" I look up at him. His eyes, still swollen and blackened from past abuses, are tired but clear. "You were so confused before, but now you seem yourself again."

"My head's better. My arms and legs ache from that long bucking…as usual. My back and mouth are torn up." The corners of his weary smile, I can see, are still oozing blood. "I'm pretty weak. But the food and the sleep helped. If we march tomorrow, I'll be ready."

Carefully I hug him closer, so as to avoid paining his bandaged back. "I'd better get back to the campfire. The more injured I appear, with any luck the less rush there will be to leave. I'm sure Sarge will be back at some point to ask me about last night, and he might be suspicious if he finds us together again."

"Ian? One thing before you go. I remember what I forgot. I remember what George did to me before he knocked me out. He did things that…" Drew falls silent, looks away, and squeezes his eyes shut.

"What did he do? You mean besides what I already know? The bucking, the cutting, the bayonet gag? What the hell else did he do to you?"

"Not now, Ian. Tonight? Will you stay with me tonight? Will you be able to? I'll tell you then."

"I will, by God, whether it makes Sarge suspicious or not. But tell me now. Did he...did he...?"

I can't bring myself to say it. Instead, I touch the curved rear of Drew's trousers, staring up at him, suddenly terrified of the answer. I can feel his hard buttocks beneath the garment, those pale mounds dusted with golden hair, that beautiful place I've stroked, licked, tasted, and rested my cheek against. "Oh, God, no, Drew. Did he...did he..."

Jeremiah's voice is at the tent entrance. "Boys are coming back, Ian. Better get on out here."

"No, he didn't," Drew mutters low. "That gift's still waiting for you. But he... I'll tell you tonight. Get out there and look like the wounded war hero you are." Drew pats the back of my trousers with a crooked smile, then takes a handful of fabric. "Skinny-assed Reb. Ain't nothing to grab back there. What you need's a few months of regular biscuit breakfasts."

"When I get you home," I say, "I'll bake you biscuits myself. With all the honey you want. No more goddamn hardtack for us!"

Leaving Drew in our tent, I take my invalid's place by the fire. Jeremiah, with a guilty crease to his brow, covers me with a blanket. A few campmates return from the woods, shaking their heads and muttering about damn Yankees. None is leading a horse. Rufus reappears, giving Jeremiah and me a quick grin before starting on lunch preparations. "Couldn't find horse nor wheel. Too bad," Rufus says with a deep sigh for the rest of the camp and a wink for Jeremiah and me. "But I did find these. More wild onions to go with the last of these beans I been soaking to cook." Rufus stirs up the fire noisily, humming to himself. "Now you just stretch out there and stay put. I'll carry some victuals to your Yank, don't you fret."

The afternoon following our soup-bean lunch I for the most part lose. My head wound's a good excuse to do something my life as a soldier has rarely allowed save during the long, dull days of winter quarters: I curl up under the blanket and I nap, I nap, I nap. I'm deep inside the luxury of a cozy doze when a hand's weight falls across my brow. I open my eyes to find Sarge squatting by my side. Even as badly as he and George have treated Drew, there's a quick pang inside of me for deceiving him this way. Lying is not honorable, it does not agree with a man's duty to country and kin, Sarge would tell me if he knew my heart today. And much of me would agree with him. I guess I'm learning love and honor can't always coexist.

I muster a smile. "Sir, what time is it?"

"Near evening, nephew. All of us just got back."

"And did you find the horses?"

Sarge nods. His fingers probe my head and find my wound. His touch is almost gentle, but I grimace nonetheless. "Yes, Ian, it took all day, but we found them. The gunfire last night scattered them far and wide. The cartwheel is still missing. I've sent George on to Buchanan on his retrieved mount to see if a wheel can be commandeered. How do you feel?"

"Really weak, sir. That Yank tried to stave my head in."

Sarge sighs, settling into a camp chair by my side. He opens his flask, takes a long sip, shares it with me, then sits back and sighs again. "This delay is very poorly timed. We have got to get to Petersburg." He rubs his brow. "The city's still under siege, and I fear it will fall before we get there. Not that a company as severely curtailed in strength as ours will be much help, but, still, we should be there. The thought of our men behind those lines, in those trenches for months... God help us all."

Abruptly he rises. "I know so many of them. I pray for them every night. I pray for General Lee and for that beautiful town. I pray for our nation. And I pray for you, nephew." He smoothes his gray moustache, gives me a faint smile, and looks into the fire. "I want to hear from you what happened last night. But not now. I'm weary to the bone. I'm just glad that you're not seriously hurt." He turns away, then turns back. Running his hands through his hair, he says, "I assume the prisoner is secured?"

"Yes, sir, he's cuffed and shackled still, in my tent. Last Rufus checked on him—I haven't had the strength—he's unconscious."

"No matter," Sarge says. "He's of no consequence. If anyone asks for me, I'll be in my tent. With any luck, George will find a wheel, or a new cart. He's always been good at requisitioning...both the living and the dead."

I lie back, staring up at a purple sky gone wavy with gusts of smoke coursing off the fire. I think about Petersburg, smoke rolling off its damaged homes and church steeples, boys like me sprawled bleeding behind the earthworks or thrown high in the explosion that created the Crater, women in the town hiding in basements, listening to the sounds of artillery day and night for months, while I lie here, warm beneath this musty blanket, head throbbing, thanks to my own careful plotting, and, mere yards away, the man I love—safe for now, thanks to my scheming—sleeping half-naked and entirely beautiful in his rusty bonds. I would sacrifice the South for him. I would sacrifice the world.

—

CHAPTER SIXTY-TWO

—

I stay by the fire till I'm sure Sarge has retired. George, luckily, is still nowhere in evidence. Probably off stealing a cart from a local while relishing the permissive vicissitudes of war. When most of the boys have retired to their blankets and the others are playing cards by the ebbing fire, I rise, muttering, "I need to piss," to no one in particular, then, after relieving myself in the woods, make my wobbly way back to Drew.

"Boy? You awake?"

"Yes, sir. I been waiting for you, Reb." Drew's just a voice in the dark, then a big dark heap beneath a blanket, and then fuzzy chest-flesh and hard arm-bulge beneath my searching fingers. "Let me hold on you, hero," he says. I acquiesce, snuggling myself into the nest his arms make, letting him spoon me from behind.

"Your poor head," Drew says, kissing my scalp. "I can't believe you took a musket-butt to buy me time."

"I'd do a hell of a lot more than that," I say, thinking again of Petersburg, and of how many years I've fought in this war. "When we get to Purgatory, I've got a promising future to insure. I've got Southern biscuits and Yankee butt to look forward to."

"Yeah, yeah, all this talk of my butt..." Drew sighs.

"Better than talking about the bloody battlefields we've both seen, right?" Drew's body is here, between me and Antietam, the Wilderness, Gettysburg, the sights I can't forget, comrades scattered in the ditches, pastures full of corpses, the screams of the wounded caught in a forest fire. His furry, famine-lean form is the only certainty I can grasp. "I save your ass, I own your ass," I say, just to hear Drew laugh.

"Yes, you do." Drew obliges me with a nervous chuckle. "I promised. Though now..." He shifts uncomfortably.

"What? What's wrong? Did George do something that has made you feel different about the way I...the way I want to love you?" I turn in his arms to face him. "Tell me. You've put me off too long."

"Wait, Ian. First things first. First, I want to say...I do realize what you'll be giving up for me if you help me escape as you've promised. I do. I know how much this war means to you. I guess I have some sense, having fought you Rebs, well, I guess I have some sense of how much you've given up, how long you've fought and how fiercely, how much you've lost...like the Valley I helped torch, God forgive me. And I want you to know how much it means to me that you're willing to try to get me free, even if it means..."

"Leaving the war. Yes. Desertion. Leaving my friends and kin."

Neither of us speaks for a while. Drew pulls me closer.

"I can do it. I will. I don't know whether I'll be a better man or a worse for doing it," I say. "I don't know what's happened to my honor. It'll feel like betraying my homeland. But I love you. I can't change that. If we stay in camp, soon you'll die. And I'll do anything to save you."

Another long silence. We shift around into our customary position, with Drew's back nestled against my chest. I run my fingers through his hair, then I squeeze his firm rump and say, "Back to your beautiful butt. Tell me about George, dammit. I need to know what he did to you."

"Yes," Drew says. "All right. But...it's shameful."

"Drew, buddy, tell me. Why be ashamed? You were certainly in no position to—"

"But I did fight him. I did! Didn't you see his eye?"

"The black eye? I wondered about that. What happened?"

"Right after you left to prepare for that poor boy's funeral, George showed up here. He smelled like liquor. I was alone, cuffed and shackled as usual. He had two of your camp mates with him. They dragged me out of the tent into the woods and tried to buck me."

"Oh hell," I snarl, gritting my teeth. "Why didn't you call for me?"

"I, I was too proud, I guess. I'm tired of being a helpless maiden always needing to be rescued by my little Rebel. So I gave them some fight. That's when I caught George in the eye with my fist. Damn, that felt good, after all the grief he's given me. But then one of his buddies punched me here"—Drew takes my hand and lifts it to his puffy right cheek—"and then George, he pulled a knife and held it to my throat, so I had no choice but to settle down. That's when they bucked me and tied that bayonet in my mouth. When the other two left, that's when George..."

Drew stops. When he begins again, his voice is shaky. "He unbuttoned my trousers and pulled my cock and balls out, Ian. He tugged on them hard. I begged him to stop. Then he played with them with the edge of the knife, nudging them around. He...he told me that, for a Yankee coward, I had a pretty big...set. He told me he'd cut them off the next time he got hold of me. He pinched my nipples so hard I bit down on the blade of that bayonet till I was drooling blood just to keep from screaming. He told me the next time he had me alone, he was going to poke me like a woman. He even...he shoved his hand down inside the back of my pants and fingered me...my hole. Told me after he was done using me, he'd find another bayonet that would...fit me down there...would fit up inside me."

A low sob breaks loose. "Then he took his knife to my back, and it was all I could do not to cry, but I knew my tears would give him more satisfaction, so I just bit down on that blade and kept quiet as long as I could. When I decided I couldn't take any more and I started shouting for you, that's when he hit me in the head."

"Oh, Drew, I should have been there. Oh God. I'm so sorry." I hug him closer, close to sobbing myself. "I let you down."

Drew clears his throat. "It's not your fault, Ian. He hates me because he wants me, I think. He hates himself for wanting me. I think he wants me like you want me, like I want you."

"Drew, you know that...that I would never hurt you...here." I stroke the curve of his behind through the threadbare trousers. "That's why I'm waiting. Till you're ready. And till we're somewhere safe. I would never, ever hurt you. Please don't let George... don't be afraid of how I feel for you, of how I want you. God, yes, I want to lie with you, I want to...take you so badly, but never, never against your will."

"I know that, Ian. I do. I have to admit I'm a little afraid, more than before, but...all jokes aside, you pretty much do own me, after all you've done for me and plan to do for me"—his hand takes mine, placing it on the iron collar locked around his neck—"so, if the time comes that we're safe and away from all this, then...I'll keep my promise."

"I wouldn't hurt you here either," I say, taking one of Drew's nipples between thumb and forefinger. "God, I love your chest. I love the strength of it, the thick hair. I cherish your sweet little nipple-buds."

Drew laughs softly. "Well, you've gotten a little rough there—as I recall, you gave 'em a good chawing before you sucked my prick—but somehow rough felt good. I know you won't ever hurt me. Your touch has given me nothing but wonder, Ian, and delight."

"God, we sound like folks out of the Song of Songs," I snicker, running my fingers over his belly, probing his navel. "And I can never have enough of you, Yank. You're like a feast to me."

"Wine and bread?"

"Yes. Or, better, buckwheat flapjacks and maple syrup." I smack my lips.

"Ummmmm," Drew murmurs, sounding both sleepy and hungry.

"Your body reminds me of a Roman god's I saw once in a book of myths. It's as if you've fallen to earth, as if I'm touching a god," I whisper. "Or Christ's body. I've told you this before. When I see you tied and suffering, I see Christ. You're like religion to me. Your face and muscles and fur...you're my cathedral, my church."

"Mmmmm. Southerners and their sweet talk..."

So drowsy, that mutter, pulling me from my romantic reverie into wartime practicality. "As much as I'd like to taste you all over again," I say, gently squeezing the mossy swell of Drew's breast and nuzzling his neck through its veil of thick hair, "it's time you got your sleep, buddy. We're likely to leave for Purgatory tomorrow, if that vermin George returns with a new wheel or cart, and, knowing his capacity for intimidation and thievery, he'll be doing just that."

"Yes, sir..." Drew cuddles closer and soon is fast asleep. I lie there, holding him, seeing artillery explode over Petersburg, a battlefield where my company and I are badly needed. I imagine cutting George's throat, throwing his body into a creek as I did that poor Yank I stabbed to death just days ago. I remember the maps in Sarge's tent, and the path to freedom I've planned: into the mountains, up a long creek, down a big river, and on home.

—

CHAPTER SIXTY-THREE
—

It's mid-morning when George returns. We've had reveille and another sparse breakfast, this time of leftover beans. Sarge has been pacing in front of the campfire, drinking acorn coffee, checking his pocket watch, and muttering to himself, obviously eager to get on the road. I've managed to sneak some food to Drew and am leaning against a tree trunk cleaning my pistol when there's a clattering sound in the woods, a few scattered shouts, and then George appears, grinning triumphantly, driving into camp a new cart drawn by two sway-backed mangy mule mares. His own horse follows, tethered to the back.

Reining the mules to a halt, George swings down. Sarge steps forward with a smile. The two men shake hands. "Found 'em in a pretty little place right outside Buchanan, foot of Purgatory Mountain. The farmer gave me some trouble, Sarge, but I was able to persuade him that his country needed this mule-cart more than—"

George's proud explanation is cut short, for he makes the mistake of patting the left mule's gray rump. She bucks and kicks, narrowly missing George. The hoof catches Sarge's coffee cup, knocking it out of his hand. For the next few minutes, the air's tinged blue with a long string of vulgarities as George attempts to discipline the mule and the mule attempts to kick the traces. The other mule joins the fray, biting and braying, until Sarge takes a stick to the animals' ears. A few quick, sharp blows, and the beasts subside.

"My God, they're high strung," George grumbles, as the left mule tucks back her ears, lifts her head into a ear-splitting bray, and musters a final half-hearted kick at Sarge before falling to on a clump of new grass.

"Always are," Sarge chuckles, retrieving his dented tin cup. "God's thunder would be hard pressed to compete with a voice so tremendous. I myself have descended to profane language only a handful of times, and each time was inspired by the recalcitrance of mules. Ian, fetch Jeremiah and you two help George empty the old cart and load up this one. We leave by noon."

We're halfway through our task when Left Mule lifts her head from peaceable grazing long enough to take a bite of George's ass. George yelps, drops the box of hardtack, and swats the mule's flank. She snorts and returns to her green breakfast.

We can't resist. "George, buddy!" I say, slapping him on the back. "Looks like you finally found yourself a girlfriend. She thinks you're some sweet eating!"

"Damnation, Ian," Jeremiah joins in. "That critter don't know how close it came to poison fodder. One bite of that haunch, and it'd be four stiff legs in the air for sure!"

Jeremiah and I laugh so hard that George, red-faced, stalks off with a snarl. "You boys should know better by now than to laugh at me. Finish the job by yourselves, you bastards." He's off, rubbing his butt, in the direction of Sarge's tent.

By noon, as Sarge has insisted, everything's loaded up, the last tent struck and folded, the fire doused. Drew sits in his ever-present cuffs and shackles at the base of a little maple, leaning back against it, the customary rag knotted between his teeth for the march to come, another tether-rope hanging from his wrists ready to be attached to the cart. I'm checking the contents of my haversack. The men are lined up, ready to depart.

"Fortuitous, this delay, as far as the prisoner's concerned." Sarge's voice at my back. His hand on my shoulder: the weight of family, the gravity of blood and homeland. "He looks like he might make the march."

I turn, dislodging his hand, sensing accusation in his tone. Before I can reply, Sarge says, "Prior to our departure, I want you to help George with something."

My mouth twists. I want to spit. Instead, I wipe my lips with the back of my hand.

"Off with you. It won't take long." Sarge nudges me forward. There's George, smiling his rat-toothy smile, standing at the wood's edge. "We need us a log," he says, licking his thin lips.

Our sullen-silent search doesn't take long, though I don't know why we're hunting firewood here when we could gather it at tonight's camp at the base of Purgatory Mountain. Within minutes, George has found a moderately heavy fallen branch about six feet long. "This one," he says, with inexplicable glee. He takes one end; I take the other; together we carry it back to where Sarge waits. I make to heave it onto the cart, but George abruptly drops his end, crosses his arms, and stands beside Sarge, face flushed.

Confused, I'm about to ask what's going on when Sarge whips out another of his curt orders. "Nephew, fetch the prisoner."

Something's happening, something I don't understand. I help Drew to his feet, take his elbow, and lead his shackled shuffle across the little clearing to stand before my uncle.

"Ian, George just told me something interesting. He said that the farmer from whom he borrowed the mule-cart lost a barn to the Yanks' torches last fall. The farmer described the leader as tall and blond. As he put it, a 'Yankee Goliath.' George thinks it might have been your Yank here."

"Absolutely not!" I blurt out before I can think.

"Oh? How would you know what that boy was doing before we captured him?"

"I don't." I square my shoulders and take a step back. "It just seems to me, in the time I've observed the prisoner, that he wouldn't be the sort to, to..." The memory of Drew's confession, the way he helped Sheridan do what he did last autumn, claws at me, filling my throat like acrid smoke. Is George right?

George is quick to take advantage of my momentary befuddlement. "Well, Yank, what do you say?"

We all look up at Drew. If it's true, and if he feels so guilty that he confesses, this tattered company of Rebel boys will tear him apart before we ever get to Purgatory.

Drew stares into my eyes. "Huh uh." He bites down on the rag, teeth flashing in the gray light. He shakes his head vehemently. "Huh uh. Huh uh."

"Let me take the rag out," I say. "Let him defend himself."

"How about a vote?" George says. "How many of you boys think this Yank's guilty as hell?"

The entire company is standing about us now, listening, scratching their heads. George raises his hand, glaring about at what's left of our once-fine, once-handsome, once-confident band. One by one, the hands go up. Only Jeremiah, Rufus, and I are holdouts.

"Shit, boys, this Yank ain't bad atall," Rufus mutters. "In fact, I like him a damned sight better than some of you." He spits in George's direction, turns on his heel, and heads off to secure the pile of cookware atop the cart.

"He bandaged me up. I'm his enemy and he bandaged me up," Jeremiah says quietly. "I ain't going to assume something bad about the man just because *George* says that a farmer I *never met*—"

"Vote taken, Sarge," George interrupts.

"Yes, indeed." Sarge clears his throat. "George has suggested for this crime further torment. Strap him to the stick."

I step forward. "Haven't we done enough to make this boy suffer? Haven't we—"

"Enough, or he can stay here. You understand me? Beneath the sod." Sarge's right eyebrow cocks, the angle of a buzzard frozen in mid-flight.

I step back. Drew's eyes meet mine, then he bows his head.

"On your knees, Yank. You, Ian, unlock his manacles. You, Jeremiah, help George bind him," says Sarge. "If we keep up our pace, we should make Purgatory by dusk."

Sharp click of keys in shackles. Gently I pull the iron off Drew's wrists and ankles, then unknot the rope-tether. He drops to his knees, massages his chafed flesh, then nods me off, as if to say, "Move on now. I can handle this."

From the cart seat I look back. George and Jeremiah hoist the thick branch onto Drew's shoulders and then rope his wrists and arms to it. "Git on up, Yank," George growls.

Drew's brow furrows. He grunts, tries to rise, sags beneath the wood's weight, then, heaving himself to his feet, straightens up, white teeth gnashing the rag and grim determination stiffening his features. George shoves Drew forward and ties his slave collar to the cart, the bugle cheerily lines out the "Forward" call, I snap the mules' flanks with a whip I find on the cart seat, and we're on the move, the last leg of our long journey to Purgatory.

—

CHAPTER SIXTY-FOUR

—

Purgatory Mountain looms to the southwest, a slate-gray cairn growing slowly closer, its horizon-edges bristling with bare-black trees,
its top swathed in mist. By the time our lengthy march ends, Drew's
staggering like a drunk, bowed beneath his burden, my Yankee Christ
lurching along the way to Calvary, barely able to stay on his feet.

The sun's setting behind a heap of cloud, orange and green edging
ominous slate-grey, as we make camp at the mouth of a dell, here at the
base of Purgatory's southern slopes, where a noisy little creek drops
down over rocks to meet the river. Above us are the mountain's rocky
steeps, spotted with high stands of pine and lingering snow, and a soli-
tary buzzard riding the winds. To our east are the broad Valley and the
distant rooftops and spires marking the little town of Buchanan. To
our west are the Allegheny Mountains, like gray waves frozen in air.
And beside us is the James, a narrow stream this far inland, before it
widens and drifts down into the rich Tidewater of Virginia. We're at a
lower altitude than we've been for weeks. Here, the land seems to be
on the verge of budding. The forest's hue is gray, certainly, the same
cadaverous gray we've been slogging through for months, but here and
there are hints of green, along the limbs and unfurling from the drab
ground.

There's a blankness to Drew's eyes, a hollowness to his face, I haven't
seen before. When I untie him from the cart, he drops to his knees. I
help him lie back onto the ground—between his size and the weight
of the branch he's bound to, it takes all my strength—in a dry, satin-
sheened pile of dead oak leaves the wind has heaped here.

I unknot the sodden rag between his teeth and pull it out. "We're
there then?" Drew gasps. "The mountain? Purgatory?"

"Yes, buddy. The day's done. You rest now."

He's out like an air-starved candle. Rufus and I unload the cart, dis-
persing the supplies. Done, Rufus heads off to start up the cook-fires,
while I unpack my tent where the woodland begins. I'll pitch it here,
near this little sarvis tree. My Daddy used to say that you know spring's

near when a sarvis blooms, for it's the only kind of tree blossoming this early. This one is still leafless but in full flower, its slender gray trunk rising into a delicate cloud of white. I pull a branch down, push my face into the snow-flurry petals, and take a deep breath. The perfume's faint but feminine. As much as I love men, I've spent too many months exclusively around them. The scent of these flowers makes me miss my mother and yearn for the past, an era with less harsh edges.

"He made it, I see." The voice is like a file, a rusty spike, a needle shoved under my skin.

I turn, guy-rope in hand, to find Sarge standing over Drew. He lifts a boot, resting it on Drew's cheek. He scrapes his sole along Drew's face. A groan, a smear of mud. Inside my head, inside that sphere of twisted gray, there's a sprig, a spark of green. It will not be trampled. It will not be snuffed out.

"Strong boy, this Yankee pig. I didn't think he'd make it up the pike."

"He's weak and shaky, sir, from hunger and hard use, but he's stubborn. I suspect he can keep up for many days yet." I turn back to my task, unfolding mold-streaked tent canvas. I can no longer bear to look at Sarge. Every kindness he has ever shown me his cruelty to Drew has canceled out. If I were a hard or vicious man, the man he's always pushed me to be, I would blot him from the world.

"I'm weary of him, Ian. We can't spare the food, as fine as it would be to keep him around for the men's amusement and my practice with the bullwhip. He stays here. You understand? After seeing what the Yanks did to the Institute, I can't stand the sight of him. If it's true what George heard, that he led Yanks who burned the Valley, it's high time the man was ended."

I drop the canvas and turn. Sarge is standing very near me. His hand drops onto my shoulder, like a hammer comes down on a nail. "When we leave for Lynchburg—it should be within a few days—he stays here. Here, here"—Sarge stamps the ground beneath the sarvis—"bury him here. Or," Sarge says, squeezing my shoulder, "if the effort of grave-digging is unwelcome—why waste time and effort on such a man?—roll him into the river. I would suppose that the creatures of the James are as famished as we."

If I needed any further fuel for my resolve, Sarge has just unwittingly given it to me. I nod, avoiding his eyes. My years of obedience are nearly done.

"Remember, now that we're here, no more tent-time for him. Tonight, gag him good and tight with rag and rope and cuff his hands behind that sarvis tree. And don't forget his foot-shackles. Tomorrow, buck or hogtie him in the middle of camp. The boys could do with more distraction; they enjoyed working him over the other day."

Rope, cuff, hogtie, gag. As much as I love to see my sweet Yank restrained, I'm so sick of Sarge's repetitive orders, his continual cruelties, his unending threats. It takes all my strength to lift my gaze and meet his. Surely he can read in my face the fear and hatred I'm feeling? The plans for escape I've been making? But no. His gray eyes are as confident as usual; his gray moustache tops another crooked smile. From his pocket he pulls out a flask. He takes a swig and passes it to me. I take a swig and pass it back.

"I know the Yank's been a good bit of trouble, Ian, but you'll be free of him soon enough. Nelson's company should be here in about two days. When they arrive, we'll march into Lynchburg together, then, with any luck, on to Petersburg to harry us some Yankees. Rid us of this pig before then. Nelson's soft on prisoners. He might object to how we've been keeping this boy. As far as he needs to know, the Yankee tried to escape and had to be shot. When our scouts inform us of Nelson's approach, take that as my order to lead him into the woods and end him."

Sarge doesn't wait for my usual show of acquiescence. He turns and strides off, giving Drew a kick in the ribs on his way. Drew gasps and shudders in his nest of leaves, gazing up at me, his eyebrows pain-knit. Another few seconds, and he's passed out yet again.

Night's falling. The breeze that's patted our cheeks all day picks up, scented with distant rain. A few petals shiver off the sarvis and drift to the earth in a long, slow slant. The grass beneath the tree is green. I pitch my tent between the little sarvis and the wind. If Drew must spend the night bound outside, the least I can do is shelter him from what elements I can. Tomorrow night or the next, we'll either be dead or as far from here as luck and our weary legs will carry us.

Campfire smoke, scents of bean soup. Drew's unconscious, and so he remains while I free him from the unwieldy log, while I unwrap his bloodstained feet, then wash, salve, and bandage them. I do the same to his broad back, rubbing ointment over the scabbed furrows and swellings. Still no sign of festering, thank God. These scars, I know, he'll bear the rest of his life. Long years yet, if I have my way, long years together, night after night sleeping side by side, my fingers stroking his scars' tracery, remembering in heaven the hell in which we met.

If I have my way. If. Enough dreaming. Done with the bandaging, I cuff his hands before him, shackle his ankles, and cover him with the same damned damp wool blanket that's been warming him since he was captured. Leaving him curled in the leaves, I head out. Time to begin implementing my plans for achieving that distant heaven.

Everyone's by the fire now, ravenous after the long day, and so I take advantage of their bellies' focus and the dense dark to visit the supply tents. No extra pistols, muskets, or knives—our supplies have never been sparser. How we'll win this war I don't know—everything necessary running lower and lower, heaped higher the losses and the lacks, our efforts shaved thinner and thinner, like soft wood on a lathe—but I guess now I don't care how or if the South wins. I have a war of my own to fight and a poke to fill. Here, cornmeal and hardtack. Here, bacon. Here, ammunition for my pistol. Here, cartridges. Here, Minié balls for my rifle, to supplement Mrs. Trent's collection still hidden in my haversack. This is duty of a deeper sort.

—

CHAPTER SIXTY-FIVE

"I hear the Yank's liable to stay here. Going to feed the roots of Purgatory's trees?"

George stinks. Drew's sweat is intoxicating, George's nauseating. Perhaps the smell's telltale; perhaps evil's a chemical compound scientists could isolate. Plus the smell of tobacco is always there; he leaves a wake of it the way a slug does slime.

"You're rank. Get away from me," I snarl, dipping bean soup into a cup.

"Dinner for your prisoner, I'm guessing? Yep, give him a few fine last suppers. Nelson's due here soon, I hear tell. If you aren't man enough to blow that boy's brains out, I'd be glad to lend a prayer and a hand. Or a shovel."

I straighten up, toasting him with the steaming cup. "You're such a fucking cur. I'd throw this in your face, but it'd be a damned waste of good beans. How about instead I break your jaw? I didn't quite finish the job before. Any rearrangement of your face is bound to be an improvement." How did I get so strong and confident? What a cowering pup I used to be. Sarge would be proud, if the context for my courage were different.

George's jagged smile vanishes beneath a sour pursing of lips. "Don't try anything tonight, Ian. As sweet on the Yank as you've been, I wouldn't put it past you to plan some last-ditch foolishness to spare him. I'll be watching you. Sarge has given me leave to pitch my tent near yours."

George pours a full cup of coffee. The smile's back. "This is good and strong. I won't be sleeping much tonight." With a wink, he strolls off.

"And neither will I," I mutter. Coffee in one hand, soup in the other, I return to my campsite. Clouds have covered the stars. Thunder rumbles in the west. Drew eats greedily, cross-legged in the leaves. When he begs for more, I fetch him another cup of soup. Before I leave the fire, Rufus has sneaked me a crumbly biscuit with a smear of lard and

Jeremiah has pressed his flask into my hand. Seems like everyone's heard Drew's doom is near.

Other than a few sips, I leave the whiskey to Drew. I figure it might dull the many ways his body must be hurting. And so my bandaged boy's belly-full and very drunk by the time I help him to his feet. I uncuff him. I take his swollen hands in mine, massaging the ragged flesh that days of constant restraint have left about his wrists, rubbing blood and warmth back into him. I lead him to the latrine-trench, then to the sarvis. He staggers through the dark, shackles clanking. Heavily he sits at the base of the tree, leaning forward and with some difficulty clasping his hands behind the trunk. When I lock the metal around his wrists, he groans. The muscles of his shoulders and arms bunch with the strain. He leans back against the trunk and sighs.

"You got to gag me now, I guess. Uncle's orders, right?" Drew looks up at me, mustering a drunken grin. So calm, helpless, and handsome, his pale face in the darkness like a wild magnolia blossom.

"Yep," I say. "He ordered rag and rope this time." I don't need to add, after all our frank talks, that I relish how Drew looks—downright he-roic-glorious, like a conquered warrior—when he's half-naked, with his hands bound behind his back and a length of rope knotted between his teeth.

"Yeah, I know. You like me like this." He's reading my mind again, the clever shit. "And, uncomfortable as I am, I'm glad to give you pleasure. But, Ian?" The grin fades. He licks his lips, grimaces, and shifts against the tree, trying to get more comfortable. "Can we talk first?"

The pleading in his voice floods me with aching, an aching I can fi-nally name. "Sure, buddy. For a while. Yes, we do need to talk." My throat tightens; my temples throb. What's inside me is like the sarvis my boy's bound to: something deep-rooted, nourished by black earth, rising into something high and light, hundreds of buds bursting into white petals inside my skull.

"I didn't torch that man's house. I never led men. I never got this far up the Valley, I swear. That bastard George was lying. And what I did last fall, under Sheridan...I never led! I just did what I was told. Do you believe me? Please believe me."

I cup his cheek in my hand and nod. "Yes, I believe you. Jeremiah and I laughed at George this morning when the mule bit him. It was just his way of hurting me: to hurt you more. As usual."

Drew sighs. "Thank you. It means so much that you believe me. But, Ian? I heard some of what your uncle said when he was here before, when I was half-out on the ground. Am I gonna die tomorrow?"

I drop to my knees beside him. There's wet on my cheeks suddenly. Tears, yes, but also rain. A thin rain has come to Purgatory, sweeping out of the western hills where home and kin wait for my return.

"Am I, Ian? Your uncle said when Nelson came...he said... Shit, are you gonna shoot me in the woods?" Drew's voice slurs and cracks. "Are you...are you gonna bury me here, beneath this little tree?"

I look around, checking for witnesses. There's George's tent, only a few yards on the other side of the tree, but the tent-flap seems to be closed, and there's no candle glow. The bastard's probably back by the fire, talking nasty with his cronies. As dark as it is, no one's likely to see us. And so I stroke Drew's bushy cheek in the slow rainfall.

"If you die, I die, Drew. Let the bastards bury us together. Listen, I've been stealing some supplies, and I'm going to steal some more. I'm almost ready to get us out of here, if I can only find a way, an opening. And I've studied Sarge's maps. If I can help you escape, will you come home with me? I think I know how to get back home. Will you come with me? Will you let me hide you till the war's over?"

"You would do that?" My lips are brushing Drew's as he speaks; his whiskey-sweet breath spills over my face.

"Yes, buddy. I love you. I want to take you home. You're dressed in gray now; local folks who might see us passing through will think you're a Rebel too. They won't hinder us; they might even help us. Or, if you aren't willing to do that, we could—if we could find some of your Federals, I guess I could surrender to them, and—"

"No. Then you'd be a prisoner, and they'd send you off to a camp up north. I hear those prison camps are terrible! I don't want us separated. I don't, I don't." Drew's words are a blur of intoxication and exhaustion. His lips nibble my chin, then my cheeks. "Ian, I don't want to die. Please save me if you can. Lead me away from here. Take me home. Your home, my home, it don't matter. Just somewhere safe. I'm tired of being starved, beaten, tied, spit and pissed on. I'm tired of being terrified. I'll gladly go where you lead. I'll gladly do what you say. Just tell me what to do. Just tell me what to do."

In answer, I press my mouth against his. The kiss lasts for a long time, postponing further speech. He sobs a little against me; our tongues wrestle gently. Within the rain-moist meadow of Drew's body-pelt, my fingers find his nipples, his navel, the prominent parallels of his ribs. Then I lift my lips from his and rest my hands on his shoulders. Bound as he is, they're taut with tension beneath my touch. His big frame is trembling. His skin's filmed with cold drizzle. "Drew, just endure. All right? Take whatever comes tomorrow—whatever pain, whatever abuse. Close your eyes, bite down on your gag, and take it. I can't promise you much, other than this: soon we'll either be leaving together or dying together. I'm going to do my damnedest to make sure it's the former."

"Just in case, will you write a letter to my family for me? Tomorrow? Please, Ian?" Drew leans against me. "Just in case, I need to say good-bye."

"You bet, buddy. You speak it, I'll write it."

Drew's acquiescent as usual as I stuff his mouth with the rag and thread rough rope between his lips and around and around his head.

"Not hurting you?" I say, finishing up with a knot in the back.

Drew shakes his head. His long-uncut hair is shoulder-length now. Heavy with rain, it falls over his face like a pale veil.

"I'm leaving my tent flaps open, buddy. I'll be watching out for you."

"Huhhh," Drew grunts. Digging cloth-wrapped feet into the dirt, he pushes himself back against the tree to take some of the pressure off his cuffed wrists.

"You're so beautiful," I say, running my palm over one gag-distended cheek. "God gave us to one another for a reason. Do you believe me?"

"Uhhh huh." Drew nods emphatically, then bows his head. The rain descends in hard drops. Taking a handful of his hair, gently I pull his head back and kiss his brow. "I love you," I say. Drew groans and nods. His head drops from my grasp, lolling drunkenly. I leave him there cuffed to the sarvis, rain pounding over his naked skin. Stretching out on the dry floor of my tent, I keep watch, sipping coffee and fighting sleep for a long while. He's a pale silhouette, motionless now, sagging in his bonds, the gleam of his face hidden behind his hair. I'm sleepy already, already half-submerged in dream, it appears, for the slant of black rain seems to be shifting into specks the palest of gray, drifting around him like late snow, crystals that fleck his hair and arms, refusing to melt. Like me, I guess: too damn ornery to let go.

—

CHAPTER SIXTY-SIX

I wake with a start. Rolling over, I grab my Bowie knife. My glasses have slipped off, so everything's a blur. I grope about, find them, push them on, and peer out into the night.

No one's there. No one's hurting Drew. He's asleep, looks like, head still hanging forward, face still concealed behind a curtain of hair. His legs are bent, spread as wide as the shackle-chain permits, his heels dug into dirt. His lower back's pushed up against the sarvis trunk, his torso bent forward, his arms angled uncomfortably, unnaturally, behind the tree.

Coffee's woken me up, sloshing in my head and in my bladder. I crawl out, get to my feet, step off a ways, and piss. Sky's cloudy still—no stars—but at least the rain has ceased. Finished, I peer at my pocket watch. Two a.m. I check George's nearby tent: empty. I walk softly toward the campfire—through the tents, past the hunched forms of company-mates snoring on the ground beneath their blankets. There's George, who, despite all his previous threats, his promise to keep an eye on me, has passed out before the fire like the drunken swine he is. I can see the drool from here, dangling off his lip.

With George insensible, tonight could be the time to get Drew out of here. But there goes one of George's buddies, on sentry duty, giving me a suspicious eye before passing by. And Drew's as dead-drunk as George, in no condition to flee with me. Besides, I have more thieving to do. I wait till the sentry's well past before taking another empty poke to a supply tent; I return to my tent hefting more pilfered food and ammunition, hiding the second poke beside the first, beneath an oilcloth.

I'm about to climb back beneath my blanket when I hear Drew's moans and mumbles. Moving fast, I'm by his side. He's shaking and jerking; I squeeze his shoulder and pat his face. He wakes, eyes rolling and wild.

"Only a nightmare, buddy," I whisper, hunkering down beside him. He pants against his gag, then grunts and nods. I press my palm to his chest—deep breathing, heart pounding. And here's that dream-snow again, drifting between us, dusting his shoulders and unruly hair. I catch a falling flake on my palm and finally understand. It's one of the white petals of the blooming sarvisberry tree he's tied to. The night breeze is casting petals about my boy like a benevolent ruler might cast a beggar alms.

Or like a gravedigger might cast earth-clods upon a corpse. I suppose it's tomorrow's uncertainty that makes me take this risk. *Touch while you can,* that seems to be the message of this night beneath the sarvisberry, by the James, at the base of Purgatory Mountain. I look and listen carefully, then, reassured that we're alone in the dark, I drop to my knees between Drew's spread legs. I knead hard the hard mounds of his chest; I brush his beard with mine. Unbuttoning my boy's trousers, I pull his limp penis and balls out. I spit into my palm, apply the wet, and stroke.

Drew shakes his head, teeth clamping down on rope, gaze casting around for hostile witnesses. Despite his obvious fear, he's hardening up fast.

"Oh, yes," I say, tightening my grip around his shaft. I bend to lick curls of hair upon his chest, to lap a nipple before taking it between my lips. "Oh, yes. Keep silent and savor this," I mutter, filling my mouth with his torso's fuzzy flesh.

Drew's head falls back. He spreads his thighs wider. He bucks into my hand; his shoulders flex, his back slams against the tree trunk, evoking a fresh shower of petals; he winces as my teeth bear down on his breast's broad tenderness. My shaft-stroking speeds up. He grunts and thrusts, rocking against me. When I tug hard on his balls, that finishes him. He gives up a strangled sigh, then erupts, tiny comets of white semen arcing from my grip to join fallen sarvis petals on black earth and dead leaves.

"Not quite done," I say. Looking around cautiously, still seeing no one, I stand between his legs, unbutton, and haul out my own sex. Drew nods, grinning whitely against the rope-gag. He heaves another long sigh as I rub my penis against the soft bush of his beard, across his taut lips, through his shaggy hair. Another palmful of spit, and I'm well moistened. He stares up at me, blue eyes become black pebbles edged with mother-of-pearl in this country dark. I ride my hand for a long minute, add more spit, and pound my palm a little longer. Sweet welling, like an underground stream leaping from its long journey beneath the hills to spurt into the sunlight.

Now I've arrived, his bearded cheeks splashed with my own sticky white, his long hair streaked with my spasmodic dew. Dropping to my knees beside him, I'm breathing hard, staring into his eyes. He's nodding as I rub my thick seed over his lips, into his hair and beard, over his petal-scattered shoulders. I kiss him, tasting myself on his mouth. By the time the rustle of leaves alerts me to the sentry's approach, Drew's slumped and drowsing, the rain's started up again, and I'm back in my tent, licking my lips and mumbling my prayers. My prayers are all for more. More touch, more taste, more shared days to come.

—

CHAPTER SIXTY-SEVEN

—

I'm just leaving the tent, stepping out into dawn light and recurrent drizzle, when I hear Rufus's shout. There's Drew, still asleep in his bonds, slender petals of sarvis white sprinkled over him, caught in his torso's hair, rain-plastered along his cuffed arms and wet pants, and there's Rufus, running toward me, looking very unhappy. He's barely had time to tell me the bad news and to scuttle off when George appears between the row of tents, sporting the bullwhip and a big grin.

"What the hell's that for?" I step between George and Drew, mouth twitching. It's the protective animal in me, lips curling up over teeth, an instinctive snarl.

"I saw Rufus over here. So I suspect you know." George strokes the braided whip-leather and looks over my shoulder at Drew, still asleep against his tree. George is braided like the lash he holds: rage, lust, and hatred, all twisted up together like greenbrier vines.

"You ain't beating him," I say. "You ain't beating that boy."

"Sarge says different. You going to give me this Yankee, or you wanting me to fetch Sarge?"

"Fetch him then, you ferret-faced fuck," I shout. "You're a bald-faced liar."

Lips pursing, George turns without another word and heads toward the center of camp.

Drew's awake now. He must have heard everything, for he's staring at me, his blow-blackened eyes fear-wide. I squat beside him, grasping his arm. "Listen to me. I think you're about to be bullwhipped again. And not by Sarge. I think George has talked Sarge into..."

Drew's eyes clench shut. His teeth grit the rope. He shakes his head. He whimpers.

"Oh, buddy, I'm so sorry. I'll try to stop this. Listen, I swear, just survive this, and soon, swear to God, I'll—"

"Ian!" Sarge's voice is distant but, from the sound of it, rapidly approaching.

I stand and turn, preparing the earthen ravelin of my arguments.

Sarge strides up, looking the same way he used to when I was a child and he'd caught me pilfering a biscuit from the bread box: brow crinkled up, thin lips grim. George follows him the way stink wafts in the wake of skunk. Crossing his arms, Sarge says, "No need to doubt George. I have indeed given him permission to beat the prisoner after breakfast. The boy will be dead soon; might as well get more use and amusement out of him before then."

"But sir," I begin. "Shouldn't we spare the poor bastard a little mercy, show him a little pity in his last days? Besides, he's asked me to write a letter to his folks."

"You can do that after the whipping. Let him dictate the letter and then gag him again."

"But sir, wouldn't a Christian show...even to an enemy..."

Sarge waves off my words like a cloud of gnats in summer. "An *enemy*, Ian. We've had this conversation before. I've told you I'm weary of this softness."

"No softness, sir. Twice now you've offered me the privilege of beating the prisoner. If he must be beaten, then I'm willing to—"

Sarge laughs softly. "You don't own him, Ian. You and I don't own his suffering. No monopoly here. George is eager to learn the whip too. Such a skill would behoove him. My suspicion is that his nature tends toward it. Far more so than yours. Now, I'm off to breakfast. Will you join me? George will fetch the prisoner after we eat."

I stare at them, arrayed smilingly against me, and behind them, the drift of campfire smoke, the lines of tents, my company-mates rising, coughing, shaking off the night's moisture, eager to fill their bellies with coffee and hoecake. Hate has too many heads today. Once again I am too few, too small.

"Come with us to breakfast," Sarge says, mouth set. "Leave the prisoner here. He'll be dead tomorrow or the day after. No need to waste food on him. A gravedigger, on the other hand, needs to keep his strength up."

Before me, George snickers. Behind me, Drew shifts in the noisy brittle of leaves. He whimpers once, then falls silent. Without looking back, I follow my enemies toward the column of wood smoke, a stubborn swirl of black in the rain.

—

CHAP̧ĨER̥ ŞIXŢƳ-EIGHŢ

This must be the ecstasy of a man who, achieving heaven, finds that
his final reward has taken exactly the forms he's dreamed of. George
is clumsy with the whip for a good five minutes before he finds his
rhythm.

I suppose I could have hidden in the tent and refused to watch the
proceedings. But that devil-part of me who's fascinated by beauty's
suffering—who studied picturebook-paintings of the Crucifixion as a
child, who studied that outlaw thrashing on the barn's straw-strewn
floor, who stared, transfixed, at the blood running down Drew's naked
back the day he was first dragged into camp, strung up, and beaten—
that devil drove me out into the daylight to serve as witness, as did the
part of me who realized that refusing to watch would be just another
sign of weakness that George might use to turn Sarge against me. I do
not need to rouse further suspicions, especially with stolen goods in
my tent and escape mapped out in my mind.

When they came to fetch him, Drew fought back. As soon as I uncuffed my Yank from the tree, Drew swung at George, narrowing missing him. Two of George's Valley cronies, brought along to subdue any
possible resistance, seized Drew. He threw them off. What a joy that
must have been, after having been bound and tormented for so long,
finally to be able to use his great strength against them. But George
brought his pistol butt down on Drew's head, stunning him, dropping
him to his knees. When Drew rose, wobbly but ready to swing again,
the mouth of George's pistol poked his chest, the two men grabbed his
arms and dragged him to yet another whipping-tree.

This one's thicker than the little sarvis, thick enough to withstand
Drew's considerably brawny efforts to escape agony and the lash. It's a
shagbark hickory in the middle of camp, bark peeling off in gray shards.
Drew's arms are wrapped around it, his hands cuffed together on the
far side. He's hugging it in his pain as if it were a lover who might offer
tenderness or solace, his gagged face pressed against the trunk. Save
for the slave collar, George has him entirely naked. The bandages have

been ripped off his back and his feet. His ankles have been unshackled and his trousers have been removed, exposing both back and buttocks for punishment.

Drew's screaming. Drew's screaming. I want to stop my ears with mud, with the wax Odysseus used as he cruised past the sirens' rock. A soft rain falls upon the camp. George swings and swings; the bull-whip cracks, cracks, opens up old wounds across Drew's back and ass, maimings I so carefully medicated and bandaged, then paints the raw hues of new welts. Again the slow drool of red across white skin and bruised skin. Again the broken sobs muffled by rope and rag, the big body shaking, straining against metal, thrashing against the trunk, high branches shifting against sky as if the tree were being axed.

George has stamina. He's dreamed of this gray day, this naked body, these shrill cries for so long. We have, I realize, several passions in common. He labors on far longer than Sarge ever did. Finally, with a pant and a chuckle, he throws the whip into the leaves and rubs his forearm. Drew loses his hold on the tree; he slumps against it, then slowly slides to his knees. Down his back, blood descends in lazy lines.

"Fine job, George," says Sarge, here at my elbow. His eyes have been on me quite a bit during the whipping, gauging my responses. I've hidden my grief as best I could, allowing instead my devil-fascination to show. Let him believe what he wants: that I'm in love only with the man's pain, rather than with the man himself, the man's racked and bound body, the sweet boy-soul within.

More orders. The same damn orders. I know, I know, I know. Dead soon, dead soon. Don't waste food; don't waste medicine or bandages. Buck or hogtie, write the letter, gag, leave all day, all night, to serve once more as spittoon and piss-pot.

Sarge strides off. I stare at the prisoner, the naked and collared slave, on his knees in the grass, slumped against the hickory. I stare at the man I love, on his knees in the grass, slumped against the hickory. George pats my back as he passes. "That boy was born to be a whipping post. He's a blessing, ain't he?"

Mechanical now, as if my will had receded, gathering its forces for more opportune times. I uncuff Drew's blood-wet wrists and he falls onto a patch of new grass. Having been given a choice between two options, I choose the less painful, a hogtie here by the base of the tree. Drew's only half-conscious, but he knows it's me. He gives me no fight as I bind him. Wrists crossed behind the back and tied together. Ankles crossed and tied together. Wrists and ankles hauled close behind him, evoking a moan, then lashed together with a short length of cord, making of him a circuit, a straining circle. Blue blinking of eyes; flash of teeth gnawing rope. Then limp again. Blood and golden hair streaking his pale ass cheeks.

Sarge again. Another order, this time masked as an invitation. How about I borrow a mount and accompany him on a short scouting ride into Buchanan, just around the mountain's flank, to see what damage the Yanks have done and to question the citizens about troop activity roundabouts? Good job, says Sarge, examining Drew's wrist and ankle knots. While you're at it, says Sarge, here's another hank of rope. Bind his knees together; bind his elbows together. Like this. Very good. No, a little tighter, till he hurts. Very good, that pained sob. Very good, blond beard serving as boot brush. See? Downright immobile. Leave him in the grass to bleed. See how drizzle thins the gore.

—

CHAPTER SIXTY-NINE

—

The three of us ride in silence, George on the left, I on the right, Sarge in between us. The dirt road skirting the James River curls east around the base of the mountain, inside a tunnel of leafless trees. Then the valley opens out, and there, beneath a lowering and drizzly sky, is the tiny town of Buchanan, with the Blue Ridge Mountains looming beyond it.

"The Kanawha Canal's around here somewhere, along which Stonewall Jackson's body was brought from Richmond via barge," says Sarge, breaking the tense quiet. "Over there, across the river, was Mount Joy, a fine mansion before the Feds burnt it last summer. After they torched the Institute in Lexington, they brought their savagery here."

The history and geography lesson is a welcome distraction, since I'm fighting a nigh-irresistible urge to leap upon George, knock out the rest of his weasel teeth, drag him into the river, and hold him under until the bubbles stop. My suspicion is that Sarge invited us along in an attempt to make peace between us. If so, it's a waste of his time. I'm just thankful that Rufus agreed to watch out for Drew and defend him as much as possible from further abuse. My boy had passed out by the time we left camp, and I'm hoping the brutal whipping he received this morning will cause the rest of the camp to show him a little mercy while I'm gone.

The bridge leading over the James and into Buchanan is a rickety makeshift thing, built alongside fire-blackened stone piers around which the water curls and races. "There used to be a covered bridge here. Last June McCausland torched it in order to slow Hunter's advance," Sarge explains. "Then he swam across the river under a barrage of Yankee bullets. Quite the feat." Sarge shakes his head, strokes his moustache, and frowns. "Unfortunately, sparks rode the wind and spread the flames through town. Ah, well, Jubal Early taught Hunter and his bluecoats a lesson after that, in Lynchburg and Hanging Rock. I'd love to have been there when old Jubal stormed Washington. 'Major,' Early supposedly said, 'we haven't taken Washington, but we scared

Abe Lincoln like hell.'" Chuckling, Sarge leads us onto the shaky little bridge, past the ruined piers, and into Buchanan.

More fire damage as we trot through town: a burnt warehouse, charred storefronts. Several citizens stick their heads out from upper windows and shop doors. Seeing the gray we're garbed in, they cheer. We find a hitching post, dismount, and tie up our horses. A cold wind gusts down the street. The drizzle shifts into steady rain.

"Boys," says Sarge, tipping his cap over his brow, "I'm heading over there, to the town hall. Perhaps this mayor will be as instructive and as generous as Staunton's. You two take your rest there." He points to a tavern. "If the owners are patriots, they'll not charge you. If they do, well, I'll meet you there in a bit and pay. Not that Confederate currency will buy much...so, just in case, limit yourselves to one drink apiece."

I think of my Yank back in camp, trussed up like an animal on the ground, new wounds oozing blood. I think about the rapturous grin on George's face as he swung the whip. Gritting my teeth, I growl, "I don't want to drink with this man, sir."

"Nor I he!" George spits on the ground. "Weak cur. Yankee lover!"

"Listen here," says Sarge, voice low, gray eyes hard, looking first at me, then at George. "The bone of contention between you two will soon be gone. Do you understand? That boy will be dead soon. You, Ian, have proven too kind," Sarge says, gripping my arm, "and you, George," he says with the shake of a finger, "I might almost say that you have proven too cruel, save that that big Yank's a foe and deserves whatever suffering he gets."

Sarge clears his throat, voice edging lower. "Damn you both. How will you two fight side by side after he's dead and buried? How can I expect you to be good soldiers and to do what needs to be done—together—if you continue this way? That bluebelly is nearly a part of our past. We have a future to face. We have a country to save. God, don't be small men! After all the South has suffered, don't be small men."

With that, he turns and stalks off. George and I stand there. My hands are shaking, so I push them into my trouser pockets. How much more contemptible would my uncle find me if he knew how much I loved Drew?

"Well, shit," says George. "Don't recall when I last saw him so angry." He lets fly an arc of tobacco slobber into the street, then the chewed plug itself. "Come on. I'd rather drink with you than stand around in this goddamn rain."

I follow him into the tavern. It's low ceilinged and warm, with a small fire on the hearth. The only other customer's an old man in the back, drinking alone. "No need for money, gentlemen," says the barrel-chested proprietor behind the counter. "After all you've done for Virginia, beer's the least I can offer." Within a minute, George and I have our wet coats off and are sipping brown ale by the fire.

"I hate you. You hate me. So what do we talk about?" I wipe foam from my lip, sit back, and prop my left foot on my right knee.

"How about Petersburg?" George works at a loose tooth with his tongue, then takes a long swallow of ale. "The city's liable to fall before we get there. How can twenty half-starved men help win that fight?"

"Good question. But what else is there to do? Stop fighting?" Even as I speak, I know what a hypocrite I am. Am I a coward, preparing to turn my back on my fellow soldiers and this war we've fought so hard for years? What will Sarge say when he finds Drew and me gone? What will my parents say if I make it home with Drew? How will I live with the shame of being a deserter?

"No," says George. "We keep fighting."

"To defend home."

"My home's burnt, friend. By the likes of your bluebelly. I fight to make them suffer."

"Like you made Drew suffer this morning." I grip the mug, lift it very slowly to my lips, and take a long sip. I'd like to swig the rest of the ale and then swing the mug against the side of his head, but that'd end me up in the guardhouse or hung up by my thumbs and in no position to help Drew.

George sniggers. He curls his lip, running a finger along a canine tooth. The bastard looks like a wild dog. "Yes. Were you jealous, that I swung that whip instead of you? He cried like a girl, like a whore getting fucked too hard. The Lord's vengeance, I'd say. It was a pleasure being God's scourge. Truly. I made you suffer too, didn't I? I know how fond of him you are."

"I think you're fond of him too. In some twisted manner. I think you hate him so passionately because of that fondness. I think his good looks and his suffering excite you."

"I think his good looks excite *you*! Are you implying that...are you questioning my manhood?" George hisses, slamming his mug down on the table between us.

"Your manhood?" I stretch, making an exaggerated show of relaxation. "What's to question?"

"If there's anyone here who's displaying unnatural desire, it's you, Ian Campbell. So tender with a man who's helped ruin our land, who—"

I lean across the table. "You wanted to poke him, remember? So righteous when you're sober, so nasty when you're drunk. Wanted to ride him like a woman, you said. Sarge says that's called sodomy. I can't imagine how a man as holy as thou could conceive of such practices."

George is bug-eyed now; any second, mad-dog foam's liable to bubble from the corners of his mouth. "That, that would have just been a brutal punishment that such a pig deserves. How *dare* you accuse me of...that sin? Nothing's more revolting or less natural. And how dare you question my faith?"

"Your faith? A Christian who beats a man bloody and proposes to rape him?"

"I *am* a Christian, which is more'n I can say for you," George spits. "You have a heathen Indian for an aunt, for God's sake! I can't even imagine the beastly sins someone as rotten as you dreams of indulging in. You...you're damned, Ian, no question of it. A hell-bound sinner! Snugged up in your big cozy tent every night with the enemy. If anyone's likely to be indulging in such abominations, it's you." George takes a last gulp of beer and once again slams his mug upon the table.

"Now you're the one who sounds jealous."

"Jealous of weakness and of sin? If you weren't Sarge's nephew—"

"You'd what? Punch me? Or, rather, try to punch me? We both know how far you'd get." I snort and roll my eyes.

"There are other ways to teach you a lesson. I'll find a way yet."

"Drew told me what you did to him before you cut his back. Touching him. His cock, his rear. Is that the kind of beastly sin you're talking about, George?"

George jumps upright, so abruptly that his chair tips back and hits the floor with a thud. His face is twisted, flushed. He couldn't look any uglier. "That's a damned lie! A monstrous lie! By God, Ian, you've gone too far. I'm going to make you pay!" Snarling, George spits on the floor at my feet.

I stand. "No," I growl. "I think you're the one who'll be paying."

"Gentlemen, please," the bartender beseeches. "No trouble."

"Sir, thank you for the ales. Your kindness is much appreciated. Apologies for the bad behavior. George, how about we continue this conversation outside?" I rub my knuckles and smile. "I think I'm going to kick your ass to the far end of town and back."

George turns pale. "Now, Ian..."

"Ha! You look like you're going to faint. Who's the cur now? Who's the coward? Forget it. You're not worth the time in the guardhouse."

I gulp the last of the ale, grab my coat, and stride out into the rain. I'm barely off the stoop when Sarge appears around the corner.

"Let's go, Ian. The mayor said that tomorrow he'd send along what cornmeal the citizens could spare. Some root vegetables too. Let's head back to camp. Have lunch with me. How about bean soup and biscuits, a little ham from my private stash? Where's George?"

I lift my face into the rain, catch the storm on my tongue, and wipe cold droplets off my hot cheeks. "He's feeling a mite delicate," I say.

—

CHAPTER SEVENTY

The ham I saved from lunch is wrapped in a kerchief so it won't create a telltale stain in my trouser pocket. Cross-legged in the grass, I sit by Drew while he dictates his letter, and, when no one's in sight, I sneak him tiny bits of the meat. He chews fast, then continues speaking.

There's little paper in the camp, and no ink. I've erased the last pencil-written letter my parents sent and am scrawling Drew's words across that smudged and dog-eared sheet. My writing desk's the back of a plate I balance in my lap. We're taking our time, because I know some of my crueler company-mates are waiting their turn to release a few frustrations—in the form of spit, piss, and blows—so the longer this dictation takes, the better.

Drew's hogtied still, as Sarge demanded. He lies naked on his left side, facing me, head resting in the new green gathering over the earth as April draws nigh. The sun's out; the drizzle's retreated. Sun-slant embraces him, as I at present cannot: his gold-glitter chest and belly fur, the bush of gold about his limp sex, the rough hemp rope knotted about his limbs, the bloodstains that hours of the rope-gag's chafing have left in the corners of his mouth. He's half-addled yet from the beating George gave him, but a sense of urgency animates him nonetheless, a sense we share, of time running out. He mumbles, stammers, groans, and shakes his head, fighting back waves of pain, trying to gather his thoughts. His eyes cross and close; he dozes; he jolts awake and continues. His words slog forward like soldiers in mud ankle-deep. I listen, I write. He licks his lips, takes a deep breath, and mumbles more. When his arm grows numb beneath him, he shifts onto his belly, then, after a while, onto his right side, trying to lessen his discomfort. I adjust my position according to his, the way sunflowers follow summer sun.

"Dear Folks," it reads so far, "I pray this letter reaches you and finds you well. You know I cannot write. I guess I have always been better at baling hay and eating pie than school. But I have a buddy here. His name is Ian. He's a Rebel. He's writing this for me. I guess you wonder how I came to be speaking to a Rebel. This is the bad part. I am a prisoner at present. I have been treated hard and cruelly for many days. Most of these men hate me, for I am their enemy and they are mine. But Ian is no foe. He is my friend. He has been kind to me. He has fed me and bathed me and tended my wounds. I would already be dead if not for him."

I read it back to Drew. He nods. I look around, see no one, and slip him more ham. I rub his numbing hands and feet; I wipe blood from the deep new wounds across his back and buttocks. Settling back down, I take up the pencil. We continue.

"I may not make it home. And this would be a true pity, not so much for myself, but I know you need me back to keep up the fields and the farm. And I know it would grieve you greatly if I die here and am buried far from you. We are all in God's hands, I know, I see for sure. So if this is the last you hear of me, if I am never to see home again, then know I love you and that I spent my last days in the care of a true friend. Your son and brother, Drew."

I read it back. Drew approves. I fold the letter, easing it into my trouser pocket. I feed him the last shard of ham. He chews and swallows, tears oozing from his blackened eyes.

"Wipe my cheeks, Ian. Please? Don't want anyone else to see."

I do so. I've dried his face and am putting away my handkerchief when George swaggers into the clearing. I stand, taking my usual stance between Drew and any danger.

George leers around me at Drew's exposed privates. "That Yank's big everywhere, ain't he? I'd like to kick that thing between his legs right off, but ain't got time for that now. Sarge is asking to see you at his tent. And he says to gag and tether the Yank and bring him along. Time he took a walk."

"Walk? What do you mean? What's going on?" Clenching my fists, I take a step forward.

George frowns. "No more chances to punch me, you scrawny boxer-boy. No more chances to sweeten this prisoner's days…and nights. The scout says Nelson's about here. Time this bastard took a long walk in the woods."

Oh, God. It's not time to walk, it's time to run. But got to get Drew untied first, so he can run too.

"All right," I say. Bending down beside Drew, I fill his mouth with rag and rope. His eyes are welling up again. He emits a stifled sob.

"Go on," I say to George, as casually as I can. "Tell Sarge I'll bring him right along. Got to untie his feet and knees first."

"That's quite all right. I ain't got other appointments. So I'll just escort you both." George seems far too satisfied for my comfort and is showing far too many of his sharp snaggle-teeth. He pats the pistol on his hip. "See, Sarge and me, we don't trust you any more, Ian. We have reason to believe you're not the upstanding soldier you appear to be."

"What the *hell* do you mean by that?" What do they know? A snake's twisting in my stomach. Something slimy and cold. It won't keep still.

"You'll find out here soon enough. Get on with it."

Hands shaking now, I pick at the knots, loosening and removing the rope binding Drew's ankles to his wrists. More knots, hard to pick apart, slow to give, about Drew's ankles and his knees. I take my time, thinking, thinking.

George has his gun out now. "Leave his top half tied. Tether his neck."

"Let me at least fetch his trousers."

"No need for those. Naked will do. Naked he came into the world, and naked he'll leave it. Let's go. Sarge is waiting."

Gripping Drew's elbow, I help him rise to his knees, then his feet. He looms over us, blue eyes wide and edged with wet silver. I loop a tether-rope around the slave collar and knot it.

George pushes the pistol into my ribs. "I told you I'd make you pay. You shouldn't have said all you did in Buchanan. Not when you had so much to hide."

"Goddamn you," I say, as evenly as my fear will allow. "What have you—?"

"Get on now," says George. "You'll see directly."

Drew walks beside me; George walks behind us. We leave the little clearing about the whipping-tree. Over the tents I can see coils of smoke rising, a buzzard drifting, and the white cloud, disintegrating, that blooming sarvis makes.

—

CHAPTER SEVENTY-ONE

—

Sarge is sitting in a camp chair before his tent, taking in the sun. The pokes of supplies I stole are there at his feet. He rises at our approach. There's a look on his face I've never in my life seen there before.

"Stay here," I say to Drew, dropping his tether.

Walking toward Sarge, step by step I sift through a long array of possible lies. They're all hollow, purposeless, like a hickory shell picked clean. Let me come to the truth at the end of this. Let me die with it.

I stand before my uncle now. He crosses his arms; I cross mine. Our eyes meet. I do not drop my gaze. Let me be a man about this, finally. Let me not shame myself.

"George found these bags in your tent, Ian. What have you to say?"

There's something else beneath the tight rage in his voice. Something else.

"Say it. Say it before us all. Nelson's nigh. We don't have a plentitude of time. You were planning...what? To help this boy escape?"

"Yes, sir."

Sarge's mouth goes slack for only a second before returning to its usual set firmness. "I'm your kin. These men are your comrades. The punishments you deserve... Shall your face be branded? Shall it be hanging or the firing squad?"

"You're a cruel, cruel man, sir. You're no Christian. This Yankee boy, I've come to care about him. He doesn't deserve what you've made him suffer. The Lord's made him a friend to me."

"The Lord? I doubt it. So where were you going? Over to the enemy?" Sarge rubs his forehead and shakes his head. Far away, something booms. Thunder, no doubt, ready to soak fresh grave mounds.

"You've heard all you need to know, sir. I have nothing more to say."

"I've known you since..." His voice rises and breaks. "How could you do this? How could you betray your country, your kin?" Sarge turns away, rubbing his eyes. "After what happened to Ariminta?"

It's as if a sword blade wept or a boulder keened. That he could be hurt? Impossible.

"You'll be hanged, Ian," Sarge whispers into a rising breeze. "I'll see to it. No more favors for family. I won't be accused of favoritism. I've tried to show you how to be a man, a soldier..."

Sarge faces me, himself again. "George, bring the prisoner over here."

Choking sound behind me. I turn to see George yanking on the tether, dragging Drew forward by his neck. He shoves Drew to his knees beside me and presses his gun's barrel to the back of Drew's head. Once more, thunder booms to the east.

"I will pardon you, nephew, if you finish him here." Gripping my shoulder, he pats my pistol in its holster. "Put a bullet through his skull and drag him into the woods. We have little time. Nelson's due. Renew your loyalty. Show me your remorse. Wipe out his memory. Let us both forget him."

"But, Sarge, Ian's...he's...he's guilty as hell. What he's done, it's nigh onto desertion! It's treating with the enemy!" George is sputtering.

"Shut up, private. Ian, do it. Do it, and be pardoned."

I look down at Drew. He stares up at me, tears glistening on his face. He nods.

"Look! Look there! He *is* your friend. Even *he* agrees this is best."

My hand falls on Drew's shoulder. Sarge's hand rises from mine.

"No, sir. I won't do this. If you're going to murder him and have me hanged, I'd just as soon you ended us here, together. One grave'll do for both of us."

Sarge's face stiffens, skin a gray bark. "You will be hanged, as is proper. He, on the other hand..."

Taking Drew's tether, he hands the rope to George. "Take him to the woods."

George smiles. "Come on, Yank. It's finally time." He jerks the rope. Drew chokes and huffs, stumbling to his feet.

"No!" I've seized George by the back of the neck when I feel Sarge's pistol between my shoulder blades and his breath in my ear.

"Easy, nephew. Don't make this worse. George, get on. Get it over with."

I stand stiffly. "Do it, uncle. Damn you. End us together."

George shoves Drew. Drew trips over one of the stuffed pokes, then rights himself.

Thunder booms closer, just over Purgatory. A shout goes up at the far end of camp. Rufus runs into the clearing, screaming, "Yankees! From the Valley! Yankees!"

It's pure grace, this chance. Sarge lowers his gun, surprised. I pivot on one heel, catching my uncle on the chin with my elbow. His pistol goes flying. Another blow, this one a fist into his gut. He staggers backward. I punch him in the jaw. He spins, slams into the side of his tent, and he's down.

I turn. George points his gun at me. Drew, yelling against his rope and rag, slams his torso into George's shoulder. Off-balance, George fires. The ball whizzes past my head.

And then, behind me, a force and a flame catch me by the waist, lift me up, and throw me down onto my face. Clods of earth are flying, and yellow sparks. God has brought his bullwhip down, his hammer, his thunder-dark palm. I am nothing now, nothing but a gray grub sheltered by Southern soil.

—

CHAPTER SEVENTY-TWO

—

Something muffled, a voice. Muffled like my senses. I turn like a worm in a cocoon, onto my back. I open my eyes. There's his sweet face hovering over me. My brother, my lover, naked and bound. So beautiful, the bush of his beard, the blue of his eyes, the rope between his teeth. I smile at him, reach up, touch his red-dewed cheek.

The earth rocks beneath me. Earth or sea? Sea rocks, not earth. What river or lake bears us up? We are riding a river home.

Drew's roaring. Got to get that rag out of his pretty mouth. Don't understand a thing he's saying. Pull that bloody gag out and kiss him hard.

I grip Drew's naked thigh, hoisting myself into red mist, flakes of fire. I stare up at Drew's face, at the mud and blood and tangled hair, and the mist begins to rise, as it does back home, the Greenbrier River on autumn mornings.

Drew's my support, the tree-hairy hill-slope from which cometh all strength. I clamber to my feet. Shaking Ian, brittle Ian, sway of winter weeds. An ache stabs my shoulder blades, jabs my right side. Here's a hole in my raggedy gray uniform jacket; here's blood. Where has youth gone? Is it night or afternoon?

I look around. There's George, asleep on the ground. There's flame arcing in from the east, a comet flying over the camp, descending with a thud and a boom. Where is Sarge? Where is his tent? There is only a hole. I walk to its edge, look down into steam, a black chute, a few sunsparkles and smolders.

This is the smoking crater of God's war-will. This is the goblet of bones and gobbets.

Ah. Now. Yankees. Now I see. I once was blind but now I see. The narrow, snarled stream of seconds favors us for once. I snatch up the pokes, grab Drew by the arm, and run. Smoke swallows the sunlight, casting our flight into shadow. Behind us, another shell makes flying flame and leaping earth of our camp.

—

CHAPTER SEVENTY-THREE

My tent's still intact, here beside the little sarvis. Inside, I seize haversack, oilcloth, cartridge boxes, rifle, and blankets. No time to dismantle the tent and take it with us. Loaded down, I emerge. My naked giant grunts, flexing his roped arms, wanting release. "Soon," I tell him. "Let's get out of here first. Keep close behind me."

Only yards away, another shell drops, and more earth goes flying with a fiery boom. My company-mates are darting every which way, shouting, crazy-eyed. No sign of Jeremiah or Rufus. As we pass the whipping-tree, I bend in my flight, snatch up Drew's trousers, and keep running. About us, walls of smoke where tents used to be, the whizzing of bullets, the crash of shell-splintered tree limbs. Behind us, gunfire, screams, the screech of shells.

Camp's edge now. The paddock's empty, the horses scattered in terror. "Goddamn, we got to walk it." I curse and spit, then lead us west into the woods, toward the mountains. There's a narrow road here skirting the James, a rough groove of mud through steel-gray tree trunks. We run along it, finally out of range of the Federal artillery. Already my armful of burdens has me panting. "Craig Creek. We got to get up the James, get to Eagle Rock, get on up Craig Creek." I'm muttering, more to myself than to Drew. "Why, oh, why, couldn't there be a horse or two? 'My kingdom for a horse.'"

That's when we hear the thud of hooves in front of us, around the bend of the mountain's base. "Oh, damn! Off the road!" I grab my naked Yank by the elbow, hustle him into the woods, and shove him onto the ground beneath the thick evergreen shade of a rhododendron bush. "Lie still," I whisper, lying on top of him. At the last minute, I scoop handfuls of leaves over us as makeshift camouflage. It feels good to feel his scarred and scabbed nakedness beneath me, even as my heart's beating hard in the face of death or capture.

They pass us at a full gallop, a blur of blue. Federal cavalrymen, damn it, at least ten of them. Heading in from the west, heading toward the skirmish, too intent on the sound of artillery to notice us there in the leaves. They're barely out of sight when I help Drew up. "Can't go up the river now," I gasp. "Got to avoid your buddies in blue. Got to go up the mountain till things die down." I look up, at the layers of fog on Purgatory's peak, at the arduous slope awaiting us. At this point I want to bury our damn supplies rather than lug them, but there's nothing to be done for it.

"Ian!"

Shocked, I turn toward the sound of my name. It's Rufus, running with a heavy limp along the road in our direction. Behind him is a sole blue-coated cavalryman, a thin, clean-shaven man with a confident grin, riding a dapple-gray, trotting only a few yards behind Rufus.

Now Rufus stumbles and falls. Now the Yank sees Drew and me. The grin disappears. He pulls his pistol and aims at us.

"Down!" I drop my load, push Drew to the ground, pull my pistol, aim, and fire.

The explosions seem simultaneous. The Yank's ball grazes my left shoulder—quick rip and sting, as if a bent twig, released, snapped back to slash me. The Yank falls from the saddle. "Oh, God! Oh, God!" He's gasping, convulsing in the muddy road.

Poor bastard. I have no time for his suffering. He might have comrades near, near enough to hear the pistols' reports. I move toward his horse, hoping to grab the bridle and get us a faster way out of here, but the damned thing rears, bolts, and gallops east.

"Hell," I growl, then "Come on!" I shout, helping Rufus to his feet. "Hand here some of that load, Ian," he says. Gratefully, I pass him the pokes of stolen supplies, help Drew up, and off we three lope into the woods. Behind us, the Yankee horseman has fallen silent.

"Uhhhhrrrr!" We're barely off the road when Drew nudges me and growls, brow folded up with understandable impatience.

"Yep, buddy, yep. You've waited long enough. Hold on, Rufus. Let me free him." I pull my knife but think better of it—who knows if or when we might need the rope? Sheathing the Bowie, I finger-fumble the knots loose. Elbows, wrists, neck tether. The rough cords fall from him. He's free. After long days of captivity and abuse, my boy is finally free.

Drew sighs. He stretches and flexes. The muscles of his shoulders and arms ripple. He massages his bloodstained wrists. He picks at the gag's knots behind his head. "Here, here," I say, helping him. The rope goes lax, dropping over his chin. Reaching up, he jerks the rag out and stuffs both rope and rag into his poclet. He smiles down at me, working his jaw around, wiping blood from the corner of his mouth. "Damnation, Reb... It's about fucking time." Then, incongruously, he seizes my hand and shakes it hard.

I laugh and wince. My shoulder's smarting now.

"Oh, damn! You need bandaged."

"Not now, Drew. We got to get up the mountain and out of danger's way first."

By the time we stop, panting for breath, we've crested a little leaf-strewn promontory topped with a table rock about a third of the way up Purgatory. Behind us and below, the battle continues. In the distance, yellow flashes, pillars of gray smoke shot through with black. From the east, suits of blue are streaming around the foot of Purgatory, too many to count. From the south, a sparse gray cloud rolls down the Valley, no doubt Nelson's forces come to join our company. We Rebs are outnumbered as usual. But I guess that doesn't matter now. Now I have Drew, and he and I have more pressing business.

"Let's see that wound, Reb." Drew's big hand, patting my back.

With Drew's help, I peel off my stained uniform jacket. He examines me, staunching blood. "Ain't bad," he says. "Either that man was a damned bad shot, or you're a damned lucky grayback." With a wink, he adds, "Thank God."

"Here's your pokes." Rufus hands them to Drew, then sits on the ground with a pained huff. "Y'all need to keep on."

"You ain't coming with us?" I say.

"Naw, Ian. I ain't no deserter. That company's all I got. Though I'm thinking there's little left of it after this rout. Plus I think I got some grapeshot in my leg. Something's hurting me bad."

Grape, yep. That must be what's paining my back and bloodying my side. That must be what's streaked Drew's face with crimson.

"Ian?" Rufus starts to speak, stops, starts again. "I'm pretty sure Sarge..."

"I know." The blood keeps welling up, staining my undershirt, trickling down my arm. "It's my fault."

"'Tweren't nobody's fault! I saw what happened! You had to—"

"Don't want to talk about it. Did you see what happened to Jeremiah?"

"Yes!" Rufus' face lights up. "I think he got away. We made it out of the artillery fire together, then he peeled off across a field and headed north. Said, since it seemed to him Sarge was dead and our company done for, he was gonna head back down the Valley, maybe borry a horse, see if he could find Miss Pearl."

Jeremiah. Sweet, furry, loyal friend. "Damnation, that's good to hear! But what about you, buddy?"

"I'm gonna hide up here for a while," Rufus says, "see how things end up down there. But you...you can't let this boy get captured again. If there's any chance Sarge or George are still alive...they'll be wanting to track y'all down, though last I saw Weasel-Teeth, he was sprawled ass-up in the mud and is liable to be a prisoner of the Yanks by now. Or a damn homely corpse. Either way, them's his just deserts. Anyway, I s'pect you were hoping to get this big ole Yank away from here. So go on. Git on now."

"Drew? Should we go or stay?"

Drew's still rubbing his wrists. He stares over the edge of the table rock and down the hill, where the blue uniforms mingle in distant shouts with the gray. Even in this extremity his sunlit nakedness, set against clouds and mountain horizon, stuns me. White skin, golden hair, scarlet wounds. My chest clenches; inside me the sarvis petals gleam, pure white in spring sunlight. It's a blessing and a miracle, to feel such delight. We're here together, free from constraint and cruelty. For now, at least, we've evaded death.

"You—you could go back," I say. "We could stay here and see who wins. If the Feds prevail, you could—"

"'Scuse me, Rufus," Drew says, turning from the vista. His hands fall upon my shoulders. He bends down and kisses my forehead. He wraps his arms around me, then kisses me on the mouth.

"Oh, Lord," Rufus whispers, looking away. "George was right about you two. He said y'all were..."

Drew laughs. My naked Yankee throws back his head and laughs. Then, slipping his big arms beneath my back and beneath my knees, he picks me up as if I were a baby.

"Shit, Drew," I mumble. My half-hearted squirming is for nought.

"I guess we're sodomites. Yes sir," Drew says, pressing me to his chest so hard I gasp. "We are sodomites indeed. Rufus, bless you for your help. But you're right. We got to get on now. Come on, little Reb. I ain't ever seen West Virginia. Take me on home. You got some pies to bake."

—

CHAPTER SEVENTY-FOUR

No pies for a while. If we get back to the Greenbrier and my family farm, hell, you bet. My kin always has dried apples on hand. But there's a damned long ways between here and home. For now, it's the same cursed hardtack. We take a few bites—this batch seems free of weevils, praise God—before taking our leave of Rufus.

"Goodbye, friend. I hope, well, I hope somehow we meet again."

"Yep." Rufus, eyes lowered, steps back when I try to hug him, so I simply shake his hand.

Drew shakes his hand as well. "I'd like to thank you for all the food you've slipped me during...my trial. Your kindness helped me survive, Reb, and I won't forget it."

"'Tweren't nothin,'" Rufus mumbles, dropping Drew's hand. "Y'all get on now. Good luck to you. I'll pray for you." He lifts his head, shakes it sadly, and manages a small smile. "Yes, I will. I will indeed." Then he turns and limps down the slope, grabbing saplings to slow his awkward descent. He looks back once. In a few minutes, he's disappeared among the gray forest trunks.

Drew pulls on the trousers I retrieved, cinching them with his rope belt, before tearing off a bit of my undershirt sleeve to wrap my shoulder wound and helping me pull my jacket back on. Using the yards of rope that had bound him, we form improvised packs, tying the pokes and blankets on our backs. I hand Drew my haversack and two cartridge boxes. Painfully, I shoulder my rifle, another cartridge box, my cap box, and my canteen. "We have a few hours of daylight left, boy. Let's circle the mountain and make camp on the western slope. Tomorrow, if things are less explosive down below, we can make the river trail and head up the James."

Drew nods. We set out, making our way around Purgatory's uneven slopes, moving through thick forest and over broken boulders. To our left, far below, the river flows, a smooth gray, edged with willows leafing out in green. To our right, far above, the mountain rises into cloud. Day fades; the booms of artillery grow distant and finally cease. Drew, barefoot, moves as fast as he can, cussing as the rough terrain tears at his soles. When he falls, I lift him up, wipe blood off his feet, squeeze his hand, and lead us farther along. While light lasts, we need to put as much distance as possible between ourselves and the Valley's skirmishes.

My Yank and I keep going till the sun's disappeared behind the western mountains, the forest's filling with chill shadow, and only a little light lingers high on Purgatory's slopes. Above us, in the boughs of huge oaks, birds settle, preparing to roost. Drew and I separate, looking for a dell, or a pile of leaves sheltered by a rock overhang, or a hollow sycamore trunk where we might spend the night.

Nothing in this direction but more rock, a few melting patches of old snow beneath a hemlock grove, and a tiny stream welling up between exposed roots and trickling down a narrow gully. Night's falling fast. The sky above me is indigo, the west smeared with red, the evening star glimmering above black humps the distant mountains make. We have so far to go.

I'm about to turn back when I hear the unmistakable click of a rifle being cocked.

"Keep real still, Reb." The voice is right behind me. "Hands up. Turn around."

I obey. A Yankee sharpshooter, on a rock outcrop a few feet above me. On one knee, long rifle aimed at my head. Unkempt rusty beard streaked with gray, blue uniform, blue cap cocked over his eyes.

"My captain's got a good pair of field glasses. He said he thought he saw a few Rebs heading up here."

"I'm done with this war." My gullet feels lined with briers. I clear my throat. "I'm on my way home."

"You're dressed in Rebel gray, aren't you?" With a lithe leap, the man descends. He stands before me now, tall, lean, and menacing. Smiling, he presses the cold muzzle of the rifle against my forehead. I swallow. I close my eyes.

"Yes." Sweat's tickling my brow. I want to wipe it off, but if I move, he might shoot me. "Yes, sir."

"Then you aren't going home, whatever sort of Rebel dung-heap that might be. You're coming with me. A prison camp's your future, son. Elmira. Or Johnson's Island. Or maybe I should just shoot you here and spare us both further trouble. Where are your mates?"

I open my eyes and stare into his. If it's my time to die, at least I'll go loving Drew. "I'm alone. No one else."

"I doubt that. On your knees."

I kneel in the leaves. Please, God, don't part me from Drew like this.

"That's a good little Reb. Now why don't you unload yourself of those burdens? Slowly."

The man backs up. The cool muzzle-metal leaves my brow. Now it's aimed at my heart.

First I lay down my rifle in the carpet of fallen leaves. Then my pistol. I unshoulder my pack, canteen, and cartridge boxes and drop them beside my firearms.

"Bowie too."

Hands shaking, I'm fumbling with the Bowie's sheath when I hear Drew's hoarse voice.

"Sir! Please, sir! I'm a prisoner of war. This man has been holding me."

There's the rustling tread of feet across the forest floor. Drew appears from behind a laurel bush, his hands in the air.

"You're a liar." The man steps back, trying to cover us both. "You're a Rebel too!"

"Sir, I'm wearing gray because my Federal uniform was ruined and then stolen. I'm from Pennsylvania, sir! I swear it. I rode with Sheridan last fall." Drew takes two steps forward. "I helped him burn the Valley."

The sharpshooter takes another step back. The mouth of the gun wavers between Drew and me.

"I fought at Yellow Tavern and Trevilian Station, sir. They took me prisoner outside Staunton, sir, nearly two weeks ago. They tied me, they beat me, they cut me, they pissed on me, they starved me. See? They've kept me collared like a slave. See?" Drew tugs at the iron locked around his neck. "Don't doubt me, sir. Here's proof! Look!"

Drew slips his pack off his shoulders and turns, displaying his scarred and welted back in the twilight.

"Oh, hell, son..." The sharpshooter lowers his weapon and shakes his head, staring at Drew's extensive maiming. Then he turns from Drew, aiming the muzzle at me. "You fucking animal," he growls low. "All you Rebs are animals. I've heard how you treat your prisoners. My buddy died in that shit-hole Andersonville."

"Sir, if you boys hadn't shelled that Rebel camp today, this one would have shot me through the head." Drew takes another step forward, pointing a finger at me.

"Then that's what this one deserves. Why bother taking him prisoner?" Again, the Yank levels his aim at my brow. Sharpshooters are the best shots, I think, almost casually. And at such close range, surely I'll die before I suffer.

I have time for a second's surge of nauseating doubt—wondering if, all these weeks, Drew's been waiting for his chance to turn on me—before my Yank leaps. His big frame slams into the stranger's; the rifle goes off, there's the keen singing of a richochet, and then Drew's wrestled the gun away and sent it flying into brush. They scuffle for only a few moments, the sharpshooter cussing like wildfire, before Drew's fist slams into the side of the man's head and he falls still.

"Up, Reb!" Drew says, climbing off the prone body. "If this man had buddies, they might be near." He tugs off the man's shoes, finds them too small, curses, and drops them. Hurriedly he searches the man's pockets, pulls out a wad of paper, and unwraps it.

"Oh, look! Cheese!" His eyes gleam; he licks his lips. "I'll save it for later. And, look! Ammunition! Here!" He tosses me the Yankee's cartridge box. "Handy, handy." He peels the uniform jacket off the fallen Fed's limp body, tries to pull it on, and swears. "Damn it! *Damn* it! Doesn't fit. All right, we'll keep it. Might be able to use it at some point. Guess I shouldn't be wearing blue anyway, if I'm going to pass as your Rebel buddy."

"I...D-Drew?" Relief's swamping my head, turbid as the Greenbrier River's spring floods back home. I sway a little. I wipe the sweat off my brow. "Damn, boy, bless you, I—"

"As many times as you've saved my Yankee ass, it's about time I returned the favor," Drew says, stripping the man's undershirt off before stuffing both it and the jacket into his pack. "Did you really think I was going to turn against you? Hell, you should know better than that by now. Get on up." Drew hauls me to my feet. I stand, legs shaking. "Here, here." Drew hands me my firearms, then lopes into the brush long enough to retrieve the sharpshooter's rifle. "Another gun, that's what we needed. Come on, Ian. Follow me. We still got to find some shelter, some place to spend the night."

I stand there for a moment, trembling. A cold breeze pats my beard. I look down at the man who almost took my life. I bend down to him and press my hand to his bared chest. He's still breathing. I wonder where he grew up, who loves him back where he calls home, whether he'll survive this war. Then I rise, shoulder my provisions, and follow my savior into the shade of hemlock boughs.

—

CHAPTER SEVENTY-FIVE

"Here! Here!" Drew shouts. I follow the sound of his voice, loping up and over a low ridge, leaves rustling beneath my feet. He's standing in the cove below, among a scattering of moss-coated rocks and patches of lingering snow. The two largest boulders lean together like fond comrades, shoulder to shoulder, in the shadow of encircling hemlocks. I slide and stumble down the slope till I reach Drew's side.

"Here, Ian. Look," Drew says, pointing. "A cave." Between the two boulders is a low entrance, a leafy ramp descending into the dark.

I light a candle stub. Cautiously we crawl inside. It's a shallow little grotto, low ceilinged, snug and dry, the floor blanketed with musty leaf mold. No vermin we can see. Too early in the season for snakes. Wedging the candle upright between two stones, I begin unpacking the oilcloth and smelly wool blankets, making of them a little nest. By the time I'm done, night's thick outside, the entrance a black almost as dense as the black stone above.

No cook-fire tonight. We're not far enough away from possible pursuers to risk it, and it's too dark now to gather wood. Cross-legged, we sit side by side inside the cave, chewing our cold dinner of hardtack and the unexpected luxury of Yankee cheese. Candle wax drools onto stone; candlelight jumps and flares; spasmodic shadow shifts over Drew's bloodstained face. Outside, there's complete silence, broken only by the sound of wind kicking up leaves. From near-death and the smoking holes of destruction we have been delivered, to this chamber beneath the forest. My prayer is sheer gratitude, unspoken but heartfelt.

Done eating, Drew assumes a position I've seen many times since we met, arms folded over his bare chest, trying to warm himself up. From my haversack, I fetch my flask. We take turns, small sips, careful to leave some for the future. Drew sighs, leans shivering against me, then slips to the ground, tugging a blanket over himself and resting his head in my lap. We look into one another's eyes for a while.

"Oh Jesus, this feels good," Drew says, smiling up at me. "I've been so cold for so long." With one hand, I stroke the hair off his brow. With the other, I intertwine my fingers with his.

"You did it, Reb," Drew mutters. "You did what you said you'd do. You saved me."

"And you saved me," I say. "George would have blown my head open. So would that Yankee sharpshooter."

Still smiling, Drew closes his eyes. "I'm so damn tired," he says. "Now that I'm free, I badly ache to return the pleasuring you've given me, but…"

I trace his beard-framed lips with a fingertip. "Later, Achilles. Right now, this here Patroclus should examine your wounds. We both got cut up pretty bad in that explosion. And the lash-marks from that beating George gave you need tended too. I have the last of the salve, the plaster, and some bandages in my haversack."

"Later, Ian, please? I'm so sleepy… Just climb under this blanket and hug on me, buddy, all right? I just need warmed up and held." That beseeching little boy again. A hook in my heart.

I blow out the candle—one of many limited resources we must carefully conserve—place my glasses atop my haversack, and slip beneath the heavy wool. The earth's hard and lumpy beneath my back, despite the oilcloth, but a cave's discomfort is far sweeter than a comfortable camp-cot now that we're free and safe. Drew stretches out on his side, clinging to me, big head on my shoulder. I wrap an arm around him. "You're so warm," he sighs. We lie quietly, listening to the rustle of leaves in night wind beyond the cave-mouth. My fingers roam over the bushy fur on his chin, the rough ridges of his whip-ravaged back.

And his slave collar. I'd forgotten it. I tug at it. "You want me to take this off? I have the key in my haversack."

"Not now," Drew says, huddling even closer. "You once said you wanted to own me, remember? Well, here I am. Here we are. I'm free, thanks to you. And I'm yours to own, if you'll still have me. We're here together, safe inside the earth. I owe you my life, Ian. I cherish you…as a comrade and as…and as a lover. I'll follow you through these Southern hills of yours for as long as you'll have me."

I roll over onto my side, facing him. He nuzzles my cheek, then continues, voice small and tight.

"I'll wear this collar for a while." From his pocket, he pulls out the rag with which he'd been silenced so often. He smoothes it, folds it, and knots it around his neck. "This'll hide it, so when or if we run into folks, they won't ask any questions. Guess a white man wearing a slave collar might raise some eyebrows. Once we get back to civilization, I'll keep it in your haversack, but right now I want to wear it. " His arms encircle my waist. "This iron used to show I was a prisoner of war, your company's whipping post. I was locked away, inside this ring, without choice or chance of escape. Now it means you own me and that I give myself to you freely. If that's what you still want?"

"Yes," I choke out, thankfulness a dry ache in my windpipe. "Oh yes. Oh yes. If you're sure."

"I'm sure," Drew whispers against me. I fondle his collar, his chin, the hair sprouting in the pit of his neck. Soon he's fast asleep.

—

CHAPTER SEVENTY-SIX

—

"Ian?" Drew's whisper wakes me. His hands shake my shoulders. "Ian."

I bolt up, panting. "Drew, watch out! He's here!"

"You were dreaming," he says. "It's all right. Ain't no one here."

I fumble for my knife in the dark. I seize and unsheathe it, brandishing it at the night outside the cave.

"He was here! Sarge! He was right there!" I point at the cave's mouth, where a shaft of moonlight stretches like a pale arm. "He was watching us!"

"Naw, Ian, naw. He ain't here." Drew pulls me down, slips the blankets my nightmare must have dislodged back over us, and embraces me. I rest my head on his chest. The thick fur tickles my nose, my cheek. I ride his breath's rise and fall, the thud of his heartbeart.

"S-Sarge was there, where the moonlight is. He was hunkered down, watching us. His face was white and his eyes were black, like clumps of coal."

"Shhhh," Drew soothes, rubbing my back, my neck. I shiver. He rocks me. "Shhhh."

"T-There was no tent left. Just a b-black hole where I'd shoved him. He was kind to me. He was kin. I—"

"Shhhh," urges Drew, patting my cheek. "You've comforted me so often. Let me do the same for you."

I drift off to the soft caress of his fingers running through my hair and his strong hand gripping mine.

—

CHAPTER SEVENTY-SEVEN

—

I rise, leaving Drew still sleeping peacefully in the heap of blankets, and climb out of the cave. It's near dawn, overcast, cold, the sun not yet risen, the forest gray and silent. Steam rises from my stream of piss. Among the carpet of dead leaves about me, green tendrils and sprouts of early weeds rise. I'm tucking myself in when I hear, just up the mountain, men's voices. I slip behind a rock, peering up. Blue uniforms wink among the trees.

I'm under the boulders in an instant, shaking Drew awake. He jerks up from our warm nest, blinking, his head barely missing the low ceiling of the cave. Shawling his bare shoulders with a blanket, he crawls out with me. The voices are more audible now, getting closer.

"More Yankees," I say, pointing up the slope. "Probably sharpshooters. Maybe sent like that last one to find us. Let's go," I whisper, turning back to the cave to collect our belongings. But Drew doesn't follow. He's looking around, brow furrowed.

"Come on!" I urge, tugging at his elbow.

"No. Wait now." Drew's gaze narrows. It's a rock he's looking at, a big one. He strides over to it, bends over, clutches it with both hands, grunts and heaves.

"What are you doing? We need to leave now. Let's head down the mountain."

"Ian," Drew pants between deep breaths. "We can hear them from this distance. So they'll be able to hear us tearing through these dead leaves. Just wait. I have an idea." Another heave, a muffled cussing, and the rock's dislodged. He pushes it, rolling it toward the cave. I doubt that any other man I've ever met would have the strength to do what he's doing.

"Holy God," I gasp. "You really are Achilles!"

Drew grins and huffs. "I'm going to seal the cave behind us. Just in case they come down here. Let's just hope the fallen leaves hide our tracks and the rock's too."

I slide down the earthen ramp into the cave. Drew follows, backing up, then falling to his knees and dragging the rock in place behind him. The light disappears, save for a thin rim edging the stone. It's how I've heard eclipses of the sun described.

We're huddled together now, Drew with the sharpshooter's confiscated rifle, I with my pistol unholstered and at the ready, our ears straining. Beyond the stopper of the great stone, the voices grow closer still. Three or four men, I reckon. Someone laughs; someone coughs and spits. The strangers pause just outside. Oh, God, are they about to make camp?

"Gimme some cracker, Paul." The rim of light around the great stone diminishes; the Yank must be leaning back against it, only feet from us. "Let's take a breakfast break."

Drew's hand squeezes mine. We keep still. I close my eyes for a few seconds, trying not to pant.

There's a rustling as men settle haunches into dead leaves and dig into haversacks. Someone hums, then breaks into song, a soft, sad tenor.

> Let us close our game of poker,
> Take our tin cups in hand,
> While we gather round the cook's tent door,
> Where dry mummies of hard crackers
> Are given to each man.
> Oh, hard crackers, come again no more.

"Lord, yes. I'm sick of wild hills and short rations." The Yankee just outside our cave sighs. Crunch of cracker between teeth; resigned chewing. "I think I'd kiss Jeff Davis' ass if it'd get me some brined beef, turnips, and Boston brown bread."

My belly gives a low growl. Drew grins at me and rolls his eyes. I poke myself; the growling subsides.

Another deep sigh. "No Rebs left up here, boys. The cowards are probably hightailing it toward Richmond as we speak. How about we head into Buchanan and see if there's any ham or flour to requisition in the name of Old Abe?"

Mumbles of assent. The Yank's shadow lifts from the stone door. There's a kicking of leaves. "Hand over that canteen," someone growls. The tenor takes up another song.

There's a spot that the soldiers all love,
The mess tent's the place that we mean,
And the dish we best like to see there
Is the old-fashioned white army bean.

To our relief, the sounds fade. For a long time we sit tense and un-speaking, still clasping hands in the dim light, till we're certain they're gone.

"Close call, Achilles." I chuckle. "And I think I'd kiss Abe Lincoln's ass for a pot of those white beans...cooked for hours with some sow belly or side meat." My hungry sigh's an exact echo of the Yank's.

"Everyone we meet will be an enemy," Drew says low, kissing my hand before releasing it. "If they're Rebels, I'm at risk, despite these gray trousers I'm wearing. If they're Yanks, you're a prisoner. And all of them are liable to string us up if they find out we're sodomites."

"Yep," I say, holstering my pistol. "That's why I'm leading us up into the mountains. It's rough terrain, and it'll take us a long time to get home. But if we take the easier routes, if we make our way up the Valley or try to move west along the Midland Trail, we're bound to run into soldiers at every turn. We're safer among the beasts of the mountains than among men." I tousle Drew's mess of hair. "Let's stay in here a little bit till those Feds are well gone. If they find that buddy of theirs you knocked out, they'll be back up here searching for us. You want some breakfast?" I open a poke and commence to rummaging. "Just hardtack, I'm afraid. Once we get deeper in the mountains, we can risk a fire, and I'll make you some flapjacks. No frying pan, but I could try to use the mess pan I stole. I have some wheat flour in—"

Drew's fingers squeeze my shoulder. "Breakfast would be damn fine... later. But, since we're stuck here in the dark for a while...right now, I want to get you naked."

I turn. Drew's grinning down at me in the subterranean murk. He tugs his slave collar. "Yes sir, this does mean you own me. But come on, little Reb," he says, unbuttoning my jacket. "Don't the owning go both ways? Don't I own a little of you too? And ain't it time I gave back some of the sweet you've given me? I can't wait any longer. Time I took full advantage of my new-found freedom."

"*Now*? It isn't safe. What if they come back? What if—"

"They ain't coming back. We'll hear 'em if they come back."

With that, he's pushing off my jacket, tugging my undershirt over my head. He kisses me, then pulls me down with him onto our rumpled blankets. "I want to do to you what you did to me," he sighs, unbuckling my belt and slipping my pants and my underclothes down to my brogans. I'm hard and aching now, cock bobbing in the dim light. He takes my naked throbbing in his fist, rubbing the head with his thumb. I groan, bucking into his grip. He pushes me down against the earth and mashes his bearded mouth against mine.

"I'm ready to taste you," he mutters into between kisses.

"But I ain't clean. Haven't bathed in days."

"I couldn't give a damn." He presses his face into my armpit and breathes deep. "Smells like forest, like barnyard. Smells downright tasty."

"All right. Just keep quiet, in case someone outside—"

"Nothing to worry about there, Reb. They're long gone, and I plan to keep my mouth busy with better things than talk."

He's as good as his word. His tongue plays over my lips, laps my beard, and descends to my torso. Pretty soon he's sucking my right nipple softly. I press my hand against the back of his head, pushing my chest harder against his face. It's been years since a man touched me this way.

"Does it feel good?" Drew whispers. "Am I doing it right?"

"Hell, yes," I moan. "You're wonderful, Drew. Just keep it up."

As he sucks, his hand's ranging over my cock, flicking the head, squeezing and stroking the shaft. "I love your hard little muscles. I love all this bear-fur on your breast," he says, resting his face in my chest hair, kissing it before shifting his attentions from one nipple to the other. "And here on your belly," he says, ruffling the fuzz there before filling his mouth with my chest-flesh again.

"If...you...don't...stop," I grunt, fucking his fist, tugging at the long hair falling around his face.

"Oh, no, you don't," Drew mumbles. "Not yet. I got other explorations in mind."

I gasp, gripping his head hard as he licks the tip of my cock.

"Ummm," he growls, wrapping his arms around my waist. "Like salty satin..." Another few laps, then he takes the head into his mouth. He sighs, sucks, and inch by inch pulls me farther into him. I slide inside till I'm bumping the back of his throat. He gags. "Easy," I say. "Hold still for a bit; get used to it." He looks up at me, nodding, grinning around my cock and sucking in air before tightening his lips around me. I look down at him in the sparse gray light, at his wide blue eyes, his unkempt hair, his red lips and blond beard wrapped around my flesh, his mouth stuffed full of me. So sweet, manly, and submissive: an amalgam heaven-sent.

"You couldn't be more beautiful," I say, touching his face. Just as my sex fills his throat, awe at the sight of him fills mine.

"And you couldn't taste better," he mumbles. "I think I like your meat better'n pie." He takes a gulp of air, then starts in again, tongue flicking about the head, mouth moving up and down the shaft. More choking, more gagging—"Sorry!"—then he's at it once more, chewing and slurping, nibbling and nuzzling. A few stabs of discomfort as his teeth catch me; more mumbled apologies. We find a rhythm. He tightens one arm about my hips, kneading my balls with his other hand. I stroke his hair, his beard, arching up into his wet mouth.

He pulls off, gasping, saliva dripping off his chin. "Hhhuuhhhh! Let me catch my breath." His cheek rests against my hipbone; he wipes his lips, then his spit-moist hand takes up where his mouth left off.

I gaze down at him, humping his fist.

"That's quite the grin you got there, Reb. You sure as hell taste fine."

"That's quite the mouth you have, Yank. Just take your time. Those western hills can wait."

"You know I ain't ever...sucked a man before. But since I met you, since you first sucked me, I've been eager to try. I want your seed bad, Ian."

He's on me again, mouthing the head, taking the whole thing down his throat till he's choking again, then pulling off, letting me cool down, then beginning anew.

I'm seriously hurting now, aching for release, and he knows it. He rolls us onto our sides and I hammer his face in desperate earnest, arms locked around his head, his drool slicking up my thighs. Then I'm bucking and shaking, choking back a shout. "Ohhh, hell, here we go," I warn, burying myself inside him, and now my rapture's filling his mouth and he's gasping on my semen, coughing, softly laughing, gulping down each of the several waves he's coaxed from me.

"So that's how a man's seed tastes," Drew says, smacking his lips, then climbing up to fall wearily beside me. His arms encircle me; he pulls me to him, my back to his chest. "A damn sight better than hardtack or white beans." He chuckles. "A regular diet of Ian ought to keep my strength up for the trip ahead. You don't mind if I take a regular sip from you, do you, Reb?"

"As long as I can do the same," I say. "How about, after I hug on you a little, I return the favor?"

"Yes, sir," Drew says, squeezing me hard in his arms. "You're more than welcome.

"Tastes like strength, doesn't it?" Drew's voice is full of wonder. "A man's seed tastes like strength."

—

CHAPTER SEVENTY-EIGHT

—

It's a sacrament, the sort of worship pagans once celebrated in caves like this. Drew's stretched naked on the oilcloth, on his back. I lie between his spread thighs, massaging his welted ass cheeks and his testicles, then with a fingertip nudging his fuzzy hole. His sex-flesh is heavy, hard, and thick on my tongue. Moaning, he rides my mouth, big hands gripping the back of my head. It takes no time at all. He explodes, liquid spasms that fill my mouth and throat, making of me an overfull goblet, my lips and chin a trickling brim. I gulp Drew down as if he were wine or bread, manna meant to see me through the wilderness. The last gush I hold in my mouth, savoring the taste for a few seconds before swallowing. Then I'm wiping my beard of a few spilt droplets; Drew's chuckling, murmuring thanks, and kissing the top of my head.

It takes a while, washing Drew's wounds with canteen water, anointing them with plaster: face, chest, back, buttocks, foot soles. Then the wrapping of makeshift bandages about his torso, loins, and bare feet. "Feels good," Drew sighs, patient as I move his body this way and that. He takes his turn, working the salve's cool soothe into the stinging wounds the grapeshot left between my shoulder blades and along my side, the red-oozing groove the cavalryman's ball cut along the crest of my shoulder. A few minutes later, both bandaged up, we're dressed, packed, and ready to continue our journey.

No sounds outside, so Drew grips the stone. He strains, heels sinking into earth. "Damn," he gasps. For a second, I'm afraid he can't move it, that we're entombed here, to slowly starve together, to breathe our last together, our bones fated to mingle forever in this dark room.

"Let me help," I say, licking my lips anxiously. We're both soldiers. Surely we deserve a better death than being buried alive.

"Naw, I can do this, believe me." Drew gives me a tight grin. "I got to impress my little Reb with my muscles." With that, he puts his shoulder to the rock and gives a bass grunt and a heave. The great weight rolls back, reluctant as a hound might be, forced to give up its bone.

Out we crawl on our knees, blinking and squinting after the time spent together in subterranean dark, firearms at the ready. No one. We breathe deep the fresh air. We stand in the pour of morning sunlight, brushing the cave's dirt off our knees, looking out through the gray forest, new green rising here and there through carpets of leaves. Cloud shadow and sun skip across the hillside. A cold wind shakes the green-tipped boughs, tugging at a strip of bandage that dangles from Drew's hip. No sign of humanity; we could be the only two men left on earth.

"Here," I say, fetching each of us a piece of hardtack. Quietly, we chew on the stale crackers. "Damn, I want some coffee," Drew grouses. "I'd even be thankful for that acorn swill you Confederates brew."

"There might be an inn at Eagle Rock," I say. "With any luck, we'll get up there by nightfall. We should be able to beg us up some victuals, maybe even a pair of shoes for your poor tore-up feet. Folks are pretty kind, and they'll feed Confederate soldiers if their larders have anything left at all. You just keep quiet, and let me do the talking. You don't sound like you're from around here, you know. You Yanks talk funny."

Drew chuckles. "Us?! You Rebs sound like you've got molasses stuck between your teeth. Like you're chewing honeycomb."

I study Drew's mischievous grin. He's so damned handsome, bare-chested and hairy in the sunlight. The smears of dirt and bloodstained bandages just highlight his heroism, how precious and fragile he is. I turn, heart brimming, and point down the mountain. "All right, clever brute, we should head that way, I think, and—"

"Ian." Drew's voice is barely a whisper behind me. "Turn around. Turn real slow. Look."

The panther is a few feet above us, crouched on top of the boulders that formed our shelter. It's a golden brown, the color of autumn oak leaves and winter broomsedge. It stares at us, long tail twitching. Whiskers bristle from its long snout.

"Back up," whispers Drew. "Real slow."

I do so. So does Drew. As I move backward, I reach for my pistol.

"No. No, Ian. No. Just keep moving."

Twigs pop beneath my brogans; leaves give off a brittle crunching. Each noise makes me wince. The big cat curls a lip. I catch a glimpse of fang. Then it sits up. It stares at us, black-edged eyes as golden as Drew's chest hair. It blinks. It lifts one paw, licks it, then it turns, leaps off the side of the rock, and lopes down the hill without a backward glance. I can hear its progress through the leaves for only a few seconds. Then the forest is silent.

"That's the way we need to go, right?" Drew says, wrapping an arm around my waist. "After that cat?"

"Oh, damn. Well, yes. But let's us wait just a bit and let that King of the Painters get ahead of us a safe distance." My thighs start up a fine trembling. "Lord, that animal could have—"

"No malice there, little Reb. Just power. I'd rather meet up with an entire pack of mountain beasts than any more of your graycoat friends."

"Or any more of your bluebellies, remember?" I gingerly pat my bandaged shoulder. "Like you said, anyone we meet might prove to be an enemy."

We shoulder our packs and our rifles. Down the hill we pick our way, taking in deep draughts of air. Almost immediately we come out on another table rock, a flat overlook facing west. I point toward the remote ridges of the Alleghenies. They look like frozen surf, still painted the blue-grays and brown-grays of winter, fringed with the black silhouettes of trees. Here and there, like moored clouds set against those distant dun slopes, are the white puffs of blooming sarvisberry trees.

"We follow a creek, then a river, and we'll be home."

"How long?"

"Depends on whether we can procure a horse, on what kind of obstacles we encounter. Goodly number of days, I'd say, on foot. A week? Two? I can't say."

"But you'll take care of me, Reb, right?"

I look up at Drew. The wind's strong up here; it ruffles his shaggy hair.

"Hell, yes." On my tiptoes, I give his cheek a quick kiss. "Okay, boy, let's go," I say, tightening my pack. "We got a long, long way to travel."

"Yes. But Ian?"

I turn to find Drew staring out over the valley of the James, toward the distant mountains. The sun's risen high enough to bathe their pinnacles in light.

"Do you think anyone will remember us? Will imagine us?"

"What do you mean, buddy? Our families and friends will always remember us, even if we...even if we don't make it home. I know it'll be dangerous, but we got to try, we got to—"

"No, I mean the men who come." Drew swallows hard, resting the butt of the rifle on the rock beneath us. "Who will come to be born.

Men like us. Men who, well, touch one another like you and I touch. Like in the Whitman poems you read me. Like in *The Iliad*. It's a comfort thinking that they are there, somewhere. That they might be there, long after we're gone, there thinking of us. Looking back for us. From some more fortunate place."

I wrap my arms around my lover's waist, this big, scarred boy from Yankee-land, my erstwhile foe. I kiss his breastbone, the fur soft against my face.

"It's a comfort indeed. I'd say it's a surety. And, by the way, I feel pretty fortunate, war or not. The war led me to you."

Drew kisses my forehead. "Yes. Whoever those men are or will be, I wish them all the blessings you and I have found together. I hope they know somehow that we were here."

With that, Drew shoulders his rifle and we descend in the very direction the painter-cat vanished. In a little while, we're on the road again. We follow the James upriver, here where the valley widens, here where it narrows again. We pass huge riverside sycamores, stone walls marking an abandoned homestead, a burnt cabin we cautiously skirt. For a few minutes we rest beneath another blooming sarvisberry. The petals drift about us; I daub blood off Drew's feet. We each take a gulp from my canteen, and then we resume our journey. Behind us, the stony head of Purgatory recedes from sight. Before us, the mountains of home await. There we will find shelter. There, with luck, we will share long years together after this bloody war is done.

—

BIBLIOGRAPHY
—

I read many books in order to educate myself further about the Civil War (or the War of Northern Aggression, as we Southerners sometimes call it). Here's a list of some I found especially helpful.

Rebel Cornbread and Yankee Coffee: Authentic Civil War Cooking and Camaraderie—Garry Fisher
Cooking for the Cause—Patricia B. Mitchell
Confederate Camp Cooking—Patricia B. Mitchell
I Rode with Stonewall—Henry Kyd Douglas
Chickamauga and Other Civil War Stories—edited by Shelby Foote
Life of Turner Ashby—Thomas Almond Ashby
The Civil War—Geoffrey Ward with Ric Burns and Ken Burns
Hardtack and Coffee: The Unwritten Story of Army Life—John D. Billings
A Different Sin—Rochelle H. Schwab
Civil War Virginia—James I. Robertson, Jr.
The Stonewall Brigade—James I. Robertson, Jr.
Soldiers Blue and Gray—James I Robertson, Jr.
Wearing of the Gray—John Esten Cooke
An American Iliad: The Story of the Civil War—Charles P. Roland
A Taste for War: The Culinary History of the Blue and the Gray—William C. Davis
The Story the Soldiers Wouldn't Tell: Sex in the Civil War—Thomas P. Lowry, M.D.
The Life of Johnny Reb: The Common Soldier of the Confederacy—Bell Irvin Wiley
The Life of Billy Yank: The Common Soldier of the Union—Bell Irvin Wiley
The Civil War Paintings of Mort Künstler, Volumes 1-4
Facts the Historians Leave Out: A Confederate Primer—John S. Tilley

ABOUT THE AUTHOR

Jeff Mann grew up in Covington, Virginia, and Hinton, West Virginia, receiving degrees in English and forestry from West Virginia University. His poetry, fiction, and essays have appeared in many publications, including *Arts and Letters*, *Prairie Schooner*, *Shenandoah*, *Willow Springs*, *The Gay and Lesbian Review Worldwide*, *Crab Orchard Review*, and *Appalachian Heritage*. He has published three award-winning poetry chapbooks, *Bliss, Mountain Fireflies*, and *Flint Shards from Sussex*; three full-length books of poetry, *Bones Washed with Wine*, *On the Tongue*, and *Ash: Poems from Norse Mythology*; two collections of personal essays, *Edge: Travels of an Appalachian Leather Bear* and *Binding the God: Ursine Essays from the Mountain South*; two novellas, *Devoured*, included in *Masters of Midnight: Erotic Tales of the Vampire*, and *Camp Allegheny*, included in *History's Passion: Stories of Sex Before Stonewall*; two novels, *Fog: A Novel of Desire and Reprisal* and *Purgatory: A Novel of the Civil War*; a book of poetry and memoir, *Loving Mountains, Loving Men*; and a volume of short fiction, *A History of Barbed Wire*, which won a Lambda Literary Award. He teaches creative writing at Virginia Tech in Blacksburg, Virginia.